Big Daddy

Mark Brumby

Published by Hit the North
Mill Wharf
Tweedmouth
Berwick upon Tweed
Northumberland
TD15 2BP

Mark Brumby has asserted his right to be identified as the author of this Work in accordance with the Copyright, Designs and Patents Act 1988.

A catalogue record for this book is available from the British Library.

ISBN:978-1-0685747-6-4

This novel is entirely a work of fiction and, except in the case of historical fact, the names, characters and incidents portrayed in it are the work of the author's imagination. Any resemblance to actual persons, living or dead, events or localities is entirely coincidental. All rights reserved. No part of this publication may be reproduced, stored in a retrieval system, or transmitted, in any form or by any means, electronic, mechanical, photocopying, recording or otherwise, without the prior permission of the publishers.

For my family, near and far...

Copyright © Mark Brumby

Also by Mark Brumby
Always Adam

www.hitthenorth.info

'The distinction between the past, present and future is only a stubbornly persistent illusion.'

Albert Einstein

'A nuclear crisis is not a worst-case scenario, it is the worst-case scenario.'

Annie Jacobsen, Nuclear War: A Scenario

HIT THE NORTH

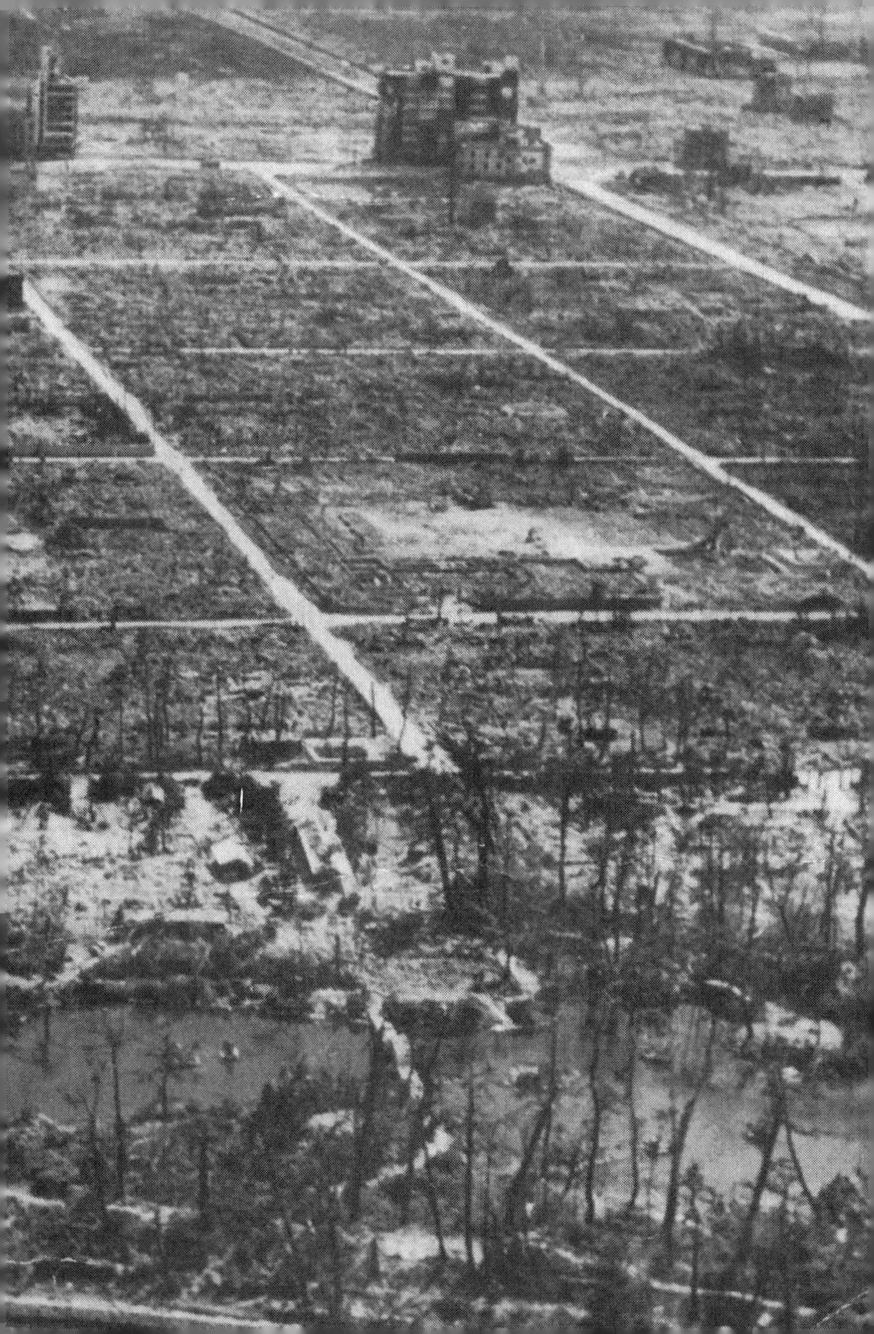

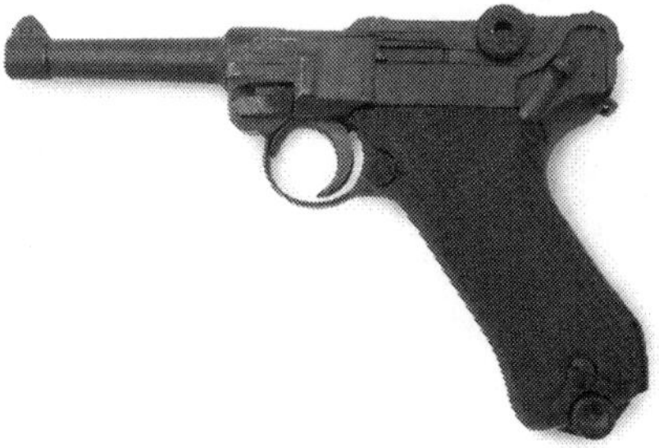

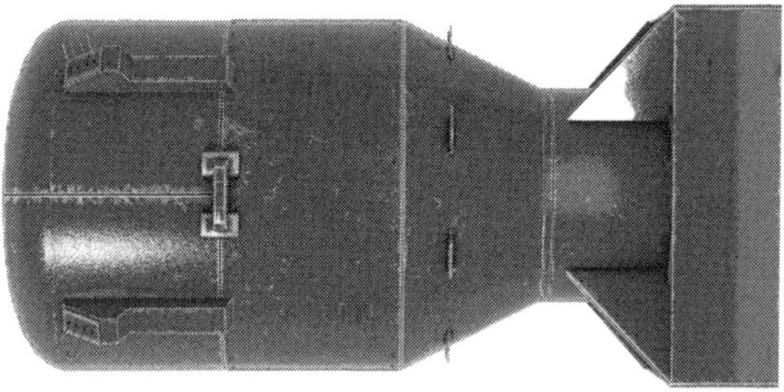

1997
Prologue

It was the perfect time of year. The pink time when the faint scent of cherry blossom hung in the air and the promise of the year had not yet been broken. It was then that the visitor came.

Yoshi Kasaga squinted hard against his poor eyesight, the distant sound of chanting in his ears as the hazy movements before him transformed themselves into the shape of a man. At home with his dreams, this apparition seemed different, somehow more familiar, somehow more real; the white robed figure approached and sharpened further. The visitor was about his own height and build, perhaps a little older, his features similar, the grey-flecked blue-black hair a little longer, tightly bound. He bowed slightly and slowly held out his hand, an object held between forefinger and thumb.

Kasaga was supremely unafraid. This was his fate, his destiny and he looked down at the hand before him, reached slowly towards it. His nails gently caressed the object and he smiled. It was a Compact Disc.

Eighteen months later...

Thursday 25, October 1999
One

The young man watched as the dust played and eddied in the slanting early morning sunshine, then closed his eyes. He was hot, he was very hot, his breathing shallow and fast, sweat blistering his skin as he forced the air down into his lungs. He steadied himself and rose to his feet, walked to the mirror hanging on the wall by the door of the small room and inclined his head slightly to one side. The spidery, grime filled cracks partly obscured his view and moving his head to one side, he felt strangely disembodied as his own grey eyes looked back at him from the glass.

****

Elsewhere, it was much colder, the riveted boat low in

the water, its sail down. It had just twenty benches, but it was full and, as the men bent and pulled silently on their rag-swathed oars, their breath hung white in the still air. It was dark and a heavy fog was creeping along the banks of the River Humber from the North Sea bringing with it a frost, the first since the leaves had fallen.

Six hundred feet above the river the first tongues of fire were beginning to lap around a building on the hillside. One of the men swore quietly; older than many of the others, maybe thirty-five, he stood thickset, his fair hair scraped back into a ponytail, a coarse red beard partially covering the ugly pockmarks on his cheeks. He shifted his position slightly to ease the ache in his left leg and looked again at the glow set against the otherwise black night sky. He could sense the excitement in the boat, but the fire was a bad omen.

The night and the fog were his friends, they shielded him from his enemies, but he had lost sight of the other boats, and it had become suddenly very cold but still, they had won the race; theirs would be the prize. He peered once more into the gloom.

Now behind them, the oil jetties, wharves and merchant shipping of the busy ports on either side of the river had slipped by unnoticed. So too had the huge towers of the Humber Bridge, once the world's largest single span but now swallowed up by the fog and the red-bearded man shifted once more. Had he turned, he might have seen the dragon's eyes, the powerful red lights atop the bridge, used to warn helicopters and light aircraft of its presence, still dimly visible through the gloom.

But he did not. The boat continued to move silently inland.

Drifting a little, as it approached the river's northern

bank, the water still brackish and tidal even this far from the sea, the boat's shallow keel scraped against the filthy river bottom. The men knew what to do. All but four of them lowered themselves gently over the boat's side, stifling curses as the cold water numbed their bodies then, slowed by the sucking mud, they strained to drag the craft towards the shore. Grunting with the effort, the men still in the boat pushing down hard into the mud with their oars, reducing the friction against the mud, the boat moved. Slowly at first, then more rapidly and within seconds it was beached then expertly secured to a wind-sown silver birch tree that rose above the waterside mist the bottom of its trunk lost to sight.

Moving quietly through the shallow water, the red-bearded man glanced at the riverbank, at the mound of debris, the shit and filth that indicated the normal high tide mark of the water and nodded; it had begun to ebb.

It would not re-float their boat for several hours, but he needed to be sure; he did not want her to become too heavily beached, but she could not be allowed to slip her moorings and disappear. He pushed her hard with his hand. She rocked gently but he was satisfied. He pulled sharply on the securing ropes then moved away from the main body of men and raised his head. He strained to listen; there was no sound.

Redbeard winced as he turned to speak. He favoured his right leg, and, in the damp of the fog, his limp was worse. He spoke softly and, as his breath billowed white around him, the men became more attentive, strained to hear his words, nodded silently then four of their number broke away from the group, jogged the few yards back to the boat and clambered on board. They pulled at bundles wrapped in rags and, straining against their weight, they placed them on wooden disks, an arm's length across and two inches thick. These they passed out of the boat then carried them back to the main group and put them down on the white-white grass.

The men unwrapped the bundles and picked at the tools in silence, a tension building amongst them. Redbeard had spoken; he had led them this far, protected them from attack and, as he limped purposefully up the gentle hill towards the A63, the distant fog-deadened hum of traffic barely audible, they followed him without question.

The little moonlight reflected from the fog glinted on the objects that the men were carrying and Redbeard stopped, one man moving ahead of the group. He had the loping gait of a man used to travelling by foot. He made distance quickly and was lost to the fog.

Alone in the darkness, the leading man approached the road. He shivered; the dew had settled on the nettles and long grass and had begun to freeze, and he narrowed his eyes. He was not a stranger to this land, yet things had changed. Certainly, it was later in the year, it was much colder but there was more than that. He paused, stared intently at the object that stretched before him and reached out his hand. He touched it, the warmth from his fingers melting its thin coating of frost. The man smiled, looked at the shape of his hand imprinted onto the crash barrier then cocked his head to one side.

Now he could hear them. His colleagues were coming up behind him and he was their eyes, he must not stop. He turned back to the direction that he had been travelling and frowned. A sound, unfamiliar, strange to his ear and it was approaching, getting louder, moving quickly.

His frown deepened and, as he looked up, some 400

paces to his right, the monster rounded a bend in the road.

It was huge, its fiery eyes lighting up the mist and the man's stomach began to rise within him. He was afraid but he welcomed the feeling; he would fight and, as the familiar excitement began to drive all other thoughts from his mind, he climbed over the crash barrier. He weighed the weapon in his hand and walked into the path of the beast.

Five miles to the east there had been excitement for a different reason but now, after a few hectic hours, the queues at the rides and attractions of Hull Fair, the largest travelling funfair in Europe, were beginning to thin. This was Thursday; it was payday for many workers, one of the busiest evenings for the week-long fair but now the evening was drawing to a close and groups of people, mostly young, were making their way back to their cars and coaches, early leavers from the nearby pubs and restaurants swelling their numbers.

Patrick Kirkby wiped the condensation from the coach's window and nodded to himself. He had counted them off and now he had counted them back on again and they were ready to leave, to return to Goole, some thirty miles to the west of Hull. It was a boring run, dull, always uneventful but it would take only thirty-five-minutes and then he would be home.

He revved the engine, a warning to the thronging pedestrians and the coach began to move, edging its way slowly through the heavy traffic. It was always busy near to the Fair itself but soon the coach was through it and moving smoothly; Anlaby Road, the site of Hull City's old football ground, the practically named Fiveways Roundabout then rapidly through the built up suburbs to the west of the city, the traffic now light.

Kirkby took a deep breath; they had only been travelling for a matter of minutes but the early attempts of the coach's happier revellers to strike up a song had come to nothing. Some were talking quietly amongst themselves but most of the tired passengers were beginning to doze, and Kirkby was pleased. He had been a coach driver for nearly twenty years and now he was more bored than tired; he didn't want to hang about. He smiled and nodded again. It was another Thursday night without a drink, but the money was good, and the traffic was not as bad as it might have been. He had enjoyed the Fair himself and now he had the football to look forward to on Saturday. His mind began to wander; his team, Sheffield United, was playing at home this weekend and his two boys, Danny and Liam, were almost as keen on the game as he was.

The speedometer flickered green; they were doing 45 miles an hour. That was acceptable in a 40-limit thought Kirkby his mind turning back to his boys; it was amazing just how quickly they were growing up. They could look after themselves now, at least for a while and he might be able to snatch a pint in a pub by the ground while they had a sing with the crowd outside. It should be a good-natured affair, Gillingham wouldn't bring many supporters with them, there would be no trouble. Easing the coach around the steep right-hand bend before the Forte Crest Hotel, Kirkby smiled. He flicked on his right indicator, pulled onto the main carriageway of the A63 and began to accelerate.

The fog was thick in patches, but Kirkby could see the Humber occasionally to his left. It was a shitty river, brown and muddy at the best of times and he stifled a yawn. The petrol station which he had passed a thousand times would slip by to his left in a few moments, he was sure that he was OK for fuel, but he looked down, glanced at the fuel indicator then raised his eyes; it had taken less than a second.

'Jesus Christ!'

Kirkby gripped the steering wheel hard, his nails biting deep. A man was standing in the road no more than eighty yards ahead of the coach. His eyes wide, Kirkby slammed his right foot down hard on the brake. Visibility was poor. At 100 yards he would have seen a rabbit or a fox, at 200 a set of brake lights but the man had come from nowhere. Kirkby felt removed from his body, he was looking down on himself, observing his actions, judging them but this was not his fault!

His mind racing, blood thumping in the driver's ears, the coach began to judder as the anti-locking mechanism cut in. Kirkby's hands locked on the wheel before him.

He couldn't swerve, there might be ice, and he rose in his seat as he stood bodily on the brake, his entire weight pressing down on the pedal, the first of the passengers thrown out of their seats, still half-asleep, tumbling down the aisle behind him.

'Get out of the w-a-a-a-ay!'

The screams had started. The passengers were frightened, some of them were hurt and time slowed to a crawl as the scarecrow of a man looked up at the coach. Kirkby could see the man's head, then his face, his eyes bulging, but it was not fear, more like anger, he made no attempt to get out of the way. Instead, the man's face began to contort into a grotesque mask. A fury seemed to possess him; his mouth opened, and he bellowed with rage, he raised his arm and hurled the object in his hand.

An instant later the coach struck him.

The broken body cartwheeled down the road. Kirkby wanted to close his eyes, but he could not as it tumbled along the concrete, rolling, diminishing in size then hit the metal central reservation barrier, mounted it and rolled to a halt amongst the scraps of tires, broken exhaust pipes, drink cans and other roadkill that littered the dirty grass between the two lanes of traffic.

Patrick Kirkby, his foot still clamped on the brake, fumbled for his hazard warning lights, his hand shaking.

He had never been involved in a fatal road accident before, but he knew that the man must be dead. He flicked on the lights and forced himself to take a breath but there was no escape, it would not leave him. He had killed a man!

Eerily silent, the only noise the rhythmic clicking of the warning lights Kirkby breathed out slowly. Behind him a woman sobbed. Then another began to cry, and the coach filled with a gentle weeping as the driver looked at the broken windscreen in front of him.

Of course! The dead man, the idiot, the cause of this, had thrown a stick!

The film of plastic, bound within the glass of the windscreen to prevent it from shattering dangerously, had done its job well and Kirkby looked at the window more closely. The stick had almost broken completely through, but something was not right. It was not a stick. Metallic, it looked too heavy. Reaching out his hand, Kirkby fingered the object gently, tilted his head. Solid, definitely metallic, it was an axe! The driver felt the heavy blade, moist from the fog and frowned.

Time had slowed again; Kirkby could feel it. The coach was silent once more, stunned, then it began. The crashing of glass, then an awful howling and screaming, part human, part animal, first from outside the coach and then from within it. The coach driver blinked hard as he struggled to comprehend. He turned his head as dark shapes began to pour through the gaps where the coach's windows had been, and he felt a dull pain in his arm.

Open-mouthed, he felt a second blow to his head and the steering wheel flew up at him, hit him hard in the face.

The man who had wielded the axe looked down at the blood-soaked driver and smiled. The hatred had gone, but he was not satisfied, he wanted more. He had never seen one, had only heard tell of them and the dragon had awed him. Olav had died and he would be mourned when the time was right. But Redbeard also felt a surge of pride, even jealousy. He ran his hand through his dirty blood-smeared hair and smiled again. Terrible though it had been, their revenge was incomplete.

Redbeard looked around him, rallied his men. Silvery, metallic, not mere flesh and blood. The monster had slowed to a halt only fifty paces away from Olav's body, would have eaten him. But Redbeard had not allowed it, had had no hesitation in ordering his men to attack the beast. It had killed one of their own and the men had grabbed greedily at the swords and axes, as the remaining bundles had been unfurled onto the wet grass.

They had left behind several ornately carved yew longbows, had split into two groups and had fallen upon the monster from the rear, hacking at it, tearing at its skin. The red mist before their eyes, they had slain the demons in the demon's belly. They had screamed, had tried to run but, as a small van had ploughed into the back of the coach, blocking both westbound carriageways of the road, the slaughter had begun.

****

Seated in the lounge bar of the large public house, Laptop ran his hand through his hair, his fingers slowed slightly by the grease. He did not notice and returned to nursing his half-pint of cider. He swilled it around his glass and, his nose wrinkled in distaste, regarded the person opposite him once more.

Although it was the nearest pub to his house, the young man had not been in the King's Head often, did not feel at home in pubs. He found them strange, somehow foreign places but it was clear that his drinking companion that evening had no such problem. The horrible man was halfway down his second pint of bitter, a whisky chaser already by its side.

Laptop was Graham Dennis, but he had been Laptop for many years and sometimes failed to respond to his real name. He was twenty-six years old, but age didn't interest him. Computers however, did. He had been born with them, had lived with them all his life, could never imagine a time without them and he treasured them, particularly the way that they allowed him to harness the power of the Internet and, whilst he travelled little, he could interact seamlessly, in theory at least, with any other person on the planet.

Graham had never had a job, at least not one that provided payslips, pensions or a company car but he was good at what he did and jobs, some of them very lucrative, tended to seek him. He had money, the drawers of the cheap plywood desk on which his computer sat in the front room of his modest house were testament to that.

They held cheques, uncashed payment for various pieces of freelance computer work that he had undertaken but they were not important. Nor was the recognition, it was the job itself that mattered and, like a dog with a full belly and a warm blanket, he was happy. He rarely, if ever, thought about tomorrow.

Laptop smiled and raised his glass. He allowed the warm cider to brush his lips but did not drink. He had had enough, wanted to get back to work. He and his client had arrived in the pub only twenty minutes earlier, having spent most of the day in front of Laptop's computer screen and already he was eager to return. He had found the work fascinating. He had been asked to investigate an apparently massive increase in computer traffic emanating from the vicinity of two American airbases in East Anglia. The client had insisted that he be there personally.

Whilst Laptop knew that such work bordered on the inappropriate, probing Government systems was a challenge that he found difficult to resist. He believed in a global community, Governments shouldn't have secrets.

Soon, they would be unable to keep what secrets they had managed to preserve and, he had comforted himself, he need not hand over any information if he had any ethical qualms. Besides, his client was a journalist, not some faceless 'political' and Laptop had recognized him, had seen him interviewed on television in the past.

At twenty past ten that evening Laptop had still been struggling to make sense of the information frothing from his computer screen. He had not wanted to show his frustration, and he felt hopeful. There had appeared to be a heavy repetition of data and sequences suggesting that he, with the help of the several powerful code-cracking programs that he had written, was near to unravelling another problem. Thankfully it was a familiar feeling. This was what he did, what he lived for. To Laptop it was better than sex; to him this was sex!

Laptop swilled his drink once more, caught the dying froth and shuddered. He did not like working with other people, but he did like to share his victories. What pleasure other people found in sharing a good bottle of wine or in the appreciation of a work of art, Laptop found in sharing and overcoming computer problems. He watched his companion drain the last of his beer and shuddered again. He caught the journalist's eye and tried to smile.

Bird-like, Melvin Lesch's head bobbed up and down and he smiled back then looked away. His ever-moving, watery eyes were the colour of strong piss, and his thin, greasy hair suggested that he spent too much time in dark places and did not trouble to find his shower very often. Often jacketed but never smart, his few shirts often bore traces of his last meal but on this occasion his cheap red polyester tie appeared to have escaped. A small man, insignificant in some people's eyes, he found his looks an asset, enjoyed being underestimated. He glanced at the computer hack, nodded again as the smile faded from his lips.

Earlier, at the geek's house, Melvyn had been frustrated, had not understood a word of what had been said to him, but he understood people, had felt Laptop's sense of excitement, had hoped that a breakthrough had been imminent and how he deserved it! It had pained him, almost beyond endurance, but he had attempted to look interested whenever the spotty youth had caught his eye. Thankfully, that had not been very often, but the nerd was a professional and, in a way, Lesch had respected him.

'See those readings?' Laptop had asked earlier. The youth had continued to peer intently at the flickering screen of his computer, his fingers still busy at the keyboard. Of course, Lesch had been able to see it, he wasn't blind, but it meant nothing to him, a mass of figures moving, apparently at random, from left to right, but there had been something about the tone of Laptop's voice that had made him pay attention; Lesch had been interested. 'They just shouldn't be doing that!' Laptop had continued enthusiastically. 'It's as though they're in a rush to say something.'

Lesch had lent what encouragement he could but had not been willing to share what information he had. A contact at the Home Office, a nice chap but one with a weakness for slow horses and fast women, positive attributes in a journalist, had suggested that the Americans had been involved in some sort of clandestine operation in East Anglia, an operation that they were keen to keep secret from their British hosts.

Melvyn had seen it as a challenge. His head cut through the air again and he smiled, his eyes on Laptop.

Now this computer geek, swilling his inch of warm cider around his glass, was going to provide him with the evidence that he needed to get a piece published. It would grab the headlines; prove to the world that the cosy relationship between Prime Minister Berwick and President Sutton was nothing more than a convenient sham. It would be a piece in one of the Sundays perhaps, a big two-page spread in the 'Times' or the 'Telegraph', even the 'Observer', a piece with his photograph at the top of it. 'An exclusive report by investigative journalist Melvin Lesch.' It would make him.

Melvyn despised computers and he had struggled during the evening to keep it from his face, his expression ranging from one of vague puzzlement to total incomprehension. Whilst he recognized their value, he had always wondered how anyone, even the sad youth opposite, could get any enjoyment out of working with them. However, whilst the sticking plaster on his chin suggested that it wasn't safe to leave him with a razor, he had been assured that the boy knew his stuff.

Melvyn tapped out another cigarette, his third since they had arrived in the pub, he was making up for lost time. He lit it, drew in a lungful of smoke and exhaled it carelessly in Laptop's direction. He had ached for a cigarette all evening but had forced himself not to toy with the packet in his jacket pocket. In his experience, cigarettes tended to upset computer nerds. Now it was different but earlier, Lesch had wanted to get his money's worth out of this one. He remembered Laptop's words distinctly, smiled at the memory.

'You see these patterns that are beginning to emerge?' he had said but had been unable to elaborate further. A blinding flash of light and an extremely loud bang had cut off the youth's words. Melvyn had been stunned, had fallen from his chair, been unable to see, his eyes adjusting only slowly to the darkness as the smell of burnt plastic had filled the air. Melvyn had been afraid, but he did not judge himself too harshly, who wouldn't have been? He remembered screaming, watching as Laptop had recovered, had dusted himself off and had straightened the spectacles that had slid down from his ears and were hanging across his nose and mouth. Unable to speak, his mouth slightly ajar, Melvyn had looked on as the younger man had scrabbled at the switches on the wall.

Melvyn had almost laughed with relief; Laptop had been concerned about his computer! They had nearly been blown to Hell and the boy was checking and rechecking his stupid grey boxes, beseeching God that his trip switches had saved his hard disk. Finally, almost sobbing with relief, the geek had declared himself happy that his material had not been ruined. Melvyn had known that he should have shared the boy's emotion, but he just couldn't; he had been ready to finish for the evening.

Melvyn had risen to his feet and twitched the net curtains. Something red, a fire perhaps, glowing on the horizon, had caught his eye. Although he quickly lost interest, it was to change his life as, just over a mile away and silhouetted against the night sky, perched high on the Wolds, the chalk hills of East Yorkshire that rolled gently down towards the Humber, a television transmission station had fared far less well than Laptop's computers and a fire, a beacon to the boats on the river below, had taken a firm hold.

The journalist had been ready to leave, had flicked at the curtain again and it had worked, Laptop had agreed to the pub. Melvyn sat back in his chair and nodded, blowing more smoke in the direction of his companion.

Not that he cared, but the geek still appeared to be a little annoyed at his weakness, but Melvyn ignored him. He could check his kit when he got back, do whatever people like him did during the hours of darkness.

****

Inspector Bielby put his wallet back in his pocket and

turned towards the young police officer, his eyebrow raised. The boy had just moved across from uniform, Simpson or Sampson, something like that, more enthusiastic than impudent. 'Say again?'

'The radio sir. I think you should hear this.'

'You do, do you?' said the Inspector; there was something about the boy's voice. 'Well don't just sit there, turn it up!'

'Incident on the A63. Vicinity of the Melton traffic lights,' echoed the disembodied voice of the female radio controller around the CID office of Hull's Queen's Gardens Central Police Station. It was 10.58pm.

Inspector Bielby picked it up immediately, the sense of urgency, fear mixed with anticipation. The hairs on the back of his neck began to prickle as he caught Sergeant Price's eye then looked away. His face had betrayed him, had read it in the other man's eye, felt somehow dirty, sullied by his excitement at what could turn out to be a major disaster, a human tragedy.

'Further reports of a fight,' continued the operator. 'Confirmed injuries and several deaths...'

'Fucking hell!' Sergeant Price's cup, brim-full of scalding hot tea, slipped from his hand and clattered to the floor.

Bielby caught the Sergeant's eye again, registered the relief on the older man's face. Bielby was in charge, they could settle back, leave him to take the strain.

The Inspector drew himself up to his full height, held in his breath and looked around the room as the radio crackled. Fifty-two now, perhaps a little overweight but every inch the professional policeman, still he needed time. He turned from the expectant faces to the radio. 'Repeat that!'

'Incident at the Welton traffic lights on the A63,' said the radio operator. She seemed calmer, and Bielby sensed rather than saw Sergeant Price smile. The operator had recognized Bielby's voice, and the Inspector remembered how it felt. She sounded young, this was a real career-fucker staring her in the face and the sooner a senior officer acknowledged it the better. She stuck to the short-clipped sentences of her training, conveyed the maximum information in the minimum possible time. 'Coach at the head of an accident with several light vehicles. Cause unclear but reports of fighting at the scene. Civilian doctor confirms at least fifteen dead. Traffic units ETA two minutes.'

Bielby shook his head sharply, maybe he had misheard but the faces of the officers around him told him that he had not. He looked at Price, began to bark orders, turning from one police officer to the next, talking to them personally, each officer sure that they had been especially chosen for the task.

'Warn Traffic to approach with extreme caution. Body armour and helmets. Check that the medical services are up to speed and get Fire to the scene. Tell them not to approach until given clearance by us.'

Bielby patted his jacket pocket and pursed his lips irritably; he would kill for a cigarette. He turned to an officer, a female Sergeant. 'Tell them to keep checking with us for the all-clear and not just sit there like bloody idiots. Ring Goole and get them to block the M62 west and keep West Yorkshire informed. Alert the armed response teams and get me a driver.'

Just under ten minutes later the car carrying Inspector Bielby and Sergeant Price drew up alongside the stricken coach. It stopped by one of the three traffic police cars already at the scene, their flashing blue lights reflecting eerily off the fog, sirens wailing plaintively. The Inspector got out of the car, sniffed the air, damply metallic.

'Who's in charge here?' Bielby did not wait for an answer. 'Turn those bloody sirens off and where's the ART? Who are you?'

'Patterson, sir,' said a uniformed Sergeant. 'We got here at 11.05. No sign of the assailants.'

The sirens died. The silence intensified by the thick fog. Bielby glared at Sergeant Patterson then switched his attention to the 52-seater coach, looking at it closely for the first time. Illuminated by the lights of the cars trapped in the jam behind it and by the flashing lights of the police vehicles that had approached it from the front, it looked alive.

Bielby's feet crunched on the broken glass of a dozen windows as he walked towards the coach, but he appeared not to notice. He saw a man, a medic of some description, his back to him, moving from what looked like one pile of clothing to another. The man rose to his feet, a haunted expression on his blood-streaked face and rushed past the Inspector without looking up. He slowed as he approached what looked like another untidy heap of rags and stooped down beside it. The heap stirred slightly and began to moan.

The silence broken, other moans became audible, but the Inspector shut them from his mind, turned back to the coach, absorbed the detail, picked out a man with his back against its front wheel, a football scarf tied tightly around an arm that ended at the elbow. Bielby patted his pocket again, glanced at Price then turned and began to walk towards the devastated vehicle. He rounded the front of it, darker away from the harshest of the lights but he could see that the few remaining windows were cracked and heavily smeared with dirt, some of it from the inside. The indescribable mess of death.

Reaching the door, Bielby climbed into the body of the vehicle. Watching his feet, he wrinkled his nose against the heavy smell of blood, diesel oil, vomit and fear and then raised his eyes. It was not a pretty sight. Standard police jargon; he'd used the phrase dozens of times during his career, and it was almost always true. From the macabre sights forced with relish onto rookie coppers right through to the really disturbing murders but the coach was truly dreadful.

Bielby shut out the emotion, turned off his feelings and soaked it up. It was his job.

Some yards further down the aisle of the coach, a traffic policeman, himself no stranger to violent death on the highway, struggled to draw breath. In his hand he held a severed arm. The Inspector looked on as a second traffic cop rushed towards him, eyes wide and bulging in a grey face. The man stumbled, almost fell as he caught something heavy with his foot, rolled it down the aisle.

A head. A woman's head, its sightless eyes open, it came to a rest against the Inspector's foot and the young traffic cop retched helplessly into his hands. He pushed past Bielby and fell out into the night air, his shoulders sagging as he slumped against the side of the coach, his outstretched arm supporting him as he whooped in great gulps of air and was sick again.

'Well, what a mess,' said the Inspector quietly. He was alone, took in what he could then exhaled gently through his teeth. 'What a fucking mess.'

Retracing his steps along the aisle, the Inspector reached the front of the coach, his feet clinging to the sticky carpet. He passed the driver's seat, torn and blood-soaked, the steering wheel hideously bent and slowly descended the steps, his feet once again crunching on the glass of the coach's many broken windows. He looked about him. The ambulances had arrived, there was no immediate threat, and he waved in the teams of paramedics. They ran past him, Bielby was sure that there were no living victims still in the vehicle, but they had to do their job. He raised his hand to his face, rubbed his chin and looked at the ground before him. Frowning, he stooped and lifted something carefully from his shoe. He looked up, saw Sergeant Price and Sergeant Patterson and beckoned them over to him.

'Check that the scene is secure, Price,' he said. 'Sergeant Patterson, speak to the radio stations. Get them to keep vehicles off this road but don't give them any details. You'll have to remove those cars somehow,' he added, waving in the direction of the traffic jam behind the coach. 'Check for witnesses first and get some scaffolding and tarpaulins up, we'll have a media circus here within the hour.'

Apparently deep in thought, the Inspector furrowed his brow, held out the sticky, discoloured ruby earring that he had taken from his shoe. 'Give this to the Crime Scene Examiners, would you? It belongs to a lady on the coach, she won't be needing it now.'

Two

The young man was sweating in the sub-tropical heat. He was afraid but he knew what he had to do, what he had been trained to do. Hell, maybe even what he had been born to do, and he would do it, he would do it for his country and for his family and for himself. He tore himself away from the mirror and moved towards the door turning one last time to check the room. Satisfied, he nodded. It was the way that he would like it to be found if he did not return.

****

A mile to the north of the A63, their breath billowing white above them, the group of tired and excited men moved quietly across the frosty field. Away from the water the fog was a little thinner but still they could hear little of the noise from the road below.

The men's weapons were dirty, but they walked with the light step of satisfied men; they were happy. It had been terrible, but they were proud. They had slain a dragon, had freed its spirit, released the demons in its belly and the story would ring forever around the fires of their homeland. Their children would know it by heart, and their children's children in the years to come but the fight was not yet over for they had heard the dying dragon's screams after they had left. They had seen its fire turn blue and begin to flash as the smaller dragons had arrived, snorting fire and wailing.

They had come to avenge their dead and the men would face them, kill them, free them from their torment.

Many demons had poured from the bellies of the smaller dragons, they had waved sticks that lit the night around them and soon they would come. Still, thought Redbeard, the corners of his mouth edging into a smile, if today were a good day to die, then the men would die content and together and live forever in Valhalla.

Redbeard was as excited as his men as he peered intently into the fog before him. He had recognized the first faint traces of wood-smoke on the cold night air several minutes earlier and now he could feel the fire drawing them towards it. They were drawing close, could hear voices, the sounds of a feast, had sensed the presence of the building before it loomed out of the mist before them and, as Redbeard and his men approached it the leader came to a halt, looked up, his eyes drawn by the creak of old wood against metal.

It was a sign, a picture. It was an image, a warning hanging on the stout post, a picture of a man's head and it wore a crown. It was a King's Head and now Redbeard was certain. They had found the castle of their enemies and there would be soldiers.

Redbeard crouched, strained his eyes against the night then waved his men to either side of the castle's door and moved cautiously to the rear. More dragons, smaller, some silver, others blood red, still more dark like hairless boars but they slept, their demons gone.

They would be in the castle and Redbeard knew what he must do. He and his men would take the stronghold. They would kill the demons, free their spirits, and he thanked the Gods for giving him this task.

Inside the pub, the atmosphere was extremely convivial as it often was towards closing time. Most of the evening crowd knew each other and only Laptop and Melvin Lesch and a young couple talking intimately in one of the pub's discrete corners were not regulars.

The lights were low, and the comforting chink of glasses and the buzz of conversation filled the air. There had been no hurry to clear away the glasses but now, Edward Saunders the landlord of the King's Head public house, was beginning to observe the licensing laws.

'Drink up please, Ladies and Gentlemen. It's well past closing time. Haven't you got homes to go to?'

Saunders voice was surprisingly high-pitched for such a large man and a gentle groan arose from the drinkers. A small group of them, however, was ignoring the landlord completely. Together, as if by a signal, they began to point excitedly at the television that had been flickering in the corner of the pub largely ignored, all evening.

'Turn it up, Eddie,' shouted one of the men. He pointed at the television. 'It's about Melton. There's been a fight...'

Well used to the excuses used in order to extort another drink, the landlord looked at the men questioningly, but something about the tone of the man's voice told him that he was serious. Saunders reached under the bar for the remote control and turned up the volume.

'...in Melton, in East Yorkshire,' said the announcer, his voice growing louder as the green bars ascended towards the right of the screen. 'We will be broadcasting more details throughout the night as we get them.'

The news bulletin faded to the normal schedule leaving the small group of drinkers looking at each other blankly.

'Is 'Newsnight' still on?' shouted the man who had spoken earlier. Saunders shrugged his shoulders, but he was interested. He reached for the remote control again. He was about to switch to BBC2 when a shadow shot across one of the two large bay windows at the front of the pub.

Saunders turned his head as the glass of both windows imploded simultaneously. Objects began to fly through the shattered windows, jerking the net curtains first this way and then that. Stones thought Saunders dimly, they'd never had problems with vandals before but what else could it be? The Landlord blinked hard, an image of feathers in his mind; it was dark, surely not an owl? Several owls?

Arrows, now there could be no mistake, were springing from the furniture, from the fittings around the bar and Saunders shook his head. He could hear the faint whiz of the goose feathers as the shafts flew past and a thumping sound as the heads struck home, but he was rooted to the ground, could not move. Light fittings and bottles behind the bar were shattering, then larger objects began to fly and a huge axe, spinning in the reduced light, struck a tall man, a lorry-driver whom Saunders knew well, full in the back. The man sank to his knees and gasped, slumped forward, his eyes rolling in his head as, around him, the air was filled with a dreadful inhuman screaming.

His mouth open, Edward Saunders cowered instinctively as the windows darkened and the bodies of nearly three-dozen men poured through them, blocking the light from streetlamps outside. A large pillar obscured him from the intruder's view as the axes began to swing, to hiss through the air.

Saunders screwed his eyes shut. He was in a dream, a nightmare, but this was his pub, he had to do something.

He forced his eyes open, looked up at the bar above him and tried to breath, to steady himself. Another scream and he flinched as a bloody hand fell onto the bar above his head, a wedding ring on its ring finger. He looked away and closed his eyes, shut out the sound and crawled towards the hatch down into the cellar below, liquid spattering his back and then he was there.

Edward Saunders bit his lip; he knew that the hatch creaked, but he had no choice, it offered safety, a haven from the hell around him. Face contorted, eyes still tightly closed, he pulled up the hatch, froze at the slightest noise then forced himself to pull it further and slid, face first, down the steep steps. He hit the cobbled floor of the cellar, turned as rapidly as his sixteen stones allowed and locked the hatch behind him.

Sweating and shocked, nose wrinkling involuntarily at the smell of stale cat shit around him, Saunders slid down against the whitewashed wall, allowed himself to breathe and slowly opened his eyes. He raised his hands.

Blood-spattered, they were shaking, and his chest was damp. He looked down, felt his stomach rise, his head begin to spin as he saw that his shirt was wet with blood, but he felt no pain; instead, a strange relief.

He was not running. He was injured, was going for help. Slumped amongst the familiar barrels and crates that he worked with every day, Saunders tried to calm himself, forced himself to breath slowly. The shadows in the cellar were deeper, more threatening than he could remember them and still he could hear the screams, footsteps and the thumping above his head. But he felt a little steadier.

'Think man, think!'

The sound of Edward Saunders' voice startled him, made the landlord jump but it was strangely reassuring, and he rose unsteadily to his feet, fearful of the stab of pain that he was sure would come. But it did not. The blood on Saunders' chest was not his own. The flush of relief that he felt was tinged with disappointment as he pushed open the door to the cellar's second, smaller room.

Saunders peered into the darkened room, felt for the light switch. This was his hide-away. It was where he came to get away from it all, from the punters, from the brewery, from his creditors, even from his wife and, as the light flooded the room, he saw what he was looking for. He wiped his forehead, smeared the lorry-driver's blood across his cheek then looked back at the small table. His pipe, the car keys and, behind them, a cup of coffee, stone cold now, the milk forming a thick skin on the top and a magazine. Next to them, his mobile phone...

Edward Saunders stumbled to the table and scooped up his car keys and the 'phone. His hand trembled, the relief pounding through his body as he jabbed at it hard with his fat fingers. He lifted it to his ear but there was nothing.

Saunders felt his head throb and noticed the phone was dead. But he had charged it that morning, had used it only once. He looked at it closely, accusingly but, even without his reading glasses, he could see that it was on. He peered at the small screen, screwed his eyes in the poor light then held it a little further away, tried to make sense of the dark grey letters. They cleared a little and came into focus.

No signal.

Of course, there was no signal in the cellar. Saunders raised his hand to his head, massaged the bridge of his nose and tried to think; he would have to go outside.

Outside!

He looked up at the ceiling, the rolls of fat riding up on his neck and cocked his head to one side, steadied his breathing, tried to improve his hearing, but there was nothing. He looked from the steps that led back into the bar to the flimsy ladder that led up to the hatch that opened into the street above.

Saunders eyes fell from the hatch. He shuffled to the corner of the room and slumped on the floor, wrapped his arms around his knees and began to sob. He could hide, need not climb the ladder, could wait for help, but then he heard a moan from the bar above. It grew, built steadily into a wail, more voices behind it and he knew that he had no choice, he had to do it, had to force himself to brave the outside world.

Another scream and Saunders began to rock slowly backwards and forwards, shaking uncontrollably. He was frightened, he was going into shock, but he forced himself to think, could he really hide? He could say that he had tried to help, had been about to leave, but then he heard it; a light noise, a scraping from above his head and he knew, they had found hatch.

Eddie Saunders was not a brave man, but, as his sobbing subsided, the fear of not doing what he knew to be right grew within him. Sweating now, head bowed, he rose to his feet, wiped his sleeve across his face and turned off the light in the cellar. Light or dark, he knew the room better than any man alive. He moved across it, took a hold of the ladder, the wood cold against his hands and climbed slowly up to the second hatch through which the beer barrels clattered every week.

Only four steps and Saunders' head bumped gently against the hatch. He gritted his teeth, checked the mobile was in his pocket, pulled out the large fob of keys that rarely left his person and allowed himself a deep breath.

The keys opened all the various doors and cupboards throughout the pub, but he knew them well, picked out the one that he needed and slid it quietly into the padlock that secured the bolt above his head. He listened intently, straining his ears for the slightest sound outside and twisted the key. It turned easily. He removed the padlock and slid back the bolt, cringed at the barely audible metallic scrape. He waited, slid the bolt fully back and pushed the hatch up a fraction of an inch. He tilted his head to one side, improved the angle and looked out into the street. He could see nothing.

The streetlights had failed an hour earlier but now they were back on and, after the darkness of the cellar, Edward Saunders blinked hard. He pushed the cellar hatch a little further, held his breathe and listened but heard nothing. He patted his pocket. His car keys and the mobile telephone were there, and he pushed the hatch a little further.

Edward Saunders let out his breathe, climbed another step when the cellar hatch was torn from his grasp.

Saunders gasped, it was a tiny, feminine sound, cut off as a hand grabbed his hair, pulled him roughly upwards and he felt a heavy blow under his right arm.

Saunders was dimly aware that someone had kicked him. But it was more than a kick. Then another blow in the middle of his back and the pain shot through him, paralysed him and he groaned as the two men who had struck him kicked the shafts of their axes hard, drove the blades deeper into his back and chest and heaved with all their might, dragged the landlord through the delivery hatch and into the street outside.

Saunders's mouth burned as the bile flooded up from his stomach. Confused, he could not register what was happening to him, felt he must be badly hurt, frowned at the dreadful tearing noise from deep within his body as he was dragged across the rough pavement. The pain stabbed at him again, blinded him, but then he felt nothing.

The landlord was moving, the rough ground tearing at his skin but he had gone, he had left his body and the cheer from the men around him seemed strangely distant. Saunders' vision was blurring, he could see only a flashing white lights as the short sword was driven into his body and the rough rope wound tightly around his neck. He heard himself begin to choke, but it was not him, this was happening elsewhere, in another place to a man he did not know. He blinked weakly as the blows rained down upon his face.

Blood spattered from Edward Saunders' mouth onto the men around him. His knees would not support him when as he was hauled him to his feet and he buckled and fell as he was dragged the short distance to the stout pillar that sprouted from the grass outside the pub. The choking rope tightened further as his feet left the ground and his body swung in an arc as he opened his eyes for the last time.

Saunders was vaguely aware of objects moving past him as he rose into the air, but his eyes were beginning to glaze. His head pounding, his own hands, broken-nailed, clawing at his face, scrabbling with the rope around his neck as the urine spilled from his leg and pattered to the ground.

The fog had cleared a little. The stars were now visible in the inky sky as the landlord's hands fell from his face and his senses momentarily sharpened. The sky spinning gently above him, there were sounds, the last that he would ever hear, creaking wood, a protesting rope, his attackers, grunting, straining as they hauled him up to swing and kick beside the sign of the King's Head and, in the distance, the wail of a police car. A cheer then nothing as the first of the arrows thumped into his chest.

Less than two miles away, on the A63, Inspector Bielby sat in the commandeered patrol car deep in thought.

Around him, even the individuals responsible for dealing with disaster and death every day of their lives went about their business in the slow and deliberate fashion of people in a state of shock.

The Scenes of Crime Investigators were there, measuring and recording, the flash of their cameras reflecting from the fog. The injured had been ferried by ambulance to hospitals in Hull and Goole and the members of two Armed Response Teams had arrived and were disconsolately kicking tyres.

Bielby had dragged his Chief Constable from a social function in Beverley to tell him what had happened. The Chief had not been happy but was now on his way to the scene. Worse in Bielby's opinion, the first reporters had begun to arrive and, as the cameras had begun to whirr, the Inspector's mood had deteriorated appreciably. The scaffolding and canvas screens had not yet been erected, and he lacked the manpower to keep the journalists away. Several had seen the scale of the tragedy. They were demanding answers, but Bielby had none to give.

The men who had committed this atrocity were still in the area, of that the Inspector felt strangely certain. He had ordered a sweep of the countryside to the west, north and east of the road and had called out the River Police from Hull to cover the water to the south. He had insisted that his men wear body armour and had called in more armed officers from West Yorkshire. They were expected to arrive shortly, but he was worried, he was very worried; he knew in his bones that the evening was not yet over but, like the death of an elderly relative, when the news came, it was still a shock. The patrol car's radio broke the silence.

'Incident reported at the King's Head public house. Armed youths reported fighting with knives. Can any units...'

Bielby grabbed the handset. The King's Head was only a couple of miles away. 'This is Bielby,' he barked. 'Approach with extreme caution and wait at the scene for armed backup. I do not, repeat not, want any dead heroes tonight.' He wiped his brow and stuck his head out of the car window. 'Did everyone get that?' He turned to Sergeant Price and the driver, jabbed sharply at the car then turned his attention back to the radio.

'Who rung it in?'

Bielby sensed a hesitance before the radio operator spoke. 'A member of the public from the pub toilets on a mobile 'phone. He's still on the line, sounds scared...'

'Keep him there,' interrupted Bielby. 'Any details of the attackers?'

'No, sir. The man heard the fighting and took a peep. Says there are dozens of them, axes...'

'Thank you,' said the Inspector as he tried to attach his seatbelt in the lurching car. He smiled grimly as Chief Constable Ronaldson's large black Rover flashed past them, travelling in the opposite direction, then tried to concentrate, stared without seeing first at the radio then at the frost-gripped countryside. He tried to weigh the possibilities.

It must be the same people, but who the hell were they?

Maniacs obviously, Hull had its share, but how could a gang like this exist without drawing attention to itself? It was not credible. And why were they doing this?

What possible motive could there be?

Less than three minutes later, the Inspector's car pulled up in front of the darkened pub. The Volvo's tires and suspension had paid a heavy price for its speed, but a dozen police cars and the two ART vans had beaten it to the scene, their occupants crouching by the sides of their vehicles, conversing in whispers, waiting for a lead, a lead that Bielby knew he must supply.

Bielby climbed out of the vehicle and, his hand on the Volvo's roof, he surveyed the scene. The fog was thinner here, the pub less than fifty yards distant, but it was the gently swaying body of the Landlord that drew all eyes like a magnet.

Eyes tracked from the Inspector to the hanged man and back again and Bielby knew beyond doubt, this was his show, what he did next could cost lives. He had to keep his men safe, slow everything down to a more manageable pace. He raised his hand to his chin.

More emergency services vehicles were arriving. They would wait, secure the pub, calm things down and talk them out, but a sound interrupted the Inspector's thoughts. Laughter. Base, unpleasant, it floated across the still air from the pub and then a scream.

Another police car screeched to a halt and its driver, a young policeman with a boyish face, jumped out. His arm frozen in the process of putting on his cap, he looked at the body of the Landlord.

Another laugh, waiting was not an option. The officers nearest to Bielby jumped back, startled, as the older man seemed to spring into action. He gestured towards the two Armed Response Teams then stabbed at the pub. 'Get your people ready to move.'

The ART vans edged towards the pub, the Inspector walking by their side, their silent blue lights flashing, lending a movement to the dripping body of the Landlord. The vans drew to a halt and Bielby, a loudspeaker now in his hand, fumbled briefly a switch before holding it out to Sergeant Price. The sergeant switched it on and handed it back.

Bielby took a deep breath. The pub now silent, he raised the loudspeaker to his mouth. 'This is Inspector Bielby of the Humberside Police Force. There are armed police outside. I want you to come out of the building in single file, with your hands raised and lay face downwards on the road. Do not make any sudden movements. I repeat; we are armed police officers. Do you understand?'

The Inspector's voice was level, reassuring and authoritative, its volume a surprise to some of the officers closest to him.

A slight breeze moved the curtains at the pub's glassless windows and its sign creaked under the weight of the landlord's body as Bielby strained to listen.

Nothing. Then voices, an indignant snort and a thump. It sounded again, a man chopping wood and then again, then a cheer and, seconds later, an object flew through one of the building's broken windows, landed heavily on the pavement and rolled to a stop in the street. Bielby did not need to look to know what it was but still he did. It was a head, the head of a young man, its lank greasy hair matted with blood. It had a sticking plaster on its chin.

Coarse laughter from within the pub broke the stunned silence as the thumping started again and Bielby's mind was set. He felt relieved, he knew what to do, had no choice. He turned to the ART Sergeant.

'Get in there now,' he said calmly. 'And Sergeant, we're not the judge and the jury here. I want this ending as peacefully as possible but take no unnecessary risks.' He turned to Sergeant Price. 'Get another twelve men ready to go in, check their body armour and helmets personally.'

Seconds later, crouching and hugging the ground, the two ARTs moved towards the pub. The door was off its hinges, the large bare windows would provide further easy access and there were no signs of a barricade. Several officers circled around the back as a second cheer sounded form within the pub and an object bumped across the frozen grass.

It rolled into the gutter and the ART Sergeant, crouched by the pub's right-hand window, radio already in his hand, caught Bielby's eye. The Inspector nodded and the Sergeant raised his radio to his mouth. 'Go, Go, Go!'

The first armed officer rose to his feet in front of the window by the side of his Sergeant then stumbled and fell backwards, clutching an arrow embedded in his body armour. Stunned but unhurt he fell, was trampled by his colleagues as they poured over him. Bielby's stomach churned as he bit down hard on his lower lip and the sound of automatic gunfire rang out.

Friday 26 October 1999
Three

Charles Bertrand Warner opened the door firmly. It bumped against his foot, and he closed it more carefully, walked down the short corridor and out into the bright morning sunshine. It was a little after 6am, but it was already hot, had been hot all night. Christ, thought Warner, it had been hot forever. The young man took a deep breath and felt his mind began to sharpen. He could hear the birds, and a slight puff of wind caught his face, lifted the hair from above his eyes. The luxury was appreciated, but it intensified the oppressive heat when the stillness returned. Warner raised his head and the building that he sought rose up before him, squat and grey against the brilliant blue of the summer sky. He gritted his teeth and began to walk towards it.

****

Baring his teeth, Jeremy Whittleton turned his head to one side, squinted and examined them closely in the bathroom mirror. They could be a little whiter, but they weren't too bad he thought as he held in his stomach and turned to one side. Jeremy was thirty-seven and in reasonable shape, still as fit as the job allowed him to be and he squinted at his reflection. He still had a full head of black hair, he patted it down, a little grey at the temples but he didn't look too bad, even at 5.30 in the morning.

Jeremy was Global Head of Equity Research at Stretton Goldberg, the influential London-based stock broking firm now owned by a large German bank. He loved his job, and, in fairness, he was rather good at it, keeping the dozens of plates for which he was responsible spinning with the skill of a veteran circus performer.

It was a rare talent, well rewarded, but he had felt a distinct sense of unease for some time now and he shook his head. Maybe he was getting old? The periodic trips to visit the bank's operations worldwide had lost their appeal and, after fourteen years, he was finding it difficult to get out of bed at this ungodly hour.

Turning back to the mirror, Jeremy wiped the last of the shaving foam from his face, wrinkled his nose at the blood-flecked flannel's unpleasant smell and pushed it to one side for the wash.

Now he could hear Caroline, in the bedroom next door. She always got up with him, that was a blessing, but her voice was drowned out as he began to brush his teeth methodically, thinking of the day ahead. He finished with a flourish, spat the toothpaste into the basin and splashed his face with cold water. He could hear Caroline more clearly now, calling his name, she sounded concerned.

'Caroline?'

Jeremy turned towards the bathroom door a little too quickly. He staggered slightly and his head began to swim. A drink after a successful day at work always seemed like such a good idea at the time, but he regretted it now, he always did. Still, he couldn't pull a sicky no matter how awful he felt; it just wasn't done. He hadn't had a day off work for years and it was more important than ever that he be in the office today. Not only to set an example but to tie up the loose ends that needed attending to before he set off for Tokyo mid- morning. He let his head clear and walked a little more steadily towards the door.

'I know that pub,' said Caroline, without looking up as Jeremy entered the bedroom. She was sitting on the bed bare-shouldered, her dark hair still down. She pulled on a fawn blouse and pointed to the television flickering quietly in the corner of the room.

'Which pub?' Jeremy felt a flicker of interest, but the thought of pubs was not a welcome one.

'Look,' said Caroline. 'It's the King's Head near Elloughton. You remember? The one on the road to Hull, set back off the road with the big Beer Garden, the pub where you broke the bar stool?'

Jeremy did remember. They had visited the large pub near the A63 with the views over the River Humber last summer and Jeremy was still sure that it had not been his fault. He had sat on a stool in the beer-garden, the leg had broken off the bloody thing and he had fallen flat on his back, spilling most of the drinks on the tray that he had been carrying. Everyone had laughed.

Rather too enthusiastically as he remembered it and he could still see Caroline's happy smiling face looking down at him as the beer had soaked through his shirt.

'So what's been going on?' He imagined the pub burning down. It was not an altogether unpleasant image.

'There's been some kind of a massacre,' said Caroline, the genuine concern obvious in her voice.

Jeremy felt a pang of guilt at his earlier thought.

He walked towards the television, images of flashing blue lights and stretchers being urgently borne towards ambulances filling the screen, haggard-looking rescue workers dashing to and fro. He had seen a snatch of the report earlier and had assumed that the scenes were being beamed from Japan. There had been trouble there for several days now and it was weighing heavily on his mind. He would be there himself in less than twenty-four hours and there were stories of foreigners being dragged into the violence and beaten up in the streets. It could be a nightmare. At the very least, the transport systems would be shot to pieces, but he had no choice, he had to go. He glanced at his watch then back to the TV. 'What on earth's happened?'

Caroline continued to stare intently at the television. 'It's awful, nearly fifty people dead so far and they're still counting. They don't seem to be giving details, looks like some sort of fight.'

Fifty people?

Jeremy shook his head and moved to sit down next to Caroline. He checked himself, looked at his watch again and felt another pang of guilt. He would have to pick up the details from the screens at work. He looked at the back of Caroline's head, read her concern in her posture.

Jeremy wanted to hold her, to comfort her, but he didn't like goodbyes, and they had argued. Caroline had been worried, did not want him to go to Tokyo, but at least this news this would push Japan off the screens for a while and he would only be away for 10 days. He put his hand on Caroline's shoulder, and she turned towards him.

He smiled, kissed her lightly on the cheek then reached for his bag, did not see his wife turn away. He zipped the bag closed, shouldered it and left the bedroom.

Moving as quietly as he was able, Jeremy looked in on the girls, Emily and Virginia. Eyes closed, unaware of the world about them, of the troubles of humanity, sleeping soundly they were beautiful, innocent and he smiled.

Jeremy was still smiling as he walked into the kitchen, flicked on the kettle. The girls were his pride and joy; he loved them with all his heart. He turned on the downstairs TV.

'...now risen to forty-eight,' said the voiceover, 'and is expected to rise further. The death toll from the earlier incident involving the coach now stands at twenty-eight...'

Bus crashes as well? Jeremy made the tea and listened as the news moved on to events in Tokyo. He paced pensively, his mind jumping between the tasks of the day ahead and the news bulletin.

The newsroom handed over to the Meteorological Office and Jeremy knew that it was time to leave. He hesitated, rubbed his chin. Caroline was still upstairs, but he didn't want a scene. He could ring her during the morning, and he'd be back before they knew it. He walked to the mirror in the hallway by the front door and straightened his tie thankful that he looked significantly better than he felt. Now he could hear Caroline moving around upstairs, he picked up his shoulder bag, his briefcase was still in the office and took Caroline's car keys from the hall table. 'Goodbye Caroline,' he shouted up the stairs. 'Say bye-bye to the girls.'

Jeremy listened for a moment but heard nothing, looked at his watch again and left the house without turning off the television. He was sure that Caroline would be fine, but still he felt uneasy, even fearful. They were growing apart. He loved his wife, was sure that she loved him, and she was his best friend, his lover, the mother of his children, but still he knew that they needed to work at it, he could feel the strain. They should have a holiday; they owed it to themselves, but, as Jeremy turned his back on the house, he shook his head. For the moment he had no choice, he had to work.

Jeremy shivered and tutted at the ice on the windscreen of the car. He rubbed at it briefly with his bare hand but did not have the time to scrape it properly. He opened the door, got in and, the rear windscreen still heavily iced over, did not see Caroline, standing in the doorway, dab at her cheek with her handkerchief.

Less than ten minutes later Jeremy pulled into the car park of the railway station at Bishop's Stortford. He slid a little on the ice but straightened up easily enough and patted the small car's steering wheel. He had had to take Caroline's car, a nice little Golf, bought only that spring and he was relieved to see that his own, a seven-series BMW, was still where he had left it in the car park the previous day. He parked as close as he could to it, the heavy frost on its windscreen announcing to the world that he hadn't picked it up last night. He'd drunk far too much but now he had to remember to ring Caroline to tell her to use the spare keys and get a cab to the station to pick up the Golf.

She would be angry, and it was another reason to feel guilty. Caroline might even have to make a second trip to collect the BMW tomorrow and he owed her an apology, a proper one. He was slipping, he had to make it up to her.

Jeremy bought his newspapers, nodded to a couple of casual acquaintances, took up his usual position on the platform and glanced at the headlines in the 'Financial Times'. The previous night's violent events in Yorkshire had not made it into the early editions, Japan's financial problems were still the lead and Jeremy waited for his travelling companions to arrive, his mind now firmly on the day ahead.

****

Returning to the bedroom, Caroline Whittleton pinned up her hair. She had heard the car over-revving outside, the gravel peppering the wall as Jeremy had driven away, but she put it out of her mind. Turning sideways, she regarded herself in the mirror; the blue line had confirmed it, she was expecting again.

It was not yet 6am, this was the part of the day that she usually most enjoyed, but Caroline could feel her eyes filling with tears. For years, she had hated getting up at such an ungodly hour but since the girls, she had seen it as a positive advantage. They were still asleep, the nanny had not yet arrived, Jeremy had left for work, and she had the house to herself, for a while at least. She could plan the day ahead; an hour and a half every morning allowed her to hit the ground running at work, but today she felt no lift, no buzz of anticipation. Was it the baby or Jeremy?

Jeremy must be concerned himself, news of the violence in Tokyo was everywhere, but he hadn't taken the time to say goodbye properly. His career should not, could not, be allowed to become more important to him than their family, their marriage. With a third child on the way they had too much to lose, but they had their holidays to look forward to, maybe they could refresh things then, keep them alive. In the meantime, Jeremy had this trip to Tokyo and then another in November to New York, but if they could spend Christmas together as a family in Australia, they had something tangible, something real to look forward to.

And Jeremy didn't know. Caroline hadn't yet told him that she was pregnant, felt a certain satisfaction in knowing something that he did not. She looked back at the mirror and smiled, moved closer to it and examined the tiny wrinkles that had begun to appear around her eyes. She was still attractive, there was no grey in her hair, her skin was smooth and unblemished, and her body was good. It always had been, and it didn't frighten her. She'd worked hard to get back into shape after the girls and her skin had begun to lighten again now that the summer had gone. She liked it neither more nor less, simply welcomed the change.

Caroline's natural father, whom she had never known, had been West Indian, her mother a clerk in a small insurance agent's office in Leeds. She had always spoken fondly of Caroline's father, still did but she had married Oliver when Caroline was less than two years old and, to her, he had always been dad. He had been a solicitor, unrepentantly middle class and Caroline had often wondered how on earth his world and that of her mother had ever collided. But, for whatever reason, they had, and the couple had had a very happy marriage.

'Lucky to have found a man at all but even his name is boring,' her grandmother had said to her mother one evening when they had thought that Caroline was not listening. And she had been right, but Caroline had loved Oliver as much as any little girl had ever loved her father. Oliver had died in a car crash when Caroline was fourteen and her last words to him had been harsh. Cutting, teenaged and thoughtlessly hurtful, she regretted them bitterly.

Life after her father's death had been tough at times, although not financially, his life insurance policies had seen to that. There had never been any hiding the obvious differences between Caroline and her two half-sisters and she had never sought to do so. Still, there had been the occasional snigger when she had introduced them for the first time but, overall, Leeds had been a pleasant place to grow up in the 'seventies and, although she had not lived there for the best part of two decades, Caroline still had fond memories of it as her hometown.

Caroline smiled; her father, Oliver, had made her what she was. He had helped to set her on the course that had led her to excel at school, had given her the confidence to accept the offer of a place to read Natural Sciences in Cambridge, to follow it with the doctorate that had ultimately led to Jeremy and the life that she now lived, and she loved him still. He was with her every day.

Caroline lowered her eyes; she did not get back to the north nearly as often as she would have liked. Her younger sisters had both followed her to Cambridge and, as all three were still associated with the University in one way or another, she was not short of friends in the south, but she felt strangely alone, inexplicably unhappy.

Descending the stairs, walking silently into the brightly lit kitchen, Caroline switched off the television and turned on the radio. Classical music, woodwind, she switched channels and tapped the teapot. Still hot, she made herself a drink, walked through to the study, turned on her computer and logged on to the laboratory mainframe the news bulletin from the kitchen now little but background noise.

****

Six o'clock and, one hundred and forty miles to the north, thick-headed, his mind dulled by lack of sleep Inspector Bielby frowned at the blood on his shoes. He steadied his breathing, held up his right hand and squinted as he examined his nails. He picked at the browning blood and shook his head.

The storming of the pub had been a short but violent affair. No perpetrator had laid down his weapons when ordered to do so and most of them had died at the scene. Bielby shook his head again. The blood on his hands would wash off. He had warned his men not to act as judge, jury and executioner away from the lights of the television cameras and, even after the terrible sights that had confronted them in the pub, he believed them when they said that they had not.

Bielby had been through the events in his mind, had turned them this way and that, had thought of little else, but still he had few doubts that he had been right to storm the pub. The King's Head had been an abattoir, a charnel house, worse. The majority of drinkers had survived the attack, but twenty-four civilians had been pronounced dead at the scene.Another two had died since as well as two police officers.

The Press had got hold of the numbers, but Bielby had clamped down hard where he was able and no information about the perpetrators had yet leaked out. Still, he had been unable to prevent several journalists getting other details, some of the names of the victims, the nature of their injuries and how he hated them, the hacks and the police officers, selling information for drinks, for petty favours or worse, for pathetically small amounts of money.

But he knew that it made for good copy. Several of the victims had been beheaded and one man had been found draped over the bar like a tailor's dummy, his arms nailed to the wood. He was dead, his lungs exposed and pulled from his body. Some sort of ritual, one of the reporters had speculated, a 'blood-eagle'.

Of the more than thirty perpetrators, only twelve were alive and all were injured and under heavy police guard in the Hull Royal Infirmary. Three were not expected to survive and none had asked for a lawyer or tried to communicate with the police or the hospital authorities in any way.

That would come, Bielby was sure, but, for the moment, his major concerns lay elsewhere. He had spoken to two newly widowed women during the night, had comforted the partners of his injured officers but he felt dirty, cheapened, had not been able to give fully of himself, he still had work to do. There were reports that one or more of the perpetrators had escaped from the King's Head, had disappeared into the fog.

Bielby rubbed his eyes, opened them and looked at the starkly painted wall in front of him. He had remained at the pub until 4am, had handed over to Inspector Walker, a capable but dull colleague also from the Queen's Gardens central police station and had then come, with Sergeant Price, to the Infirmary to be with the seven officers who had been injured in the storming of the pub.

The last of the men was now stable, Bielby had sent Price home an hour earlier, but still did not feel able to leave the hospital himself. He looked up as a nurse bustled past, rummaged in a cupboard beneath the reception desk and walked past him again carrying a large bottle of bleach and a tin.

'Lousy head to foot, they are,' said the nurse to no one in particular. She caught Bielby's eye and tried to smile. 'Never seen anything like it.'

Too tired to smile back, Bielby stared blankly at the nurse's retreating back.

****

Striding purposefully into the Oval Office, US President George Sutton hid his tiredness well. The diminutive Larry Edelman, his National Security Adviser, was struggling to keep pace and the seven other members of the President's National Security Council were clearly taken by surprise by Sutton's unannounced entry into the room. They failed to rise to their feet until the President was almost at his desk.

'Sit, sit.' Sutton ran his hand though his hair, turned to Edelman. 'Larry, tell me this isn't as bad as it sounds.'

Edelman cleared his throat. 'I'm afraid I can't do that, sir. It's serious, more than thirty perpetrators this time, almost a hundred dead.'

President Sutton sat, rubbed his chin, worked the stubble with his thumb. It was 1am in Washington and he was tired. He tried to keep in shape, to work out, but it was hard to make the time. Youthful they called him, but he felt every day of his forty-four years.

Still, bed was a distant prospect and the three-day weekend in New England that he had promised Lizzy and the boys was likely to be cancelled. George junior and Bradley were at college, had only agreed to go to please their mother, but Patrick and James would be devastated. The President raised his head. 'An accident? A co-incidence?'

Edelman hesitated. 'No, sir, we think not.'

Four

Charles Warner opened the door to the dull grey building. He breathed deep and entered, the corridor warm and humid, ahead of him the door to the room held open by a red fire extinguisher. He straightened his jacket and walked in. A large fan whopped slowly above the young man's head, moved the stale air from one place to another but did nothing to lighten his mood of the four men already seated. They were facing the front and turned to follow Warner's progress to his seat. He caught the eye of the man closest to him and his face twisted into a difficult smile.

****

George Sutton raised his eyes from the papers before him. His advisers, apart from Larry Edelman shifting uneasily in his seat, waited for an invitation to speak seemed to have little to say for themselves as he looked from face to face.

The room was crowded, but the President had never felt more alone, more in possession of something that set him apart. In addition to Edelman, Daniel White and Alex Reinhardt, the President's two personal advisers on national security and economic policy were present, alongside Linda King and Dick Turner, Sutton's Secretary of State and Secretary of Defence. Jack Scott, the Chairman of the Joint Chiefs of Staff, was seated on one of the couches. Next to him was the Attorney General, Tony Rodriguez. Gerry Buchanan, the Director of the Central Intelligence Agency, was standing by the door that led to the President's private study and dining room.

Maria Hernandez, the US Ambassador to the United Nations usually present for such briefings, was in New York and Joey Kline, the Secretary of the Treasury, was in Europe. The seat that the sixty-two-year-old Vice President, Walter Peacock, had made his own was empty. His loss already being felt acutely, he had been killed in a car crash in Arkansas two weeks earlier. The President looked from the vacant seat to Edelman and nodded.

To avoid the recurring dilemma of who really controlled US foreign policy, the President had adopted a policy of almost total openness with his National Security Council. This usually had the effect of reducing the relative power of his National Security Adviser but there were still occasions when things were managed on a more ad-hoc basis. This had been one such occasion and, smoothing his few remaining hairs across the top of his head, Edelman took a deep breath.

'Mr President, there have been two serious incidents in the north of England perpetrated by a group of over thirty individuals. These incidents have left almost seventy civilians, most of the perpetrators and two police officers, dead,' said Edelman. He paused and Sutton watched as his National Security Adviser caught Linda King's eye. 'The attacks appear to have been carried out by individuals who arrived on the shores of the River Humber in a Longboat which the British police found about a quarter of a mile from the first incident. The perpetrators were armed with swords, knives and axes as well as bows and arrows and the attacks occurred in East Yorkshire, an area that suffered from major Viking raids and later immigration over a period of two centuries around a thousand years ago.'

Sutton looked at his advisers in turn as Edelman paused, stroked a strand of black hair back across the top of his head and swallowed hard. Secretary of State King was glaring at him, surprised, undoubtedly, but waiting for a chance to strike, willing him to make a mistake. President Sutton shook his head. He stepped in, broke it up. 'Questions, Linda?'

The Secretary of State looked at the President and shook her head, the corners of her mouth turned down.

'Reenactors? Possibly racist but lunatics, obviously?'

Sutton turned back to Edelman, spread his hands.

'Larry?'

Edelman pursed his lips, looked at the President, raised himself to his full height and continued. 'We believe that these people may, in fact, be genuine Vikings. If they follow the pattern...'

'Whoa, whoa!' Linda King looked from Edelman to the President. 'George, where are we going with this?'

'This isn't a joke, people,' said Sutton. 'I suggest that you hear Larry out.'

Secretary of State King sat down slowly, and Edelman continued. 'These may be individuals brought from the past by means which, as yet, we cannot explain...'

'George, this is a big leap!'

Sutton's eyes held those of his Secretary of State.

'Linda, we can do this either with or without you.' '

I'm sorry, George,' said Linda King, once again resuming her seat. 'Larry, please.'

'After analysing data from a series of incidents, culminating in those of earlier this evening, we believe that a series of phenomena, possibly orchestrated, possibly not, have led to the appearance of individuals and now a group of individuals in the north of England. These individuals, to all intents and purposes, appear to have come from the past...'

Edelman's voice trailed off; his confidence shot. He sat down, began to mop his forehead as the members of the NSC began to exchange glances. One by one, they turned to the President and George Sutton rose to his feet.

'Go on, Larry. Let's get this all out. If this is orchestrated, are we saying that the Brits are the intended targets?'

Edelman smiled and rose to his feet, ignored the glances. Most of those present had not taken part in the briefings over the last six weeks, were ignorant of the facts. The National Security Adviser's hand trembled as he smoothed his hair, but he cleared his throat and continued.

'We don't know at this stage, sir, but the events have all taken place there. The energy pulses, the appearances too, the rocks and the animals...'

President Sutton glanced at Linda King. 'I'll have to ask you to take this at face value for the moment, people. We'll do the background later.' He turned back to Larry Edelman. 'Should we tell the Brits?'

Edelman blanched, shook his head. 'With respect, sir, tell them what? That we believe a group of Vikings have been whisked through time by a person or persons unknown?'

'I'm aware of the problems, Larry, but what hope have we of containment if we don't work with them?'

'That is a consideration, Mr President,' said Edelman. 'But to tell them may, well...'

'May what, Larry?'

'May suggest that we've been carrying out an investigation in their back yard...'

'And haven't we?'

'We do have active elements in the UK,' Edelman said, his discomfort clear. He glanced towards the door and the small, unremarkable man in the corner of the room shifted his position, cleared his throat discreetly. He ran his fingers through his thinning reddish-brown hair and Gerry Buchanan, the 48-year-old Director of the CIA's friendly eyes caught those of the President.

'Yes Gerry?'

'Whalebone, sir,' said Buchanan slowly. 'A low-level operation, non-intrusive.'

'And?'

Buchanan cleared his throat a second time and the President flinched. 'There's a possibility that it's been compromised.'

Sutton looked down at the desk before him, shook his head. 'Give us the facts.'

'As I said, Whalebone is a low-level op. Nothing dirty, it's been running in the UK for several weeks. We were about to withdraw our people, but we may be too late, we've lost contact with a couple of them and, in the light of that, you may like to consider sharing some information with the Brits before they work things out for themselves.'

Sutton said nothing, turned to the window. The view of the head of the CIA was clear, deniability was no longer an option, and the President turned back, surveyed the sea of mostly blank faces before him.

'Larry, make preparations to tell the Brits and don't hold anything back.'

****

Carter Lockyer had finished his physical audit.

Nothing serious, thank God, but each movement revealed some new minor injury, and he had lost one of his shoes. Even more bizarrely, he had lost a sock and, all things considered, he had felt much better. No doubt, he thought as he leaned back in the Spartan wooden chair, unshaven, his dark brown hair, matted and dirty and his roll-neck black sweater badly torn at both elbows, he looked a mess. He rubbed his chin and wondered where it had gone wrong.

Operation Whalebone had blown up in his face. Lockyer had not heard from his partner, Lesley-Anne Kohl, for almost three hours, had to hope that she could salvage something from the wreckage, was safe as he, seated at a table in a small room deep underground in Paddington Green police station, most certainly was not.

He had been taken some forty minutes earlier. Now

he had to minimize the blowback and that was going to be no small job. His nationality they may have guessed from his flight, but he had been disturbed that they had known his name, and he still did not know where he was.

Lockyer had been blindfolded, but he had only been in the car for four or five minutes so he could not be much more than a mile from the US Embassy. Added to that, the faint rumble of underground trains meant that it was probably Paddington Green. Normal procedure, it was what he would have expected, there was nothing to worry about. Lockyer tried to steady his breathing, was disappointed that he could not.

Lockyer pursed his lips and nodded; the professionalism of the agents who had taken him had been impressive.

They had done their job well, but now it was imperative that the situation was not allowed to escalate any further. It was not in his interests that it did, not in the interests of his country, not even in the interests of the British themselves, if only they could see that, and he would do his best to prevent things from becoming any more complicated than was strictly necessary. He nodded again and smiled, rubbed his bruised chin as it came back to him. This was still a 'no shots fired incident'. He had liked the phrase and wanted to keep it that way.

Just under an hour earlier, Carter Lockyer had found himself staring down the barrel of a gun as he had left the nondescript office inside the building close to the Ministry of Defence in Whitehall. It was to have been a standard bag-job, not too nasty, nothing wet about it, but he had been caught, camera in hand and Lockyer could still picture the wide, surprised eyes of the man behind the gun.

The CIA man's instincts had taken over and a shiver ran down his spine as Lockyer remembered how he had immediately slammed the door in the armed man's face, burst across the office and thrown himself without hesitation through the window that he had opened earlier to provide an exit route that he had not expected to use.

Lockyer had known that the drainpipe was there, had tested it, knew that it should be able to support his weight, but as he had raced down it, he had felt sure that it would come away from the wall, but it had not. He had reached the ground safely and had crossed the grass, gained the anonymity of the bushes, his breath white around his head, before the first voices had been heard at the window behind him. But he must have been observed. There must have been at least a couple of spooks behind him from the start and the chase was on. Lockyer had exited the gardens, crossed Horse Guards Parade, skirted St James's Park and then crossed the Mall. He had not believed that he was being followed, had cut to the left and entered Green Park and paused for a few moments to assess the situation.

Had the man been a simple security guard? Lockyer had doubted it at the time, still did. Guards in the UK were very rarely armed, even in sensitive buildings, which meant that he was likely in the business, a fellow spook!

Although there had been no signs of a pursuit, Lockyer had taken the small automatic weapon out of his pocket, had scraped a hole in the frost-crusted earth of the Green Park flowerbed, and covered the gun over. He had pin-pointed the spot then had crossed Piccadilly and headed into Mayfair.

Less than a quarter of a mile from the vast American Embassy in Grosvenor Square and safety, Lockyer had begun to relax when he had sensed that he had company.

Looking around, he had caught sight of two men emerge from the heavy shadows by one of the grand Georgian buildings in Berkeley Square and begin running soundlessly towards him.

Professionals, pavement artists for sure, Lockyer had begun to run himself. Breathing heavily, he had made Mount Row, Carlos Place and could see the Embassy, was only yards from safety when the hand brushed his shoulder. Lockyer had spurted on, had made another ten yards when the hand had swung up again, had taken a firm hold of his hair.

Lockyer winced at the thought, Christ, but it had hurt!

His eyes had immediately filled with tears, but he had kept on running, had used his momentum to gain the few remaining yards but the man holding him allowed himself to fall, to be dragged along the ground and Lockyer had found himself pulling the weight of a large man with his hair. He had gasped in pain, had slowed and sank to his knees as the second agent grabbed his arm, pushed him to the ground. Lockyer rubbed his jaw; he had felt his face hit the pavement, strong hands pulling his arms behind his back. A knee in his back, he was winded and could not speak, but he had heard a voice clearly.

'Hey, what gives?'

It had been an American voice and Lockyer had twisted his head painfully towards it, had seen the white-belted Military Policeman slowly descend the Embassy steps.

'I'm an American citizen,' Lockyer had said before he had been able to stop himself. Now he could curse, it had been a mistake, an unforgivable lapse of discipline.

'Get...'

A large hand had clamped down on Lockyer's mouth, a length of sticky tape replacing it almost immediately. He had felt the man's weight shift above him.

'Stay there, soldier. The UK starts at the foot of those steps.'

Lockyer had felt the ratcheted plastic cords being tightened on his wrists even as the man was speaking and, from nowhere, a black bag had appeared and had been pulled over his head.

'This is a no shots fired incident,' the Scottish voice had said. A hand had patted Lockyer on the head. 'Let's keep it that way, shall we?'

Lockyer had heard the MP unbutton his gun holster, knew that the boy had only seconds to live. He had not been able to warn him, but it seemed that he had not descended any further down the steps when Lockyer had heard a car sweep into the square, its tires squealing as it slid to a halt nearby followed by the unmistakable sound of an automatic weapon being cocked. Then another.

Lockyer had tried to cry out, a life was about to be snuffed out. It would be handled discreetly of course, a car crash or some such but then the sound of studded boots on flagstones then a second American voice. 'Meissner, what the Hell are you doing out here?'

A muttered reply and something tightened around Lockyer's feet. The spooks were turning their attention back to him; that was good. A strong hand-held his head down as he felt his wrists being attached to the plastic cord around his ankles.

'Get your hand away from the weapon son,' the Scots voice had said. Hesitation.

'Get the Hell inside, Meissner!' A second American voice and the boy's life was safe.

****

In East Yorkshire the young police officer took off his helmet and ran his hand through his damp hair. The cold clawed at him, sought out his exposed skin and he put the helmet back on, looked up at the eastern sky; it had not yet begun to lighten. It was 6.45am and, though it was a little less cold by the side of the River Hull, the muddy, slow-moving tributary of the River Humber from which the city of Hull took its name, a freezing fog had crept in and was blanketing most of the city.

The town seemed to be asleep. The fog had deadened what little sound was about and Constable Andrew Bielby had been struggling to prevent his mind from wandering for some time. He blew on his gloved hands, an automatic gesture and stamped his feet. He could scarcely feel them, longed to be out of the cold, but would do his job. And the overtime would help. There had been plenty for anyone who wanted it since the two incidents to the west of the city, many police officers had returned to their stations during the night, were now keeping a watch over the city, were freezing in silent corners as he, himself, was doing.

Two, maybe more, perpetrators had escaped from the King's Head the reports had said, and, during the early hours of the morning, despite the deathly quiet that had settled over the city, nerves had been stretched to breaking point.

Bielby stamped his feet again, shuffled from the doorway of the office building at the junction of Scale

Lane and High Street in which he had been sheltering; there had been nothing for hours. The nightclubs and restaurants had emptied relatively peacefully, the odd scuffle, but nothing out of the ordinary and, by the time that the scale of the tragedies had become known, the town was asleep, the centre virtually deserted.

Grave-like, it had remained very quiet for the rest of the night leaving Bielby and, he hoped, dozens of young officers like him, to shiver as they squinted periodically into the fog. He knew that colleagues were positioned throughout the city, trusted them to do their jobs and knew that he was not really alone but a non-emergency radio blackout had been imposed, and he had begun to feel very isolated. He shuffled a little further from the doorway, looked across at the Manchester Arms Hotel and remembered his father's words. 'It's the same for everyone in the beginning,' the old man had said. 'Give it a chance and you'll know if it's really what you want to do within a year or so.'

Andrew Bielby's father was often right, but the younger man already knew that this was what he wanted to do. He would stick it out, had immediately appreciated the camaraderie, had made real friends but, from time to time, he still wondered whether having a father in the business was an asset or a liability. The faint smile that edged across his face broadened then disappeared as the young officer's radio crackled into life, but it was nothing.

There had been a disturbance near the Marina, an old, converted dock that was now home to several hundred small pleasure boats, the report said. Routine but not to be ignored, youths probably, nothing serious but Bielby was pleased for the interruption. Hoping to be asked to investigate, he acknowledged the report but was told not to leave his position.

Frustrated, Bielby frowned, strained his ears against the deadening fog for any sound of movement. Nothing. Then a buzz, nothing more but as he listened, he thought that he could hear voices. The fog could be playing tricks on him, but then, he was sure. The youths were coming closer.

A shiver of excitement ran down Bielby's spine. He peered into the gloom again and made out the shapes of three, then four people approaching, shrouded by the fog, but now backlit by a yellow sodium lamp buzzing in the damp air. They were much closer than he had imagined, one of them was waving something, a car aerial.

Bielby turned away and radioed in their location as quietly as possible then turned back to the youths.

Talking loudly, their accents local, they were making no attempt to keep out of site and Bielby felt a flush of disappointment. Still, they had not seen him, arguing about money, the tallest of them lurched down the side of an ugly grey-brick, 1960's building towards the Old Harbour and the river Hull. The others followed.

'Four youths moving by the side of Oriel House towards the River Hull,' whispered Bielby softly into his radio. 'Keeping them in visual contact. Look to be moving north, direction of Wilberforce House.'

Bielby turned off his radio. Not that they were paying the blindest bit of notice to what was going on around them, but he did not want it spluttering into life and attracting their attention. There were four of them, after all, not small either and launching a policeman into the foul river might round off their evening nicely. He undid his truncheon's Velcro fastening and walked silently to the river's edge. The youth's had begun to argue amongst themselves.

'What the fuckdya do that for?' said the youth in the blue jacket.

The tallest youth had launched a mobile phone spinning towards the waters of the river below, but there was no splash. He sniggered loudly, peered at the brackish, tidal river. It was low, exposing filthy humps of the mud banked up against the wharves of the warehouses by the water's edge and leaving the river as a narrow, fast-flowing ditch in the middle. Bicycles, shopping trolleys and much worse had disappeared into the dark sucking mud and the mobile telephone had already vanished, leaving nothing but a small black hole. Soon that too had gone.

'It coulda been worth summat,' said the blue-jacketed youth.

The group came to an unsteady halt as the tall youth grinned widely. 'It's worth fuck all now!'

The youth hooted at his wit and staggered towards an alleyway that led back up towards High Street. He laughed again, unzipped his flies and began to urinate forcefully onto the cement floor. Tailing off to a messy dribble, he sniggered, zipped himself up then stopped to peer into the darkness of the alley.

Bielby frowned, watched the youth intently as he furrowed his brow, tried to focus his eyes. He had seen something, a movement. Bielby flicked on his radio but could not tear his eyes from the scene before him. The youth was turning, was about to speak to the others when he grunted suddenly, staggered backwards towards the river clutching his stomach.

'Kev?'

'Kevin?'

The tall youth began to shudder strangely, his feet drumming on the wooded wharf as he took another unsteady step backwards.

'Kev, stop fuckin' around...'

Unthinking, acting on instinct and reaching for his radio, Constable Bielby was moving towards them. He was in plain sight, but Kevin Wood could not turn his head.

Nor did he appear to have heard his friends' voices. He looked down at the dark liquid oozing between his fingers and began to judder, to tremble violently. He took another step backwards away from the alley, tried to turn but could not.

Another step.

Then another as the shape of a man emerged from the shadows. Then Kevin Wood pitched backwards, over the edge of the quay and into the filthy black ooze banked against the river's western wharves.

Immediately, the clinging mud began to suck at him, to draw him down.

A foghorn warned traffic somewhere on the Humber but Bielby, still walking towards the stricken youths, paid it no heed. His eyes, instead, were drawn to the boy in the mud. They could still save him. His hands were fluttering like a bird's wings, he was still alive, but they needed to get to him quickly.

Unblinking, Bielby watched as the youth moved his lips.

No sound emerged. Noticeably weaker, his arms had fallen to the mud, his fingers now trembling over his stomach and Bielby gagged.

Even in the half-light, Bielby could see the wound and,

although the youth was not struggling, he was beginning to sink, water flowing back into the depression that his body had created in the mud, beginning to pour into the boy's mouth. He coughed weakly, tried to move, but by the time the water covered his eyes, he no longer had the strength to blink.

'Kev?'

Still the youths had not seen Bielby approaching. The officer pulled his radio around to his mouth.

'Kev, we'll get a rope, we'll get you out.'

There was no rope, the mobile phone had gone, they would not pull their friend from the mud. The youths looked on in silent horror as the river took their friend, smoothed over the impression that his body had made, left no trace of his existence.

Footsteps and the three youths turned as one. A bearded man.

Walking with a limp. Moving towards them.

Filthy, bedraggled, an object in his hand.

Constable Bielby was twenty yards behind the man, the youths maybe ten yards in front and, again without conscious thought, the young policeman was closing the gap.

His mind numbed by shock, by six hours of exposure to the penetrating cold, Bielby registered the sword swinging lightly from the man's hand, held casually and it seemed so natural, an everyday tool of the man's trade, but it still drew his eye. Perhaps a yard in length, thick and heavy, somewhat rounded at the end.

Bielby feet carried him on, he clawed at his radio. 'Assistance urgently required; River Hull; behind Oriel House. Five suspects, one man injured in the river, another man with a sword.'

His voice somehow firm, Bielby felt an urgent desire to vomit.

'Stop there!' The constable's right hand fell to his truncheon. He pulled it from his sheath, slipped his handcuffs into his left hand, both steel restraints protecting his knuckles. 'Lay down the sword.'

The red bearded man spun to face him, inclined his head, weighed him, took in the small, wooden nightstick and smiled.

Bielby shivered as the man turned his back.

Target selection. That was what they had called it; all predators did it, chose between their targets, ranked them in their order of importance and Bielby was under no illusion; he was a target too.

Time slowed. A glance behind him, a smile then the Viking turned again and charged the youths, his sword raised in his right hand, a ribbon of blood fluttered from its tip and two of the youths broke, shot with a terrorlent speed along the wharf but the youth in the blue jacket stood his ground his fingers closing around the something in his pocket. He pulled it with a flourish.

A knife.

A small, pathetic knife and he was too late, was a thousand years too late. He could only scream and raise his hand as the carbon steel of the Viking's sword sliced through the damp air.

The sound carried. Full bodied, a golf swing without the crack of club against ball. Rather softer, soggy and Bielby felt sick, inadequate, humbled. It went against God, against everything that he had ever believed to do what the man had done, to hack at living flesh but he could not flee. He was a police officer, would rather be anything else but he forced himself to open his eyes, to move towards the crouching figure, now stabbing forcefully at the shape on the ground.

Bielby pushed away his fear, tried not to think, began to run and raised his nightstick before him. He passed the spot where the first youth had been attacked, splashed through the blood and urine, began to scream and the bearded man smiled. Bielby had not seen the second man, slumped in the alleyway, his blood-drained fingers fumbling with his bow.

Redbeard raised his sword, spread his feet and braced himself for the assault, crouched slightly but Andrew Bielby shuddered to a halt. Quizzically, almost disappointed, the Viking rose to his full height.

Andrew Bielby had heard a faint buzz as the goose-feathered arrow shot through the air, had heard the dull thud as it had buried itself deep in his left thigh, but he felt no pain. Still, his leg would not move and, as he looked down, saw the arrowhead, like a tent-pole, holding the heavy wool of his trousers far away from his skin he felt his head begin to swim.

Bielby looked from his leg to the smiling Viking and laughed out loud.

Comical, his life was about to end as brilliant black and white zigzag shapes flashed before his eyes. He retched in to his bloody hands, sagged and sank to his knees.

The Viking's smile slipped. He raised his sword and began to run. An unearthly scream cut through Andrew Bielby's shock, assailed him, terrified him but still he felt removed from the situation. A murder was about to happen.

His.

'Young Policeman Killed by River.'

He could read the words as the sword scythed through the air.

In another world, Bielby held his baton above his head, shut his eyes.

The bullet caught the Viking in the centre of his back. Parts of it passed through him, the force of their exit splattering blood and shards of bone onto the wharf and the young policeman kneeling in front of him. Other shards of metal had torn through his heart, lungs and liver and he crumpled immediately.

Driven on by his momentum, the Viking's sword continued its descent. It struck the young officer's baton, shot viciously to the side and skinned the knuckles of the man's left hand before clattering to the ground.

His hands still held before him in supplication, Bielby opened his eyes, dropped the baton then slowly lowered his hands. The handcuffs shielding his left hand were bent, scarred by the sword-blow and bloodied but he smiled and looked at the bundle of rags, so recently a man, which lay before him. The killer's eyes were open, and the young policeman watched as they began to fade.

Five

The instructor waited for the men to settle. He drew a deep breath. 'There'll be plenty will try to stop you,' he said, his voice steady. 'But you've been chosen to deliver this package, and that's what you're going to do.' Warner's knuckles were white, his nails digging into the palms of his hands. He forced himself to stop, looked around at the faces of the men whose lives would depend upon him. It was just a matter of time. In seven hours it will all be over.

****

Inspector Bielby had still been at the Hull Royal Infirmary when the details of the incident in the town had been relayed to him. He was not surprised, was relieved that the police marksman stationed on the Myton Street Bridge had found his mark, but his world had collapsed when Inspector Walker had rung him some minutes later to tell him that Andrew had been involved.

He had seen it so often in other people, now felt it himself, the numbing, cold, creeping other worldliness of the deepest shock. He had fought against it, knew that his boy had been involved but what did that mean? He had pulled himself together, knew that there had been fatalities, people had died, but it was out of his hands.

He was the relative of a victim, he would be amongst the first to know and, if he hadn't heard the words, then the worst couldn't be true.

Andrew would be twenty-two next month. No longer a boy but Bielby could remember the day that he had been born, had taken his first step, said his first word, started school yet now he was a policeman. There were risks, but now, as a father, Bielby realized that he had never been prepared to contemplate what that could really mean. He raised his hands to his face, pushed back the tears. He had seen it in parents before, denial followed by a slow acceptance, an overwhelming grief but he had prayed, harder than he had ever prayed before, that his boy would be alive. Disgrace, injury, he could live with anything but let him be alive.

In his years as a policeman, Bielby had delivered bad news, sometimes sickeningly bad news, to hundreds of people; but he had received none. True, there had been a broken limb and stitches here and there, but the minutes that followed Walker's phone call had been the worst of the Inspector's life. He had been lost, alone and he had felt an intense desire to talk, to share his misery with another human being.

Bielby patted his jacket pocket; no cigarettes and this was a hospital after all. Should he ring Kathleen and tell her? No, she would know the news soon enough, good or bad. They had had their differences recently, but the least he could do was to leave his wife these last few minutes before her world fell apart.

Images from the coach and the Kings Head flooded his mind, severed heads and the blood. The fifteen minutes before Walker had rung to confirm that Andrew was alive had been the longest of his life. Bielby had cried, had called upon God, had tried to shut out the glare of the camera lights outside the hospital, the incessant shouted questions.

The Inspector's dislike of journalists had grown into a burning hatred. Those already camped outside the hospital had been kept behind hastily erected barriers, forty yards from the front doors of the casualty department, but more were arriving every hour, London based, foreign correspondents making their way north. Dozens now, there would be hundreds by the end of the day, and they could cost lives.

Bielby rose to his feet and walked to the door. He raised his eyes, looked past the thronging crowd. Numb, deaf to the shouts as the nearest journalists recognised him, he watched the ambulance pull into the hospital car park, blue lights flashing. Heads turned as one as the vehicle swept around the car park in a large arc. It turned ever more sharply, arrived with its rear doors facing the doors to the casualty department as, the photographers fighting for their pictures, night turned to day, and erupted into a flashing wall of light some ten feet high.

The doors of the ambulance opened, and a stretcher was passed out to the medics already by the vehicle's side; they lowered it onto a gurney. More flashes, the second shape inside the ambulance, white-shrouded, dead, brought temporarily back to life. Bielby felt his legs began to fail beneath him.

Looking away, the Inspector sought out the live patient, recognized the familiar features of his son. Andrew Bielby was moving, very much alive but pale, very pale. He was talking to the paramedic by his side, the man's orange trousers blood-drenched, torn at the knees and the Inspector swallowed hard. He could picture it clearly, the man, tending to the injured, kneeling in blood, his son's blood. The Inspector's knees buckled, and the floor rushed up at him, struck him hard in the face.

Andrew Bielby looked up from the gurney on which he was laying. There was a fuss in the hallway, a man, middle- aged, being helped to his feet. His father. He caught his eye, the Old Man's concern all too obvious and he felt the first sting of a tear. He tried to smile, blinked it back. His father looked relieved, tired, angry and Andrew felt a rush of warmth.

Now, the lancing pain had ebbed to a throb, and he didn't feel too bad, could move his arms and legs. He did it again to reassure himself, but his left leg was numb, moveable but somehow alien. He held up his heavily bandaged left hand as the gurney began to move, was wheeled towards his father. He waved his hand.

'No more violin lessons...'

His father nodded, pursed his lips and turned to the paramedic, the man now holding plasma bag above Andrew Bielby's gurney.

'His thigh wound is a little more serious, Inspector.' The paramedic looked down at his own legs. 'Don't worry, it's a soft tissue wound, this isn't all his blood...'

'Otherwise, I feel fine,' said Andrew. He felt a little drunk, his face began to cloud over, and he looked at his father. 'I was so scared, dad, I was so scared...'

'He'll be OK, Inspector,' said the paramedic. He pulled a plastic curtain to one side, pushed the gurney towards the nearest inspection bed with scrubbed up doctors and nurses waiting for him.

'He's in shock, weak from the blood loss, but he'll be all right, believe me.'

The paramedic leant over and put his hand on the Inspector's shoulder and Andrew watched as his father's lip began to tremble. The older man turned away, his head lowered, his shoulders heaving silently. Tears ran the length of his nose, pattered softly one by one onto the floor of the ward.

The faint sound musical to his ears, Andrew could hear them. He was alive, but he felt removed. He felt his father's hand on his shoulder, and he raised his eyes, watched as a young nurse rushed past, her shift over.

She looked at them, a boy and a middle-aged man, crying in the hospital's casualty ward and he smiled as she turned, carried on her way.

****

Two hours to the south, in Cambridgeshire, Caroline Whittleton was late. It was unprofessional, she was angry, and it was Jeremy's fault. He'd taken the car and hadn't even thought to mention it.

Caroline's Project Manager, Dr Brandon Bryce, stood on the steps to the laboratories, raised an eyebrow as Caroline approached but she felt sure that he wasn't checking up on her. Brandon just wasn't like that, but some sort of explanation was necessary, pulling up in a cab always looked so seedy. It suggested driving bans, illicit liaisons or repossessed cars.

'Car, Brandon. Jeremy took it.'

'I beg your pardon?' said Dr Bryce absently. His glasses slipped to the end of his nose, and he blinked rapidly. 'Ah, Caroline! What was that?'

'Oh, it's nothing,' said Caroline. She walked past Bryce, forced a smile and entered the laboratory.

****

It was lunchtime and the diplomatic wires between London and Washington had been hot for some time. What had started as a polite enquiry from the British as to whether the Americans had a man missing in London, had fast become ugly. Theodore Kettle, the American Ambassador to London, had become involved by mid-morning, obliging the British to pass the matter quickly up the line. The professionals had reluctantly handed over to the politicians and here too, the affair of Carter Lockyer threatened to go to the very top.

The British Home Secretary, Julian Ryde, had been closely involved in the handling of the outrages in East Yorkshire throughout the night. He had visited the incident room in the Queen's Gardens police station in Hull and had not slept. To be dragged back to London to deal with a diplomatic incident, particularly one involving the Americans, had not been on his agenda.

Still, he was a professional. He had freshened up, had called in Kettle, and was now running through events as they had been described to him with an almost theatrical indignation. The righteously outraged victim, he was thoroughly enjoying himself.

Pausing for breath, the Home Secretary looked down at the large frame of Theodore Kettle. The man's plump knees were well spread to allow room for his ample belly to sag between them but he was still smiling good-naturedly and Ryde felt a flash of annoyance. He and Kettle had been acquainted for thirty years, had drawn strength from their mutual dislike since they had been at Oxford together and now the horrible fat face was smiling up at him. Florid, large nosed, tufts of hair at each nostril, Ryde found himself wondering how the man managed to draw breath.

Ryde straightened his tie automatically, pulled his thoughts back to the matter at hand but winced slightly as he turned. At least the excitement had taken his mind off his health and that could only be a good thing. He had been diagnosed with pancreatic cancer earlier in the year and had been told that it was untreatable. Inoperable the doctor had confirmed when Ryde had pushed him to spell it out in English. Only 20% of patients survived for more than 12 months after diagnosis and almost all of those were the operable cases.

The Home Secretary looked at the back of Kettle's thick, bristly neck and tried to push his personal problems from his mind. He had ignored the vague abdominal discomfort that he had felt over Easter, had put it down to over-exercise; but he had not been able to ignore the later signs. His urine had begun to darken, and his bowel motions had become irregular and lighter in colour. It was serious, he had known that, but it had only been when Jenny had noticed that he was losing weight that he had relented and had gone to see the doctor.

But by then it had been far too late. The tumour had metastasised. It had spread to the liver, to the blood vessels around the pancreas and the Home Secretary had been told that he had only a few weeks to live. That had been in August.

It was late October now and Ryde didn't feel too bad. Still, he was a realist. 'I don't think we'll pay the golf club fees in advance,' he had said to Jenny only last week trying to lighten the mood. 'Speak for yourself!' she had replied.

She was a tough old bird, Jenny. He'd had the devil of an argument with her when he'd decided to decline some of the treatment that had been suggested. It was undignified, directed at some of the symptoms of the disease rather than at the disease itself and, when pressed, the doctors had agreed that the side effects could be seen by some as being worse than any benefit that could be hoped to achieve.

Sure, that Kettle's back was still to him, Ryde breathed deeply, caught the cheap American's Cologne and wrinkled his nose. Apart from Ryde's own family and one or two local party workers in Teesside, only the Prime Minister knew of the Home Secretary's condition, and he wanted to keep it that way for as long as possible. He turned his attention back to the US Ambassador.

'Tell me Theodore,' he said, his expression pained. 'Do you make a habit of spying on your friends?' Ryde looked at Kettle and raised his eyebrows but gave the American no time to answer. 'Of course you do, how foolish of me! Israel, Germany and of course the French but I'm hurt Theodore. I'm really, deeply hurt that you should spy on us just when we were getting along so well!' Ryde paused, raised his eyebrows. This almost made life worth living.

'Let's stick to the facts, shall we?' Kettle said calmly, his flaccid blue eyes focused on the British Home Secretary. 'You say that you have an individual...'

'Oh, but I can assure you that we do have an individual, Theodore! He's as American as Apple Pie, I tell you!' Ryde smiled. Apple pie was English, of course, but it suited him to argue otherwise.

'Whatever!' said Kettle looking directly at Ryde again, the Englishman's eyes a little yellow. Ryde saw the hatred. He liked it. 'So, you think you have an individual,' drawled the Ambassador, emphasizing his south-western accent, 'who may or may not be an American citizen and who may or may not have been in certain premises. An element of reasonable doubt there, Julian, wouldn't you agree?'

Ryde smiled. Much as he wanted to take the American's whatever and ram it down his throat, that was not an option. 'This is the UK, Theodore. It's your patch. If he does turn out to be one of your spooks caught with his pants down, who knows what newspaper could end up with the story. Remember the security guard is still in hospital, poor man. Broken nose, God knows how many stitches and his wife, and four children are by his bedside. He's a Gulf War veteran, probably a hero who fought side-by-side with your chaps in Iraq only to be damn nearly killed by one of them while just doing his job. Won't look good, Theodore. It won't look good at all!'

Kettle had whitened appreciably. Ryde was beginning to warm to his task, was contemplating another attack when the American played his trump card.

'Anyway Jules, let's get down to business, shall we? Would the Prime Minister accept a call from President

Sutton at 2pm on a matter of the utmost urgency?'

Ryde gritted his teeth at the Jules but hid his surprise well and a full thirty seconds' silence followed the question as the Home Secretary viewed it from all angles. There was no comeback. It would go to the very top. That let Kettle off the hook, for the moment at least but this was interesting. He turned to the American and smiled, his eyes cold. 'I'll check and get back to you.'

Kettle smiled. 'Well, I'm pleased to have had this little chat, Jules,' he said, rising to his feet, effectively bringing the meeting to a close himself. 'We really must do it again some time.'

Ryde smiled warmly and walked to the door. He opened it and held out his hand. 'We really must.'

Theodore Kettle left the room, and Ryde closed the door behind him. His smile faded. Kettle was a real pro. He had played his cards well and Ryde was angry, but he was also intensely curious. Yes, the Ambassador was a bastard. Copper Kettle, they had called him at Oxford. A draft dodger, later a flag-waving armchair soldier complete with a chest full of medals but there Ryde had the advantage. He had flown Sea Harriers during the Falklands War, had had one aircraft shot out from under him and another so badly damaged that it had spent the rest of the conflict under repair. Still, that counted for little now. He rubbed his chin, looked at the telephone on his desk and slowly picked it up.

'Get me the Prime Minister's office would you please, Hilary?' Ryde stretched, kneaded the small of his back. 'Then get hold of Special Branch and Peter Whinney at MI5.'

****

Deep beneath Paddington Green police station, Carter Lockyer knew nothing of the outrages in Yorkshire, nothing of the diplomatic row that had burned the wires between London and Washington, was aware only of the lights and the incessant questioning of the two men who sat opposite him.

His head was spinning. He did not know how long he had been held. There was no clock in the room and his wristwatch had gone. Glimpses at the watches of his interrogators suggested ten hours, but he was a professional and they could have been spun, set to mislead him.

His jaw set, his eyes narrowed. Steal too much time and he would spot it a mile off, too little and it wasn't worth the deception, but Lockyer had to gain time, time for colleagues to cover trails, to remove embarrassing evidence, to begin the political process.

But these men were professionals too.

Lockyer had told them nothing. He could keep it up for hours, had nothing to be afraid of, but he'd taken a knock when his face had hit the pavement. He could still be concussed, and it might affect his judgement, weaken his resolve. He must concentrate.

They seemed to be certain that he was an American and his own people would be making strenuous efforts to get him out. The whole thing could still be passed up as some big misunderstanding. He would be out in twenty- four hours but that could be a very long time.

'Why the Debonet building, Carter?' they had asked him a hundred times already. 'Why room 306?'

Lockyer shook his head. He was hungry and he felt like shit. He had skinned his knees in the fall outside the Embassy and the plastic cords had chaffed his wrists.

His hair had come out in clumps where the heavy Brit had swung from it and now, he had a splitting headache. His elbows were badly grazed, he'd chipped a tooth, his tongue had swollen up where he had bitten into it, and he desperately wanted a cigarette. He shook his head again.

It was the little things that wore men down. The forward sloping chair, the back pain, lack of sleep, the broken nails and splintered teeth. General discomfort. He had been told it often and knew it to be true. He was beginning to smell.

'Look, gentlemen,' said Lockyer. He raised his head, his eyes very blue in the harsh light, his voice, lisping past his swollen tongue. 'This has all been a big mistake. We both know that I'll be out of here in a few hours so let's try to show a little understanding, shall we?'

The shorter of the two men, squat, malevolent, regarded Lockyer coldly. 'No-can-do, Carter.' Lockyer raised his eyebrows, his expression pained. 'We don't know yet whether or not you died outside the Embassy.'

Lockyer's expression did not betray the flutter that he felt in his stomach. The man was bluffing. He must be, this was England. But people did disappear. He said nothing, forced himself to relax for the benefit of the cameras behind the mirror on the wall.

Less than an hour later, Carter Lockyer was released. He felt abused, somehow dirty. He declined the offer of a shower and change of clothes before shuffling, his shoes lace-less, to the US Embassy car that had been sent to pick him up. He had failed, felt that he had let somebody down but, in truth, he knew that he had not.

Six

Duty. Sometimes it weighed heavy, was hard to bear. Warner steadied his breathing, looked up at the clock on the wall at the front of the room. Its hands were moving mighty slow and, watched by a dozen pairs of eyes, a large fly buzzed ponderously past it. It flew over the young man's head before heaving itself through one of the partially open windows and was gone.

'You don't need me to tell you that you'll be making history,' said the older man. 'Today will be remembered forever...'

****

By 2pm London time, all the necessary preparations

for UK Prime Minister, Donald Berwick and US President George Sutton and their respective advisers to speak to one-another had been made. It was to be a videoconference, although the preference of both leaders for a face-to-face conference was not shared by some of the older advisers on either side of the Atlantic who shuffled, for the most part very uneasily, behind their respective leaders.

The members of the President's National Security Council that had been present for the earlier Oval Office meeting were there and had been joined by Maria Hernandez, US Ambassador to the UN, and by two specially invited advisers. Naked without their white coats, the scientists were in disguise, President Sutton had said, in a failed attempt to relieve some of the tension in the room.

In the Cabinet Room in Downing Street, the UK delegation was considerably smaller and lined only two thirds of one side of the huge boat shaped table that dominated the room. Despite the attacks outside Hull, Donald Berwick had insisted that Julian Ryde, in his capacity as Home Secretary, take part in the videoconference and Susan Burnell, the Foreign Secretary had also been obliged to make herself available. Also present were Peter Whinney and Robert Smith, Director Generals of MI5 and MI6 respectively, and Alistair MacDonald of the Special Branch. Morgan Jones, the Prime Minister's Press Secretary, stood discretely behind his political master, a portrait of Sir Horace Walpole looking down upon them both. There was not a scientist, not a science degree, in the whole room.

The sound of coughing drew everyone in the Cabinet Room's attention to the large flickering screen at the end of the table. It cleared to show the President of the United States, and his advisers arranged around the President's desk in the Oval Office apparently preparing themselves for the meeting that was about to take place.

'Plenty of them!'

The Prime Minister ignored his Home Secretary. 'Maybe they want to apologise en masse...'

'Julian, please!

Prime Minister Berwick turned back to the videoscreen, scanned the faces in Washington He pursed his lips.

For the most part it was the normal White House team. The President looked as though he hadn't slept, and Edelman was unshaven. Still, something did not look quite right, and a tall, rather untidy man caught the Prime Minister's eye. He could not place him, did not feel that he had not seen him in the President's company before. Beside the tall figure stood a much smaller, plump man. Both men stood some distance from the politicians and looked a little out of place.

'Looks like a cheap wedding photograph!'

'Julian!' The Prime Minister gestured to the screen. 'The volume's off, Prime Minister,' said an unseen aide.

'Keep it to yourself, Julian,' said Berwick. Ryde raised his eyebrows, and the PM turned to the sandy-haired, middle-aged man to his left. 'What about the technicians?'

'They'll have headphones on when the meeting begins,' said Alistair MacDonald, head of Special Branch, his gentle Scottish brogue unmistakable. 'They'll not hear a thing.'

'Everybody OK?'

Around him, heads nodded, and the Prime Minister

straightened his tie. He gestured to one of the men by the screens to turn on the volume. Several of the Americans on the screen looked towards the camera, they had clearly heard London come to life.

'What's the weather like George?' asked Berwick after a moment's hesitation.

'Weather's fine, Donald,' said George Sutton. 'Thanks for taking the call.'

'No problem.'

The President glanced at his advisers. 'I hear that one of my countrymen may have found himself in your care?'

'You could say that, George.'

To the President's left, Larry Edelman had raised his hand to his forehead and President Sutton turned, looked at him, before continuing. 'It would be helpful if we could resolve the matter quickly, with as little fuss as possible.'

'Consider it done,' said Berwick. 'You'll have him back within the hour.'

Behind the Prime Minister, Julian Ryde spluttered, coughed into the glass of water that he was holding to his lips, the first drops beginning to darken the blue cotton of his shirt.

'Thank you, Donald,' said President Sutton. 'A misunderstanding.' He looked at his advisers and turned back to the screen. 'But there is something else.'

'Do go on,' said Berwick.

'This may be the most foolish thing that I have ever said,' said Sutton. His team around him shuffled uncomfortably. 'In many ways I hope that it is. Maybe you would allow me to try to explain.'

In the UK Cabinet Room glances were exchanged as the President drew himself to his full height. 'For several weeks, we have been recording energy bursts in the region of two USAF bases in Cambridgeshire.

'Initially, we suspected espionage or an attempt to interfere with our military capability. But no signs of any break-ins were ever found and, at first, the pulses never affected the aircraft or any of our systems. Much of it is pulse hardened, and, with the exception of radar tracking equipment, nothing was damaged.

'These energy bursts continued at irregular intervals and then we became aware that they seemed to coincide with bizarre reports in the local newspapers. It took a while, of course, we had to filter out the normal, run- of-the-mill rubbish, but it looked as though a pattern was beginning to emerge.'

'Bizarre reports?' prompted Prime Minister Berwick from London.

'First there were the rocks, discovered in previously barren fields near Cambridge. Not very exciting, but they got a mention. Still, the ice that appeared in Helmsley, North Yorkshire, got a little more attention. It was a bit odd, I believe?'

Donald Berwick looked at Julian Ryde. The Home Secretary hesitated before speaking. 'Yes, it was a little strange,' he said. 'The locals called in the Home Office. The ice weighed almost three tons and must have been dumped there by some sort of crank.'

'Go on.'

Ryde made a face then continued. 'It contained no traces of pollutants meaning that whoever dumped it there must have cut it from several feet below the surface of one of the poles or from a remote glacier. We still don't know why.'

President Sutton nodded, looked down at the papers

on his desk and then back at the video screen. 'And the wild boar in Hertfordshire?'

'Yes?' replied the Prime Minister.

'They were hunted into extinction in England several hundred years ago, were they not? In which case, where did it come from?'

'From a wildlife park, I would imagine?'

'Possibly,' said President Sutton. 'And possibly not. The pulses continued, got a little stronger and things got much worse. Two Scotsmen murdered a police constable in Derby last month, you recall?'

'Tragic,' said Berwick.

'Certainly that,' said President Sutton. 'The perpetrators were violent, strangely dressed men, I believe. Insane, obviously, but didn't they seem to want to destroy everything English, to be fighting a race war?'

Again, Prime Minister Berwick turned to his Home Secretary. Julian Ryde nodded, and President Sutton continued. 'No links were established, but these incidents, spread around the UK, maybe overseas as well, always coincided with an energy pulse near to the USAF bases then yesterday, we recorded a larger burst of energy. Stronger, more pervasive, several bits of kit were damaged and the incident in East Yorkshire occurred.'

'What are you saying George?' said Donald Berwick from London.

President Sutton seemed almost reluctant to continue. Larry Edelman, the National Security Adviser shook his head, and the President looked away. 'Please bear with me just a few moments longer. When one of my sons was about five years old, he told me a joke. He said 'Daddy, what's brown and sticky?' I wasn't sure that I wanted to know the answer, but I asked him, nonetheless. His answer was 'a stick!"

Blank looks in the UK Cabinet Room. The British officials waited politely for the President to go on whilst the Sutton's own advisers shifted behind him, avoided eye contact with each other and with the politicians in the UK.

'Well, what I am trying to say is that sometimes the most obvious answer to a question is the correct one,' said President Sutton. He paused before continuing.

'If you receive a bloody visit from a group of people who arrive in a Viking Longboat, dress like Vikings, talk like Vikings and behave like Vikings, then what should one call them?'

Silence. A cough. The shuffling of papers and Julian Ryde broke the silence. 'Vikings?'

'You said it Mr Ryde.' President Sutton looked at the video screen intently, he said nothing further for several seconds. When he spoke, he did so slowly and without interruption. 'Did these people have any dental work? Were they lice-ridden? What language did they speak? Were they all unshaven? Did any of them have medical scars? Inoculations? Did any of them ask for a lawyer, or communicate with the hospital staff or with the police in any way?'

There were no bemused smiles on the faces of the British inner cabinet. There were expressions of genuine concern. Prime Minister Berwick turned towards Julian Ryde. 'Well, Julian?'

'I must admit, Prime Minister, these were not the first things that we looked for,' said the UK Home Secretary, his voice deadly serious. 'The live suspects have been removed from the Hull Royal Infirmary. We haven't made their whereabouts public. They're under sedation, still violent. The autopsies have begun on the dead perpetrators, but we have had no word yet on the results.'

'Find out would you,' said Berwick. Ryde nodded. 'Any communication with them?'

'None that I'm aware of.'

'When these results are in, you may decide to conclude,' said the President from Washington, 'that all the evidence suggests that these people are genuine Vikings. I'm told that the eastern part of Yorkshire suffered from sustained Viking attacks and then extensive settlement over a long period?'

'That's correct,' said Julian Ryde, again the first to speak. 'York was the capital of Viking England. It was reached via the river Humber, which is fed by the Ouse amongst other tributaries. Hull is nearer the mouth of the river. It was originally called Wyke, a reference to its original Viking inhabitants.'

President Sutton said nothing, and the silence grew.

Morgan Jones, the Prime Minister's Press Secretary broke it. 'Re-enactors? Lunatics? Even then there are inconsistencies. The weapons used, for example. I thought that the longbow was invented by the Welsh in the thirteenth century?'

'Well King Harold wasn't shot in the eye by a carrot was he!' snapped Julian Ryde. 'Short bows were common four thousand years ago, the Greeks, Romans and Chinese all used them extensively and long bows as we know them have been found at Nydam Moor in Denmark. The longer weapons were most likely first used by the Vikings.'

Jones glared at Ryde, but did not hold his eye. He looked away and patted the cigarette packet in his pocket and looked at the Prime Minister pleadingly.

Berwick shook his head before turning back to the screen. 'Where are you going with this, George? Some sort of cult? Or are you saying that these people rowed across the North Sea?'

In Washington, President Sutton raised his eyes from the desk in front of him and looked at the video screen. 'No, Donald, that's not what I'm saying. I'm saying that these might be guys who woke up yesterday morning in the tenth century and died yesterday evening in the twenty-first.'

In the UK Cabinet Room, Donald Berwick paused before he spoke. 'Mentally?'

Sutton raised his eyes, shook his head. 'I realize this takes some believing. We'll mail over what we've got, a summary anyway then what say we get together again? Around 6pm your time?'

Donald Berwick looked from the video screen to his closest advisers. When he spoke, his voice had a disembodied, calm quality. 'Yes George, I think that would be a good idea.'

The screen faded.

For several seconds, there was silence in the Downing Street Cabinet Room. Berwick turned to Julian Ryde, but the Home Secretary spoke first. 'I'm sure we've got people working in this area.'

'Then I didn't imagine it?'

Julian Ryde shook his head, and the Prime Minister nodded and held up his hand. He turned to the video conference technicians, looked at Alistair MacDonald then motioned them to take off their headsets. 'You'll be needed again later this afternoon, gentlemen. For the moment though, Emma will look after you.' Berwick glanced at McDonald then back at the technicians. 'I'd rather that you didn't leave the building.'

As the two technicians left the room, the Prime Minister's frown deepened. He had known Sutton for nearly ten years, since he was simply a run of the mill Senator, and on the whole respected his judgment. He could be ill, but the President's advisers had looked serious enough and there had been some very steady hands there, Linda King, for example, and Turner and Scott.

Gerry Buchanan, the man's reputation in Vietnam, Guatemala, Iran, Iraq and a whole host of other dangerous and unpleasant parts of the world well known within the intelligence community, had also been there and had appeared to support his President. Berwick had an immense respect for that man. He turned to Julian Ryde. 'Thoughts?'

'We have to treat this seriously, do what due diligence we can in the time available.'

'Alistair?'

'I agree, Prime Minister.'

Berwick looked around the room. More nods. They were waiting for him to take the lead. He turned to his Press Secretary. 'Morgan, get me a still from the video will you please? Liaise with whomever you think necessary but get me the names and a brief résumé of everyone there. Start with the individuals that you know least well and don't waste too much time on the National Security Council members.' Berwick nodded towards the door and Morgan Jones left the room. The Prime Minister turned to his Home Secretary. 'Julian, see that this American is released and get him back to his Embassy then see who we have working in this area of physics. I can scarcely bring myself to say it.'

'Time travel?' said Ryde. 'I'll get onto it right away.'

A slight smile played upon the Home Secretary's lips and Berwick winced. 'I take it that the Americans are OK?'

'Of course he is, Donald, he's fine. There was a fight in front of his Embassy. Nothing too serious but a welcoming committee of journalists would be best avoided. He may have one or two bruises.'

'Handle it will you?' said the PM, then, turning to the room in general. 'We'll meet back here at 4pm for an internal briefing, hopefully get some scientific input before we get back on to the White House at 6pm. OK?' More nods and Berwick turned once more to Julian Ryde. 'Make sure that the scientists have signed the Official Secret's Act, for heaven's sake, Julian. And make them as user friendly as possible, would you? We're going to need to understand what they're talking about.'

****

Alone with their thoughts since the earlier videoconference, there was an air of anticipation when the British Cabinet took their seats once more around the large table in the Cabinet Room at 4.15pm.

'Well, Ladies and Gentlemen,' said the Prime Minister as the gentle shuffling began to subside. He looked from face to face around the table. 'I've checked the date and it's not April 1st so, unless we have some evidence to suggest otherwise, we must take what the Americans are saying seriously. Morgan, what about the advisers present in the Oval Office?'

Morgan Jones rose from his seat at the Cabinet

table and prepared to speak, he puffed out his chest. He did not have a regular place at the top table of British government and had temporarily taken the Chancellor of the Exchequer, Sandy Patel's seat. He cleared his throat and looked around the room, apparently pleased to have the attention of everyone present, even Julian Ryde. He handed out large copies of a still photograph taken from the earlier videoconference.

'Aside from the President and the other members of the National Security Council whom I'm sure we all know well, these two individuals,' Jones jabbed with a pointer at an enlargement of the photograph pinned to a flip chart behind him, 'are Professors Clayton Jobber and Myron Klutz, distinguished physicists with a history of articles published on the relationship between energy and time. Nothing on time travel.'

Jones's rich Welsh voice was still ringing from the walls as he looked up. The mention of time travel passed without mention, his audience still apparently devoting to him their full attention. There was little indication that any believed the reference to be amusing.

'Julian,' said the Prime Minister turning to Ryde. 'Do we have people, and can we get them here in time to speak to Jobber and Klutz?'

Morgan Jones sat down; the spotlight had left him.

Ryde smiled at him as he took the floor. He cleared his throat. 'Yes. We have a government funded facility in Cambridge that I'm told is leading edge. We've got the project head, Dr Brandon Bryce and his chief physicist Dr Caroline Whittleton coming in. They should be here around 5pm. I've no doubt they'll be able to enlighten us somewhat, but it'll be a shock to them, they've not been briefed.'

The Prime Minister knew Julian Ryde well; he pondered the half-question. 'Perhaps best that way. We can judge their reaction to the suggestion, and we can't give them details that we don't have. Tell them that it's a vitally important but controversial suggestion that we would like them to comment on. Given the nature of their work, they might guess what it's about, but I'd rather not tell them anything further at this stage.' Ryde nodded and the Prime Minister continued. 'And the perpetrators?'

'The injured are still in Hull, the dead are in Cambridgeshire. It seems appropriate now, but we had decided to move them there before we heard about the American airbases. As the President suggested might be the case, those in custody appear unable to speak modern English but do seem to understand some Danish words. We haven't had any historical linguists in there yet, I was a bit reluctant to spread the net too wide...'

'Do it,' said Berwick. Ryde nodded and continued. 'The first autopsies have been completed. Both the living and the dead appear to be reasonably clean but have evidence of recent lice infestations. None of them have any obvious medical scars and none have any evidence of dental work or inoculations...'

'Could these be lunatics from some sort of commune?' interrupted Berwick. 'Dangerous drop-outs from either somewhere in the UK or the Continent?'

'It's possible,' said Ryde. His tone suggested that he did not believe it likely. 'But the absence of inoculation scars or dental work does suggest that these people have not had any contact with what we would call civilization since the day that they were born. Hence, their parents must have been involved and the chance of that being the case for over thirty individuals is very remote.'

Prime Minister Berwick nodded. The discussions continued and it was a sombre-faced Prime Minister who took the call at 5.20pm telling him that Dr Bryce and Dr Whittleton had arrived in Downing Street. He requested that they be shown straight up to the Cabinet Room, steepled his fingers beneath his chin and craned his neck to look out of the window.

The weather was closing in; it was beginning to get dark. A light tap at the door and Berwick rose from his seat as the door opened and Dr Whittleton followed by a hesitant Dr Bryce entered the room. Mixed-race, she was much younger than he had imagined.

****

Caroline Whittleton knew that sponsors were a Good Thing. They provided finance, other resources, encouragement and occasionally valuable technical input, but couldn't they just leave the professionals to their research once the cheques had cleared? Wasn't the knowledge that they were funding groundbreaking research enough? Caroline knew that she was being unreasonable but, with the Prime Minister of the United Kingdom clearly looking her up and down, she couldn't help it, and Brandon looked even worse. He looked intensely miserable. Bill Gates, he had earlier suggested, the tone of his voice suggesting interference of the worst sort, was rumoured to be interested in the commerciality of some of the Microsoft sponsored projects in and around Cambridge.

Bryce squinted at Caroline again through his thick glasses, the sweat glistening on his prominent forehead, and Caroline sighed; sometimes she envied him. His myopia protected him from the worst of any alien environment and, although he was chronically nervous, his life sometimes seemed reassuringly simple. Fifty-five years old, he had devoted his life to Physics and particularly the relationships between time and space, but he was not a political person. Younger physicists had passed him by on the career ladder, Caroline would soon pass him herself, but still, he appeared content, happy in his work. He had been Caroline's boss now for seven years, first on the teaching staff of the University and, for the last four years, as the head of the Trinity Park project.

For the moment, however, boss or no boss, Caroline would have to carry him. She looked around the Cabinet Room and felt the faintest flutter of excitement. Even Brandon would have had to admit that a call to see the Prime Minister was intriguing, but what was this about?

The huge crowd of journalists, several of whom had banged on the windows of the government car as it swept through the iron gates into Downing Street, had shaken them both badly but now they were here. It had not been pleasant. 'Hey pop,' one of them had shouted at Brandon, 'who's the black chick?'

'Welcome to number ten, Dr Whittleton, Dr Bryce,' said Donald Berwick, the Prime Minister. He indicated two seats at the end of the table and smiled, just an ordinary man. 'Please take a seat. I hope that the ladies and gentlemen of the Press didn't cause you too much trouble?'

Caroline shook her head. Dr Bryce said nothing, and the Prime Minister continued. 'I'd just like to remind you both that you've both signed the Official Secret's Act,

I'm sure you're familiar with what that means. Please repeat nothing that you may hear here this evening. In particular, say nothing to the Press. It's the safest option. To do anything else is almost always a mistake. They'll speculate on your accent, your appearance, your job, your age and, before you know it, they'll have your shoe size on the front page of tomorrow's newspapers.'

The PM was smiling but he was serious, and Caroline Whittleton smiled back. She had never been warned about her behaviour so politely in her life, but she was intrigued, could feel her face beginning to flush. A briefing was one thing, she could understand it, the Government after all was their ultimate paymaster, but at such a high level!

The Prime Minister's smile faded. 'I'm informed that you are this country's leading experts on time and its relationship with mass and energy and that your work is at the very cutting edge globally,' he said. 'Is that a fair comment?'

Dr Bryce's discomfort seemed to reach a new level of intensity. Blinking hard, bird-like, his head began to bob, and he turned to Caroline, his lips pursed.

Caroline smiled her encouragement but could read the signs. Brandon was not going to speak, probably could not speak, indeed was unlikely to utter another word until they left the building, and she nodded. She turned to the Prime Minister, peered over the rim of the thin glasses that she occasionally wore to aid her close vision. 'Yes, I think that our facility could fairly be described as one of the best in the world. As I believe you know, Professors Jobber and Klutz also run a first-class facility in Massachusetts and we think there's work of a similar nature going on in Russia, although I believe they've had a serious problem with funding recently.'

'You speak regularly with the Americans?' said Berwick. 'I have spoken to Jobber on occasion,' said Caroline struggling to keep the inquiring tone out of her voice. 'Though I mostly get through to his associates. I know of his reputation, of course, and have followed his contributions to scientific journals, but Professor Klutz I've never met.'

'And what do you make of them?'

Caroline frowned. 'They've got a pretty high profile in some circles, particularly Jobber. There's a series of videotapes of presentations given by him in the US and many of my colleagues swear by them. He's brilliant, of course but he has something of a reputation for, well...'

'Please go on.'

Caroline shuffled. 'For presenting his work theatrically, popular science videos and the like. Nothing wrong with it, I quite approve but he's renowned for his antics in the lecture theatre.'

Caroline paused and Berwick continued. 'What you are about to hear may or may not sound fantastic to you but I would ask you to bear with us. What we need is your scientific opinion as to whether or not what we are about to suggest is feasible.'

****

One time zone to the East, some eighty miles from Poland's borders with Belarus and the Ukraine, it was as black as pitch. Low cloud hid the moon, and the sharp, strangled bark of a fox broke the silence.

The damp air promised rain to come but the fallen leaves were still dry, eddying and rustling on the single tracked road, scraping harder and harder against the tarmac until, suddenly, energized, stirred violently by an unseen hand, they flurried fiercely, threw themselves into the ground and burst into flames.

Crackling fiercely, the burning leaves silenced the fox as, forty yards away the wheels an unfamiliar vehicle hit the road for the first time. Slewing to one side, the wheels span viscously and the tracks that covered half the vehicle's length clawed at the road surface, tore up a great swathe of tarmac.

In the darkness of the vehicle's interior, his eyes wide with shock, the driver wrenched hard on the vehicle's steering wheel. The night had closed in. It was much darker than it had been earlier, he must have lost his line but now he had regained it, the danger passed.

His error unnoticed by his sleeping colleagues, the man smiled and raised his hand to the leather thong that hung from the hook protruding from the grey metal of the vehicle's shell above his head. His fingers rubbed at it but he felt ashamed and his nose wrinkled in disgust. His hand fell back to the wheel as, even in the darkness, he could see the charm only too clearly. It was an ear, a human ear.

Seven

The clock ground relentlessly on. It swallowed the seconds, digested the minutes and flowed like a river, constant and steady, reliable, it would never end.

'It's made in America,' said the instructor. He slapped the flip chart with his pointer, glared at his audience. 'And we're in the export business.'

He paused for laughter but there was none.

****

Now seated in a small Downing Street office adjacent to the Cabinet Room, Caroline Whittleton's shoulders sagged. She was shocked, deeply disturbed, had not for a moment linked her work or the work of any other scientists with the awful events in and around Hull.

It was awful, but was it possible? Could anybody have made it happen?

Yes, she had told the politicians, and she still believed it. It was feasible, remotely possible in the most literal sense of the word but was scarcely credible. Nobody, no group of people could have been so far ahead of her without her knowing, without her hearing of their progress. We were talking of years, decades even but the evidence, if such it was, was compelling. Yes, she had insisted, tons of wood, thousands of pounds of flesh really could have been transported over 1000 years of time. It was possible.

They had not wanted to believe her and Caroline could not blame them. She shook her head again, closed her eyes, weighed it in her mind. Had it happened? Had it really happened? And if it had, then who had done it?

She and Bryce were not close, Jobber and Klutz appeared no closer, so who? The Russians? She doubted it. Were they British? Possibly and if they were not, then why had these events occurred in Britain? Then behind the 'how?' was the 'why?' Not for the academic glory surely? Caroline had not had time to explore the question earlier as Julian Ryde, the Home Secretary, reading from the screen of a small mobile telephone, had effectively broken up the meeting. There had been another one, he had said, another burst of energy near Cambridge and with that, she and Dr Bryce had been asked to leave the Cabinet Room, had been ushered out and now, beneath the shock, the questions were beginning to build.

Caroline gently massaged her temples. There had not been the faintest hint of anything like this in the scientific journals. There were so few scientists who were even remotely capable of such progress and Caroline knew them, at the very least knew of their work and they could quickly be discounted. So had the work been carried out in secret and if so, why and again, by whom?

'Dr Whittleton?'

Caroline had not heard the door open, did not hear the voice.

'Dr Whittleton?' Caroline started. She looked up.

Brandon Bryce was already on his feet, the man who had shown them into the waiting room a few minutes earlier standing patiently by the open door. 'The Prime Minister has asked whether you could both step back in.'

'Of course,' Caroline said. She felt embarrassed, looked at Dr Bryce and tried to catch his eye. She could not and he looked horrified, his eyes flickering from side to side as they walked the few yards back to the Cabinet Room. Suddenly Caroline felt very alone. She smiled what little encouragement she could.

'Please,' said Prime Minister Berwick, indicating two chairs as the aide led Caroline and Bryce into the room. It had changed. At the far end of the table, a large screen had been erected and now showed the Oval Office in the White House. Caroline looked at it and frowned.

People were moving, she could hear voices, it was a live link. She sat down.

'Good evening, Dr Whittleton. Dr Bryce.'

The voice was American, vaguely familiar. Caroline looked around the table and then at the video screen once more, it was the President of the United States. Her eyes widened. 'Good evening, sir.'

President Sutton smiled then looked away. 'You registered it, Donald?'

'Yes,' nodded Berwick. 'A burst near Cambridge.'

'We've got nothing more. If we hear anything, we'll let

you know immediately.'

'Let's hope it's nothing,' said Sutton. He paused, then continued, addressing a wider audience. 'I'm sure that several of you have doubts as to my sanity but I'd be grateful if you would bear with me and, to that end, I'm pleased that Dr Whittleton and Dr Bryce have been able to join us.'

'I wouldn't like this to become a physics lecture, ladies and gentlemen. but I think that we should spare a few moments for Professor Jobber. He'll run us through the state of the various theories regarding time then maybe your people could add their views, Donald? Over to you, Professor. Please treat us gently!'

In Washington, the camera panned around, and a tall man rose to his feet. The physicist regarded his President oddly, pulled a set of half-rimmed glasses from his pocket and slid them onto his long nose. He turned, stared from the screen as the camera closed in on him.

Caroline recognized Professor Jobber immediately. He was wearing what had become his trademark dark green corduroy trousers and a brown check shirt. His jacket was hanging open, seven or eight pens crammed into his shirt pocket, stains where ink had seeped from them over the years. His rather long dark-brown hair was pushed back over his ears where it had begun to curl, and he had the beginnings of a beard. The man looked as though he had not slept for a week. He cleared his throat.

'For all of recorded time, people have been fascinated by time itself. They have studied it, measured it, tried to hold it back but they have rarely asked the most fundamental question of all. What is it?

'Defining time without using the word itself is almost impossible, indeed its very measurement is difficult enough. We quantify it by reference to the movement of our planet, its rotation upon its own access or around our sun but to a visitor from another planet, that means nothing.

'However, it does illustrate an important point that we all accept without thinking but which I will cover in more detail later. We always measure time relative to something else. Indeed, we have no choice, and, in this case, we use the universe around us but this leads to some fascinating questions. For example, if the earth slowed down would time itself move more slowly? And, more fundamentally, if the universe itself did not exist then would time also stop? Before the Big Bang, did it not exist?

'I'm getting ahead of myself,' said Professor Jobber. Gravity ever his enemy, he pushed his spectacles back up to the bridge of his nose until, seemingly satisfied that his audience was sufficiently attentive, he continued. 'Back to definitions. I think of time as one of several physical phenomena, dimensions, which separate things, one from another. In this way, it is similar to other dimensions. For example, we know that the most obvious way in which a person can avoid a speeding train is by being in a different location. That is by physically moving along one of the first three dimensions, above, to the side of or away from the train itself. However, he can also avoid it by being in the same location but at a different time.

'Yet time can do much more than separate one thing from another. It can separate an object from itself in a different form. It is the difference between a human being and a pile of dust, between wood and coal, between shellfish and limestone. It is the difference between ice and water and here a link with energy that I will cover later can be quite clearly seen. Energy will speed the change from the one state to the other and the greater the amount of energy expended the less time is required for the transfer. The link is easily proven; but I'm getting ahead of myself again.' Jobber's glasses had slipped to the end of his nose again. He left them there and leaned forward, peered over the top of them at his audience.

'Sir Isaac Newton postulated most clearly the Classical view of time, and his view held sway for almost two and a half centuries. He held that time was a river, a permanent, measurable, one-way flow. Obvious, yes? But we now know that he was wrong. Many intelligent people invested a great deal of time and some of them their entire reputations in the defence of Newton's view of the Universe. As you might imagine, they were reluctant to give it up, but they were doomed to failure, the classical view became increasingly difficult to defend.

'By the end of the nineteenth century, some physicists began to believe that time was not necessarily a constant. But if it wasn't, then what was? Surely something had to be? Like a child, whose feet had lost contact with the floor of the swimming pool, they needed something that they could hang on to, another constant, something which they could rely upon, a theory to fill the gap left by the apparent failure of Classical physics. They searched, frightened by what they might find and then, in 1887, the Michelson-Morley experiment provided what they were looking for, a true constant, the speed of light.'

Jobber paused, sipped a little water from his glass.

He looked at the sea of faces before him and took a deep breath, the patient teacher of grade school physics. He continued, 'If a man looks at his infant son, the image striking his eye is travelling at the speed of light. So, if he runs towards his son at, say, 15 mph, then the image must be striking his eye at the speed of light plus 15 mph. Right? Wrong! Nothing, nothing at all, travels faster than the speed of light. You can take that as a given or I can prove it to you here and now, but the scientists had found the constant against which they could measure everything. They were delighted but what they now held to be true had implications. Everything other than the speed of light, even time, even reality itself, had therefore to be relative, relative to the speed of light.'

Again, Jobber paused. Again, he drank from his glass and Caroline frowned. She had seen it before, had watched the tapes of the Professor in action but still she was fascinated. Jobber turned once more to the screen and continued. 'This was the anchor point that the scientists had been looking for decades, and they began to build upon it. If the speed of light was constant then, by definition, time was not. It might simply be a dimension, a fourth dimension...'

'Einstein, right?' It was Jack Scott, President Sutton's Chief of Staff speaking from Washington. Reminded of a presence other than the Professor, heads turned towards him.

'Wrong!' Over loud, a hint of triumph in his voice, Jobber was smiling. 'The science fiction writers were ahead of the game. It was H. G. Wells, in his book The Time Machine, written in 1895. That's ten years before Einstein's Special Theory of Relativity and a full 20 years before his General Theory was published in 1915.'

'But Einstein did say that time was a fourth dimension – didn't he?' Crest-fallen but no fool, Scott persisted.

'Yes, he did. Now it is received wisdom that time

is a dimension and last night I believe that that was demonstrated in the north of England.

'Think about it. Before it arrived, the only medium separating the waters of the River Humber from the boat on which those killers arrived was time. Not height, or breadth or width but time. Indeed, it is time that separates this very room from the Indian villages of the 16th and 17th centuries, or from the swamps and forests of the dinosaur age. Nothing more, nothing less and, for whatever reason, in East Yorkshire last night, more than thirty men, tons of timber, crossed the medium of time. The medium was breached, torn, call it what you will but don't look so surprised, it's a medium like any other, made to be crossed, it must happen all the time.'

Caroline felt Prime Minister Berwick look at her. She turned, caught his eye and nodded. Clever wordplay, theatrical, delivery but this was now mainstream thinking.

'I am not asking you to believe that these men moved from one dimension to another,' said Professor Jobber. 'That really is science fiction. I am simply suggesting that they moved within time, that time, like any of the other three dimensions, can be affected by energy and how radical is that? It's well understood by the basest of creatures. The smallest child waving a rattle knows it well. By expending energy, he can move his rattle up or down, from side to side or backwards and forwards. So why can he not move it through time? Why should time be so different?'

'I'm suggesting that it is not, that, whilst we may not be able to do it ourselves, it should, in theory, be possible. Indeed, Einstein went significantly further when he introduced the concept of space-time. If time was relative, he asked, then what was it relative to? The speed of light, his colleagues suggested, but Einstein was not convinced. He, and many of those who followed him, showed that it might be relative to numbers of things, that energy, mass, gravity and speed could all effect time. They could bend, warp it, stop it even. Maybe even make it go backwards.'

Jobber, his glasses forgotten, sipped his water, glanced at the screen. There were no questions. He continued, 'But what about time travel? Driven by the science fiction writers, the dreamers, the theorists, that has always been the big question. Some say that the evidence is all around us and, before you scoff, they may be right. They point to the pyramids of ancient Egypt rising from the lifeless sand or those of South America as examples of either time travel or of alien visitation and, although I happen to think that they are wrong, we cannot discount either possibility completely. Certainly, I would readily admit that Einstein's General Theory of Relativity did not dismiss time travel. Indeed, it suggested that it was possible, even likely. But not easy.'

Again, Jobber paused. The shadow of a smile playing on his lips, he pushed his glasses back up to the bridge of his nose. In London and Washington, silence. 'In a one-reality environment, Einstein suggested that time would stand still for an object that was travelling at the speed of light...'

'One reality?' It was Julian Ryde who had spoken.

Professor Jobber regarded him patiently. 'Yes. One reality at a time, I think. We'll cover multiple realities in a moment. As I said, at the speed of light, time stops. Indeed, Einstein did suggest that, if it were possible for objects to travel at greater than light speed then, for the objects concerned, time would run backwards.'

Behind Jobber, National Security Adviser, Larry Edelman, shifted in his seat. 'But what about black holes and wormholes and...'

'A little ambitious at this stage, I think,' said Jobber. 'But we'll get to that shortly. As I said earlier, modern physicists believe that energy, mass, gravity and speed can all affect time but that these relationships are linked. Indeed, that makes sense if one considers how they are measured which is effectively relative to one-another. Gravity, for example, is a function of mass.

'So, let's make a leap. How are black holes created, do wormholes exist and, if they do, then can they, as many people suggest, facilitate travel through time?'

Jobber paused but he was not inviting comment; he continued. 'The gravitational force created by a star is huge. If it were not for the nuclear reaction, the ceaseless explosions at its core that transform hydrogen into helium and create a huge outward pressure, then many of them would simply implode.

'In fact, that's exactly what does happen when a star becomes tired, and the energy created within its core becomes insufficient to counter the effect of its own gravity. They implode, suck themselves into a speck of dust and become black holes. But in a Universe of almost infinite variety some, perversely balanced stars, stop half-way as the energy within the star remains sufficient to prevent the implosion becoming total. These become white dwarves or neutron stars but those that collapse fully, shrink to the size of a pinhead and become black holes. They have an almost unbelievable mass and, as a result, have a huge gravitational pull from which not even light can escape.'

'Run that by me again, would you please,' said Jack Scott. Caroline felt for him. 'I'm sure I'm not the only one who's struggling here.'

'The escape velocity, here on earth is about seven miles a second,' answered Professor Jobber, staring at the Chief of Staff, clearly wondering where to begin. 'That holds for objects of any size and effectively means that a bullet fired vertically upwards will not shoot out to the stars because it is not travelling at more than seven miles a second. Instead, gravity will win the gravity-speed battle, and the bullet will fall back to earth.

'The escape velocity on the moon is lower because it has a weaker gravitational pull, and on the sun, it is higher for the opposite reason. Indeed, our sun has an escape velocity of about 100 miles a second, even if we were able to get there, we couldn't hope to leave the surface, but black holes are many millions of times denser. Their gravitational pull is unbelievably strong producing escape velocities of more than 186,000 miles per second and that, ladies and gentlemen, is the speed of light. Hence nothing, not even light can escape from a black hole and, given that light has been sucked in, held captive, not allowed to escape, time will stand still.'

Professor Jobber looked around the Oval Office and at the screen to London. Jack Scott caught his eye and smiled. In London Caroline Whittleton looked at the Prime Minister and nodded. This was mainstream. Jobber continued, 'In a single reality environment, this place where space-time ends is called a singularity. The laws of physics as we know them do not apply...'

'Surely they're fixed,' said Larry Edelman. 'The laws of physics I mean?'

'Narrow-minded...'

'Particle chauvinism,' said Caroline Whittleton in London. She could not stop herself. The assumption that everything we see is everything there is...'

'Thank you,' said Jobber. 'We assume that what we can see, what we can understand is all that exists. Now is not the time to talk about dark matter, but that's rather arrogant approach, don't you think? Men thought for thousands of years that the earth was flat. They knew that it was, it was obvious that it was, they could see that it was, but they were wrong. How can we be sure that we are right about the laws of physics? Have we been everywhere in the Universe, seen everything? How can we condemn the ancients as fools whilst making the same arrogant mistake ourselves?

'Still, even if the fundamental laws of physics hold on the surface of a black hole, and I'm as certain as I can be that they don't, then we can still assume that time stands still and that a singularity is created.

'Within this singularity, at the heart of the black hole, we will find a wormhole, a passageway, one that leads from the black hole through which we have entered to another black hole in a different time and place within our universe, or even in a different universe.'

'A fiction writer's dream,' said President Sutton.

'That's right,' said Jobber. 'It's the concept of hyper-space, widely quoted in fiction but it's science fact. Finding wormholes is not easy but controlling them is an altogether bigger problem. They are thought to be unstable, may last only for milliseconds and may not be large enough to permit the passage of any more than a few particles through hyper-space from one time to another. Indeed, there may be many other problems. The wormhole would probably destroy anything that passed through it, and we have no way of knowing when or where the particles would emerge but, having established the theory that these things exist, the rest is merely detail...'

'Can these things be built?' asked President Sutton.

'I had never imagined that they could be, no,' said Jobber. 'But I'm open to persuasion. Still, these are former stars that we're talking about. Creating a black hole of our own would take more energy than is available on the whole of our planet. Either that or we'd need a new source of energy, a source much more powerful than anything that we currently have.'

Donald Berwick nodded. 'So, these people might have discovered a new source of energy?'

'If this is really happening and it's being coordinated, then that's possible,' said Jobber.

'And you mentioned that there may be other ways of warping time. Speed or energy?'

'Yes. Einstein showed that as objects speed up, the rate at which time passes for them slows. If the object were to move at the speed of light, then time would stop, if it were to move faster than the speed of light, then time would go backwards...'

'But that's impossible?'

Jobber smiled. 'Unfortunately for the would-be time-traveller, Lorentz showed that as speeds increase, the size of an object diminishes and its mass increases. If the speed of light was achieved then, whilst the object would shrink, its mass would increase to the point where its own gravity would cause an implosion. I cannot see how we could ever hope to control such a process, the black hole could destroy our solar system, but, as I said earlier, once a principle has been established, everything else is noise.

'So, our options are narrowing. If utilizing a black hole is too difficult and travelling at the speed of light is not realistic, then that leaves the use of energy,' said Jobber. He paused, raised an eyebrow. 'Or manipulating multiple realities. You agree with me of course, Dr Whittleton?'

Caroline hesitated. She was being used as a prop. She knew the arguments well, but they led nowhere. The silence grew and she spoke. 'Yes, although I can see no easy options. Relativity theory shows us that both mass and speed can bend time and Einstein also thought, as do I, that energy could also affect time either directly or indirectly through the creation of a wormhole. To this day, it has never been proven. Indeed, we have never come close to proving it and may never be able to.'

'Yes, yes, thank you,' interrupted Jobber. He seemed keen to speak again, irritated by Caroline's negativity. She smiled and the Professor continued. 'Maybe somebody else has proved it for us, Dr Whittleton. Certainly, it is hard to think of any other rational explanation for these appearances.'

Julian Ryde gagged. 'Rational?'

'I realize that some people listening now will lack the scientific knowledge to grasp what I am saying,' said Jobber; he was dangerously calm. 'But in layman's terms one way in which to prove a theory is to disprove any other reasonable conclusions and I believe that we can do that in these cases. How else could these events possibly have happened?'

'I'm convinced that everyone present would like to hear what you have to say, Professor Jobber,' said the Prime Minister, pausing to glance at Ryde, the latter's head bowed. 'Everyone. Do please go on!'

Jobber looked at the video screen, dared a challenge

before he continued. 'Energy of sufficient intensity to warp time would probably need to be nuclear, although that's not absolutely certain, and evidence of its use in these situations would surely have been found. There are some theories that intense magnetic fields could be used, or energy from another, non-nuclear source. We're talking about almost unbelievably large amounts of energy here and it would need to be controlled, extremely accurately targeted and, as the energy was pulsed a man-made wormhole, effectively a door in time, could be opened.'

Jobber seemed to expect trouble. He glared over the top of his glasses, focused on the video-screen. The faces that stared back were intensely serious. He continued. 'In theory, once this door in time had been opened, anything could come through. Junk, vegetation, anything or nothing, but in practice the objects and groups of people that we have been observing have been getting bigger. It would require unbelievable precision to reach through the wormhole, the infinitesimally small door and pull something through. But that does appear to have happened, what other explanation could there be?

'Questions?'

'None.' It was Prime Minister Berwick who had spoken. 'Let's get this all out in the open.'

Jobber pursed his lips, nodded. 'It is likely that the size of the object picked up and the speed of its movement at the time that it was targeted could be limiting factors in its transportation as could the degree of precision required for targeting. However, and I think you'll agree, Dr Whittleton, the span of time over which it was transported would have no bearing.' Jobber paused and Caroline nodded. 'Indeed, some of the first objects to appear may also be the oldest. For example, the ice could have come from the last ice age. Remember, it was totally pollution free and, if it did, then it must be more than ten thousand years old and the rocks could be even older but, immobile as rocks and ice are, they would have been easy targets.'

'Targeting suggests intelligence,' said Julian Ryde in London.

'Indeed, it does.'

'The hand of man?'

'I would expect so.'

Ryde looked away from the screen, caught the Prime Minister's eye. 'Please go on.'

'As I said, the span of time over which the objects could have been transported is not a limiting factor. This is because, effectively, time is curved. Circle two points on a sheet of paper, six inches apart, bend that paper and, to anyone living on the paper, the circles, although they are almost touching one-another, are still six inches apart. Time is like that sheet of paper, but it is bent in an infinite number of directions meaning that any one microsecond of time is equidistant from any other microsecond irrespective of whether they are separated by what we understand to be a minute or by a million years.'

Jobber pause, sipped his water, his audience was silent. He smiled slightly and continued. 'So, let's reflect a little more on what time is. Over a million years a continent, Africa for example, behaves like a rice pudding. It sinks, spreads out and, over a billion years, it behaves like a liquid. Time really does separate an object from itself in a different form. It is the key and it's all around us, but, if it is curved, then it doesn't take a great deal more imagination to believe that every point in time is touching every other point but think what that means. It means what has happened in the past is still happening now as is everything that will happen in the future. I'm sure...'

'You're moving a little quickly,' said Julian Ryde in London. He turned to Donald Berwick. 'With your permission, Donald, could we go back a little?' Berwick nodded and Ryde turned back to the screen. 'You mentioned multiple realities?'

Jobber pursed his lips, shook his head. 'Dr Whittleton, perhaps...'

Caroline Whittleton stood up. She took off her glasses and put her notes down onto her seat. She did not need them. She regarded Jobber coolly before beginning to speak. 'One of the most popular time travel scenarios in science fiction involves a person becoming involved with an earlier version of himself, or with his mother or his grandmother. This creates a paradox. If the time traveller kills his mother, then he could not have been born and could not have killed his mother. But he does exist, because he killed his mother, etc.

'Such paradoxes mean that either, backward time travel is not possible or that the 'chronological protection agency' never makes a mistake. No time tourists are allowed or, alternatively, it might mean that a parallel universe has been created...'

'Parallel universes, multiple realities,' said Larry Edelman from Washington. 'The same thing, right?'

'Pretty much,' said Caroline.

'And what the hell is the chronological protection agency?'

'One of Stephen Hawking's less serious suggestions,'

said Caroline. 'But getting back to parallel universes. We could have two universes, two realities, one in which the time traveller's mother is alive and one in which she is dead. Effectively a Schrödinger's cat scenario.

'Quantum physics holds that multiple realities are possible and leads on to several interesting conclusions,' Caroline said. She could see Professor Jobber from the corner of her eye on the screen to Washington. He was moving foot-to-foot, clearly keen to speak again. Caroline ignored him.

'We can think of one point in time, similar to a very short trunk of a tree. Above the trunk are a million branches, a billion branches, an infinite number of branches, and below it there are an infinite number of roots. Now if you project that mental picture from two dimensions into three, then you begin to see what the theory of multiple realities is suggesting. Every point on every one of the infinite number of branches and roots, is itself a trunk that has an infinite number of branches feeding into it and an infinite number of roots leading from it. Everything, every point in time is in effect a focal point around which everything else is built.'

Caroline looked at the screen to Washington. She knew that she was losing people but continued again before Professor Jobber had a chance to speak. 'I'm afraid that that's as easy as it gets,' she said. 'A second, even more radical suggestion is that all these realities could exist at the same time; effectively in a fourth dimension. Not only is there a parallel universe in which you did go back and kill your own mother, but the universe in which we live also exists at all its earlier times right now. Hence, as we speak, the future has happened already, the Second World War is still being fought, the Roman Empire still exists, and the dinosaurs are still the masters of the planet. In this environment, one could effectively slide from one universe to the other, giving the impression of time travel...'

'A sort of virtual time travel?' said Julian Ryde.

'Precisely.'

'But what about moving back in time,' the Home Secretary asked. 'Is that possible? And if it is...?'

'And if it is, then why haven't we been aware of time tourists visiting us from the future?' interrupted Professor Jobber from Washington. He tugged hard at the hair curled behind his ear. 'In the Multiverse, the environment in which an infinite number of parallel universes might exist side by side, then it would be no more difficult to slide into an earlier universe than it would be to move forward. Of course, that's just synthetic time travel, virtual time travel as you said but if it is possible, then the question still needs to be addressed. Why have we found no evidence of it taking place?

'Non-visitation could be telling us that multiple realities cannot exist, but, on the other hand, it is almost impossible to prove a negative. However, I believe we are agreed that, in a single reality environment, it would be much more difficult to move backwards.

'Indeed, putting moving faster than the speed of light to one side for the moment, the past has already happened and, intuitively, it seems impossible to believe that we could change it. Still, there are scientists who believe that if one were able to travel through a wormhole, then it would be possible to go back in time...'

'Although some suggest that it would not be possible to go back to a point before which the wormhole did not exist,' said Caroline in London.

'Yes, yes,' said Jobber. 'And wormholes may only exist for a fraction of a second so there would be little chance for the time traveller to change history.

'Others have suggested that there is an as yet unidentified scientific reason why backwards travel within a single universe is not possible,' Jobber continued. 'As Dr Whittleton suggested, Stephen Hawking, for example, has commented on the potential existence or otherwise of a chronology protection agency that protects one time period against interference from another.'

'A sort of space-time police force?' suggested Linda King, the State Department boss.

'More a God,' said Julian Ryde.

Jobber nodded. 'Certainly, an infallible being, one who has never made a mistake, never allowed his guard to slip, even for a moment. But even if there was no chronological protection agency, and travelling back in time is not against the laws of physics, there are other reasons why we may not see the evidence; it might only ever be done once.

'By this we mean that the first person with the ability to move backward in time would have a unique opportunity to prevent others from following, to eliminate those who might become a threat to him or her in the future, Dr Whittleton or myself, for example and, that being the case, we would never know that there had ever been any interference with our time line. For us, it would have already happened, we would swear, as we do, that backwards time travel was not possible...'

'So, is that what you're suggesting has happened? Has that one person achieved it?

Jobber paused, squinted at the screen, made out

Julian Ryde. Once again, he pushed his spectacles up to the bridge of his nose, but Caroline sensed the Professor was playing for time. The silence grew. 'Possibly.'

'Dr Whittleton?'

'I've had no time to consider the question, Mr Ryde,' said Caroline, 'although, as you can see Professor Jobber and myself are very much alive.'

There was a pause before the British Home Secretary continued seriously. 'So, it either hasn't happened or, and I mean no offence, it has happened, and you were not deemed a threat?'

Caroline nodded and Ryde continued. 'And if we take the view that backward travel is not possible, then how can one bring objects and people forward from the past? Surely by doing that we are changing history?'

'In a single reality situation, the objects or people will already be gone,' answered Professor Jobber from Washington. 'They disappeared in their own time. The Viking Longboat, which appeared in Yorkshire yesterday evening for example, must have been lost a thousand years ago. No more than a few dozen families would ever have mourned its passing, but it must have been recorded. The person who did these things had to get his information from somewhere, but it was already gone. There will be none of the fading photographs of the science fiction films showing individuals disappearing from the past, no heroic attempt to remove Adolf Hitler, because if we were ever going to do such a thing, then it would already have been done, his name would mean nothing to us.'

A silence descended on both sides of the Atlantic before the Prime Minister spoke from London. 'Fascinating, but could we return to the present, the energy bursts? Are they the trigger or a side-effect of what you suggest has been happening?'

'Could be either,' said President Sutton. He looked at Jobber.

'The energy pulses near our airbases in Cambridgeshire have been one of the few constants and have always been followed by something. That's how we first got on to the phenomenon.

'Initially, we thought that the appearances were part of a British experiment, something covert. Our people had followed the bursts, detected a pattern, the energy always expended around Cambridge but, until the incident with the longboat, there had never been any evidence found in the area where these objects appeared.

'On Thursday there was. The TV station, the localized blackout but still we imagined that the majority of the energy necessary to trigger the event was expended remotely, in the Cambridge area. And now there's been another one.'

In London, Prime Minister Berwick turned from the screen to Julian Ryde. The Home Secretary shook his head then glanced at Alistair MacDonald, nodded towards the door and the Special Branch chief rose and left the room. Berwick shook his head. 'We've nothing on it yet.'

President Sutton continued. 'As the events have become more dramatic, the objects larger, the energy expended has increased. With the latest occurrence, the Viking Longboat, in addition to the several hundred houses in the area that lost electrical power and the television transmission station that was destroyed there was much greater damage in Cambridgeshire. Even some of the hardened systems were corrupted.'

'Sorry to change the subject,' said Julian Ryde after a short silence. He glanced from President Sutton to Professor Jobber. 'Do you believe that these people ever go back?'

'Certainly, we don't have the ability to send them back,' said Jobber. 'Not with the technology that we have available to us at present.'

'So, they stay?'

'They are human beings like you or I,' said Jobber. 'Although they may do things which, though normal to them, make it impossible for them to function in today's world.'

'I think that's an understatement,' said Ryde. 'So, what do we do with them?'

It was a rhetorical question. Jobber simply shrugged and held up his hands.

The President cleared his throat, and the camera panned around to him. 'So that's where we're at people. You know pretty much what we do now. The data regarding the energy pulses near our bases is being collated and we'll get it to you as quickly as possible, but maybe at this point we could ask our scientific advisers to leave us for a few moments?'

'Of course,' said Donald Berwick. He pressed a button beneath the table in front of him and, almost immediately, the door to the Cabinet Room opened. He turned to Caroline and Dr Bryce and Caroline felt a flush of disappointment. 'Dr Whittleton, Dr Bryce? Julian, perhaps you would be kind enough to show our guests a little of the house?'

Ryde rose to his feet. If he was disappointed himself, he did not show it as he smiled at Dr Bryce then turned to Caroline. He gestured towards the door. 'Shall we?'

Caroline and Dr Bryce followed the UK Home Secretary out of the Cabinet Room and the doors behind them. Ryde was immaculately dressed, Caroline noticed, and much taller than he appeared on the television. He turned to face them.

'I'm sorry,' he said, his voice assured. 'Please forgive me, but we haven't been properly introduced. Julian Ryde. I have the pleasure to serve as Her Majesty's Home Secretary. I'm delighted to meet you.' Ryde shook Caroline's hand firmly then turned to Dr Bryce. 'Although I must say that the circumstances of our meeting leave a lot to be desired.'

Tight-lipped, Dr Bryce blinked ferociously, and Caroline smiled, looked more closely at the Home Secretary and frowned. His skin had a yellow tinge, and he walked stiffly. He was not a well man. He seemed to sense that he was being scrutinized, looked Caroline in the eye and smiled. He turned and led the way along a landing to a staircase that swept down to the ground floor.

'We may have to return to less pleasant matters later,' said Ryde. His back was to the two Cambridge physicists and Caroline looked around her. She imagined that they were moving towards the front of the building. 'But for the moment, maybe you'd like to follow me?'

Caroline nodded, politely at the Home Secretary, but her mind was elsewhere. She had seen the black front door of number 10 Downing Street a hundred times on the television, but had never thought that she would walk through it yet there it was, below her on the ground floor, a policeman seated by its side. She scarcely noticed the portraits of the previous Prime Ministers that decorated the wall as they descended the stairs.

'...originally two buildings,' said Ryde. Caroline chided herself for missing his introduction. 'It's much larger on the inside that people believe.

Although there was a house on the site previously, the present façade, and that of number eleven, were built in the 1650's by an American property speculator, George Downing. Of course, he wasn't American then. Rather an Englishman living abroad, but he was a bit of a spiv. He sold the houses on and the last private householder to live here was a Mr Chicken. It's true, I swear but he left in 1735 when Sir Horace Walpole moved in and it's been in the family, so to speak, ever since.'

The Home Secretary stopped in his tracks and Caroline watched as he took a firm hold of the stair's handrail. The politician's knuckles whitened, muscles tightening in Ryde's cheek. Caroline tried not to stare; it looked like a stomach problem of some sort. The Home Secretary tried to smile. He continued. 'Of course, the room we've just left is probably the most famous one in the building. Much extended in the late 18th century, the table is a relatively recent addition, but the 23 chairs are the same as those used in Gladstone's day and Churchill's broadcast announcing the end of the Second World War was made from the exact spot where George Berwick was sitting. Indeed, from that very chair.'

Caroline reached the bottom of the stairs and let her hand rest on a large globe. She turned to Julian Ryde. The house was overwhelming, but her mind was elsewhere. 'This is for real, isn't it?'

'A present from President Mitterand,' replied the Home Secretary, looking at the globe. He ushered them into an adjoining room. 'The globe that is, not the world. I think that that was beyond even Francois' gift and yes, it is. This is very much for real.'

****

Almost two hours later at 9.15pm, Caroline and Dr Bryce were asked to return to the Cabinet Room. Caroline ached for a radio, for news of any sort. She had heard nothing of the outside world since late afternoon. Surely, they would have told her if there had been any more news, whether the burst that they had recorded earlier in the evening had led to another of these horrible events? Caroline shook her head; if it had, then how would they know? It could be distant from the source of the energy itself, Hull had proved that, and they might never be truly sure. It could be anything. She entered the Cabinet Room ahead of Bryce and Donald Berwick stood to greet them. The Prime Minister was alone, the video screen turned off. He gestured towards two chairs but remained standing. A coffee pot and two teapots were standing on a table next to them.

'Coffee?'

Caroline shook her head again, not sure what the protocol was, but she needed to know. 'Has anything happened?'

Berwick shook his head, poured a coffee. He added a little milk. 'At the moment, we're not aware of anything.' Caroline felt her shoulders relax and Berwick continued. 'The President of the United States and I believe that Professor Jobber should fly to the UK. We would like you to work closely with him. How would you feel about that?'

Caroline knew that it was not a question. She hesitated a little too long before answering. 'At the labs in Cambridge?'

Berwick nodded and Caroline tried a smile. 'Yes, I think it would be good for Professor Jobber to be here. What do you think Brandon?'

'Splendid,' said Bryce. He straightened his spectacles, his eyes magnified by their thick lenses. It was the first time that Caroline could recall him speaking since the Government car had swept them into Downing Street.

'This is a matter of national importance, perhaps of international importance,' said Berwick. 'Professor Jobber will be here some time tomorrow.' He paused and Caroline could feel herself being weighed, judged. 'In your opinion as a physicist, Dr Whittleton, why would anyone do these things?'

'To prove that they can,' said Caroline without hesitation.

Prime Minister Berwick said nothing; he smiled without humour and shook his head. 'I think not.'

****

Berwick had thanked Caroline and Dr Bryce once more and, their audience over, they had been shown to the waiting car. Caroline had felt numb, she still did, her eyes distant, unfocused. She could still scarcely believe what she had heard and, sure that her own face, mirrored that of Brandon Bryce, she tried to compose herself.

The shouting and the flashing of the journalist's cameras that had greeted them as the car pulled through the wrought iron gates at the junction of Downing Street and Whitehall was even more intense than it had been earlier. It had taken no more than a couple of seconds for the car to push its way through the crush, but Caroline had felt abused, tainted by the questions.

'What's your name love?'

'In to see Duncan, were you?'

'Give us a smile!'

There had been female voices as well as male and then, as the car had pulled into Whitehall, the flashguns had been pressed up against the windows, names shouted out to elicit a reaction. It had been horrible.

The car was edging its way into the strand, the traffic thinner and Caroline turned to Dr Bryce. His eyes still wide with surprise. Once again, he seemed unable to speak and she sat back as they headed east, swept rapidly through the City of London towards Bishopsgate and the A10 to Bishop's Stortford and Cambridge.

Caroline looked at the driver, tried to relax. He and his front seat passenger exchanged a look, the passenger obviously the senior of the two, something in his body language and Caroline noticed that the car had a second rear-view mirror fitted, the type often found in the cars used in driving schools. The front seat passenger was checking it periodically.

Tired as she was, she had not meant to stare when the man caught her eye, a flash of blue even in the dim light. He smiled, his eyes flicking from the road ahead to the rear-view mirror and back again; he seemed to be looking for something. Embarrassed, Caroline looked away, checked the rear window but, as Haringey gave way to Enfield, she saw nothing out of the ordinary. She turned once again to Dr Bryce and broke the silence.

'So, what do you make of it, Brandon?'

'Very interesting,' said Dr Bryce. He blinked rapidly and frowned.

Caroline nodded; she could think of little to add and

Bryce was clearly in no mood to talk, he rarely was. She had not expected him to comment on the human misery, the plight of the victims of the previous day's attacks, but the power, the almost God-like power that the knowledge of how to do such things would bestow upon a person, was almost beyond words. Her mind turned to the politicians. Did they know what they were dealing with? This was more important than tax cuts and sound bites, was probably more important than everything! Berwick had seemed to understand the gravity of the situation and Julian Ryde's grasp at such short notice was impressive; maybe they would rise to the challenge, but what could they really do?

Caroline lowered her eyes. She would have to work on the project full-time, of course, drop everything, focus fully and the Americans, when they arrived, would make a real difference but Brandon, his eyelids buzzing like a winged insect, might struggle. She would have to run the operation. Jeremy was not there, she had the girls to think about, but she had no choice.

Caroline's mind was still racing when the car pulled into Bishop's Stortford. Brandon was going back to Cambridge and Caroline thanked the driver. He nodded and she caught the eye of his passenger once again. Sandy haired, mid to late thirties he smiled and, as she walked up the short path to her front door, Caroline felt strangely reassured.

Terri, Caroline's regular babysitter, was standing expectantly just inside the front door, her coat draped over her arm and Caroline felt that she should apologize. She nodded and said nothing, took the envelope from her pocket, slipped in another £10 and held it out. Terri nodded sullenly and left without a backward glance.

Caroline had expected no less. She walked into the house, music blaring from the sitting room and looked at her watch. She turned off the CD player then picked up the remote and pointed it at the television to turn it off as well when, her finger poised on the button, she changed the channel instead. The news was still on.

The East Yorkshire story must have played already, but she could catch the headlines at the end of the bulletin. Surely if something new had happened it would still be running, but there was nothing and the broadcast moved on to Japan.

The riots in Tokyo were getting worse and Caroline felt a wave of guilt, she was pregnant, and Jeremy knew nothing. She looked at her watch again and sat down. Her husband would be almost there by now, she should have told him before he left, but they had argued. She shook her head and turned back to the television.

Tokyo's financial markets were still in free-fall, apparently, and a lot of individuals, not just the very wealthy, had lost their life savings. There had been renewed violence, with more to come and she had not wanted Jeremy to go and now two foreigners, an American and a German, had been reported missing.

Caroline briefly looked in on the girls, came back downstairs, switched off the TV and pulled the sheet of paper that the Downing Street staff officer had given her out of her pocket. She picked up the telephone, dialled the number and a brusque sounding woman answered almost immediately. She seemed to know who Caroline was, needed few details. 'We will have someone around to look after the children at 7.30am. Will a nanny and a nurse be sufficient?'

'Yes. Thank you,' said Caroline. 'Seven thirty?'

Caroline put the telephone down. She checked the locks, climbed the stairs slowly and set her alarm clock for 6.30am.

Saturday 27, October 1999
Eight

'*We know it will work,*' *said the older man. 'Some of you've seen it. For most, it'll be a new experience. You'll see things that you've never seen before.*'

****

It was 8.15am and, four miles to the east, Kazimierz Dolny was now almost completely awake. The postmen had finished their first rounds, and the shops were beginning to open as the half-tracked armoured personnel carrier pulled into the village square by the tiny stream that fed the Vistula and drew sharply to a halt, the tarmac on the road tearing up in neat folds.

The vehicle was gunmetal grey and was strewn

with implements, fastened securely and in many cases dampened by blankets and rags. There were shovels and buckets, a broom, several canvases, a tent and what looked like a tin bath. There was even a bicycle lashed to the front of the vehicle in pride of place with three dead chickens strapped to a spare wheel, their feathers fluttering in the gentle breeze. Several guns protruded from the vehicle, relics, two large MG34 machine guns to the front and two smaller machine guns, one to either side. The grey canvas roof was drawn down, the vehicle's passengers not visible.

The market pitches set up for more than an hour, the square was busy. The first housewives, silent, beginning now to point at the halftrack, had been buying fruit and bread, checking the availability of other goods for later in the day, but the first bemused glances had turned to looks of disgust as the villagers recognized the markings on the vehicle's side. An old man spat noisily as its guns swept the square.

The canvas sheet that served as a roof for the APC began to move. A flap was thrown open towards the front of the vehicle and a head appeared. Helmeted, mid-grey, the head turned, took in the square and, as the man raised himself up, his green-green jacket became visible. Unshaven, very young, the man was slim and of medium height, his head held high, his chin out, perhaps a little arrogant. At his neck a small cross glinted in the slanting morning sun.

The man disappeared into the vehicle and a buzz of gossip filled the square. It stopped abruptly as a loud metallic clang rang out, the doors at the rear of the APC striking the body of the vehicle. Some villagers flinched, others began to register concern as, first the man who had looked around the square, and then several of his colleagues moved swiftly through the hatch and jumped onto the cobbled square.

Uniformed, the men, most only boys, looked tired and dirty, dishevelled but, as the first man out of the halftrack barked an order, they snapped to attention.

He spoke again and the men already out of the vehicle ran to different corners of the square, other bodies from within the vehicle tumbling out behind them.

****

Andreas Studer drew himself to his full height. He was twenty-two years old. More than a decade an orphan, he had spent a quarter of his life in uniform and could remember little else. He was a Rottenführer in the 3rd SS Panzer Division, 'Totenkopf', and he thanked God daily for giving him the chance to fight for his Fatherland.

Studer's father had died by his own hand. Andreas had only been a boy at the time, nine years old but even then, he had been under no illusions. It had been the British that had killed him; the British and the other enemies of the Reich, the French and the Russians, above all the Jews. The old man's small savings had been wiped out by years of inflation and his army pension had become worthless. He had lost a leg fighting for the Fatherland in the Great War, had been physically and mentally broken by his experiences in the trenches.

His chin jutting a little further, Studer was certain.

His father had been no coward, had never been work-shy but he had not held down a job after the war. He had suffered, was poor, but had always told his children that the humiliation of their country at the hands of their enemies in the years after the Armistice had been much worse than anything that he had suffered in the mud of Flanders or in the years since.

No, the elder Studer had maintained, the Reich had been betrayed, betrayed by its Jew politicians and its weak, effete business leaders. Traitors, they had themselves been manipulated by the French back in '19 and worse had been to come. The French had taken back Alsace and Lorraine, temporarily, thank God and the filthy Slavs had pushed their borders to the west, made room for the Bolsheviks. Andreas's father had been thirty-one years old when he had died, leaving four sons to be raised by his consumptive wife. She was had tried but had been feeble, had lasted less than two years and the Reich had become the only parent that he and his brothers had ever known.

It was a matter of great regret to Andreas that his father had not lived to see the Führer come to power in '33. His mother had disapproved at first, a filthy little Austrian she had called him, but Hitler had promised all Germans a better life and the young Studer, bright-eyed, his heart thumping in his chest, had determined to make that promise a reality and what a start! He and his brothers and his countrymen had destroyed the French and pushed the English back to their stinking homeland. They had beaten the Russians and would force them to accept their defeat once the Reich had shortened its line. Then they would show them. It would be June '41 all over again and this time, this time nothing would stop them. He looked around the square and caught the eye of an old man. He was well dressed, suspicious, Jewish...

****

With his back to the converted synagogue, its congregation long gone, Andrzej Luczak had watched the Germans arrive. His mouth had fallen open, and he had rubbed his eyes.

Luczak might be old, more than seventy, but his memory was good. The uniforms of the men were mud-encrusted, stained but somehow familiar looking and then the certainty had begun to build. He had watched, had been unable to tear his eyes away, but had been afraid of what he might see. Then he had frozen, had not been able to move but now he forced himself to look, a little higher, up the arm, to the shoulder and there it was, the eagle! He looked at the collars of the young man's jacket and the years fell away. Silver beading on the left and yes, there they were on the collar to the right, two silver S's, angular and menacing. Andrzej Luczak began to urinate.

Luczak's German was good. A gentile, his maternal grandmother German, five years of occupation during the war and fifty years of German television, first the dreadful rubbish from the East and more recently German national television had made him fluent but these were words and phrases from his childhood, from a past that he did not want to remember.

'Halt...'

Luczak had heard it many times before... 'Papers!'

...often followed by the sickening thud of rifle butts striking flesh and sometimes running feet, a moment of freedom followed by a burst of gunfire...

'Papers...'

...and the dogs and the awful martial music, blaring from loudspeakers attached to the sides of some of the military vehicles, military vehicles just like this one.

Andreas could almost touch it. Horrified, he reached out his hand.

****

Andreas Studer looked around the square suspiciously, watched as the old man, his hands held before him, frightened yet curious, edged towards the APC. Animals, sheep, these people were lower than that. True, he and his colleagues had done their job well, had been ruthless in the cull, but still there were still so many of them!

Certainly, the towns around here were Judefrei, the Jews had gone, and they had made up around a third of the population, but the Poles were little better. All that work and still so much more to do! Andreas cocked his head to one side, his eyes narrowed. There was something else.

The Square looked unfamiliar. Its church looked as though it had been recently repaired, and Andreas laughed out loud, harsh and cold. Poles! They couldn't feed themselves, died like flies but still they rebuilt their churches! His eyes caught those of the well-dressed old man, his bony arm still reaching out towards the APC.

'Papers!'

The Rottenführer unslung his MP40 machine pistol and moved towards Andrzej Luczak. He grabbed the old man roughly by the lapels of his coat, pushing him away from the halftrack.

'Papers, I said. Are you deaf?' The quality of the overcoat, the shine of his shoes; the man had clearly soiled himself and he was too old. He should be dead, the dirty Jew bastard! 'You do have them? Or are you a Communist, a People's Commissar?'

'No sir! No sir!' said Luczak, his German heavily accented, rusted by lack of use. 'I am Andrzej Luczak sir, a humble carpenter! Now retired. I am no communist, sir!'

The German pulled the old man around, pushed him backwards against the rear of the Armoured Personnel Carrier. 'I believe you, old man,' he said softly. 'Of course, I believe you but where did your German come from? Did you learn it in Russia? Where are your papers?'

'I...I...I, here they are!'

Luczak pulled his identity card from his pocket and held it towards the Rottenführer. Studer snatched the plastic ID card from his hand, the magnetic strip catching the light.

'What the Hell do you call this, you communist pig?' The Rottenführer bent the ID card between his finger and thumb, felt it snap back into shape and handed it to the man to his right. He gestured towards the door of the APC. 'Get in and don't steal anything. Tobler, keep your eye on him.'

The old man was dragged from his grasp and Studer looked around the square. The peasants were regarding him strangely. Fear and a scarcely concealed panic but also contempt. Were these people mad? Did the rabbit no longer run from the hound? Still, he was unafraid. Several of the younger men began to move towards him from the direction of the small stream but that meant nothing. Studer turned his back on them. He did not see the police car enter the square.

'Achtung, Partisanen!'

The old man temporarily forgotten, Studer span around, saw the police car. He said nothing, but his men knew what to do. Sturmann Horst Heller and Oliver

Wengler had already fallen to the floor with their MG34 and the remainder of the men had fallen back to the side of the APC and behind a small fountain in the centre of the square as the police car drew to a halt. Two officers got out and a few people ran towards them shouting and gesticulating towards the Germans. The policemen looked up, the taller of them moved his hand down towards the leather holster at his hip.

'Feuer!'

The MG34 buzzed like an angry insect and several lighter weapons crackled for an instant. The police car jerked to and fro, a hundred flakes of paint flying from it, ripped upholstery, dust and fluff floating in the air.

Masonry dust drifting on the light breeze, the sound of the now idle weapons washed from wall to wall in the square for several seconds. Then it was quiet, the silence broken only by the crash of falling glass as the window of one of the buildings behind the police car tumbled, intact, to shatter on the cobbles of the market below.

Studer was in little doubt that the men were dead, the immediate threat neutralised. The taller one, the one that had tried to draw his weapon lay grotesquely across the bonnet of the car, flaps of torn clothing, some soggy with blood, lifted by the breeze and the second was inside. He had been pushed back through the vehicle's broken window, his feet alone visible, but he was dead. In addition, two villagers lay in front of the vehicle, one of them groaning softly, moving, the other still.

'You filthy bastards!' shouted Studer, rising to his feet. He was almost spitting with rage. He nodded to Sturmann Heller, jerked his head towards the police car and the Sturmann jogged over towards it. The eyes of the villagers followed him.

'We tell you again and again and still you shelter these people!' said Studer softly as Heller reversed his rifle and rammed the butt into the body of the tall policeman. He nodded, walked over to the moaning civilian, smiled and reversed his rifle. Holding it by the barrel, he raised it high above his head and swung it down hard.

'You see what happens?' said Studer. Walking towards the back of the APC he gestured towards the police car. He took off his helmet, tossed it into the vehicle, reached inside and grabbed Andrzej Luczak roughly by the lapel of his overcoat. He pulled him out of the vehicle, dragged him towards the centre of the square.

'Fools!' said Studer. He was calmer now. He ran his hand through his short blond hair, spiky with sweat and he stared into the old man's eyes. He pushed him backwards towards the fountain. 'Why do you make us do these things?'

The villagers had clearly welcomed the partisans and now they had to pay. Studer looked around the square then back at Andrzej Luczak, the old man's hands hanging limply by his sides, his eyes lowered. He had stopped moaning and Studer swallowed hard.

This would be his first, at least this close, but it had to be done. He reached to his waistband for his Walther HP Automatic and pulled it free. Without a word he raised it to the old man's head, pushed it roughly into his cheek and pulled the trigger. The metallic click rang around the square.

'Scheisse!' hissed Studer. He banged the gun roughly against his hand and held it once more to the old man's head.

'May God forgive you,' said the old man in Polish. 'And have mercy on...'

A shot rang out as the Rottenführer pulled the trigger for a second time and the old man crumpled to the ground. Studer swallowed again, set his jaw and glared at the nearest peasants. He dared them to hold his eye yet several did and Studer looked away.

'Heller, take Kaiser and get back over to those Partisans. Find out what you can. Get their weapons. Funkel get on the radio again. The rest of you, see if you can find some food.' The Rottenführer walked slowly back to the half-track. He turned and watched Horst Heller pull open the jacket of one the dead policemen; a knife in his hand, he took a hold of the man's ear.

'And Heller? We'll be taking two of the bastards with us.'

Heller clumsily tried to hide his knife from view. He grinned and saluted sloppily as, around the square, a gentle sobbing broke the silence.

****

Caroline Whittleton had woken early feeling a little sick; she had not slept well. The events of yesterday had disturbed her, kept her awake into the small hours and now she was occupied planning the day ahead as she went through her morning routine. She felt a pang of guilt as she thought about the girls. With their father away, they would be devastated.

Emily had been pleading all week to go to the Woburn Safari Park and Caroline had not said no. She had known that Emily had read it as a maybe and had allowed the hope to build but, by 7.30am, she was keen to get back to the labs. She would have to be hard and there had already been tears.

The girls had been up when the child minder and the nurse arrived. They clearly suspected something, and Caroline had had to turn away, force herself not to look at them but, thirty minutes later, she could still hear their sobbing as she slowed her car to a halt in the car park of the Trinity Science Park. She tried to push the girls from her mind, gathered up her briefcase and the papers, some loose on the car's front seat and entered the labs.

'Anything on the energy burst from last night?'

Dr Bryce turned, frowned then shook his head. The sleeves of his lab-coat were rolled back, a definite sign of excitement. 'No, but we've to expect Professor Jobber in about two hours. Apparently, he was in a bit of a state, he hates flying and I must say, I know how he feels. Until today he hadn't flown for twelve years, they had to sedate him.'

Caroline slipped off her old Barbour, walked to the equipment cupboard behind her desk and took out her white lab coat. It was more than Bryce had said in a week; he was about to speak again but Caroline beat him too it.

She was direct. 'Can it be done, Brandon?'

Dr Bryce sat down at one of the workbenches and rested his chin on his hands, silent for several seconds. He smiled, tried to look worldly, nodded his head and looked at Caroline over the top of his thick glasses. 'Yes,' he said. 'I really think it could be done.'

Caroline respected Bryce and he was rarely so emphatic. 'But how, Brandon? How could anyone make such progress without this lab, or Jobber, or Klutz or anybody else knowing anything about it?'

Bryce had no answer and Caroline sat down. It was theoretically possible but fantastic. It was beyond belief, yet the evidence suggested that it had been done! Caroline opened her computer, clicked through to her mail and was pleased to see that the detailed information she had been promised regarding the previously recorded energy pulses had arrived. She alt-tabbed away from her home page, something about Poland scrolled across the screen and she gestured to Dr Bryce to come and look at the data. He would have received the data too, but she felt the need to talk, and she felt his breath on her neck. He was about to speak when Caroline glanced at her watch; she wanted a chance to summarize their results before the Americans arrived.

'What time will Jobber be here?'

Bryce considered the question seriously. 'About 11am.'

****

In his room in the Hotel Seiyo in the Ginza district of Tokyo, Jeremy Whittleton rubbed his eyes. It was almost 5.30pm. He had not meant to fall asleep, but he hated flying east, and he had not slept well on the BA005, the 1.40pm British Airways flight to Narita.

Jeremy walked over to the window and pulled back the net curtain. He was on the better side of the hotel, away from the Shuto Expressway. Before him sprawled the shops, art galleries and boutiques of Ginza, beyond that the whole of Tokyo, the Hama Rikyu Palace Gardens and Tokyo Bay. He leant forward and craned his neck to the right, he could see the top of the Sony Building, its garish lights beginning their daily assault on the night sky. Letting the curtain fall, Jeremy turned and picked up the phone on the small writing desk by the side of his bed.

'Declan O'Donnell here,' boomed an Australian voice, the rising intonation unmistakable.

'Declan? It's Jeremy. Are we still on for a beer?'

'Sure, mate. I've been trying to contact you for a couple of hours.'

'Sorry, Dec, I've been dead to the world. What time?'

'About half seven? I've got a few things to do.'

'Sounds fine,' said Jeremy; he could have done to have made it a little earlier. Still, he could ring Caroline, he needed to apologize about the car then he could eat early at one of the excellent restaurants in the hotel itself. In any case, the bars in Shinjuku and Shibuya didn't close until five or six in the morning; so there was no rush. He rang reception, reserved a table at the Italian restaurant then checked his watch.

He punched in the number for Caroline's Cambridge lab.

The ring tone sounded only once then switched to the answer-machine and Jeremy left a brief message. He hung up and tried Caroline's mobile. Again, there was no answer.

Nine

'*Don't stick around to watch,*' *said the instructor, serious now. 'It'll get pretty hot, and you'll have less than a minute. At your speed and distance, we think you'll be OK.*'
'*You think?*' *muttered Charles Warner under his breath.*

****

President Sutton was shattered. It was 4am and he had not slept for 45 hours. Ashen faced, he shuffled the grey photographs gently, looking first at one and then another.

Despite having been taken by a satellite in low earth orbit over eastern Poland, the photographs were surprisingly clear. The German half-tracked APC was clearly visible; shapes that were obviously people could be seen around it.

The President looked up, sought out Gerry Buchanan, the CIA chief. Behind Buchanan stood Dick Turner, the President's Secretary of Defence and Jack Scott, the Chairman of the Joint Chiefs of Staff. Some little way from them, Larry Edelman finished a hushed cell phone conversation. The men were clearly very concerned.

'Are we sure?'

'The radio traffic suggests that there has been an attack on the village of Kazimierz Dolny by neo-Nazi extremists,' said Buchanan, his voice betraying no emotion. 'There have been some fatalities.'

Dick Turner tapped one of the photographs in front of the President. 'This appears to show an SPW, a Schützenpanzerwagen or armoured personnel carrier. A half-tracked vehicle, I'm told it's probably an SdKfz 251, a German design from World War Two that ceased production in 1945. It was widely copied around the world in the War.'

President Sutton hesitated; he looked up at Gerry Buchanan. 'So, these could still be look-alikes, could've got hold of some vehicle and be living out some sick fantasy?'

'That's correct, sir,' said the CIA chief, his tone flat. He clearly did not believe it.

Sutton shook his head. 'Carry on.'

'Neo-Nazis have been a problem in the eastern part of Germany but there has never been anything like this, certainly nothing by German extremists in Poland.'

'What's your opinion?' asked Sutton, raising his head.

Buchanan seemed reluctant to speculate. The CIA director said nothing. President Sutton looked directly at him, raised his eyebrows. 'Let's have it, Gerry.'

'Information is very limited, sir,' said Buchanan.

'But I think the Germans would have had some advance intelligence if this were a planned neo-Nazi attack. There is a very real possibility that this event is linked to those in the north of England on Thursday evening.'

Sutton massaged the bridge of his nose, slowly opened his eyes. 'And what's happening now?'

'We're still sifting information from several mobile telephone calls, sir,' said Buchanan. 'We know that the killings in Kazimierz Dolny were reported to the police in Pulawy, the nearest town of any size. The perpetrators appear to have taken two local youths with them, but police reinforcements should be in the area in the next few minutes. Unfortunately, we won't have such a clear shot from the satellite because of low cloud moving over the area. Dick?'

'We believe that the nearest Polish Army units are near Lublin, some fifty kilometres away,' said Dick Turner, taking his cue from Buchanan. 'It's still a local affair, we don't think that the police have requested military help yet, but they probably will...'

'And the Germans authorities?'

Turner looked at Buchanan, he nodded. 'Polish-German relations have been very good for several years,' said Gerry Buchanan. 'They're particularly warm at the moment so it's likely that the Poles will report the facts to Berlin as a matter of some urgency, whether or not they believe the perpetrators to be German nationals.'

Sutton turned a particularly graphic photograph with his finger, pushed it across the desk towards his Defence Secretary. 'How many men are there in one of these things?'

'That depends on what it was carrying, sir,' said Turner. 'Set up to lay mines or configured for bridge building, it may just be a two-man crew plus maybe two engineers but if it was troop carrying then maybe a dozen men in total. On the other hand, if it was being used in a battlefield emergency, withdrawing troops for example, then it could be carrying up to twenty, even twenty-five, heavily armed men.'

'Do we have any clues here?' asked President Sutton.

He glanced at the photographs in front of him again, wrinkled his nose in distaste.

'The only reports have referred to 'several' armed men but eye-witness reports are notoriously unreliable,' said Gerry Buchanan. 'From the satellite photos, I'd say there were 20 or more.'

'Jesus!' The President shook his head, his eyes closed. 'Anything we can do to help?'

'I think they can handle it, sir.'

'You think?' Buchanan nodded and the President continued. 'Do we tell them anything?'

'Ultimately we may have to, Mr President,' said Buchanan. Behind him, Larry Edelman pursed his lips. 'But for the time being, I suggest that we say nothing. The authorities need to deal with the situation on the ground and their response to the most obvious conclusion, that this is a motiveless attack by neo-Nazi extremists, would likely be the same if we told them what we suspect. Indeed, if we did tell them, it might slow their response, cost lives.'

'Thank you, Gerry,' said the President. Gerry was rarely wrong, but silence had its price. Sutton turned back to the photographs on his desk, looked at the strangely angled bodies and at the armoured personnel carrier. He rotated one of the pictures slowly, then pushed it gently away.

****

In what had been the General Government of Poland, the Nazi administrative area that included Kazimierz Dolny, it was 12 o'clock noon and Andreas Studer had just finished eating. It was still cold and bright, but clouds were beginning to build to the north-west.

The rain was coming and Studer breathed deep, looked around him with some satisfaction. The men had eaten, and their current position was not too bad at all.

The Rottenführer had left Kazimierz on the Pulawy road, moved the half-track to a more defensible position in a small wood. The trees had yet to lose the last of their leaves, they would give some limited protection from the air and the deserted farmhouse by the side of the road would be even better. It had no roof, but the cellar and two outhouses would be useful if he was forced to hold his ground.

And visibility was good. The one road out of the village in this direction bent a little but it ran north-easterly in open view and the river Vistula gave them some cover to their left. Hence, any approach other than by the road would have to be made over the open ground to their right or from the air.

Studer took off his tunic, tested the cold water in the bucket in front of him. Generally, he was pleased with his handling of the situation so far. Sturmann Heller and the others had spent a few minutes questioning some of the peasants in the square, but the mood had turned ugly. Heller was no diplomat, and one man had been shot. Heller had insisted that he had produced a knife.

True or not, Studer nodded to himself. He had

twenty-four men under his command, and he didn't want to risk their lives dealing with these filthy animals. More appropriate reprisals could be taken later.

The two Polish boys that Sturmann Heller had grabbed from the square sat cross-legged by the side of the APC, their heads down. Heller was standing over them whittling at a stick with his knife. He began to hum one of the tunes that he had picked up from the radio to himself and Rottenführer Studer smiled.

Still, he was concerned. Funkel had still not managed to raise anybody on the radio, the Russians had been interfering with their broadcasts for many weeks now, but never for so long and the airwaves were full of unfamiliar music, English and Polish voices. At one point, Funkel had picked up a German signal, but it was broadcast only, it would not acknowledge their call sign, had prattled on instead about gardening. Keeping spirits up on the Home Front perhaps, but of no use to Studer or his men. The Rottenführer had told Funkel to carry on trying and had posted men at points two hundred meters to the front and rear of the APC on the road, and also at the edge of the copse of trees but still, his unease had grown.

True, his men were battle hardened and there was no enemy armour in the area. Lightly armed Partisans should not be too much trouble and even regular troops, which should not be in the area anyway, would find it difficult to knock out the APC without a fierce fight, but something was not right. He had pondered the situation, was cursing the radio when Oliver Wengler, a keen youth of eighteen with a tiny Swastika pinned to his breast pocket, slid to a halt before him, saluted hastily.

'Sorry Rottenführer,' blurted the youngster, his face

red. 'Tobler reports six maybe eight enemy vehicles approaching at speed from the north marked up like the partisan car in the village...'

'Armour?'

Wengler was already turning, making to head back to his post. He stopped himself. 'No obvious heavy armour, sir. Distance two K's, ETA ninety seconds...'

Studer jumped to his feet, the men waiting for him to speak, tense beneath their disinterest. 'Heller, watch the prisoners. Kaiser, take three men and remain with the APC. Tell Schmidt that we're dealing with an enemy to the north. The rest of you, get your gear and come with me.'

The young German picked up his MP40, grabbed a half-full ammunition box from the rear of the APC and ran in the direction of the oncoming enemy, Wengler ahead of him, the rest of his men clattering behind. The box was heavy and getting heavier. Twenty seconds then thirty and Studer was tiring but he had made it and then he saw him, Jan Tobler.

The youth turned to him, his face flushed with relief. 'Eight vehicles, Rottenführer. Light armour and civilian vehicles, partisan cars. They're out of sight, won't be more than a few seconds.' Even as he was speaking, he unslung the MP34 ammunition belt from around his neck, the machine-gun three meters away on the top of a low wall that offered some protection and from which he could sweep the road to his front.

Studer nodded, he approved of Tobler's position. He turned to Johannes Fischer, a pasty youth of nineteen. 'You, you're ammunition man for Tobler. The rest of you take cover by the MG and watch your fields of fire.'

'Anti-armour?'

'Yes you, don't fire unless I order it, I want the vehicles stopped with small arms. I don't want any flame and smoke to give them cover. Everyone OK?'

All around nods, the strain showing on the young faces but nothing from the road. A heartbeat or an age, it was the same as the men waited but still nothing and then the sound of a siren.

Then another and Studer squinted through the rear sight of his MP40 as the first of the vehicles rounded the corner some four hundred meters away. Moving at around 100 kph, brightly coloured vehicles, of a design that the Rottenführer did not recognize and marked up as police cars he let out his breath slowly. He could not miss.

As Studer's breath hissed from his lips, the barrel of the MP40 began its slow descent. Steady as a rock, this was what the Rottenführer did well and now he could see them clearly.

The vehicles were marked in Polish. They were clearly a threat to his men, but still Studer hesitated. The Russians were less than 40 kilometres to the east, there had been talk of the Poles rising to liberate themselves for weeks and partisans now often wore uniforms. The Russians or the Americans must have shipped in these vehicles but now was not the time to consider the matter further. He made out the shape of a man in the leading vehicle and gently squeezed the MP40's trigger, watched as the shape jerked backwards sharply.

'Feuer,' shouted Jan Tobler, his words lost in the crackle of small arms fire about him. His MP34 buzzed, coughed viciously and Studer squeezed the trigger of his MP40 again.

The front of the leading vehicle erupted into a cloud of dust. It swerved sharply to its right, struck the low wall by the side of the road, swung to its left and mounted the embankment, bumping along for several meters before hitting a rocky outcrop and crunching to a halt. Behind it, showers of glass burst from the second car as it sheered to its left and screeched against the rocky embankment. Sparks trailing behind it, it slammed into the back of the lead car, catapulting two bodies through its shattered front window. They seemed to hang in the air forever before tumbling earthwards, bouncing over the bonnet of the lead car and falling to the ground motionless.

The remaining police cars were attempting to brake, swerve to avoid the holocaust, but the automatic gunfire was relentless. Hunched but still firing his weapon, Studer moved out into the open meadow to his left between the low brick wall and the Vistula with several of his men. They poured withering fire into the side and rear of the convoy, turned the insides of all six remaining police cars into a maelstrom of razor-sharp glass, shards of metal, flesh, blood and bullets. Seconds later, the shooting stopped.

The Rottenführer held up his hand, cautioned his men but he was elated. It could not possibly have gone better; the partisans had returned not a single shot! He gestured towards the low wall that ran between them and the devastated convoy of vehicles, led his men to cover, but it was deathly quiet.

Studer waited. Still nothing and then the smaller sounds; a spinning wheel, an already shattered window giving up some smaller pieces of glass, the clicking of a hot exhaust pipe and then a groan.

The Rottenführer waved his men over the wall. They spread between the cars, flowed like a field grey river and occasional single shots began to ring out. Within another minute, the entire area was secure and Studer allowed himself a smile. Thirty-one partisans were dead.

'You three, stay here,' said Studer. 'Collect their weapons but leave the vehicles where they are. We'll use them as a roadblock; the APC can move them easily enough later and no smoking! The rest of you come with me.'

The young German turned, walked back towards the APC, the radio unmanned by its side. He scratched his chin, waved to Horst Heller and pointed towards the two Polish boys.

****

Caroline Whittleton leaned back, stretched the muscles in her shoulders. She had already fed the data into her computer; several men and a motor vehicle in Poland, approximate weights and it appeared to make sense. The burst had been more powerful than any previously recorded, larger than before the appearance of the Vikings and much bigger than the very earliest readings and Caroline frowned. She looked at the man seated opposite her.

A dazed Professor Jobber had arrived, dishevelled and exhausted, shortly before 11am. He had said little and, in Caroline's opinion, his appearance had hardly improved in the thirty minutes since he had slumped into the laboratory chair. The American, seeming to sense that he was being observed, rubbed his eyes and looked at the brief résumé that Caroline and Brandon Bryce had prepared earlier.

He grunted, slowly looked up, his large brown eyes puffy and bloodshot. 'Is this all that you have?'

Caroline looked at the Professor over the top of her thin glasses and tried to stem her welling anger. Time had been far too short to do their work justice, but what they had produced was a fair summary of their progress to date. She looked directly at Jobber, tried to keep the anger from her face.

'Of course that's not all we have!' Caroline's spoke slowly, her voice level. 'It's a summary for Christ's sake.' Jobber snorted and Caroline held her breath, counted to ten looking at the top of the greasy-haired American's head as he read on. 'Where's your material?'

'We're having it all electronically mailed, of course,' said Jobber. He scratched his ear absently. 'That way we should be able to avoid the problem of incomplete information.'

'Oh, I'm sorry, I didn't realize that you had solved the problem,' said Caroline. 'If you haven't then your work, by definition, cannot be complete.'

Jobber raised his eyes from the printout before him, arched an eyebrow. He smiled stiffly. 'You have a point.'

Caroline felt the tension lessen in her shoulders. She and Brandon had heard the story already, had found it hard not to empathise with the hook-nosed American.

Jobber had told his political masters that the only way they would get him on an aircraft would be to drug him and they had taken him at his word, his military overseer engaging him in conversation whilst a medic had rolled up his sleeve.

Rather than ask the man to desist, Jobber had enquired as to what he was doing and had been given a full and honest description of what was happening whilst simultaneously being injected with a potent sedative.

The Professor's will had weakened. He had walked,

as best he was able, cheerfully onto the large military aircraft and now, suffering from what must have been one of the worst hangovers of his life, he looked like a shadow of the man that Caroline had seen on the screen to Washington the previous evening.

Caroline allowed herself a smile. Jobber was rubbing his upper arm, and she could imagine the slight swelling caused by the injection, the annoying itch. The American caught her eye, his smile gone. He looked back down at the work before him. 'So, make the necessary preparations for the receipt of the information, would you?'

Caroline stood up, any sympathy that she might have felt, gone. She cleared her throat and Jobber raised his eyes, peered over his half-rimmed spectacles.

'Listen to me, Professor Jobber, because I only want to say this once,' said Caroline. Jobber sat up a little straighter. 'We have been requested to work together, and my team and I will do our utmost to make that collaboration a success. However, I feel justified in demanding a similar commitment from you and from your team. Do I make myself clear?'

Brow furrowed, pouting, Jobber grunted. He looked as though he was about to lay an egg. He opened his mouth but, initially, no sound emerged. He tried again. 'Sorry...'

'Don't mention it.'

Ten

Charles Warner watched as the instructor gathered his papers, his briefing over. He breathed out slowly and looked around at the drawn faces, strained lips attempting smiles over tightly clamped teeth and he knew; he had to set an example. He nodded and stood up.

****

Rottenführer Studer felt sick. The excitement of the assault had passed and now he was deeply worried. His men were relying on him, they were in a hostile land, enemies gathered on all sides, and he looked at the sky.

The wind was picking up, the air wet, and pocket-sized, mid-grey clouds were skittering beneath the boiling black sky to their west as Studer looked at his watch, turned it towards the light of the east, the better to see its face.

It was almost 1pm and Funkel had still not raised anybody on the radio. There had been more signs of activity to their north and there had been an attempt by a strange looking civilian car to approach their location from the village to the south but Otto Schmidt, the man covering the approaches from that direction was a trained soldier, had done his job well. He had seen guns in the car; peasant's shotguns and he had opened fire.

The vehicle had crashed some three hundred meters from the APC and Schmidt had been putting occasional rounds into it ever since. The petrol-soaked metal had refused to catch fire, but Schmidt was sure that he had hit the driver. Still, there were others and several shots, ineffectual from shotguns at that range, had peppered the APC with pellets.

Studer's men were becoming more edgy, and he did not know what to tell them. The radio appeared to be receiving signals, but they were strange, foreign and something about the village was beginning to prey upon his mind. They had been in the square for only a matter of minutes, but certain pictures of it kept coming back to him. His division had been through Poland on its way to Leningrad in '41. They'd been back in the Godforsaken country for some months now and Studer knew it relatively well, was sure that he had been in the village before, but it had changed.

It was far too prosperous, the people not initially afraid and the shops and houses had looked different.

The stores were well stocked with food and there had even been a pet shop. A pet shop! In the middle of a war, it beggared belief but he had seen it and there had been some sort of huge wall outside the village, a monument perhaps, covered with gravestones and Stars of David?

And still there was something else. It eluded him, teased him but then he had it; many of the houses had had antennae on their roofs!

Why would peasants have antennae? What innocent use could they possibly have for them? This must be an enemy communications centre, a stronghold mocked up to resemble an ordinary village! That would explain the difficulty making contact with the outside world, the response of the peasants, their apparent lack of fear, everything.

But what should he do? Studer fingered the Iron Cross at his neck. What would Sepp Dietrich or Reichsführer Himmler expect of him and his men? What would his Führer expect?

The Rottenführer leaned against the APC, ran quickly through the options. Remain where they were and continue to try to reach their Unit on the radio? Yes, but they had not been successful so far and, although the cover was good, their present position might be difficult to defend during the hours of darkness. They had flares, but not enough to light the whole area for an entire night. Alternatively, should they break to the north? The enemy might not expect that, but the ruined partisan vehicles on the road would slow them, betray their escape and Wengler had reported evidence of enemy activity on the road beyond them. Then again, should they try to break across open country? The half-track was good over rough ground, but the river to their west and the high ground to the east might limit their progress.

The village? Studer considered it, turned it in his mind. They would have the element of surprise. It could work. With sufficient daring, it would work!

The decision made, Studer felt a wave of relief course through his body and his tension began to melt away. They would move back into the village, hit the nest of saboteurs hard and fast! His men would be more than a match for lightly armed partisans or communist commissars, they would reel under his blows, collapse in defeat and he had demolition charges in the APC. If they were quick and forceful, they might be able to liquidate the whole village, level it, remove it from the map.

The young German stroked the Iron Cross at his throat.

It was only a Second Class, admittedly with bar but a First Class would do nicely. They would announce it in Erkner, his home village, some few miles east of Berlin and his brothers would be so proud.

Studer nodded, rose to his full height, was about to tell his men to gather around him, to share in the news when he heard it, a chattering in the sky.

The Rottenführer turned his head, strained his eyes to locate the source of the sound and there it was, an aircraft! Approaching from the north, large, relatively slow moving, he had never seen anything like it before and it was approaching front on, he could not see its markings.

The aircraft appeared to hover, its huge blades thrashing the air and the Rottenführer grabbed at his MP40. Focke-Wulf had produced such hovering machines, one had flown the English Channel and Flettner had improved the design, but Studer had never seen one, had had no idea that they were this large. It was huge. Open-mouthed, he watched as the machine descended, landed on the road beyond the destroyed partisan vehicles.

****

Initially, the Polish authorities in Pulawy had been too shocked to react but now the machine had begun to move. Vehicles following in support had observed the devastation of the convoy of police cars on the Kazimierz Dolny Road, but the cause of the destruction had not been immediately obvious. Reports from Kazimierz claimed that a Nazi Schützenpanzerwagen had arrived in the village and that the occupants, about twenty men, had shot dead two policemen and four civilians. Police units had been dispatched towards Kazimierz from both the north and the south and those approaching from the south had made the village. They had confirmed the murders there but the emergency services approaching from the north had been violently assaulted, more than thirty men killed.

The authorities had been sceptical. It simply could not be true but further observation had suggested that the destruction was real, the perpetrators now occupying a small copse of trees and a series of abandoned buildings just to the north of the village. Still, such devastation was hard to believe and neither the alleged perpetrators, nor the APC were visible to either the observers behind the convoy or to the police units approaching cautiously on foot from the village.

Neo-Nazi extremists were not unknown in Poland, but there had never been any violence on this scale. It was unbelievable, horrific. The German authorities had been notified shortly before 10am and, as the scale of the incident had become apparent, Foreign Secretary Joachim Studer had offered military assistance.

Studer was popular in Poland; he was seen as a friend, had been a supporter of the country's application to join the European Union, a sponsor after their membership had been approved and there was no desire in Warsaw to humiliate him. All parties desired a speedy end to the current problem, but the German Foreign Secretary had exceeded his authority and had boarded a Tiger HAC army helicopter, forcing an unscheduled visit upon his Polish hosts, approaching Kazimierz Dolny from the north at a little after 1pm.

From Foreign Secretary Studer's vantage point, five hundred feet above the Pulawy, Kazimierz Road, the SS APC was not visible but, as the copse of trees was pointed out to him, he noticed the small column of police vehicles, strewn, unnaturally, across the road to its north.

Joachim Studer breathed deep, pursed his lips. His stomach began to flutter. Fear, he knew it for what it was, accepted that he was not a physically brave man, but many things frightened him more than the possibility of injury and he had had time on the flight from Berlin to turn the current situation over in his mind several times.

How could it be happening? There was no confirmation yet that these people were German nationals, and he prayed that they were not but, deep within him, he feared that they were.

Yet how could any German risk bringing such a disgrace down upon his country, revive such dreadful memories of the past? Surely the struggle had been fought and won, bought dear with the blood of so many millions of his fellow Europeans, Jew and Gentile, German and Slav, yet it appeared it had not.

He had to hope for the best, but prepare himself for

the worst and, if the men were German, the struggle would be to show that his ordinary, decent countrymen had nothing whatsoever in common with these violent racists and murderers.

Studer, his stomach stilled, nodded. He knew that he must talk to these people, be seen to talk to them, prove to the world that the perpetrators had nothing in common with the German people as a people. He had to show the world that Germany deserved her place among civilized nations and that she would do whatever was necessary to retain it.

A television journalist friend, Oskar Richter, and his cameraman had joined Studer on his visit to Poland.

Politically ambitious, driven as he was to show German decency to the world, the Foreign Minister needed the help of the media. Certainly, it would be good television, would elevate him in the eyes of all decent Germans but, he had convinced himself, that was, for the moment, of secondary importance.

With the slightest of jolts, the helicopter put down. His fear, for the moment, forgotten, Studer jumped from it and took in his surroundings, keen to give Richter and his cameraman a few seconds to begin filming. Sure, that they were ready, he strode purposefully towards the uniformed man with what appeared to be the largest number of ribbons stitched above his breast and offered him his hand.

As he shook Major Viktor Malinowski's hand, genuine tears of emotion in his eyes, Studer knew that he had guessed correctly. 'Do we know for sure that these men are German?' he asked, his Polish good.

If Malinowski was surprised to be addressed in his own language, his face did not betray the fact. Still, he hesitated before he spoke. 'Reports from the village suggest that the murderers were speaking to each other and the villagers in German,' he said slowly. 'The vehicle was marked with German crosses and a Swastika, the uniforms appeared to be German and bore SS insignia. What conclusion would you suggest that we draw?'

Studer flinched at the mention of the Schutzstafel, the SS. This was terrible. It was well known within Germany and overseas that the Foreign Secretary's father had had three brothers, all of whom had fought and died within the ranks of the SS, two in Russia, around Kursk, the third in Poland. Only Joachim's father had escaped military service because of his age, but even he had joined the Hitler Youth. He had been wounded in the final battle for Berlin.

'Could I talk to them?'

'You are welcome to try,' said Malinowski. His mouth twisted into a thin smile. 'However, I think it only fair to tell you that I think they will shoot you.'

'I must try.' Sure, that Richter and the cameraman had got his words on film, Studer struggled to suppress his fear and waved to them to follow him. Though his stomach was telling him differently, the thought of some Fascist monsters shooting a German politician was too ridiculous to contemplate. 'Do you have anything that we could use as a white flag?'

Malinowski's smile twisted into a sneer. He turned to one of his Lieutenants, spoke rapidly and gestured with his chin towards a group of soldiers standing a little distance away. He turned back to Foreign Minister Studer, raised an eyebrow and, moments later, a baton complete with white T-shirt tied securely to it was brought to him. He handed it to Studer.

'Thank you.'

'Herr Studer,' said Malinowski, his smile now gone. His German was good, better than Studer's Polish. 'I do not believe this to be a good idea.'

Studer swallowed hard but the blinking red eye of the camera pushed him on. He spoke in German. 'On the contrary, Herr Major. I have no choice.'

Turning, Studer began to walk towards the eight destroyed police cars. He held the baton above his head, the T-shirt tied to it fluttering in the stiffening breeze. Oskar Richter and his cameraman followed a few meters behind.

Seconds dragged like minutes. The cars seemed to be getting no closer, but the German Foreign Minister could hear his feet on the road, knew that he was moving. He closed his eyes, opened them again and he was closer, could smell something, like petrol and burnt meat.

His brow lined in concentration, Studer forced himself to continue, and he was there. He passed the first of the destroyed police cars, tried to avert his eyes but he could not. He looked directly into the vehicle, struggled to register its contents, sprawled bodies, legs and arms intertwined, blood and other matter splattered over the seats and the unbroken rear window.

Foreign Minister Studer frowned, followed a twisted arm to the shoulder, then the shattered head and he felt the bile begin to rise in his throat. He tore his eyes away, but the horror followed him, forced itself upon him. A dark pool of liquid had gathered beneath the car, and it stank; burnt meat, bullet scorched human flesh. He retched but swallowed it down, the camera was on him, and he walked on, did not look at the other vehicles. He was past them, could hear Richter and the cameraman behind him and was about to stop when a voice sounded from somewhere ahead.

'Halt pig!'

The Foreign Minister looked about him but saw no one. A low wall, a copse of trees, the owner of the voice was hidden. When the man spoke again, the voice burnt with anger. 'Who are you and what do you want?'

Foreign Minister Studer's shoulders sagged. Harsh but educated, the Berlin accent was unmistakable. 'Well, pig?'

The Foreign Minister felt a flutter of panic. Words, the everyday tools of his trade, had abandoned him and he looked around, could smell his own fear. Richter and his cameraman were some ten meters behind him, crouching behind one of the destroyed cars and the journalist gave a nervous thumbs up, nodded towards the camera, its redlight blinking. Studer summoned his courage, struggled to keep the fear from his voice. 'An unspeakable tragedy has occurred here today.' The Foreign Minister felt his stomach flutter again and this time he could not stop it, and he took a step backwards, recalled the words of the Polish Major. This man could shoot him. 'A tragedy both for Poland and for Germany and I beseech you to give yourselves up before any further damage is done.'

****

By the copse of trees, Rottenführer Studer turned to Jan Tobler, his mouth open in surprise. Tobler smiled. 'Sounds like a suicide, Herr Rottenführer.'

'You are killing for a Germany which lost its direction and decency,' said the middle-aged man on the road before them. He had begun to shake, was staring blindly into the copse of trees, his eyes screwed almost shut. He began to stutter. 'Y-y-you are bringing shame upon your country. I b-b-beg of you to hand over your weapons.'

'Give him yours, Rottenführer,' said Tobler. He grinned widely.

The Rottenführer did not hesitate. He brought the MP40 up to his shoulder, squinted down the sight, looked the man in the road directly in the eye and pulled the trigger.

The German Foreign Minister's feet left the floor, his body thrown backwards by the force of the bullet that ripped through him, his corpse smashing against the side of the partisan automobile behind him. His body slid silently to the ground.

'Traitor!' spat Rottenführer Studer. 'Tobler, take two men and deal with the two dogs that were with him. Take care, one of them has a shoulder held weapon. Bring it here.'

Tobler slid off to Studer's left. Presently the sound of voices, a scream and then the crackle of automatic gunfire.

****

In Berlin, Chancellor Willi Kauffmann turned away from the television. Studer's speech, his subsequent murder, had been broadcast to millions. They had seen his body slam against the car behind which the sheltering journalists, his head crack lifeless against the floor.

Then the terror of the reporters, cowering behind the vehicle as death approached them. The screams, the sound of gunfire and the camera crashing to the floor...

Kauffmann had liked Studer. He was, he had been a

genuine person, truly sensitive, a man who had suffered in his early life because of his family's wartime links to the Nazis and that he had been a fool and had exceeded his authority was of no consequence. It was hard to believe that he was dead. Kauffmann turned to Hans Gruber, the Bundeswehr chief. 'Finish this for me Hans. Finish it now...'

****

In Poland ninety minutes later, Rottenführer Andreas Studer, his eyes set, surveyed his position. It was 3.30pm, prematurely dark and it was raining hard, the gusty wind blowing from the northwest. They had about two hours of daylight left, and the men were excited, frightened but pleased to be active.

They would take the initiative, attack the village, they would not leave a mouse alive and Klaus Funkel, his useless radio packed away, was organizing his weapons, slipping extra ammunition clips into his pouch and hanging stick grenades from his belt. He slipped his Russian knuckle-duster onto his left hand, pushed his sharpened trenching tool through his belt, checked that his Turkish knife was easily accessible in his boot and looked up.

Rottenführer Studer was by his side. 'I hope you fight better than you operate that radio, Klaus!'

Funkel, squatting on the ground, smiled. 'You know I do!'

'Sturmann Heller!' said Studer turning away. 'Yes, Rottenführer?'

'Burn those photographs.' Studer ignored the Sturmann's pleading. 'You know the ones I mean.'

Studer didn't have the time to argue. Heller's private collection could get them all killed; pictures of the murder of British troops at Le Paradis, outside Dunkirk in '40, of countless SS special exercises in Poland and Russia since '41, they were disgusting, could earn them all a bullet in the head. He looked Heller in the eye. 'And ditch the fucking ear, you sick bastard. I don't want any shit like that on us when we go in. Gold teeth, jewellery, Russian lighters, they all stay here!' He turned to face the rest of his men, pointed to the sodden ground, spoke quietly. 'Dig a fucking hole or something. You can get it back later.'

Studer stared his men down then cocked his head to one side and held up his hand, he could hear something. The men hushed and there it was, a windy whooping sound above the blustery lashing of the rain.

The Rottenführer strained, listened again, put his field glasses to his eyes and then he had it. It was an aircraft like the one that brought the German traitor, but bigger, dark grey against a mid-grey sky.

Then there was a second; a third and then a fourth but they were no longer approaching, they were hovering to the north, beyond the ruined convoy of police vehicles. Then three smaller aircraft became visible, approaching fast.

Crouched, Studer turned to his men. 'Spread out and take cover. Watch those birds, but don't fire unless I say so.'

The first helicopter rose effortlessly, threatened to slip from view, melt into the gathering gloom, but then it peeled to the side of the other aircraft, began to move towards them again.

Studer, his eyes wide, his head tilted to one side, was

amazed; it was fantastic! It was like nothing he had ever seen, sleek, heavily laden with what must be weapons, now being followed by the other aircraft and then he saw the thing he wanted to see more than anything else in the world, the familiar black cross on a white background clearly visible on the side of the aircraft.

'I don't believe it!' Studer jumped to his feet, broke cover. 'It's one of ours!'

The men around him rose to their feet and Studer smiled broadly as the lead 'craft begin to swoop towards them, moving fast.

'We will win this war,' said Oliver Wengler, his eyes shining.

His lower lip trembling, Wengler rose to his feet, but there he died, his young body torn apart as orange flashes to the left and right of the leading aircraft lit the sky. Canon shells raked the ground in front of the copse and then the ground erupted, mud, bodies and flames shooting into the air.

****

Within minutes it was finished. After Foreign Minister Studer's death, the German Government had pleaded with the Poles to be help in the containment of the incident. It was unheard of, went against all diplomatic protocol, but Chancellor Kauffmann had been persuasive, had argued that the participation of a Germany totally opposed to the resurgence of Nazism would go some way to showing the world that this was not an incident that would adversely affect German-Polish relations.

The prospect of German military activity on Polish soil filled some with dread but the three Tiger HAC anti-tank helicopters that had attacked the copse of trees from the air, used their surface to ground HOT anti-tank missiles and their huge 30mm canons to great effect had doubtless spared Polish lives. No armour hidden in the wood could have survived the attack and several secondary explosions had confirmed the destruction of the APC.

The four CH53G troop helicopters had followed sixty seconds behind the Tigers. They had put down their storm troopers a hundred meters from the copse, ninety-six of them in total, all heavily armed.They had advanced to clear the copse, the small wood silent save for the crackling of burning wood but, as the driving rain had lashed down on the attackers, steamed their masks, men had begun to fall.

Two of the helicopters had been damaged by automatic gunfire and a volley of well-timed grenades exploding at waist height had greeted the soldiers' arrival at the trees.

The APC had been a blazing wreck; bodies littered the ground, but sustained and accurate fire had come in from the burning farmhouse and several of its outbuildings. Storming them had proved to be an expensive business.

They had finally been taken room by room, the attack not allowed to falter, but the enemy had retained control of the cellars until the last.

They had even threatened to counter-attack, showed no signs of wishing to surrender and there had been no time to bring up the tear gas. The final action had been fought in the smoke and the half-light, hand-to-hand with knives and entrenching tools.

The last man to die had been a slim youth of about twenty. He had worn an Iron Cross, second class with bar, and died with the name of Adolf Hitler on his lips. The German Army had lost more men on foreign soil in fifteen minutes than it had done in the previous fifty years.

Eleven

The eyes of his comrades were on him as Colonel Warner moved towards the door. He opened it and walked into the corridor glad to be away from their gaze and exhaled steadily. The still air was like a stifling curtain after the rudimentary air conditioning of the briefing room. He began to sweat immediately.

****

George Sutton mopped his brow. In Washington, it was a little before 10am and the President, sitting, grim-faced, at his desk in the Oval Office with Larry Edelman and Secretary of State Linda King, had watched Oskar Richter's last report, had been informed of the German military response. The President turned to his National Security Adviser.

'Who is doing this, Larry?' No response, the President spread his hands. 'Speak to me people?' Blank faces. A cough.

'Is it orchestrated? If so, then by whom and to what end?'

Edelman broke the silence but had little to say. 'Jobber's in the UK, we're doing what we can. It won't be easy...'

Edelman's voice trailed off and the President shook his head, rubbed his eyes hard. 'Do what you can. Wake me if there are any developments.'

The meeting over, George Sutton rose to his feet and, leaving his advisers to see themselves out, he walked the short distance from the Oval Office past his private study to the Oval Office dining room. He worked a kink out of his neck and ran his hand through his black hair, his eyes tightly closed. He wanted to take a shower, but he was tired and, as he looked around the dining room the floor cluttered by piles of documents and memorabilia from recent visits, his eyes settled on the camp bed.

He sat down.

****

In Cambridge, Caroline Whittleton pushed back her chair, rose to her feet. She stretched her shoulders to ease the tension that had been building steadily and glanced at Professor Jobber. Looking fractionally less haggard, the American did not look up. Despite the dreadful events of yesterday, Caroline had found Professor Jobber's wholehearted involvement strangely cheering. Brandon had been of little use, he rarely was but she felt less alone, less isolated, had immersed herself in her work.

Myron Klutz would not be coming to the UK. Caroline was disappointed, had spoken to Jobber's partner that morning but the computers in his labs would be linked into the Cambridge system and several other members of the Massachusetts team had already arrived from the States, more would follow, and Caroline had been impressed.

The laboratories had become crowded. The new arrivals had struggled to carve out niches, several adjoining buildings had been taken over, but Caroline had let it ride. She had never been territorial, her work was too important, but she had noticed the presence of an increasingly large number of security service personnel.

They had tried to keep out of the scientists' way and Caroline had ignored them, had become totally absorbed in her work. Still, she had become hungry, had broken for something to eat and now, her mind still on her work, she grabbed at the swinging canteen door just in time to prevent it from catching her on the shoulder.

A major energy source was almost certainly necessary to allow objects and people to move through time, but in theory it could be done; of that, Caroline was in little doubt. What was doubtful, however, was that sufficient energy could ever be artificially generated, let alone harnessed. There was not enough energy on or in the entire planet to come close to achieving the power that they would require, but that was a matter of scale and not of principle.

In addition, locating the objects that had been moved would require a level of sophistication that was almost incomprehensible. The manufacture, operation and direction of such tracking equipment added another, totally new dimension.

Her appetite forgotten, foreign, belonging to another world, Caroline shook her head, looked down at the tray before her and pushed the green salad, a little brown bread by its side, around her plate with her fork.

Professor Jobber was cutting enthusiastically into his pizza and Caroline frowned. After such a period of silence, her voice sounded alien, removed. 'Surely the military should be able to locate the source of so much energy?'

His brow furrowed Jobber scowled at his pizza. He folded a generous slice with his knife, speared it with his fork and shoehorned it into his mouth. His jaws working furiously, his mouth thankfully closed, he regarded Caroline strangely.

Like an exhibit she thought, but then his face softened, and he looked around the room, swallowed his food with an effort. Scattered about them, groups of scientists were talking in low, urgent tones. 'One would have thought so. Although the equipment necessary to generate the energy and track the target could be in two different locations.'

'Agreed,' said Caroline. She paused; she felt a sudden flush of guilt. The reality of it all, the victims of Thursday's events were slipping from her mind. Still, she had to go on. 'But if we leave that to one side, concentrate on the energy. That's where the signs should have been most obvious. How could so much energy be generated without leaving some traces of nuclear activity?'

Jobber pouted, shook his head. 'An intense electrical pulse? Drawing from stored energy, magnetism used to focus it more aggressively?' Jobber paused but Caroline said nothing, used the silence to draw him on. 'But even then there would be traces and we'd be dealing with such phenomenal amounts. How could any device, reliant on so much energy be targeted so accurately, be used to open a window in such a precise place at such a precise time? In the history of the world, a century is the size of a postage stamp on a football pitch...'

'Yes, I know,' answered Caroline. 'I've heard your lectures.'

Jobber's eyes flickered from his food to Caroline.

She smiled. Mollified, he focused his attention back on his plate. 'The idea of pinpointing a moment, perhaps less than a second, in the ocean of time, it is almost too fantastic to contemplate. We could be years, perhaps decades these people...'

'You're right but we're not being asked to re-invent the wheel,' said Caroline. She found the hint of despair in Jobber's tone depressing. 'We're being asked to observe and comment on what's happening, simply understand it, suggest how it can be stopped...'

'Simply?'

Caroline looked at Jobber, at his intense brown eyes, behind the colour a light. 'Of course there's nothing simple about it. It's new, another level altogether. We might not be able to replicate these events but we're not being asked to. Surely, we could hope to understand it, possibly stop it?'

'Oh, we can understand it,' said Jobber a slight smile playing at the corner of his mouth. 'Given enough time...'

Caroline continued to pick at her food but ate very little. As she and Professor Jobber prepared to return to the laboratory, one of the suited men approached them. Confident, a smile in his eyes though not on his mouth, Caroline had seen him before, the front seat passenger in the car from London to Bishop's Stortford and she looked at him more closely. Thirties, quite tall, wire trailing from his ear to disappear beneath his collar, loose fitting suit, he could be carrying a gun.

'Malcolm McCurran,' said the man. He nodded. 'I'll be with you for a while, I'll try to stay out of your way. For the moment, I've been asked to pass on a request that you make yourselves available for a meeting at 5pm. We'll bring in the necessary communications equipment, but the Prime Minister and his team would like to ask you a few questions.'

Assured, handsome in a bent-nosed, sporting sort of way, the man's accent was hard to place. Caroline nodded and McCurran left them. She looked at Jobber. Possibly jet lagged, he was much quieter in person than she had imagined. His popular science videos had left her with a very different impression. He was frowning and failed to catch her eye.

****

President Sutton was seated once more at his desk in the Oval Office. Unable to sleep, he had tried to freshen up in the bathroom opposite his private study, but he was exhausted. He rubbed his chin and looked up.

It was 11.55am, members of the NSC were arriving and the videoconference was due to begin in five minutes. Gerry Buchanan would report on the situation in Poland, after which Professor Jobber and Dr Whittleton would be invited to speak from England. They had had some time, should at least have begun to quantify the problem, be able to describe it and the politicians needed some answers. Finally, the Prime Minister and the President would speak alone for a few minutes before their advisors re-joined them.

President Sutton acknowledged Edelman, his National Security Adviser, nervously smoothing the few hairs across the top of his head and looked again at the satellite photographs in front of him. Vikings in England? That was bad, very bad but Nazis? Surely there could be nothing worse? The disgusting memories of the recent past were somehow more dreadful, more immediate, somehow simply worse than what had happened so long ago in the murk and dust of Dark Ages England. Sutton turned a photograph with his finger. The images depicting the Bundeswehr operation were slightly less clear than the earlier ones of the village itself, the weather had deteriorated, but this one showed the devastation outside Kazimierz Dolny clearly enough.

Sutton pushed it to one side and closed his eyes, the voices of his colleagues washing around him as they entered the room. He ignored them, concentrated on his breathing. Presently he heard the video screen flickering into life and opened his eyes.

Focusing on the screen, Prime Minister Donald Berwick was seated at the table in the now familiar Cabinet Room, surrounded by his closest advisers and senior ministers. A second screen, linking both the White House and Downing Street to the laboratories in Cambridge stood next to the first.

'Good afternoon, Donald, and good afternoon, everyone,' said Sutton. His voice was firm, he pushed the tiredness away but, like a persistent dog, it pushed back. 'I'm sorry that we could not be meeting under more pleasant circumstances.'

Berwick nodded. 'As bad as it looks?'

President Sutton nodded, glanced down at the photographs on the desk in front of him then turned to Gerry Buchanan. 'Gerry?'

Buchanan rose to his feet. The scrambled images from the photographs had been electronically transferred to London by secure line, printed out and lay on the desks of everyone in the Cabinet Room. Buchanan walked over to a flip chart in the corner of the room to which he had earlier pinned several enlargements, looked directly at the video screen to London and began to speak.

The Director General of the Central Intelligence Agency ran through the initial attack in Kazimierz Dolny, the response of the local police, the massacre on the road to the north of the village, the murders of the German Foreign Minister and the journalists and the final liquidation of the perpetrators in the ruins of the farmhouse.

The audiences on both sides of the Atlantic listened in silence. None of the politicians or advisers had been old enough to remember the last war personally, but several had lost relatives; most of Larry Edelman's family had been expelled from the Polish villages east of Warsaw, liquidated in the camps.

'Well, ladies and gentlemen,' said President Sutton, breaking the silence as Gerry Buchanan retook his seat. 'The situation is getting no easier. Questions?'

'Do the Germans and Poles know what we suspect?' asked Julian Ryde in London from the Prime Minister's left. Fresh, well groomed, he was wearing a dark blue blazer and a blue and white tie.

'Not at the moment,' said Sutton. 'We had intended to decide about whether or what to tell them after this meeting. In the first place, we're not sure of what we know and secondly, I don't believe that anything we could have said would have changed their response.'

'I tend to agree,' said Susan Burnell, the UK Foreign Secretary. 'But surely we must tell them now, we owe it to them and if they were to find out any other way, the consequences are unthinkable.'

'I'm sure we'd all like to tell them, Susan,' said Julian Ryde. 'But tell them what? This is the real world. They probably wouldn't believe us. The chances of a leak would be massively increased and what would it really achieve?'

Burnell reddened; she turned to continue, but Donald Berwick held up his hand. 'I can't see that it would change their behaviour,' said the UK Prime Minister. He turned back to the video screen. 'I think we say nothing.'

President Sutton nodded slowly. Behind him, Larry Edelman appeared visibly relieved. 'Dr Whittleton, maybe you could give us your thoughts?'

In the laboratory Caroline rose to speak, checked herself and looked at Professor Jobber. The American spread his hands, the corners of his mouth turned down.

Caroline took off her glasses and put them on the workbench in front of her. 'Our position is essentially unchanged. We believe that travel through any of the four dimensions of which we are aware is possible in principle and is not contrary to any of the laws of physics. If these incidents did involve travel through the fourth of those dimensions, then it would most likely have occurred following the creation of, and passage through, a wormhole at the centre of a black hole...'

'Do you really think that that's credible?' Julian Ryde held up his hands. 'I'm sorry, it's just...'

'It's OK,' said Caroline Whittleton. Beside her, Professor Jobber had begun to twitch. She caught the Prime Minister's eye and smiled. 'I completely understand how Mr Ryde feels. This would require the expenditure of a great deal of energy, an almost unbelievable amount, but what other explanation is there? The CERN Large Hadron Collider in Switzerland can generate mini-black holes, they might even be able to send quantum sized particles through these artificial singularities...'

'But a person?' said Ryde gently. 'Thirty people, a longboat, an armoured car?'

'Detail,' said Professor Jobber, rising to his feet in Cambridge. 'Scale, simply a technicality.'

Caroline nodded and turned back to the screens to London and Washington. 'Professor Jobber is correct, but it is much more than a minor detail. The team in Switzerland suggest that the energy required to create a man-sized wormhole would be equivalent to converting an object with the mass of Jupiter into energy in an instant.'

'Still possible in principle?'

'Not impossible.' Caroline looked at President Sutton. 'The amounts of energy used would be fantastic, literally mind-blowing and the bursts would need to be very accurately focused, but we believe that, given enough time, then yes, this could be done.'

Behind Caroline on the Cambridge screen, Professor Jobber smiled. Julian Ryde broke the silence. 'How?'

Caroline raised her eyes, shook her head. 'We don't know...'

'Your opinion?'

For a moment, Caroline said nothing. She raised her eyebrows. 'As a physicist, I prefer to avoid speculation, but we keep coming back to singularities, a black hole with a donut shaped wormhole at its centre, somehow held open long enough and wide enough to allow these objects to enter, pass through. Clearly, we would have noticed, could not have survived as a planet, the expenditure of an amount of energy, similar to what I suggested earlier, so I would assume the use of exotic materials...'

'Exotic material?' Glancing around him for support, Larry Edelman looked pained, somehow personally injured by the concept.

Caroline nodded, did not smile. 'Yes, that really is the terminology used. Schwarzschild wormholes, any wormholes that we could aspire to create artificially, are very tiny and short-lived. They would need to be stretched, held open by something, ghost radiation, a negative energy field created by some sort of exotic material...'

'I just can't go with that,' said Edelman.

'Carry on please, Dr Whittleton,' said George Sutton. He looked around the Oval Office. 'Let's hear it all.'

'We're observing what actually happens out there,' said Caroline, 'simply suggesting how it might have come about. All of this is unidentified, but it would be necessary to stop the wormhole from snapping shut and destroying anything within it. Just because we can't measure something doesn't mean that it's not there, but we're not close to being able to do this ourselves, even under laboratory conditions, let alone in the field.'

'So, for exotic you can read unknown,' said Professor Jobber, rising to his feet. 'This is on top of the new 'super-unleaded' fuel that we would need to create a wormhole in the first place...'

'Fantasy fuel!' said Edelman.

'Shut up, Larry,' said President Sutton. Edelman lowered his head. 'Please go on, Professor Jobber.'

Jobber looked levelly at the screen before him, still composed. He pushed a lock of hair back behind his ear and continued. 'The material may be unknown to us, the fuel might, as you say, be a fantasy but, if someone really is doing these things, then they are neither unknown nor a fantasy to them.

'Indeed, if we begin our analysis of the situation from the standpoint that time travel is occurring, apply the theory of best fit, then everything else falls into place. We would expect to see the expenditure of a great amount of energy both at the point of disappearance and appearance and that is what we have. We would also expect to find that something or someone had arrived that had not been there before, which is exactly what we have seen...'

'But how? How could they do it?' It was Julian Ryde, his tone non-confrontational, his question almost rhetorical.

'We're not in a position to offer definitive answers,' said Jobber calmly. 'They could be converting matter into energy. This could then be pushed more easily through a wormhole and be reconstituted on the other side.'

'I take your point, Professor, that if we approach the situation from the bottom up, then time travel looks more likely...'

'Yes, it solves the problem. Indeed, I can see no other explanation.'

'But going back to these exotic materials and new fuel source,' continued the Home Secretary. 'I fail to see how materials can still be unknown, can be revealed miraculously to one person, if indeed, this is being brought about by an individual or...'

Jobber held up his hand. 'You're a practical man, Mr Ryde. The little I've seen of you suggests that, but it's very arrogant of any of us to assume that we know everything, have discovered everything.

'To the scientists and theologians of the early fifteenth century, America did not exist, some still swore that the earth was flat, dolphins were fish and bats were birds. True, the fog of their ignorance did begin to thin; our ignorance may be less profound than theirs, but we don't know everything.

'What I mean to say is that the level of ignorance may have changed but not the existence of ignorance itself. The material that we're describing may not even be from this planet, the Universe is a very big place, and we can't hope to know everything. Even here on earth, the mineral rich areas of the world could still yield surprises.' Jobber paused, he looked at the screens to London and Washington and caught Julian Ryde's eye, then turned to Caroline Whittleton. 'Particle chauvinism?'

'That's right,' said Caroline. She looked at Julian Ryde and then at Prime Minister Berwick. 'It's human to assume that the boundaries of our knowledge are the boundaries of all knowledge, but we can't afford to think like that.'

In London, Julian Ryde smiled. 'It's life Jim, but not as we know it?'

'Precisely,' said Caroline.

'Could you say a few words on the size of objects that have been moved,' said President Sutton. 'Whether they were animate or inanimate, the time period over which they might be transported, any signs one might expect in the areas after the transfers have taken place?'

Jobber smiled and nodded. 'We believe that the size and movement of the target objects is a factor. Indeed, it is probably no co-incidence that they have been getting bigger and more animate over the last few weeks, culminating in the events of Thursday evening and today but as I said earlier, the time period over which the objects are transported should not be a factor.

'All moments in time are equidistant from each other, time itself has no friction but the older the objects are, the more difficult they become to locate because of the absence of written records. The block of ice found in Yorkshire could be targeted easily because, until about ten thousand years ago, the whole of the north of England was glaciated; the stones would have been easier still, but we don't believe that their location could be changed. Put simply, if a longboat was on the shores of the River Humber a thousand years ago, then it will be on the shores of the River Humber today.'

'And as regards traces in the area of the incident itself,' said Caroline, picking up from Professor Jobber, 'one might expect to see damage or interference to electrical equipment, but if the pulse of energy was targeted accurately enough, there may not be any actual burning.'

'Yes, yes, that's correct,' said Jobber. He nodded vigorously. 'And as techniques improved, there would be less and less evidence that the event had happened. In theory, time could be bent to order, the bits that popped out could be more and more accurately targeted and we would be unaware that anything untoward was happening.'

'How far are you from being able to do this yourselves?'

asked President Sutton from the Oval Office. Jobber and Whittleton looked at one another, the question not unexpected.

'Quite some time, I'm afraid,' said Caroline. 'In the absence of a major breakthrough, then quite a long way.'

'You can have any resources that you need,' said Donald Berwick from London.

'We appreciate that, of course,' said Caroline. She picked her glasses up from the bench in front of her and turned them in her hand. 'You know the people that we'd like to have here, we've got some of them already and they could help, but we can't manufacture a miracle, not yet at least, and, without that miracle I would have to say that we're years, perhaps decades away from a solution.'

Caroline had spoken quietly, Julian Ryde the first to respond. 'But this is being done? I mean, you're sure that this is being orchestrated? Can we detect the hand of man and, if so, what on earth has propelled them into such a lead?'

In Cambridge, the physicists exchanged a look and Professor Jobber paused, peered over his half-rimmed spectacles. 'Two questions. We have no answers to the second but, regarding the first then yes, we believe that there is a human fingerprint. Time is simply too vast for these events to be accidental. A random event would move nothing, the rock or the ice maybe, but not the people. Global humanity could stand shoulder to shoulder on Long Island, as a species we're a pinprick, nothing, nada and, as regards the German attacks in Poland, the odds of picking out a moving vehicle must be literally billions to one against.

'However, when we introduce the theory that the events were orchestrated, the facts fit the profile much more closely. There would be plenty of documentations, reports referring to times, locations, movements of vehicles, everything that would be needed to allow a person or persons to seek out a target and there must have been data regarding Viking attacks in northern England by reference to Saint's days, folklore etc.

'In short, the chances of bringing lumps of nothing from the past are so great that there must be human involvement. Maybe dozens, thousands, millions of lumps of nothing have already been brought from the past but the fact is that the incidents are much more dramatic now and they're occurring quickly, the one after the other. It suggests experimentation, the perfection of techniques, a plan.'

Jobber paused and looked at the screens showing his audience on both sides of the Atlantic. He was being taken very seriously. He lowered his eyes, continued. 'Of course, one thing that we do not yet know is how these objects are being collected from the past, whether they're being specifically targeted and snatched up, like a grizzly bear fishing for salmon in a river or whether a wormhole into which these objects have travelled is being created and held open.'

'Like a net?'

'Precisely, Mr Ryde.'

A silence descended. President Sutton glanced at UK Prime Minister Berwick before he broke it. 'Thank you, Professor, Doctor Whittleton, I think that will be all for the moment.'

In London Donald Berwick nodded his agreement. He turned towards the Cambridge screen. 'I believe that accommodation is being prepared for you on site?'

Professor Jobber nodded absently. Caroline seemed

less sure but said nothing. 'I'm convinced that it would be much more convenient for all concerned,' said the Prime Minister. 'The children will be looked after, Dr Whittleton. I'm sure that it would benefit your work and it's only a matter of time before the Press starts to become a nuisance. Freelancers are often the worst, it would be much better if you stayed on site, easier to keep them away.' Caroline nodded; she knew that it was an instruction, and the Prime Minister continued. 'You'll get the details at the end of this meeting. Our people will bring your things up to Cambridge.'

Caroline nodded again. Adrift, her life no longer her own, she tried to smile as the screen to Cambridge faded. In London and Washington, the Cabinet Room and the Oval Office emptied, and, for a moment, there was silence; George Sutton broke it. 'Do you buy it, Donald?'

Donald Berwick shook his head, his lips arched downwards. 'We could be the victims of some orchestrated hoax but that's looking increasingly less likely. Events in two countries involving the citizens of at least two more?' Berwick shook his head purposefully then looked up. 'Theory of best fit? If that means I buy it then yes, I suppose I do.'

President Sutton shrugged casually; he had developed a tick in the corner of his right eye. 'So, what do they want?'

'If we could work out who, then we might be partway to answering that, but we've had no contact, no demands, no threats, nothing. No boasting either, but I don't see how they can be out of the mainstream; Jobber and Whittleton would have heard something so what does that make them? Terrorists? Idealists? Religious maniacs?'

'More questions than answers...'

'And we're not in a position to answer them, but Cambridge is clearly critical,' said Berwick. 'It's the obvious place in the UK I suppose, an IT hotspot, information and technology businesses and research facilities are concentrated there but if there's anything to be found we'll find it. Whoever these people are, they could simply be there for the expertise or for anonymity. The targets could be elsewhere.' Berwick paused, looked at the President. 'We need something else, George; we need help. We can't just crash into every business premises within twenty miles of Cambridge...'

'You're sure? Sometimes can't isn't an option.'

Berwick swirled the water in his glass, nodded. 'If we have to then we will, but for the moment we're working on the terrorist angle. What else can we do?'

Neither man spoke. The low hiss of atmospheric interference and, in the Oval Office, a clock sounded the quarter hour.

Twelve

Fresh beads of sweat blistered, tickled like insects as they crawled across his skin, gathered, pooled, half-mooned beneath his arms. Where Charles Warner's jacket was folded over his arm, he could feel the material of his shirt, wet, sticking to his skin. He continued down the corridor, opened the door and emerged into the bright morning sunshine.

****

Back in her Cambridge laboratory, Caroline Whittleton's frown deepened. Pleased that they had not been goaded into making any rash promises to the politicians, there was still much to do, but they would try. And here, given their head, virtually unlimited resources, they might even make some progress but could promise nothing. The additional personnel would help. Some of the people whom Caroline had requested to be made available were true experts in their fields, people to whom she would normally have deferred but this was different.

She and Jobber would have the best brains in Great Britain and the United States assembled, either in Cambridge or with Professor Klutz in New England, within twenty-four hours and, if progress were possible, then they would make it.

Caroline shuddered at the responsibility. It was frightening but exhilarating and she looked at Professor Jobber, the American cursing quietly under his breath. He was a genius of course, of that Caroline needed little persuasion, but he was overbearing and rude, more thoughtless than positively unpleasant but she could work with him, had to make this work. He raised his hand irritably. 'Get me the measurements from the Polish pulse, would you?'

Caroline shook her head resignedly; she could see the computer print out in front of him, an unfinished cup of coffee standing on top of it. Jobber waved his hand around impatiently without looking up, clicked his fingers. 'The data's there,' said Caroline, inclining her head to Jobber's right.

Jobber looked up, over the top of his glasses and followed her eyes to the file by his side, the wrinkles on his forehead deepening. He nodded, looked away, resumed his scrutiny of his computer screen and picked up the printout, spilling the remains of the coffee onto the worktop. He began to flick through it. 'Pen? Pen?' Half a dozen pens in his shirt pocket, Jobber patted the table in front of him.

'Tell me, Professor Jobber,' said Caroline. Jobber did not respond. 'Professor Jobber? Clayton!'

Jobber continued to study his flickering monitor. 'Hmm?'

Caroline was feeling reflective, wanted to summarize their position. 'How far are we behind these people?'

Jobber raised his head, smiled at Caroline. 'I really don't know.'

Caroline gritted her teeth. She should have framed the question more precisely. She decided to persist. 'Do you believe...' Caroline stopped speaking. Once more scrutinizing his screen, Jobber was not listening and Caroline reached over, touched his arm. The American flinched, appeared to blush and Caroline seized her opportunity. 'Do you believe that we will be capable of emulating these people on say, a three-month view?'

As a scientist, Caroline could understand Jobber's reluctance to speculate. He hesitated, then spoke patiently, as if to a child. 'No, I think that your suggestion of years, decades more likely was nearer the truth. Still, as you said yourself, we're being asked to observe, not to build, and we could make some progress. If the authorities capture any equipment, for example, then we could make some real progress.'

Jobber was right, the military or the police could help, possibly get hold of something tangible. In fact, they had to, if they didn't then it might just be a blur, events moving too fast for them to keep up. The gradient of the slope that they were hurtling down might simply be too great for them to remain in control, might condemn them to react to events, fight fires without ever really knowing why. After all, their opponents could have been working on this for years, their practical experiments, tangible evidence of what they had achieved. Had these people been working to a plan? If so, then what was it and were they ready? Were their ducks lined up in a row, ready to be picked off at their leisure?

There was no way of knowing. Caroline was in the dark, the feeling both alien and disturbing to her.

****

Working on into the evening, Caroline and Jobber checked and crosschecked the data that had been collated over the last eight weeks. Jobber had two further long conversations with Professor Klutz whilst Caroline examined the relationships between the energy apparently expended and the bulk of the objects brought to the present.

It was frustrating work, their measurements too imprecise. The speed of the object might make a difference, even the weather. Caroline looked at Professor Jobber, a look of studied effort on his face. He seemed to feel that he was being observed and spoke without looking up. 'Of course, it's all happened already.'

Caroline started a little. Neither she nor Jobber had spoken for over an hour. 'I beg your pardon?' Jobber did not answer. 'Do you mean that anything that has come back from the past has already disappeared?'

'That's right,' said Jobber shaking his head at his computer screen. He leaned back in his chair and looked at Caroline, his large brown eyes clear, almost smiling. He pushed a lock of hair back behind his ear. 'But more than that; everything has already happened. Whether we succeed or fail in preventing any more of these events, everything. Bizarre, isn't it? Why do we bother?'

'Like the crew of the Mary Celeste,' said Caroline.

Jobber looked up, frowned. 'Mary Celeste?'

'The disappearances, as you said. They've all already happened, both those that we know about and many that we do not. It could explain a lot; my handbag which disappeared earlier this year from the Tube between St Paul's and Oxford Circus, for example.'

Jobber did not laugh, instead his face clouded, his eyebrows rose. 'I don't think that they would have taken your handbag. Kill you, possibly, but I think it's more likely that that was a casual theft.'

The hair prickled on the back of Caroline's neck, and she stared at Jobber, her mind ahead of his words. Backward time travel was not impossible. Her involvement, and that of Professor Jobber himself in the academic debate about time was well known, they could be personally at risk, yet Jobber was calmly carrying on with his work as though he had said nothing of importance.

When she spoke, Caroline's voice was distant, somehow removed. 'Have you had any personal items disappear in the recent past?'

'Me?' said Jobber; he was the only other person within fifteen feet of Caroline, and she fought to keep the irritation out of her voice. 'Yes you, Professor Jobber.'

'People are always removing things of mine. They try to say that I've lost them, but I always remember where I've put things down.' Caroline doubted that, but still she felt unease, a chill.

'I shouldn't worry,' said the tall American. He tried to smile. 'If they wanted either of us dead then we would already be dead. Fascinating, but they would seem to want us alive.'

Caroline sat down heavily, ran her hand through her hair. She tried to concentrate. She'd checked on the girls in the well-worn courtesy house in the grounds earlier. The child-minder seemed competent if a little brusque, but that had been hours ago, now the girls might be in bed, it must be after 9pm. She looked at her watch. Shocked to see that it was almost midnight, she had to leave.

Standing up, Caroline slipped off her lab coat and reached for her Barbour. She tossed it over her shoulder, noticed the weight in one of the pockets and pulled out her mobile phone; she had missed two calls. It would be 9am in Tokyo. Caroline hit the fast-call button that she had programmed in for the Hotel Seiyo Ginza.

****

Sitting on the bed in his room in the Hotel Seiyo Ginza, Jeremy Whittleton raised his left hand before him; it was shaking badly. He needed to speak to Caroline, to hear her voice, to talk about normal, everyday things, problems even, things that he would have normally blotted out. He breathed deep, shifted his position and fished out the small wrap of tissue paper that contained his wedding ring from his trouser pocket. He unfolded it and slipped the ring back onto his finger, his right hand momentarily stilling the trembling of his left.

Thirteen hours earlier, as his taxi had dropped him off some 500 meters south of the Roppongi subway station, Jeremy had taken the ring off. He didn't mean anything by it, it was just a habit he had told himself as he crossed the road and entered the building whose address he had been given. He took the elevator to the second floor; the doors opened onto a bar.

'Yo, Jeremy! Mine's a beer!' bellowed an Australian voice from somewhere to Jeremy's left. He turned and saw the huge frame of Declan O'Donnell heave itself from a chair at one of the tables by the window, where he had been sitting with two other men. Declan was wearing casual slacks and an open necked polo shirt. He stood 6'6' in his stocking feet and made Jeremy feel positively tiny. He'd be about thirty-two now, Jeremy thought, and there was not an ounce of fat on him. He positively radiated health in a way that only Australians and some west coast Americans seemed able to do.

Declan shook Jeremy's hand vigorously, polished off the last inch of his Erdinger Weiss bier and nodded to the barman. Handing a fresh bottle to Jeremy, he waved his own drink dangerously. 'Cheers!'

'Cheers!' said Jeremy.

They clanked bottles and Jeremy raised his drink to his mouth, it tasted good. 'Pascal and Drew,' said Declan, waving his bottle towards his companions. 'I work with the buggers, and they fancied a beer. Hope you don't mind?'

'No problem,' said Jeremy.

Two more beers and a long chat with the proprietor, a friendly German, followed before the ex-pats loosened up.

'So what's it really like here now?' asked Jeremy. The blank faces that had stared at him on the Narita Express on the way in from the airport had rattled him; he tried to keep the nervousness out of his voice. He was not altogether successful. 'We've been getting some pretty bad reports back home. Tell me they're overdone?' Jeremy was prepared for a glance, probably a wind-up, but the ex-pats' hesitation chilled.

'It's been a bit sticky,' said Drew. He struggled to smile, and Jeremy tried to weigh him up. Drew didn't look like an early panicker, but then again who did, and spooking newcomers was a well-established ex- pat sport. Jeremy let the remark go, did not want to know any more. It was only a short trip and he tried to change the subject but the ex-pats pulled it back.

'It's changed, just in the last month,' said Pascal, a Belgian, his English almost perfect. 'It's deeper than just the financial troubles. Sophie was pushed off the pavement last week, someone spat at her.'

'His wife,' obliged Declan.

People were jostled off the pavement all the time in London, but Tokyo was different. Still, Jeremy determined to put the matter out of his mind. He made another attempt to change the subject; he moved them on to money, a well-established ex-pat favourite and, twenty minutes later he felt much improved as he, Declan and the others headed out of the bar and into Roppongi.

Jeremy had visited the Roppongi district before but did not know it well. Declan and his colleagues clearly did, even nodding to a couple of acquaintances as the group wove its way through the crowds that grew steadily thicker as they approached the Roppongi Crossing.

Jeremy looked at the 'Bladerunner' scene around him, neon lights, hustlers and noisy streets full of people, the thundering two-storey Shuto Expressway ahead of him, belching out carbon monoxide onto the partygoers beneath. Yet it was only 9pm, the area wouldn't really start buzzing until much later...

'Here ya go,' said Declan propelling Jeremy into the 8-lane crossing. Jeremy found himself swept along, he looked up at the giant Panasonic screen towering above them, dance music blaring from the hi-tech speakers to its sides and then struggled back up onto the sidewalk on the other side of the road, blundering into what looked like a group of journalists, cameras flashing. There were policemen, an argument was developing, there were raised voices, bared teeth, but Declan, clearing a path for the others, good-naturedly pushed his way through.

'Gaijin!'

He hadn't imagined it, Jeremy was sure. The pushing around him intensified and he shook the word out of his head, tried to concentrate on his surroundings.

The bar was much more crowded than the last, the wall of bottles at its far end almost obscured by the mass of customers but, as he saw the wooden figure of a Red Indian by the door, Jeremy knew that he had been here before; it was the Geronimo Bar. He patted the wooden Indian absentmindedly on the head and they forced their way inside.

The small group drank their first beer without exchanging a word, unable or unwilling to make the effort to make themselves heard above the deafening noise around them then, at a wave from Declan, Jeremy, elbows bared, leveraged his way to the bar, bought the second round.

Most of the conversations around them were being conducted in English of variable quality, the crowd predominantly male. Jeremy smiled to himself as he took the beers, rubbed the pale, newly exposed skin of his ring finger and considered the stories of well-to-do Japanese girls hanging around Gaijin bars picking up foreigners.

Fat chance, he thought as he caught the eye of a Japanese man standing beneath the head of a large, sad looking buffalo that was hanging on the wall. The man held Jeremy's eye, he was about forty and wore an open necked shirt and a light-coloured jacket. Jeremy thought that he caught the flicker of a smile cross the man's face and he turned away.

'Deck?'

'Yeah?' The Australian was impatiently waving an empty beer bottle at the besieged barman. 'Time to stock up.'

Jeremy watched him and smiled. It was good to be out, but he'd have to slow down a little. It's only just after 10pm; he frowned. 'Deck, this isn't a gay bar, is it?'

'Hell, no mate, you're outta luck!'

Jeremy put his now warm bottle to his mouth, took a drink and turned sharply in the direction of the Japanese man. He was no longer there. Jeremy felt uncomfortable and Declan had still not been served.

'Shall we move on?'

'Yeah, why not?' Declan glared at the barman, banged his bottle down on the bar and waved to Drew and Pascal. They were trying to talk to a pretty Japanese girl, their attempts to ignore him increasingly futile as the large Australian bore down on them. 'Gas Panic?'

'What?'

'Gas Panic! Tasteless, huh? It's a bar,' said Declan turning towards Jeremy, a twinkle in his eye. 'You'll like it.'

They left the bar and, Drew, Pascal and Jeremy followed in his wake. Declan forged ahead, carved a path through the crowd. The traffic on the street was bumper to bumper and some young people were weaving between the cars. Others were singing and one girl fell to her knees in the middle of the road. She was helped to her feet by several of her giggling friends and Jeremy knew how she felt, he was drinking too quickly. He raised his hand, looked at his watch; it was 10.30pm.

The head and shoulders of Declan bobbed above the crowd some five or six yards ahead of him, Jeremy pushed a hawker's hand from in front of his face. Lights were flashing, tourists were pressing in, but the Yakuza licensed hawkers were the real problem, slowing him down, pushing cheap jewellery at him, shouting in bad English. Jeremy reached up to fend off the hand again as a large west African, thrust a necklace at him, held onto his shoulder to slow him down further. Jeremy pushed his way through, scowled and looked up; Declan had disappeared.

Shit! Jeremy didn't know where Gas Panic was.

Still, why should he be worried? This was Tokyo, not Beirut. He could ask for directions, give him the excuse to make it a short night. He walked on, headed away from the throb of the Shuto Expressway, the huge Panasonic screen and the crowd thinned a little; he would go back to the hotel, see Dec again in a couple of days. He looked up and his eyes caught those of a man standing on the pavement ahead of him. It was the man from the Geronimo bar.

Jeremy was not quite sure what to say or do. The man must be gay but if he was, then had he been giving out the wrong message? Should he say something? He was embarrassed, tried to smile. 'Well, look...'

The man smiled and held up his hand. 'One thing you should know about Tokyo, Whittleton San,' said the man, his English excellent.

'Yes?' said Jeremy. His own smile frozen on his face, he was still walking towards the man, wanted to get past.

As he drew level he felt the hand on his shoulder. He stopped, could feel himself begin to flush.

'Time can pass so very quickly,' the man said, holding Jeremy's eye. 'You must be certain that you do not lose what little you have.' The man smiled again, removed the hand that he had raised to Jeremy's shoulder.

'Well yes, absolutely,' said Jeremy. He shook his head, looked away and walked on, glad to be away from the man, but something was not right. He could not place it, but then he had it; he had been addressed by name!

Jeremy turned sharply but the man had gone. No big deal. Maybe he was just being friendly, had seen him in the hotel or might work at Strettons? Yes, that was it. He must work at Strettons, possibly in Jeremy's own department; he would check tomorrow. He turned and continued, but something had changed; the sidewalk was empty, the people gone. His head beginning to swim, Jeremy squinted, looked around him.

The roads were deserted, the neon lights off, it was much quieter. He could hear the Expressway. Very faint, it had been drowned out by background noise earlier, but now he could hear it.

Jeremy looked at his watch. 10.38pm, the streets should be busy, getting busier but then he realized that he had read his watch far too easily. It was getting light!

It couldn't be but it was! Jeremy looked up at the sky, felt the panic begin to rise inside him. Which way was east? He had it, and yes, it was definitely light!

His watch must have stopped, but what had he done, had he slept in the street? Surely, he hadn't had that much to drink? Jeremy patted himself down, no bruises and he pulled out the wad of money from his back pocket. Still there, as far as he could tell, a substantial wad, he hadn't been mugged but he was worried. Could he have blacked out? Was he ill?

Jeremy did not know how long he stood there, watching the street, unsure of what to do. Street cleaners, some all-night revellers passed him, stared oddly and he knew that he had to move. He walked slowly back up towards the Roppongi Crossing and immediately saw a taxi.

Relieved, he tried the door, but it would not open. The drivers operated them automatically from the inside he remembered. He tapped on the window, tried to look presentable, but the driver scowled, muttered something and gestured with his hand. Jeremy tapped on the window again, but the driver pulled away.

'Gaijin, Gaijin!'

Jeremy raised his hands to his head, massaged his temples. He squinted, registered a taxi rank some 100 yards ahead of him and began to walk towards it; there were two taxis, no queue. He buttoned up his shirt and tapped on the window of the first feeling distinctly odd; it wasn't a hangover, it was too early for that, he could still feel the beer. He heard the locks spring on the car door, and he clambered in. He looked at the small clock on the dashboard of the taxi. It was 8.45am.

The ride to the hotel had been uneventful but now, safely back in his room, the stares of the concierge and porter as he had stumbled into the hotel, still fresh in his mind, Jeremy felt numb. Tired, he needed to sleep but he couldn't, his mind was spinning and then the telephone rang. Jeremy stared at it blankly, picked it up on the sixth ring. It was Caroline.

Sunday, 28 October 1999
Thirteen

He was with her now, could feel her strength. She was so vast; shiny in parts, dark, dangerous in others and, as Warner turned to look at his colleagues, themselves deep in thought, he knew that this was not the time to talk. They had work to do. He breathed hard, nodded and took the well-worn photograph out of his breast pocket. 'Mom, this is for Patrick.'

****

Prime Minister Donald Berwick was alone in the Cabinet Room, seated in his customary chair beneath the portrait of Sir Horace Walpole. He steepled his fingers and brought them up to his face, his eyes distant. It was 6.50am and he was so worried, he had not slept. Dr Whittleton had relayed her fears for her husband's safety to her handler just after 1am and the Prime Minister had been informed immediately. He had directed that the information be passed to Washington and, whilst he had insisted that his colleagues get some rest, he had not seen his own bed since Thursday evening.

A dirty pigeon flapped past the Cabinet Room window, distorted by the thick glass but the Prime Minister seemed not to notice. He shook his head. He was exhausted and he knew it. He would have to get some rest, there was a danger that he would make mistakes, but for the moment his mind was far too active for him to relax.

Berwick had not spoken to Dr Whittleton directly, but Caroline's handler had been extremely experienced, had judged that Caroline was not prone to panic attacks and had relayed several suggestions Caroline made to her supervisor who in turn passed the information to Alistair MacDonald, the head of Special Branch. MacDonald. The Prime Minister had sanctioned Caroline's requests immediately.

Berwick rubbed his cheek, the two-day shadow blackening the skin. A faint knock and the Cabinet Room door opened.

Julian Ryde entered the room. 'Good morning, Donald.'

Berwick grimaced; he nodded to the seat by his side. His Home Secretary looked distressingly well; Berwick could only imagine what he looked like himself. 'Well rested, Julian?'

Ryde arched an eyebrow. When he spoke, his voice was steady. 'Potentially interesting?'

Berwick nodded. 'We're hoping it's our first contact.'

'Dissent?'

'That would be nice.'

'Otherwise, why warn her to back off? Subtlety hasn't been a feature to date, why not just remove her?'

Berwick shifted in his seat; maybe he should have woken Julian earlier. 'Larry Buchanan made the same point; we don't have an answer.'

'He couldn't have imagined it?'

'Dr Whittleton seemed very certain that something happened to her husband, and I'm inclined to believe her. Two of our staff in Tokyo have spoken with him and agree that he sounds credible, not too easily flapped.'

The Prime Minister glanced at the papers on the table in front of him. 'He seems to have simply disappeared, to have lost several hours of his life and there were traces of an energy surge at around 10.30pm and 8.30am Japanese time. Just faint traces picked up in the Cambridge area, just above background levels, but it fits the times that he's mentioned.'

'A warning?'

The Prime Minister nodded. 'Possibly, but I doubt it.'

'And the husband? What's he been told?'

Donald Berwick shook his head. 'Nothing. Dr Whittleton's tried to persuade him to come back but he's refused. As you might imagine, she's a bit distressed but we'll do what we can to protect him in Tokyo, we'll put a couple of men on it. We might be able to manufacture a passport problem of some sort, force him back that way, but we can't just bundle him back to the UK against his will.

'In the meantime, Dr Whittleton would like her daughters to be taken care of. She wants them moved every day and all references to where they've stayed destroyed.' The Prime Minister avoided Julian Ryde's eye and continued. 'She's also suggested that we stop recording the time, place and purpose of our own meetings; destroy the tapes of our conversations with the Americans, remove any trail that these people might be able to follow in the future and I agree with her. If this is orchestrated, if we're under attack, then it makes no sense to give these people any more information than we have already.'

Ryde nodded slowly to himself. 'So, for the record, none of this ever happened?'

'This is as strange to me as it is to you Julian,' continued Berwick, 'but if Dr Whittleton's right, then we're under threat from the future. That implies that backward travel must is possible.'

'OK,' said Ryde; he sat down slowly, his teeth gritted. 'It seems reasonable to stop the information flow; but aren't we shutting the door after the horse has bolted?'

Prime Minister Berwick felt the hairs begin to rise on his arms. He leaned back in his chair, he fully understood the comment implicit in Julian's question; they were too late, were destined to fail. He nodded, spoke slowly. 'To some extent yes, but what's the alternative? Leave the door open? And we needn't be passive in this; we can change times, alter places...'

'In which case couldn't they simply reach further back into the past,' said Ryde. 'Couldn't they grab Dr Whittleton at her graduation, or you when you first took your seat in Parliament? Yet they didn't, I survived the Falklands war, we're both here speaking to one another now. I haven't been able to absorb it all but there might be parallel universes out there in which these things did happen, we were removed, but they didn't happen here and surely there's a reason for that? They, whoever they are, must believe that our actions are no longer of any consequence.'

'Still, we have no choice,' said Berwick. His voice lacked conviction. Ryde's logic was impeccable. 'It would be foolish to give our enemies the chance to locate us whenever they wanted by giving them accurate dates, times and places. We can't simply assume failure before it's forced upon us. We're still here Julian. We can only do our best.'

'Of course,' said Ryde; he rubbed the bridge of his nose. 'So, what's the Japanese angle?'

****

Japan! Caroline Whittleton raised her hand to her nose and rubbed the red mark caused by her glasses as the door to her laboratory swung closed behind her. Why had Jeremy had to go to Japan?

The threat to Caroline's family had given her strength, she had spent most of the night in the lab, but it had been a mistake and now her exhaustion threatened to overwhelm her. She felt as though she was in a dream, her movements slowed, she was wading through liquid, and she needed to sleep. She waited for her head to clear a little, the stars to disappear from before her eyes and then began to walk towards the courtesy house, small flurries of autumn leaves stirred by the chill breeze.

It was 9.30am, a bright, late Autumn morning.

Caroline nodded to a man standing, baggy-coated, a wire trailed from his ear to the collar of his shirt, by a tree a few feet from the house and found the door unlocked. She walked inside, Emily and Virginia playing happily in the front room with Nurse Beckwith and the nanny and the latter forced a smile. The place had the feel of a holiday home about it, clean but well-used, ample but ill-matching furniture, some children's games and a stack of heavily thumbed best sellers gracing the mantelpiece. Caroline relaxed fractionally but there was no pleasure in it. By the front door, two suitcases were packed and ready to go, she was losing her family, first Jeremy and now the girls.

Caroline felt the tears begin to prick her eyes. She wanted to cry but she had to be strong. She smiled at Nurse Beckwith, kissed her daughters and gave them the notepads and pencils that she had taken from one of the Downing Street offices. She had left some sweets in the bedroom earlier and Caroline, not wanting to leave the girls for a moment longer than she had to, ran quickly up the stairs.

She was tired, emotionally drained, may have been imagining it but she felt the hairs on the back of her hands stir. Like the children's trick with the electrically charged balloon, it felt like static electricity, but someone must have left a window open. Caroline opened the bedroom door.

Bending down by the small bedside cabinet, Caroline pulled open the top drawer. She took out the sweets and began to rise to her feet when she heard the bedroom door close behind her, a key scrape in the lock.

Caroline turned sharply. Her eyes wide. A man, Asian, possibly Japanese, he was regarding her quizzically. She rose to her feet, took a step backwards. Her heart pounding, she felt calmer, knew what she must do. They had come to get her, kill her but she must protect the girls, lead the man away. Remote, removed, Caroline weighed the probabilities, how best to give her life to save the girls?

The man was in his early forties, black hair scraped back from his head, a short pigtail at his neck. Smiling, he was wearing a long dark coat that descended almost to his ankles. 'Dr Whittleton, it is a great honour!' The man's eyes did not leave Caroline's, and she felt her limbs begin to freeze. The man smiled again, more patronizing than friendly, the examination of an exhibit in a zoo.

For several moments, neither the man nor Caroline spoke. Then the man lowered his eyes, and Caroline felt her limbs free.

'Death will rain down from the skies, Dr Whittleton.' The man's mouth was twisted into a smile, but his eyes were cold. 'Then they will believe, you will see. They will be destroyed to be reborn.'

The Japanese man inclined his head, observing, studying. He opened his coat and Caroline's eyes widened further. He was wearing white silk pyjamas, baggy, traditional clothing of some sort, a huge blade held to his body by a silken belt around his waist. Perhaps eighteen inches long, it had no handle, nor was there a scabbard.

'Death will take them all and they will know the truth!' said the man as he slid the knife slowly from his belt. 'The fire will cleanse them, the earth become liquid beneath their feet, their bodies vapour. Theirs will be the supreme sacrifice, they will lead the way to salvation, the Divine Way.'

Caroline could not move her feet, she could see the girls, dead, hacked to pieces; she had to make this easy, would not scream, surely, they could still live?

The Japanese man straightened his head, the smile gone and, his coat hanging open, he regarded Caroline dispassionately. He began to slowly wind a white cloth around the part of the blade where the handle should have been and Caroline struggled to think, weigh her options. She looked around for a weapon of some sort. A cuddly toy, a small plastic lamp, a shoe, but nothing useful and she knew that she was going to die and die quietly. For the sake of the girls, she must not make a sound.

The Japanese man took out a second bandage, wrapped it around the palm of his left hand. Seven, eight, nine times he circled his hand, but still Caroline did not move.

How long would it take? Would he stab her? Hack and slash her, the life draining out of her, her brain starved of oxygen, her heart stopped without blood. Would it hurt?

The man held the knife high and looked at it, a reverence in his eye as the blade caught the weak late autumn sunshine slanting into the bedroom.

Caroline flinched, felt her legs begin to shake. Less painful than childbirth, much quicker, seconds and it would be over, but she could not close her eyes. Her lips were dry, her mouth moved slowly up and down but Caroline made no sound. These were her final moments, she would share them with her killer, but, when the man closed his eyes once more, she felt her limbs released from his grip. She took an unsteady step backwards and the man sat down.

Caroline was shocked.

She took a second step backwards, then the man's eyes once again sought out her own and she froze as the man shuffled the coat from his shoulders, allowed it to fall to the floor and pushed it under his buttocks. He was leaning slightly forward.

Caroline's breathing quickened. Her fear returned as she felt the threat to her life recede. She felt sick, began to shake uncontrollably.

The man closed his eyes again. His white shirt opened, exposed his hairless chest and abdomen and he swung the blade in his outstretched hand in an arc pointing first at the ceiling, then at Caroline and then rotated it inwards towards himself.

Caroline raised her hand to her mouth; the blade was gone. She looked up from the Japanese man's navel to his face. Dark, glittering the man's eyes were on fire, screaming, but the room was silent, and she looked down once more at his stomach, his whole body below the waist red with blood, bubbling, spilling, filling the folds of his pyjamas, tumbling in tiny waterfalls onto the floor.

Caroline began to choke. Rivulets of blood snaked towards her feet, clawed their way toward her as the man sawed across his abdomen with the knife and still not a sound.

Then a grunt and Caroline tried to look away, but she could not. Still firmly clamped in his hands, the knife was protruding from the right side of the man's stomach, below the point of his ribs and his bandaged hand slipped from it. He grunted again, screwed his eyes against the pain and a bubble of mucus burst from his nose. He grasped the knife once more turned it in his body, began to cut upwards and Caroline felt her knees buckle beneath her as something vomited from the man's stomach, pink and grey, alive. A stench filled the room as Caroline's knees hit the ground. She began to retch.

****

The pain was ebbing. Now just a whisper in his ear and Ichiro Ishimoto opened his eyes. He was satisfied, his life fulfilled; the gaijin had heard him speak and she would understand. He felt a wave of contentment wash over him, dulled the pain and he looked down at the blood-soaked knife now lying on the floor by his knees, pushed from his body when his spirit spilled out and he reached for it.

The pain stabbed at him, flooded his mind, drove everything before it but he drew the knife from the pink and red mess, so alive and thrust it into the carpet. He leant on it, looked up at the Gaijin, spoke to her with his eyes but she said nothing.

Now, the numbness was spreading, creeping upwards from his legs and grey clouds were edging in around him, threatening his sight. Ishimoto's eyelids began to flutter. He could hear distant voices. He slid forward onto the handle of the knife and his body sagged, but did not fall.

Fourteen

Warner sat contentedly in the pilot's seat, Davie Campbell by his side. The engines had been started up and, the crew carrying out their routine pre-take-off checks, he felt a wonderful release. A couple more minutes and they would be in the air, free. Warner was with his family now and they would do their job. Nothing in the world would stop them. Nothing at all.

****

The news of the shocking death in Cambridge reached the Prime Minister within minutes; it was not yet 10.30am. Still with only had two hours' sleep, he set the wheels in motion to bring forward the videoconference with the Americans from 5pm to 12 noon.

Julian Ryde had instructed the Cambridgeshire police to report on the death immediately and a four-man forensic investigations team from the Special Branch had also been dispatched to Cambridge. Two of the detectives would stay with the body, investigate the scene and report on the progress of the autopsy and McCurran was already there.

He and the other two detectives would interview Dr Whittleton and any indications of the dead man's identity, place of work or residence would be transmitted to the Cabinet Room immediately. A brief résumé of what had happened had been sent by secure electronic mail to the Oval Office.

Berwick had authorized Julian Ryde to take whatever action he thought necessary, and the Home Secretary had organized for several Special Air Service four-man units to be moved from Hereford to Cambridge. They lacked a target, but cross-referencing of the several energy bursts was now indicating an area to the south-west of the city and he thought it wise that the troops be on hand.

Glancing at his watch, the Prime Minister sat back in his chair, kneaded the back of his neck; had he forgotten anything? On balance, he thought not. What needed to be done had been done and now he must let the professionals do their job and do what he himself was least well equipped to do. Wait.

The Prime Minister rose to his feet, blinked hard. Shapes were moving at the periphery of his vision, red and yellow, morphing into the shape of fantastic beasts, and he knew that he needed to rest.

Leaving instructions with Julian Ryde to wake him should something happen, he sat on the edge of the camp bed in the holding room and took off one shoe. He paused, stifled a yawn and breathed hard. He closed his eyes, dropped the shoe from his hand and was instantly asleep.

****

Two hours later, Donald Berwick was not a happy man. Julian Ryde had instructed that the Prime Minister be woken only five minutes before the video screen to Washington fizzed into life and Berwick had been pushed to find the time to comb his hair. He respected Julian, would trust him with his life, but he felt dreadful, was sure that he looked worse. Still tie less, he ran his hand over his still unshaven chin. He felt as though he had slept in his clothes. Indeed, he had.

'Good afternoon, Donald,' said President Sutton from the Oval Office. Gerry Buchanan, Larry Edelman, Linda King and Jack Scott were seated closest to him and the camera panned round to show the remaining members of the NSC. Dick Turner was getting some rest and Donald Berwick noted with some satisfaction that Edelman was unshaven. 'How's Dr Whittleton?'

'Bearing up relatively well in the circumstances,' said Berwick.

'Ritualistic suicide?' said the President. On the screen to the UK, Berwick nodded. 'So, the Japanese link seems to be confirmed?'

'It would appear so,' said the UK Prime Minister, oblivious to the filling rooms on both sides of the Atlantic. 'We believe that the man was Japanese, but he was carrying no identifying papers, credit cards, keys or money. He did have a short poem in his pocket, about cherry blossom of all things and we're looking at it now. It's pictographic script. Japanese, I'm told. A copy was sent to you about an hour ago.

'The only other things that he had with him when he died were the clothes that he stood up in and the knife, a simple, handle-less blade. Other than that, we've got very little. Certainly no one that we're aware of has come forward to report a colleague missing in the last couple of hours but, if they do, we'll let you know immediately.'

'And the body,' said Sutton. 'Can we get anything from that?'

'The autopsy has begun but has not yet finished,' said Berwick. He rubbed his eyes, unable to catch himself in time. 'All we know at present is that the man was in his late thirties or early forties, medium height and build for an Oriental man and in apparently good health apart from the wound that killed him. In fact, he was immaculately turned out, right down to manicured fingernails and toenails.'

'So, this doesn't look like a bungled attempt on Dr Whittleton's life?'

The Prime Minister shook his head, nodded to Alistair MacDonald, the head of Special Branch. 'Alistair?'

'Probably not,' said McDonald. He rubbed his reddish-brown moustache with his thumb. 'Dr Whittleton was unarmed, the deceased was alone in her company for plenty long enough to kill her; but he didn't.'

'As regards Dr Whittleton, she's pretty shocked of course but is keen to carry on with her work,' said Berwick. 'Her girls have been removed as she requested, and she's given a statement to Special Branch already. They are staying with her in case she remembers anything else, but nothing has essentially changed from our earlier e-mail to you. 'It sounds as though the dead man's last words to Dr Whittleton were effectively a verbal suicide note. He mentioned the supreme sacrifice, his expected salvation. It's in the e-mail. If we have nothing on his identity by the end of the evening, we were considering putting his face on the television; it might spark something,' said Berwick. The PM paused, looked at Morgan Jones and then at the video screen to Washington. 'Personally, I'm not convinced. What do you think George?'

'I'm not sure it would be wise at this stage,' said Sutton after a moment's hesitation. 'The Press is a genie, easy to let out of the bottle, not so easy to put back in. Manipulating it is rarely pain-free; it might be better to keep it quiet. If this guy was looking to get caught, then maybe he didn't agree with the rest of his group, might have been trying to tell us something. Could be the others don't even know he's missing yet...'

'Yes, that's true,' said Berwick. He turned to Jones, raised his eyebrows and continued. 'As regards the death itself, we wheeled in a Japanese expert from Oxford after the incident with Jeremy Whittleton in Tokyo to see if any of the words used have any special relevance in Japanese. He's stayed on and has been filling us in on suicides like these.

'It's rare now, not unknown, but he suggested that there were four principal reasons why a samurai or high caste Japanese would have committed hari-kari, or seppuku as they prefer to call it, in feudal Japan. Firstly, it could be to avoid dishonour or capture; secondly, to follow a master into the afterlife or, thirdly, it could be ordered as a form of capital punishment. Fourthly and most interestingly, it could also be a sign of disapproval at the behaviour of a master that stopped short of betrayal. He says that the fact that this guy had no second, or Kaishaku, suggests that he felt very strongly about something.'

'Kaishaku?'

'He's the guy who steps in at the end to administer the coup-de-grace,' said Berwick. 'Usually by beheading. In this case our friend had to finish the job himself.'

'The Press would go wild,' said Julian Ryde in London. He glanced briefly at Morgan Jones; the Welshman averted his eyes. 'We can't possibly go to them but what we need to know is who this man was and what was he trying to tell us.'

In Washington President Sutton turned to Gerry Buchanan. 'Gerry, give us a rundown on Japan. What do we know about the most active sects, individuals, terrorists, etc?'

Not comfortable in the spotlight, the spymaster's body language betrayed him. He ran his hand through his thinning hair. 'Well, as regards religious sects, there are plenty of them in Japan. The country's post-war economic miracle was achieved at great social cost and has alienated large numbers of people.

'That set the scene and then the business slowdown in the nineties supplied a lot more potential recruits for these alternative groups. In addition to the dispossessed, there are organizations incensed by the relentless creep of permissiveness, westernisation, you name it; it's a mess. Hell, you can see something of the target market from the pictures of rioting on the streets of Tokyo...'

'And more specifically, Gerry?' said Sutton, a little irritation registering in his voice. He turned to the video screen, rolled his eyes.

Buchanan seemed to acknowledge the rebuke

and continued. 'I've just spoken with the NSC Staff with responsibility for Transnational Threats. They confirmed that the Aum Shinrikyo, a religious cult, has been the biggest thing in Japan for years. Their name means the Supreme Truth...

'Whittleton mentioned them,' said Morgan Jones in London.

'I believe that Dr Whittleton said that the man mentioned the supreme sacrifice,' said Buchanan. 'It could be linked, but we can't be sure. A lot of things are 'supreme' and many cults are big on sacrifice.

Still, the AUM was responsible for the Matsumo and Tokyo nerve gas attacks in 1994 and 1995 when 19 people died. They were a real threat but most of the cult's leaders are incarcerated.'

'So, this isn't them?' said Sutton.

'It's a little early to say,' said Buchanan. 'But the cult has several legitimate operations and generated a significant amount of cash from its computer shops and restaurants, as well as from greenmail and extortion.

'It was estimated that they had up to $1.5bn in cash, real estate and other assets it 1995, the bulk of which they still have. That gives them some real financial muscle and they still have some followers; it's not possible to ban a state of mind, even if most of the former leaders are in prison.

'The Public Security Investigation Agency, the Koancho, Japan's internal security service failed to disband the group in 1997 under the Anti-subversive Activities Law. They couldn't prove that the group had a political objective. The Aum subsequently changed its name to Aleph, which means 'start anew' and they did. But they still have several hundred full time members and quite a significant Internet presence.'

'Surely that can't be?' said Donald Berwick in London.

Buchanan raised his eyebrows fractionally. 'The AUM still exist; they've been financially compensating some of their earlier victims, but they've kept most of their money and they haven't renounced their leader, Shoko Asahara.

'Asahara is currently incarcerated, but the Aum did have a significant following overseas, chiefly in Russia and this was unaffected by the clamp-down in Japan. The cult's Russian members include scientists and other influential figures who were used to infiltrate the Black Market for arms in the former Soviet Union.

'Indeed, there was some speculation that the gas attacks on the Tokyo subway were a prelude to larger attacks and an attempted right-wing take-over of the country, perhaps launched from a base in Russia. However, whatever the truth with respect to what the Aum either did or didn't do in Japan, we have no evidence whatsoever to link them to the recent events in England.'

'Regarding the cult's imprisoned leaders,' said Donald Berwick. 'None of them could have been, well, removed, replaced?'

'This is new territory for us all,' said Buchanan. 'We've not spoken to the Japanese authorities but, as I say, there is no tangible evidence to suggest that the Aum Shinrikyo is involved.'

'Then who?'

Buchanan shrugged. 'There are some other very extreme groups that we do know about in Japan, some trying to import the Ebola virus, others trying to get their hands on Anthrax spores, Botulin toxin, the smallpox virus, nerve gasses and a whole host of other unpleasant weapons.

'Indeed, the Aum itself is alleged to have used Botulin toxin. We believe that it lacked the scientific expertise to use it to deadly effect but its suggestions like these that cause us the greatest concern.

'Many of these groups will use whatever is the deadliest weapon that they have to hand. They have no compunction, no qualms, no moral hindrance, to prevent them from doing these things. They genuinely appear to have the desire to destroy human life on a massive scale and when they have the means to do so, then, like the extremists of the al-Qaeda, the evidence suggests' that they will.'

'Al-Qaeda?'

'We've no evidence that they've ever been operational in Japan,' said Buchanan, 'but the Aum was bad enough. Their members released the nerve gas Sarin onto the busiest subway system in the world and fifteen stations were affected.

'They had clearly intended to kill or incapacitate thousands, probably tens of thousands of people and it took the lawyers four hours to read out the charge sheet at the beginning of Asahara's trial. The cult appeared to have little regard for life and, in addition to the twenty or so victims of the gassings, an anti-cult lawyer and his family and a public notary, up to three dozen Aum members are also missing, now presumed dead.'

'Jeez...'

Buchanan looked from Larry Edelman to the President and continued. 'Still, as always, the most dangerous groups are those that we know least about.'

In London, Julian Ryde nodded. 'What do these cults typically trade in, what do they offer their followers?'

'There are many different groups, of course,' said

Buchanan. 'Many different messages, but frequently there are common themes. Their teachings are often a garbled mixture of Apocalyptic Christian and Buddhist ideas and new age beliefs, usually with a violent edge. Their Gods and icons tend to reflect this. Shiva, the Hindu God of destruction and rebirth might feature, and they often put very little value on individual human lives. They tend to be big on sacrifice and purification, mysticism, yoga, meditation etc and the Aum, for example, still talks of Armageddon. However, until we know who we are dealing with, it might be fruitless to speculate further on what they might want.'

'You think?' said President Sutton. He turned to face Donald Berwick on the screen before him, raised his eyes slightly towards the ceiling. 'Indulge us, Gerry.'

Buchanan, however reluctant to speculate, continued. 'At the micro-level, that is within the cult itself, many of these groups demand that new members sever all links with their family. Often there's a great deal of sexual predation, frequently new members are coerced into donating large sums of money to their new 'church'.'

'So why would anyone join?'

'Very few people join what they think is a cult,' said Buchanan looking at the image of Donald Berwick in London. 'Rather they become swept up in their new beliefs and, before we start to point the finger at the Japanese alone, let's remember that this is a global phenomenon.

'The Jonestown massacre in Guyana claimed over nine hundred lives, mostly American and over seventy Solar Temple cult members died in Switzerland and Canada. In Japan, the Aum was a legally registered religion and several of its members stood for parliament. They went so far as to set up their own shadow government.'

'So, what drives them, makes them turn to violence at the macro-level?'

'To the outside world, cults are often invisible but, as you say, some can and do become violent. For the most part it is a reactive violence, often in response to a feeling of persecution, a feeling that is frequently justified,' said Gerry Buchanan. He shifted in his seat, looked slightly less uncomfortable. 'However, the level of violence is often out of all proportion to the perceived threat...'

'Like Waco?' interrupted Larry Edelman.

'Yes, but there's still a question as to which side initiated the violence there,' said Buchanan looking at the National Security Adviser. 'To some the FBI looked far from clean, the Aum is a better example. They were willing to kill thousands of people to head off an imagined threat. There's no doubt that some cults do foster, sometimes intentionally, a feeling of paranoia, a highly dangerous mixture of beliefs. They see themselves as special, why else put themselves through such discomforts and they believe that they are persecuted. They develop a willingness to resort to extreme violence to defend themselves and this can sometimes be pre-emptive. Combined with their lack of respect for human life, well, I'm sure I don't have to spell it out.'

'Spell it out, Gerry,' said President Sutton.

Buchanan took a deep breath, shifted again. 'Based as they often are on one charismatic individual, cults tend to have a relatively short lifecycle. They might typically exist during that individual's 30's and 40's and the more harmless ones, if harmless is the right word, implode.

'Others, harmless or not, begin preparing for Armageddon, building shelters, as the Aum did, and mass suicides, such as Jonestown and those of the Solar Temple, are quite common.

'Other groups, however, become externally violent. Most members genuinely believe that they are defending themselves when they attack society at large but their feelings of specialness can lead to a hatred of authority. They believe that they have been chosen and that everyone else is wallowing in sin and can go to hell, sometimes literally, and some seem prepared to actively send them there. The most dangerous cults of all begin preparing for Armageddon and then try to bring it about themselves.'

'And in Japan in particular?' asked Susan Burnell, the UK Foreign Secretary, looking at the MI6 file in front of her. 'Is there ever a criminal element? The Yakuza, for example, do they ever become involved?'

'Not often,' said Buchanan. 'The Yakuza are mainstream gangsters, although they were implicated in the murder of Dr Hideo Murai, the Aum's chief scientist. He appeared to have been shooting his mouth off in '96.'

'Any other groups?' His question unfinished, Prime Minister Berwick's voice trailed off as he read the message that had been discretely passed to him by a person not visible on the Washington screens. He took a proffered telephone, held it to his ear for several seconds, all eyes upon him. He looked up at the screen.

'It may be nothing, but I did ask Special Branch to relay information immediately from either the autopsy or their discussions with Dr Whittleton if they thought it important.

'The Doctor has given a fuller description of what the man said before he died. He referred to death falling from the skies, the earth turning to liquid and many people being burned to death, being vaporized. Any thoughts?'

A silence descended on both sides of the Atlantic. 'A nuclear explosion?' said President Sutton; he caught Linda King's eye, her lips pursed. Her views on nuclear weapons were well known.

In London, Donald Berwick nodded. 'Homemade, presumably?'

The President frowned; he looked around the Oval Office and at the screen to London. There were several nods; he hesitated before he continued, chilled as the implication of Berwick's words became apparent. 'Must be; if they'd stolen a warhead, or taken one from the past, then we'd know about it.

'We've never lost a bomb, neither have you or the French and China and the new nuclear powers seem tight. What's happened in the former Soviet Union, God only knows for sure, but we don't think that they have any weapons missing. Plenty of fuel, mules carrying plutonium in their bodies, but no weapons that we're aware of, and probably not enough weapon's grade material to make a bomb...'

'And any weapon that had been taken, removed from the past, would reappear in the same position from which it had been taken wouldn't it?' said Donald Berwick. 'Hypothetically, it would be easy to track...'

Minds all around the Oval Office and the Downing Street Cabinet Room were racing; Gerry Buchanan looked particularly worried. Seated to the President's left, he discretely nudged his Head of State's arm.

President Sutton did not acknowledge him but allowed the conversation to move on for a minute or so before he spoke again. 'Gentlemen, ladies, do you think it would be possible to break for ten minutes so that we can consider how best to use this information?'

In London, Donald Berwick looked over at Julian Ryde. The Home Secretary nodded fractionally; they would re-run the tape later. 'Of course, George,' said Berwick. 'Good idea.'

****

The screens on both sides of the Atlantic faded. In Washington, the President turned to Buchanan. 'What is it Gerry?' Buchanan looked around the room at the paraphernalia of democracy, the Chairman of the Joint Chiefs of Staff, the heads of the State Department, the Defence Secretary, the Secretary of the Treasury, the US Ambassador to the UN and the President's advisers on national security and economic policy were all present yet this was the inner Cabinet, the National Security Council. The President followed Buchanan's eyes around the room. 'It's the price of democracy, Gerry. This is the NSC, what's on your mind?'

Buchanan blanched and Sutton swallowed hard. He could feel it, taste it; this was a defining moment, a watershed. Buchanan cleared his throat. 'Regarding your comment that we had never lost a nuclear weapon, Mr. President...'

'You mean we have?' said Sutton; Buchanan rarely addressed him as Mr. President. 'We've lost a weapon. Why was I not told? When?'

Buchanan looked up, as close to panic as President Sutton had ever seen him. 'Sir, you were never told because the only instance of a US nuclear weapon not being detonated, disarmed, destroyed or put into storage was so long ago.'

'Right,' said the President. Sir was little better than Mr. President, possibly worse. 'But it happened?' Buchanan nodded. Sutton, outwardly calm, noted his obvious discomfort. The spymaster's world was one of very small, very private meetings. Buchanan shifted uncomfortably in his seat, was beginning to sweat. 'Carry on please.'

'We lost one at the end of the War, Sir.'

'World War Two?'

'Yes. We...'

'But there were only three bombs, Gerry,' interrupted Sutton again, his words more a question than a statement. 'One was detonated in New Mexico, one at Hiroshima and one at Nagasaki. Tell me I'm correct.'

'I'm afraid that's not correct, Sir,' said Buchanan looking the President steadily in the eye. 'There were fourteen.'

'Fourteen!' said Linda King, spat out the word. 'What do you mean there were fourteen? How could there have been fourteen?'

The sweat beginning to glisten on his forehead, Buchanan did not answer. He scratched the back of his hand urgently. Somewhere in the room a pencil snapped before the President broke the silence. He spoke softly, slowly. 'Why were there fourteen, Gerry? Why didn't we know?'

'It's classified material, sir,' said Buchanan.

'Never likely to be de-classified, treated strictly on a 'need to know' basis.'

'This is the Government of the United States of America sitting around this table,' said President Sutton. 'I suggest that we do have a need to know. Run us through the facts.'

'Sir, at the end of the War the US and the Brits believed that the Russians might attack the West when Germany had been defeated,' said Buchanan, his tone clipped. 'The option of attacking them first was actively countenanced so I guess keeping quiet the fact that we had more nuclear weapons was...'

'Dear God!' It was Linda King; she was shaking her head slowly.

'Keeping the weapons in reserve was deemed to be sensible under the circumstances,' continued Buchanan. 'As it was, we now believe that the Russians knew that we had more bombs, that's why they turned against the Japanese in August instead.'

'A first strike?'

President Sutton looked from Linda King to Buchanan. 'Are you saying that we understated our strength because we wanted them to attack us?'

'I don't think it was ever viewed that way, sir,' said Buchanan. 'But I guess if ever the Russians were going to attack us, then August '45 was as good a time as any. We could have finished it there and then, on German soil, five thousand miles from home and long before the Russians got the bomb themselves. We knew that it was just a matter of time before they caught up with us technologically, we only had a narrow window of opportunity...'

'What do you mean window of opportunity?' said Linda King. She glared at Buchanan, turned to the President. 'This isn't a fucking coffee blender or leaf blower that we're talking about.'

'I realize that, Secretary of State,' answered Buchanan. 'I wasn't born then, I'm just stating the facts.'

'And we would've laid waste to the whole of Europe

East of the River Oder?' said Linda King, turning back to the CIA Director.

Buchanan held his hands out, palms upwards. 'I don't know, Secretary of State. I'm just suggesting what the rationale might have been at the time. Better Germany than Kansas.'

'So, what happened to the weapons?' said President Sutton. 'You say we lost one? Just how do you lose a bomb?'

'One was detonated at the Alamogordo Bombing and Gunnery Range in New Mexico,' said Buchanan, 'one was dropped on Hiroshima, one on Nagasaki and the third, it was going to be the first, was lost when the plane carrying it went down near its target. The other ten bombs were decommissioned in the early nineteen fifties.'

'The plane that went down, the wreckage was recovered?'

'No.'

The word hung in the room for what seemed like an age.

'So, it went down in the sea?'

'It must have done.'

'How do you figure that out?'

'Because we never found the wreckage.'

'Not a piece?'

'Not a piece, sir.'

'How close to the target did the bird go down?'

'Very close, sir.'

'How close, Gerry?'

'It was over the target, sir.'

Sutton paused before asking the question that he knew he must ask. The question to which he was sure that he already knew the answer. 'What was the target?'

Fifteen

'Tokyo!' said Warner, savoured the word. He turned to his co-pilot. 'Tokyo!'

Davie Campbell nodded, and Warner smiled, thought of Patrick. Almost ten years his junior, his brother had left both of his feet on Iwa Jima earlier in the year when 26,000 of his comrades had died. The fanatical resistance of the Japanese had been a shock. More than 20,000 Japanese soldiers had fought to the death. Only 1,000 broken and starving prisoners had left the island alive, and Okinawa had been worse. 110,000 defenders had died, thousands of marines. Kamikaze pilots had sunk 24 American ships on a single day and if the Home Islands were invaded as planned in November or December then such losses would pale into insignificance. Five million Americans would land, hundreds of thousands, maybe millions, would die.

Warner's eyes narrowed. The Japanese, the enemy had been defeated on land, at sea and in the air and yet they fought on. There had been not a single mutiny or outbreak of any kind, these people would fight to the death, to the last man if their Emperor told them to. The War simply had to be ended quickly.

'We'll put the fucker down the Emperor's throat!' Warner did not swear often. 'No more Iwa Jimas or Okinawas.' Not after this day's work. Warner gently wheeled the 'Flyer and, not a cloud in the sky, the runway lay before them. He patted the crumpled photograph in his breast pocket, considered the weather. It would be raining soon in Tokyo, but more than water would fall.

****

'Tokyo!' Not a word and President Sutton continued. 'I want full details of the plane, the crew, the bomb, the crash site...'

'I have them, Mr President,' said Buchanan, 'I was, well...'

'You knew?' said Linda King. The Secretary of State slowly shook her head, closed her eyes. 'You already knew!'

'No of course not,' said Buchanan. He mopped his forehead, coughed. 'It was the Japanese link that did it, we dug out the details.'

'What do we tell the Brits?'

'We tell them everything,' said Buchanan. He looked at Larry Edelman, registered the disapproval, dismissed it and turned back to the President. 'They know so much already, but they must understand the urgency of the situation, the scale of the threat. The main threat might not be to them, but they may need to take drastic action in their own back yard.'

'I agree,' said Sutton. He looked around the room; there was no dissent. 'OK, let's get the conference back on. Gerry, perhaps you'd be ready to brief us on the plane and its crew and cargo?'

Buchanan nodded and the President motioned to turn the video screen back on.

'Hello again Donald,' said Sutton when the screen had flickered back into life. Apparently waiting politely for the President to come back and share his information with them, none of the members of the UK Prime Minister's Cabinet appeared to have moved from their earlier positions. 'I'm afraid that we have some rather disturbing news.'

Two minutes later, the Prime Minister was the first to speak. 'What does this mean, George? Where was the plane, how big was the bomb, what sort of damage could it do?'

'This is as new for us as it is for you, Donald. Gerry has some background, but he's only had a few minutes. Please bear with us.' Sutton turned to Buchanan. 'Gerry?'

Buchanan nodded and took the floor. The sweat stains half-mooning beneath his armpits already visible, he buttoned up his jacket. Outwardly unruffled, he coughed into his hand and began to speak, his voice firm, authoritative. 'The Tennessee Flyer was a Boeing B-29 Superfortress. It was piloted by Colonel Charles Bertrand Warner, co-piloted by Captain David Fraser Campbell, aged twenty-nine and twenty-six respectively.

'She took off from the then recently constructed airbase on the island of Tinian, in the Marianas, just after first light on Friday, 3rd August 1945. Initially, her flight was uneventful but, towards the end of her mission, she reported heavy AA fire, mechanical interference and bright lights in the sky and was lost over Japan just before noon the same day. She had been escorted by two other Superfortresses; they reported the lead bird hit on the final approach to Tokyo just after 11.45am Standard Japanese Time...'

'Did they make it back?' asked President Sutton. 'The crews of the escort planes?'

Buchanan nodded. 'Yes, but neither pilot is alive today. Alfred Cutter committed suicide in the 1960's, shot himself, and Jackie Peller was killed in a motor vehicle accident only last year; he was ninety years old. Both co-pilots died in their homes, killed by intruders in their homes, one in 1956, the other in 1988, but several crewmen are still alive. We're contacting them now, but I'm not too hopeful that they'll be able to add anything to their statements of nearly sixty years ago; most of them wouldn't have had sight of the outside world, a patch of sky from a gun turret at best...'

'And the reports at the time?'

'Anti-aircraft fire was surprisingly intense for this late stage of the War,' said Buchanan. 'Both surviving birds were damaged. At the time, neither pilot claimed to have seen the Flyer ditch in the ocean and, three days later, Colonel Tibbitts made it through to Hiroshima. All trace of the 'Flyer was buried.'

'Believe me, I've been there.' Julian Ryde continued. 'With the confusion, near panic of an approach under fire, much of what you'll have got back could be misleading, but the pilots must have been trained to observe, to report back under any circumstances? How many minutes were they from the target?'

Buchanan did not answer, looked at his President before he responded. He coughed. 'Less than two.'

'And it ditched in the water?'

'They thought that it had, Mr Ryde,' said Buchanan. 'The wreckage was never found, it had to be assumed that the plane had gone down in the water, the Sagaminada to the south of Tokyo and the crew had either gone down with her or been killed by civilians when they came ashore.'

'How deep is the water?' persisted Ryde.

Buchanan did not speak.

Sutton turned to him, nodded curtly.

'Not very deep sir,' said Buchanan. 'The guys who wrote the report at the time considered that, well, that the ship could have limped out, ditched in deeper waters...'

'Against her orders?'

Buchanan nodded.

'Please do go on,' said Ryde.

Buchanan looked at the President. Sutton nodded again. 'The payload was one 9,500-pound bomb. Named Big Daddy, it was a small weapon by today's standards. Still, at around 23 to 25 Kilotons, it was a little larger than both Little Boy and Fat Man, which were dropped on Hiroshima and Nagasaki in the following few days.'

In London, Donald Berwick shook his head. He hated deception, had initially been pleased that the Americans had come back so quickly, had not sought to deceive them, but now he was not sure whether his earlier ignorance had not been preferable.

Berwick knew a considerable amount about nuclear weapons, had been in Tokyo only four months earlier on a trade and goodwill visit and the vision of the equivalent of twenty-five thousand tons of TNT exploding in the centre of that city was simply too awful to contemplate. The buildings, offices, museums that he had visited would be destroyed in an instant and tens, possibly hundreds of thousands of people would die. He raised his head, looked at the screen.

'Where exactly, was Big Daddy to be dropped?' Berwick swallowed hard. Tokyo was a vast city. The target could have been the docks, the railway marshalling yards or some other lightly populated district, perhaps a demonstration by the Americans of their new weapon's awesome power. The casualties need not be as horrific as might be anticipated but, as he looked from face to face on the screen, he saw Gerry Buchanan blanch and his heart sank.

'Target One was the Nihombashi district of central Tokyo,' said Buchanan.

The words washed over George Berwick. It could not have been worse. 'Nihombashi?'

'This was intended to be a first and final strike,' said Buchanan. 'It was expected that the damage inflicted would have been so severe, so traumatic, the Japanese capital so badly damaged, that the war would have ended that weekend. The planners thought that they were saving lives, that the Hiroshima and Nagasaki bombs need never be used.'

Buchanan hung his head. He raised it slowly and looked once more at the screen. 'We all know now that the War didn't finish that weekend, the Tokyo bomb didn't fall...'

'Hasn't fallen yet,' said Berwick, his eyes closed. He shook his head. The target selection was natural enough for wartime but now, in addition to the number of important Government buildings located there, the Nihombashi district was the financial heart of Tokyo.

'If the device exploded between Tokyo Central Railway Station and the City Air Terminal then the damage would be horrendous. The Bank of Japan, the Stock Exchange and the Imperial Palace would be within a quarter of a mile of the detonation, they would be virtually destroyed and the wide streets in that area would channel the blast outwards, through the shopping districts and galleries of Ginza, through the University district of Kanda. The city would surely never recover.

To Berwick's left, his voice distant, out of place, Julian Ryde spoke. 'And the pilot's standing orders if he lost radio contact or lost his escort?'

'They were to press on with the attack, sir,' said Buchanan. 'The order to drop had already been given four minutes from the target to save the planes from over-flying the area twice.

'There were secondary targets selected on his anticipated approach route and his orders were to target an earlier site, Yokohama, or the Shimbashi or central Ginza districts of Tokyo, if he felt he could not get through to Target One.'

'So we have a young man,' said Julian Ryde. 'He's thousands of miles from home, no contact with the outside world, has received the order to drop, has standing orders telling him to press on and drop if he loses radio contact or to select a secondary target if he feels threatened or confused?' Ryde raised his eyes. 'Is there anything else that we should know?'

'Nothing good,' said Buchanan. 'Warner had a brother seriously injured on Iwa Jima and another in a PoW camp in Burma. He had reason to hate the Japanese, was nearly rejected for the flight, but they decided that his feelings towards them might be an asset rather than a liability, was thought to be the least likely of the short-listed pilots to back out...'

'So, if we reach him on the radio?' said Ryde.

'He would think it was a Japanese trick and would drop the bomb,' said Buchanan, matter-of-factly.

'And the bomb? Airburst?'

'No.'

'Ground-burst?' said Ryde, his voice rising.

'Yes sir,' said Buchanan. 'This was intended to end the war, there was only a limited knowledge at the time about the profound long-term impact on the target area that a ground-burst weapon would have.'

In London, the Prime Minister and his Home Secretary exchanged a long glance, Berwick flashing through the calculations. Twenty-five thousand tons of TNT, nine thousand five hundred pounds of bomb converted to pure energy in an instant. How many pounds of pressure per square inch would result? What size would the fireball be? What effect would a nuclear pulse have on a modern city, a huge financial centre the size of Tokyo?

Buchanan had already done the calculations. 'This was a standard fission weapon, the same as those used at Hiroshima and Nagasaki, but it was a little larger. It was intended to explode on the ground rather than at 2000 feet, as was the case for the second two drops. Although a ground burst bomb would maximize the radioactive fallout and collateral damage at ground level, it would cause less flash damage as the fireball would not be visible over such a great distance.'

'OK Gerry,' said President Sutton. He rubbed his

eyes. 'What should be expected?'

Buchanan fastened another button on his jacket. 'We have four major effects to consider; the fireball, the blast and its associated winds, the problem of nuclear radiation and the thermo-nuclear pulse.'

'Jesus!' Linda King cursed, laughed harshly. 'Jesus, Jesus, Jesus!'

The sweat beginning to glisten on his forehead, Buchanan glanced at his President; Sutton nodded him on. 'Even in a heavily built-up area, the fireball from this relatively small bomb would incinerate everything within a radius of about two hundred meters and ignite fires over a far wider area. Fortunately, most of these fires would be extinguished by the blast wave that would follow almost instantly...'

'And rubble doesn't burn very well,' said Julian Ryde quietly, almost to himself.

'No, but rubble does burn, Mr. Ryde,' said Buchanan. 'It's just a question of at what temperature.'

The UK Home Secretary nodded his agreement. 'Please go on Mr. Buchanan.'

'As regards the second effect, the blast and the resulting winds would be similar to a conventional bomb but far, far greater, many thousands of times more powerful than the IRA's bombs in Bishopsgate and the Baltic Exchange in London, for example. It's been suggested that they caused more than a billion pound's worth of damage each, but here an area greater than the entire West End of London would be almost completely flattened.

'Many of the buildings in central Tokyo were earthquake proofed. This might reduce damage, but it's still likely that all the buildings within a one-and-a-half-mile radius of the detonation would be destroyed or very severely damaged. Within this area of around seven square miles, very few people out of doors would survive and an untold number of those under cover would also die.

'The subway system would survive the blast relatively intact, even this close to the blast. The crude tunnel shelters at Nagasaki saved thousands of lives and the Nihombashi district of Tokyo has one of the largest concentrations of subway stations of anywhere in the world.

'However, there may be no warning, and the timing of the explosion would have an impact on casualty numbers. Central Tokyo has a weekday daytime population of around 150,000 to 200,000 people per square mile meaning that over a million people could be caught in maximum destruction area during working hours. Worse still, over lunchtime on a weekday, or in the early evening, we would expect up to a quarter of these people to be outside at any one time and they would all become casualties.'

'You said that the Tennessee Flyer got to Tokyo just before lunchtime on a Friday, didn't you?' said Larry Edelman.

'That's correct,' said Buchanan, 'but we have no idea at what time of day or even what time of year it might reappear.'

Buchanan paused. He took out his handkerchief and wiped his forehead, the sweat caught on his eyebrows. 'More than one and a half miles from Ground Zero, blast damage will lessen progressively, but during the daytime, there would be many tens of thousands of injuries caused by flying glass and other objects, thousands of deaths and here, between one and a half and two miles from the blast site, the danger from fire increases again.

'The thermal radiation would still be sufficient to start fires within the direct line of sight of the explosion, but the blast that followed it would not strong enough to put them out. Damaged buildings here would burn more readily that those flattened nearer to Ground Zero. There would be less rubble and more combustible debris.

'The ability of the inhabitants to fight fires at this point would be negligible and would remain so for the first twenty-four or even forty-eight hours after the blast. Calculations suggest that if fires start in only five percent of buildings, then this would spread unhindered and lead to the eventual destruction of thirty to fifty percent of all remaining buildings within the affected area.

'Most of those uninjured in this area should be able to escape into the subway system, but many of those already injured would be caught in the fires.'

Buchanan paused, looked around him before he continued. 'Both gamma and neutron radiation would result from the explosion. Already unpleasant, a ground burst bomb would irradiate much more debris and dust than would an explosion in the air above the target.

'Thousands of tons of dust, vaporized buildings, bodies and vegetable matter would be sucked up into the mushroom cloud and dispersed according to wind direction and here, still air would be least favourable as it would allow the radioactive particles to settle in large concentrations in one area. Strong and variable winds would be most helpful but it's feasible that, if there were no wind whatsoever, central Tokyo would be uninhabitable for many months, perhaps years. A clean-up operation would cost tens of billions of dollars.

'The final effect of a nuclear explosion such as this is the one about which we know least. An EMP, or electromagnetic pulse, caused by the burst of gamma radiation, could cause chaos. It can cause the failure of electrical and electronic systems over a wide area and, in a modern city such as Tokyo, the effects could be catastrophic.

'Thankfully, a ground burst weapon would have less effect in this regard than an air burst one, but in the financial district, we could expect all banking, stock exchange and debt market systems to collapse. We simply do not know what the consequences of this would be.'

Buchanan fumbled for another button. The camera following him, he walked over to the coffee table in the centre of the room, took a sip of water. He seemed unwilling to continue.

'And the projected casualties?'

Buchanan looked at President Sutton, pursed his lips. 'Of course we can't be precise. In Hiroshima, around seventy thousand people died immediately following the blast and the final toll over a thirty-year period has been estimated as high as 200,000.

'In Nagasaki, the casualties were somewhat lower due to the geography of the target area but casualties in Tokyo would be several times greater. If the explosion occurred during working hours, the figure would have to run into the hundreds of thousands.

'The sheer numbers of injured would cause a particularly distressing problem. There are not enough beds in Japan to cope with the victims of this one relatively small bomb and there aren't enough acute burns beds in the whole of the world to deal with the badly burnt.

'In any case, transport would be so badly disrupted

that the locals would effectively be on their own in the short term. It would be intolerable to watch the injured die on prime-time television, but logistically there might be no way that we could help them. They would have to endure the unendurable.'

Buchanan paused then continued. 'Food stocks would run out, the dead would go unburied, and disease would spread. Elsewhere, radioactive dust would be settling according to the prevailing winds; Chernobyl would look like little more than a dirty bonfire...'

'Thank you, Mr Buchanan,' said Prime Minister Berwick in London, his face grey, exhaustion etched onto every line of his drawn features. 'There are other effects as well, of course. As you have pointed out, in addition to the human casualties, billions of dollars of damage would be caused, and the clean-up operation would cost countless billions more. The contamination would force hundreds of thousands, more likely millions of people out of their homes. The Japanese government would need to repatriate money to pay for the rebuilding with profound knock-on effects for the world's financial systems.

'Japanese consumption would fall causing demand problems for some industries world-wide, interest rates would rise to stem the flow of capital into Japan, and we could end up facing a recession greater than anything any of us have ever known. This would not be just a Japanese tragedy.'

President Sutton rose to his feet in Washington. 'Horrific, I think we can agree, but does any of this provide us with a clue as to motive? Do we have a Japanese target and a Japanese perpetrator? If so, what's the UK angle?'

'As you said,' said Gerry Buchanan, 'we're by no

means sure of either target or perpetrator yet, far less the motive or the means...'

Sutton caught Gerry Buchanan's eye and nodded. The CIA man fastened the last button on his jacket, darkened patches of sweat still visible below the collar of his shirt. 'Run us through the angles, Gerry.'

'If the bomb is in the possession of extremists,' said Buchanan, 'then we may feel drawn to conclude that they wish to use it either to cause an explosion, or to threaten to cause one, the distinction being that between mass murder versus extortion.'

President Sutton glanced at Linda King and continued. 'I know it's awful but we're dealing with realities here. Extortion's clearly to be preferred, but we, or the Japanese authorities, should have received some communication of some sort and we've had nothing.'

'Maybe we're ahead of them,' said Larry Edelman. 'Maybe they didn't think there was any point talking as we wouldn't believe them?'

'We can hope that that's true, Larry, but we've no evidence to suggest that we're ahead of anything.' President Sutton turned back to his CIA Director. 'Demands, Gerry? What would you expect?'

Buchanan shifted. 'They could be financial, political, or any combination of the two, but we've had nothing...'

'From which you would conclude?' said Donald Berwick in London.

Gerry Buchanan did not answer immediately; he raised his hand to his jacket. The buttons fastened, he glanced towards his President. 'Two possibilities, maybe more,' he said, his words once again clipped. 'One; that the perpetrator was confident, first that we would believe that his threat was credible and second, his aims were such that he was confident of achieving them without having to spell out exactly what they were. Holding up a threatening hand to a noisy child, for example, the threat is unspoken, but both parties know what is expected.'

'Is that one or two, Gerry?' said Sutton. 'One, sir.'

'And the second?'

'The second possibility is that the intention of these people is that the bomb should explode, probably without warning, explanation or contact of any sort.' Buchanan paused. That was the worst of it and he'd got it out. He seemed to relax a little. 'In this case, we would be dealing with a madman, a man with whom negotiation was impossible. But even here, there would likely be a purpose, something that we could use against him.'

'What about timing, motive?'

President Sutton looked at Edelman, said nothing. His National Security Adviser was right. He looked back at Gerry Buchanan, nodded.

Buchanan looked pained. 'Speculating on the motives of madmen can be...'

'Tell us what you think, Gerry.'

Buchanan stared at Larry Edelman. 'The motive could be a desire for revenge against Japanese society, a cry of anguish, or an attempt to place the blame elsewhere, American imperialism for example, or onto another sovereign body, even a rival terrorist organization.

'Alternatively, it could be for some warped financial reason, to destroy the Japanese banking system, free the world of debt or cover up a robbery or a real-estate scam. We really can't know.

'Or the goal may be political, a desire to change society, explode the bomb, create and nurture the chaotic environment in which the government could be changed. We already have the makings of a financial melt-down in Tokyo and the streets are getting ugly.'

'So where does this leave us?' Julian Ryde broke the silence. 'Can we negotiate, buy time?'

'How?'

President exhaled slowly, turned to Gerry Buchanan. 'And what do we tell the Japanese?'

'I don't know at this stage, sir.' Buchanan looked around the room, uncomfortable in the open. 'Perhaps we would be well advised to say nothing for the moment. Everything that we do know is speculation, deduction at best and can we really tell them that a US warplane is going to drop a nuclear weapon on their capital at some time in the future, but we don't know when? What possible response would they have, and would they believe us? Would they abandon Tokyo, one of the richest areas of real estate in the world, on our word?'

'Or do they know already?' said Julian Ryde quietly.

All eyes on him, he shrugged. 'Just a thought.'

'There was some talk of covert Japanese Government backing for the Aum Shinrikyo at the time of the Tokyo gas attacks,' said Gerry Buchanan. 'It was investigated but never proven, put down to internet conspiracy theorists at the time.'

'But Gerry?'

Buchanan looked from the screen to his President, frowned slightly. 'But we can't ignore completely the possibility that some members of the Japanese Government might be sympathetic to the goals, if not the means of what we've been discussing.'

The President nodded. His eyes focused on the far distance. 'I think we tell Tokyo, George. The scientists as well.'

****

It was a little before 3pm when Caroline Whittleton received her first telephone call from the Prime Minister. Until only hours earlier, she would have thought it bizarre, ridiculous, unbelievable that she would be speaking to the head of Her Majesty's Government but now, her life turned upside down, her family at risk it seemed natural, somehow normal. She and Professor Jobber had taken the call on the speakerphone, had listened in silence to the news. Caroline's world had been shaken again. Tokyo! Jeremy was there, her husband, the father of her children, of her unborn child!

Professor Jobber seemed unmoved, and Caroline looked at him. From what she remembered, he was wearing the same clothes as yesterday. If he hadn't slept in them then it certainly looked as though he had and he knew nothing of her personal circumstances, seemed almost happy at the news. He nodded. 'It had to be something like this, I suppose,' he said. He pulled his tie down another inch, strained against it as though it was trying to choke him. 'A sort of Grand Slam and it was hardly likely to be an experiment for the good of mankind. I don't see that it influences anything; we must still prevent them from functioning, their target doesn't change that.'

Still Caroline said nothing, her unfocused eyes on the workbench before her. Jobber sniffed, was about to turn away when she spoke. 'You may be right Clayton, but can't you feel it? The weight, the weight of the thousands, possibly hundreds of thousands of lives that may depend on us?'

Professor Jobber rubbed his chin slowly and shook his head; he hesitated, he seemed confused, unable to focus on the question. 'No.'

Caroline looked away; she did not want Jobber to see her eyes, to judge her. Should she ring Jeremy, tell him of her fears? Would they stop her? Maybe she should tell him about the baby, say that one of the girls was ill, that he was needed in England? He loved them, of that Caroline was certain, but he might see through her and, even if he did return early, she had no idea how long she would have to try to keep him away from Japan; Tokyo was a part of his job and it might be safer now, before these people had perfected their techniques, than it would ever be again.

She turned back to Jobber, he was regarding her oddly and she felt that she should speak. 'You're right, we can only do our best...'

'Including Klutz, we have the best brains in the world here,' said Jobber without embarrassment. 'We could...'

'The best brains but one,' said Caroline quietly and shuddered. The futility of their situation was pressing in on her once again; she must be tired. Maybe it was the suicide, but she needed to sleep. 'And he's still out there.'

Jobber nodded, paused before he spoke. 'We need to destroy, not to build, to criticize, not create. That's always easier and we're a little closer than we were.'

Caroline smiled at the words of enthusiasm and looked at her watch. Her head span, she was exhausted, but at least the girls were safe, had not seen the terrible death earlier.

The screen saver on Caroline's computer clicked in. Bubbles floated aimlessly across the screen and Caroline moved the mouse absently. The screen cleared and her work, feeble, incomplete, once more stared out at her and Caroline closed her eyes. Gravity was a curvature of space-time but so what? Could time be harnessed? She didn't know. Might rotating cylinders offer the best prospect of manipulating time? Possibly. Would electromagnetic fields slow it down? Again, it was possible; but what did they really know? So little.

****

Jobber and Caroline worked on through the afternoon, checking and rechecking their data, reaching for the inspiration that would propel them forward, but Caroline could sense it, they were trying too hard. She rubbed her eyes, looked out of the window. It was dark and she was tired, more tired than she had ever been. To carry on now could be counterproductive.

It was 11.55pm and she rose unsteadily to her feet, slipped off her lab coat and put on her Barbour. Jobber grunted and, dreamlike, Caroline left the laboratory and found herself opening the door of the courtesy house. She nodded to the Special Branch agent, a new face, younger, very professional, and entered the building.

Caroline took off her coat and put her mobile telephone beside the kettle on the kitchen work surface and her fears bubbled back. Tokyo! She turned the telephone on; she had missed another call. She scrolled through her saved numbers but, before she could locate Jeremy's mobile, the telephone rang. She fumbled the buttons, answered it. 'Caroline Whittleton.'

'Hello, darling,' said Jeremy, his tone guarded.
'Jeremy!'

'Expecting anyone else?'

'No of course not,' Caroline said; there was so much that she wanted to say, but Jeremy sounded all right. 'I've just turned the phone back on, I haven't had time to ring you. How are you?'

'Fine thanks,' said Jeremy slowly. 'Yourself, and the girls?'

'OK, the girls are fine. They've gone to my mother's for a few days. I'm rather busy here, it seemed like a good opportunity for them to see a bit more of each other, but she won't be able to take them for too long.'

'I'm making some decent progress here,' said Jeremy.

'Things aren't as bad as they look on the news but, I don't want to hang around, I might get back a little early.'

Caroline tried to judge his tone, what should she say? Use her mother, perhaps say that they needed help, needed him in England? 'It would be nice to have you back,' she began. She tried to keep her voice level. She could push it further, invent an accident, maybe the car, not the girls, she would have mentioned that immediately. 'The girls are worried, they...'

'It's not too bad,' said Jeremy a little too quickly. 'There's been a bit of damage around the place, but, well...'

Caroline hesitated. 'Please come home Jeremy, we need you here.'

'I can't Caroline,' said Jeremy, again too quickly and she felt her heart sink, felt that they were both dancing around what they really wanted to say and there was still an edge, possibly even fear in Jeremy's voice. He paused and, when he continued, his voice was steadier. 'It was only ever going to be for ten days. I might be able to make it five or six. How long is that?'

It could be forever, thought Caroline. She said nothing.

Monday 29, October 1999
Sixteen

Colonel Charles Bertrand Warner turned to Davie Campbell and smiled. He had checked off the crew, they were ready. He gunned the B-29's four huge 18-cylinder Wright Cyclone engines, nodded towards the runway before him. 'We'll be in the air in a minute, Davie. It's a bullshit-free zone up there and we can get on with it, post the package.'

Exhilarated, genuinely pleased to be leaving the briefing room, the airbase, the ground crew and the oppressive sticky heat behind, Warner was with his family. When they were airborne, they were closer than family, they were everything and he was glad that he had been chosen for this job.

He had been careful, had worn the mask, disguised the depth of his hatred but now the world would long remember his name, would remember how Charles Bertrand Warner flew his B-29, The Tennessee Flyer to Tokyo and ushered in the nuclear age. This day, the 3rd of August 1945 would be the most important day of the century, would change the course of history.

Warner grinned, looked at Campbell. He looked as relaxed as ever and Warner reached across, ruffled the younger man's hair. He'd never seen Davie flap, had never seen him lose it, they had lost engines, taken shrapnel over the Home Islands earlier in the year but he was a rock.

That had been only four months ago but so much must have changed, not least on the ground. Since late March, months of attention from the USAF would have seen to that. Curtis Le May's B-29s had begun to hit Tokyo only late last year, attacking it first from Szechwan in China and later from the Marianas. It had been a while coming but they had finally taken the war to Japan, made them pay.

He knew the statistics by heart. Prior to March 1945, they had dropped only 7,000 tons of bombs on the Japanese Home Islands, peanuts compared to the 1.4 million tons dropped on the Reich, but the raids on Japan since then had been amongst the heaviest of the war, the wooden buildings had gone up like tinder, had burned and they were going to burn some more.

They were dropping 40,000 tons a month now, the target for year-end 110,000. By the fall of '46, they would have dropped more on Japan than they had on the Germans, and didn't they deserve it but it would never happen.

Warner knew that the war had less than twenty-four hours to run. It was quite a pity.

Nodding to himself, his eyes on the middle distance, Warner patted the joystick of the aircraft as the memory of his visit to the Boeing aircraft manufacturing plant in Wichita, Kansas the previous May ran through his mind.

It had been a marvel! Acres, hundreds of acres of plant

devoted to building these fantastic birds and he had been allowed to choose his own, had named it, had been treated as a celebrity for the day and the guy who had showed him around had given him advice on which one to choose. He had pointed him towards a plane that had been built by a team in peak form. 'It's not a Friday aircraft, son,' he had said, his tone conspiratorial.

'I wouldn't like a Friday 'plane, or a Monday 'plane for that matter, but don't tell the Brass that I told you so.'

Warner had known the score. A Friday aircraft could be built on any day of the week but was one completed by a gang keen to go on leave, possibly more willing to cut corners, take risks whereas a Monday 'plane was one finished by a gang that had just come back from leave. They might be rusty, and no pilot wanted to take the risk but his was a mid-week 'plane, a 'plane built by the best gang on site and they were proud of it; they had a right to be.

To Warner, the 'plane was one of the marvels of the war, a huge, 100-foot-long wonder of engineering that was his to use for the day; it was quite the second most impressive thing that he had ever seen.

****

Aged twenty-two, twenty-three next week and in the job for four years, Police Constable Gary Marshall breathed deep. He had four minutes to live.

Still proud in his uniform, the young policeman straightened his back, thrust out his chin and sniffed the autumnal air once more. Unperturbed by the bizarre nature of his job that morning, he reached up to his shoulder for his radio. 'Marshall here, I'm outside Tangen Industries, Brinefleet Science Park.'

His location report acknowledged, PC Marshall raised his hand to his chin, rubbed it, squinted at the trees stretching out in a line before him on the neatly landscaped science park. Sure, this was a poor relation to the huge Trinity site further to the north, but, as his scowl deepened, Marshall could not help finding it impressive, nonetheless.

Marshall pursed his lips, his brow knotted. They weren't fir trees. He was no expert, but that much was obvious; they had lost their leaves. Smooth-barked, they weren't horse chestnut or oak, so possibly beech and that fitted the bill.

The policeman crouched down, his knees cracking in protest, looked at the seeds on the ground, small, nut-like and encased in slightly furry husks. He stood up, rubbed his chin again and noted the two mechanical diggers positioned at the edge of the courtyard, mounds of dark brown, almost black earth piled by the sides of the road. That fitted as well. He reached once more for his radio.

Further information conveyed, PC Marshall turned off his radio a wiser man. Although he now knew that it manufactured many consumer products with which he was very familiar, FabraTech and SonaTech electronic goods and PluraPharm pharmaceuticals, he had never before heard of Tangen Industries and he was suitably impressed; it was an industrial giant.

He moved to the side of the building, more mounds of mud and he noticed the frost, still white on the grass where it was in still shadow. Walking silently, he was approaching the two large bins by what looked like the rear entrance to the facility when two men emerged silently from the bushes to the side of the courtyard.

As they walked towards him, the policeman drew his last breath.

****

In the Downing Street Cabinet Room, Donald Berwick took a deep breath, pushed the papers in front of him slowly to one side and closed his eyes. It was 11.00am and, even after the shocks of yesterday, his body had taken the decision from his hands, had protected him from himself, shut him down, forced sleep upon him and he was grateful. Berwick could not remember being helped to his bed. He had slept like a dead man and had been woken at 3am.

Briefed now on what little progress the scientists had made, he felt markedly better for the rest, had even had the chance to shower, shave, brush his teeth and grab a change of clothes, but he felt an inner tension.

He opened his eyes and looked at Julian Ryde, the older man looked remarkably well. Certainly, he had managed to snatch some sleep during the night, maybe he was a little jaundiced, but in all other respects the Home Secretary looked as though he had spent an hour or so dressing for a military parade. Berwick tried to smile but succeeded only in twisting his lips.

There was a knock at the door to the Prime Minister's private office, the door opened and Susan Burnell, the Foreign Secretary, entered the room. She was wearing no makeup, Berwick knew that she had not slept, but she did not look tired, and he felt suddenly very old. He nodded towards a seat and closed his eyes once more.

Donald Berwick had been in no doubt that it was right to share what knowledge they had with the Japanese authorities and the Government of Prime Minister Hiro Tanaka had been informed of the fears of both the British and American authorities late the previous evening. There was no going back but, in Berwick's opinion, there had never been a choice, there must be positive benefits to be gained from working together and, with some 55,000 Japanese nationals working in England, some useful pressure might be brought to bear.

There more than fifty Japanese or Korean industrial or research sites in the Cambridge area alone, all of which would need to be discretely investigated, and the Japanese authorities could now be asked direct questions about people or organizations that they may otherwise have refused to answer. Indeed, should there be a breakthrough in identifying the dead Japanese man, swift action might have to be taken against Japanese citizens or property in the UK, in which case Tokyo's compliance would be helpful.

Berwick rubbed his eyes then opened them. He shared President Sutton's surprise; the reaction of the Japanese Government had not been what he had expected. The first contacts had been with Prime Minister Tanaka's civil servants in Tokyo as the PM himself was out of the country. The Americans were assured that he would be immediately informed of the threat and would return to Tokyo, but there had been something else, the civil servants, more than usually inscrutable, had appeared resigned, almost unsurprised. The Prime Minister raised his eyes, looked from Susan Burnell to Julian Ryde.

The Home Secretary seemed to read Berwick's mind. 'Do you think they already knew?'

Berwick glanced at Burnell, the Foreign Secretary's face non-committal. 'The turbulence in the Japanese markets, the attacks on foreigners? It's possible but how?'

Julian Ryde shook his head. 'I don't know. The incidents, those that we know about, that is, have all occurred in Europe. Cambridge has been the focal point, but the idea is compelling.'

The Home Secretary paused, he seemed unwilling to continue, and Donald Berwick raised his eyebrows. 'Go on, Julian.'

'If Tanaka's Government were aware of the threat, then the knowledge would have been confined to a small number of people. The problem then, is how could this knowledge influence the behaviour of the Japanese financial markets, the crowds on the streets in Tokyo?'

The Prime Minister shrugged at Ryde. 'Your opinion?'

'The Sword of Damocles had an interesting effect in Sicily, you're familiar with the story? It was put down to the imagination of Cicero, just a fable but quite apt.' The Home Secretary smiled, and, for a moment, the spark was back. 'Damocles was a noble at the court of Dionysius, a Greek King in Sicily who reigned in the fourth century BC. He was a tyrant, a brute who ruled through fear, but he was not stupid, he knew when he was being flattered.

'Damocles laid it on thick until one day, the King offered to trade places with him for twenty-four hours. Damocles leapt at the chance, but it was only then, seated on the royal throne, that he realized that a huge sword was suspended from the ceiling by a single horsehair directly above his head.'

Berwick frowned questioningly; he was tired.

'Don't you see?' said Ryde. 'The King had hung it there to bring home to Damocles just how precarious was his position, of just how tenuous was his hold on happiness, on life itself and some say that he left it there, that he wanted to be reminded of his mortality every day thereafter. Many historians attribute his extreme brutality and nationalism to that threat, a threat of which only he was aware.'

The Prime Minister's frown deepened. He looked down at the papers before him. Japan was changing, but still he could not believe that the Government had known of the threat that they may be facing. If it had, then surely there would have been some attempt to move assets and people, maybe even the Government itself, out of the capital? Now, it may be too late, nothing could be done too quickly for fear of antagonizing whoever it was that was threatening them.

'Maybe no demands actually have to be made,' reflected Ryde quietly. 'The hand raised to a noisy child, remember? The threat need never be spelled out, need never be recognized by more than a small group of people.'

The Prime Minister nodded. The telephone rang and he answered it immediately. 'Send him in right away.'

Seconds later, the door opened and Alistair MacDonald, the head of the Special Branch, walked briskly into the room.

'Go ahead, Alistair,' said Donald Berwick. 'What do we know?'

'It may be nothing, sir, but at the moment it's all we have.'

'Give us the facts, Alistair.'

'Yes, of course,' said MacDonald. 'As we know, the dead Japanese man was carrying no means of identification, but we're getting a bit more through from the forensic examination, his clothes and shoes have given the investigators a bit more to go on. The soles of his shoes were relatively clean, so we can conclude that he walked for some distance on paved rather than muddy ground. However, deep within the patterns of the soles, the forensic examiners have found traces of both brick dust and sterile topsoil.'

'Both quite common, surely?' said Susan Burnell.

'True, but brick dust is dispersed quickly by the wind or rain so to find traces of it in the tread of a pair of shoes suggests that the wearer was very close to the building work itself.

'This is educated guesswork, obviously, but the sterile soil suggests recent landscaping using soil that hasn't had time to pick up the usual natural debris: seeds, earthworms, insect eggs, animal droppings and other detritus. It could help us to focus our search.'

Prime Minister Berwick frowned. 'Anything else?'

'Forensics have also found fragments of beechnuts in the soles of the man's shoes along with silver birch and dandelion seeds. The latter two types of seeds are light, primary colonizers of virgin soil and could be blown in from anywhere, but the beechnuts might be helpful. These are quite heavy and tend to accumulate underneath the trees that they've fallen from, they could be present at the site we're looking for.'

'Couldn't they have been picked up from somewhere else?' asked Donald Berwick.

'Yes, that's possible but unlikely,' said MacDonald. He straightened his tie, nodded to himself. 'The nuts were found deeper in the tread than the mud and the brick dust, they'd clearly been walked some distance and had been crushed meaning that they must have fallen onto a pavement or a road. If they had fallen onto softer ground, then our man would have merely squashed them into the earth.'

'Working on the assumption that the Japanese link is more than just a co-incidence, we've had police officers discretely visiting the premises of Far Eastern companies, Japanese, Korean, Taiwanese, in the Cambridge area for a couple of hours now. We've passed this information on to them, and they've been asked to note the premises' proximity to building works, particularly those involving landscaping...'

'And you've got them gazing the trees?' said Julian Ryde.

'I know it's a long shot, sir,' said McDonald. 'It might be nothing but, at the moment, it's all that we've got.'

Berwick nodded and turned to Ryde, smiled grimly.

'Cross-referencing the co-ordinates that you gave us from the energy pulses has only indicated a general area,' said MacDonald, breaking the silence. 'We're going to need some time.'

****

By twelve noon, Alistair MacDonald was gravely concerned. He had received a series of briefings on the progress of the Cambridgeshire constabulary's investigations, but they had lost contact with one of their officers. He knocked gently on the Cabinet Room door and entered the room.

Donald Berwick looked at the head of Special Branch, nodded towards a chair. 'Anything new on your missing Constable?'

MacDonald nodded. 'Marshall was last reported in the grounds of one of Tangen Industries sites to the south-west of the city centre. We've got more people there now but haven't approached the company.'

'Tangen?' said Berwick, his voice sharp. 'Julian, get what details you can on its UK operations, particularly the names and résumés of its directors, photographs as well if possible and plans of the company's buildings, lists of its products etc and any other information that you think might be of use.'

Ryde nodded, rose to leave the room.

'And Julian?' said the Prime Minister. 'Bring forward the time of the videoconference from 2pm to 12.30pm would you and check the readiness of the SAS to move at short notice. Ask the Americans if they have troops available, failing that an observer.'

'Of course,' said Ryde with a smile. 'I've spoken to Hereford within the last half an hour, they moved troops into Cambridge late last night and only need twenty minutes notice. The Americans will have troops ready within two hours but, failing that, they'd like to include an observer. They've put forward our friend, Carter Lockyer. He's cooling his heels on one of the US airbases fifteen miles from Cambridge right now.'

The Prime Minister turned his head slightly and grimaced. Ryde put great faith in the SAS and so, in truth, did he, but they worried him; they were frightening men, and they were meant to be. They were the people to whom one turned, the people who did the jobs that nobody else wanted to do or was able to do. 'Move the troops to the site would you please, tell them to stand by. Let them know that they will probably have one or more American observers with them and make sure that there are sufficient armed police in the area to back them up; they'll have to take their orders direct from the military.'

Ryde left the Cabinet Room, but was back within minutes followed by Peter Whinney, the Director General of MI5. 'They'll be ready by 1pm, sooner if necessary.'

'Good,' said Berwick. 'And the Americans?'

'Lockyer can get there before 12.30pm.'

'Troops?'

'Ninety minutes.'

Berwick checked his watch. He would brief the Americans more fully, but ninety minutes was too long. If the young policeman had not been found by the time the SAS and the police were ready, then the Tangen facility would be stormed; Carter Lockyer could go along for the ride. Nodding, Berwick turned towards his Home Secretary. 'So Julian, what do we know about Tangen?'

'It's still chaired by Benny Natsumo,' began Ryde. He shuffled the notes before him. 'Eighty-two years old, he's one of the architects of modern Japan, a larger-than-life character, but now effectively a recluse, he founded the company in 1945.

'Like a number of large Japanese combines, Tangen has interests in a huge range of businesses from the heavier civil engineering businesses such as motorway construction and shipbuilding, it built some of the largest tankers in the world in the 1970's and part of the Tokyo subway system, through to banking and insurance businesses, light engineering, pharmaceutical operations and consumer electronics businesses all over the world; Europe, north America, the Far East and some mining businesses in South Africa, Nigeria, New Guinea and Siberia. The company's three UK sites are in Cambridge, Slough and Sunderland.'

'Perfectly straight?'

'We thought so, MI5 has nothing on them,' said Ryde.

He nodded to Peter Whinney. 'Peter?'

'We have files on one or two individuals now working at their companies in the UK,' said the MI5 chief. 'But Japan has never been classified as a high-risk' country and we have nothing serious. Tangen itself always looked clean.'

'We've got people at the other two sites?'

'Yes.'

'And MI6?' said Donald Berwick, turning to his Foreign Secretary.

'We have very little on them in Japan, Donald,' said Susan Burnell, glancing down at the papers provided to her by Robert Smith, the UK's overseas spymaster. 'Japan's a friendly country after all and, for both political and practical reasons, our own operations in Japan are extremely limited.

'MI6 has always believed that the risk of damaging blowback from burnt jobs makes the risk of having a major presence there unacceptable. Regarding Tangen itself, the Koancho or the PSIA, the Japanese Public Security Investigation Agency, have given us some background, but they have never had any concerns about Tangen, had always believed that what little risk it did pose would come from its non-commercial operations; and these were previously purely domestic...'

'Non-commercial?'

'Yes,' said Burnell. 'In addition to its commercial operations the company is a massive sponsor of the traditional arts in Japan and numbers of world class museums, several with a martial theme. The company has the most comprehensive collection of sixteenth and seventeenth century Japanese art in the world. It has Japan's largest private collection of militaria. And the biggest space exploration museum outside the US. These were all thought to be risk-free, but it also has a series of 'meditation centres' throughout the country.

'These are recent additions, apparently, Benny Natsumo appears to have become much more religious in recent years, he had a serious health scare earlier last year and nearly died as the result of an unidentified infection. The hospitals couldn't help him, and he relied heavily on some alternative remedies. He's taken on some private guru...'

The Prime Minister sucked in his breath and Burnell paused. Berwick looked at Ryde. 'Get in touch with Ambassador Hirohata Julian? Prime Minister Tanaka should be back in Tokyo, Hirohata must have spoken with him, and we need to be brought up to speed.'

Berwick ran his tongue along the inside of his lips; how would Hirohata react? The Japanese Ambassador had been in Newcastle, a courtesy visit to several of his country's business interests in that region, but now he was back in London and both Berwick and Ryde knew him well. He had served with the Koancho, his country's intelligence service, had been closely involved in the operations directed against the AUM almost a decade earlier and had paid a heavy price; the car bomb that had grievously injured him had robbed him of his wife and two of his children.

Politically, the Ambassador had always argued that the interests of his country and those of the West were interminably linked and Berwick had never had any reason to doubt his sincerity. Unfashionable though his views may have become, he had remained outspoken, could have been recalled to Tokyo at any moment, his career over.

Good-natured, he spoke perfect, strangely accented English and Berwick liked him; he was a principled man. 'Carry on Susan.'

'As I said, Benny Natsumo took on a private guru, we haven't got a name yet...'

'Could the tail be wagging the dog?' asked the Prime Minister rhetorically, interrupting his Foreign Secretary once more. Burnell did not reply.

****

In Tokyo, it was almost 9.30pm. Initially pleased with the work that he had cleared during the morning, the Japanese markets had slipped badly in the afternoon and Jeremy Whittleton had become seriously concerned. He was the Global Head of Research, trading losses were not his direct concern, but he knew that the bank had had a disastrous day; they could be in trouble, but still the questions from the Embassy had continued.

'What did the gentleman say to you?'

'Did he seem tired?'

'Depressed?'

'Did he say where he had come from, what he would like you to do?'

Jeremy was perplexed; he felt that he should be flattered that they were taking such an interest in him, but whatever had happened, and Jeremy himself was becoming less sure of the facts, it had never been a crime. Yet it was being investigated as though it was, and he was beginning to feel more like a suspect than a victim.

The first man from the Embassy had wasted a large part of Jeremy's morning and a second official, a rather brutal looking Scotsman, had forced his way into the office shortly after lunch. Jeremy had run through yesterday's events for what seemed like the hundredth time but still, the official had refused to leave, talking instead to Jeremy's colleagues.

Drew had been right. Out on the streets, things were getting a bit sticky and, though Stretton's building itself had escaped damage, several of those nearby bore the scars of recent violence. Boarded up windows on their lower floors, like blackened eyes or missing teeth. Roving groups of journalists, the occasional knots of policemen and the street cleaners sweeping glass from sidewalks further contributed to the general feeling of unease.

Yet the latest riots had not even made the news, in the UK they would have slipped further, would have been prioritised according to the level of breaking stories from elsewhere in the world, put far behind the investigation into the events in the north of England.

Jeremy shivered. He would not be sorry to leave. It was late and he had done what he could for the day, but the last of the secretaries had left more than an hour earlier and he wasn't sure how to order a cab. Still, staying at his desk all night was not an option. He pushed back his chair, flicked off his computer, grabbed his jacket and took the elevator down to the ground floor. Hesitating briefly in the deserted entrance lobby before leaving the building, the thought flashing through his mind as the door closed behind him that, without his security pass, he would not be able to re- enter the building.

Something crunching on the sidewalk beneath his feet, Jeremy looked down; broken glass, scattered unevenly, glinted in the reflected light of the office blocks around him. It had not been there that morning. The street cleaners had recently passed, and Jeremy felt a stab of concern. He looked around him.

People on the street, couples even, relatively calm, unhurried, but a long queue snaked from a taxi sign some sixty yards ahead of him and he wanted to keep moving. It was a fine evening, tranquil, he could walk a couple of blocks. There would be more people, plenty of cabs.

Jeremy walked on for perhaps ten minutes, flicking his head periodically behind him before he began to relax. Edgy, he had not panicked and, as he looked around him, the faces that stared back at him drawn but unthreatening, his confidence began to return. The riots had been mostly financially motivated, he was out of the danger are and he shook his head, chided himself for his earlier concern but then he heard it for the first time. Breaking glass.

Stopping in his tracks, Jeremy turned, searched the faces of those around him. They had heard it, turned away, avoided him, a Gaijin and then he heard it again, coming from the financial district, breaking glass, shouting.

Jeremy turned in the direction of his hotel, quickened his pace, but the pavements were filling and then he heard another, different noise; a carnival, a celebration of some sort, chants and he felt the anxiety well in his stomach; he walked on, briskly, pushed, used his weight to make some headway but his progress quickly slowed.

The sounds were coming closer.

Turning his head a little too quickly, his eyes wide, staring, Jeremy could smell his own fear. He resented it, tried to drive it away, those around him must smell it too, but suddenly he didn't care, it overwhelmed him, flushed reason from his mind, he needed to get away. He struggled but could not move then sirens, a demonstration, a riot.

The weight of the people around him made further progress impossible. Jeremy struggled momentarily then, aware of his height, he tried to shrink, to force himself into a smaller and smaller space but he could not and the sounds were louder, closer.

He looked up.

He had been forced to a halt outside the Prime Minister's official residence, the noise had risen in intensity, threatened to overwhelm him and then he saw it, a screaming mob rounding the corner less than 100 yards behind him.

Sweating now, Jeremy could move neither forwards nor back; the crush was pinning him, he could scarcely raise his arms from his sides, and he felt another surge of panic, stronger than anything that he had ever known, it coursed through his body, threatened to loosen his bowels. He tried to control his breathing, forced himself to think of crowded trains, a football stadium, anything to convince himself that this was nothing out of the ordinary, but the screaming and chanting was getting closer, and he opened his eyes.

The vanguard of the placard-waving mob was now in the road, some fifty yards to Jeremy's right weaving between the grid locked cars. The banners were written in Japanese, but Jeremy could see the Arabic numerals, it was about money, about the collapsing markets and his breathing steadied; it was not racial, how bad could it be?

Some of the cars were sounding their horns, but most had turned their engines off and, the demonstrators pushing their way between them, their drivers averted their eyes, but Jeremy could not look away. He breathed deep and, the police sirens getting no closer, the crowd impenetrable, he wished the moment passed.

Jeremy had never been to a yoga class, had never meditated, but he tried to let it wash over him. Like a trip to the dentist, it would soon be over, but then the pitch of the shouting changed, became intense, furious and he looked up; a man was standing by the side of a stationery car.

He was a westerner, the car British, a large Rover and then Jeremy recognised him, the Scotsman from the British Embassy, looking directly at him. His eyes pleading, the man mouthed something, but his words were lost to the crowd.

Gaijin! Gaijin! GAIJIN!

Spittle flying from lips, faces contorted in rage, the mob now upon him but still Jeremy could not look away.

GAIJIN!

GAIJIN!

Jeremy knew very little Japanese, but he knew that word, gaijin, foreigner, outsider, usually a harmless statement of fact it could also be used differently, could be screamed as an insult, hurled as a weapon, had been used in the past to excuse the inexcusable and, as the crowd surged around the British Embassy car, Jeremy feared for the man in the car, feared for himself, for all who were different.

The Embassy man, half in the car, half out, tried to close the car door, slam it hard, but he was too late, much too late. The door struck one of the demonstrators, but did not catch and, as the man opened the door again, it was wrenched from his hand and the kicks and blows began.

Jeremy's mouth fell open; he could do nothing, not even move as the blows against the bodywork of the Embassy car echoed, metallic, from the buildings around him. Placards slapped noisily against the roof, but somehow, against all logic, the Embassy official had regained his grip on the door and it thumped shut.

Momentary silence, a roar of rage and several of the younger demonstrators began to rock the car violently, followed by the sound of breaking glass above the frantic screaming as the hands reached inside the vehicle.

Gaijin!

Gaijin!

A determined, steady chant and all of Jeremy's attention was focused on the scene before him, the sound of sirens fading into the far distance, another life. He could see limbs flying inside the car, something being pulled first this way and then that and then, as if by a conscious act of will, the suited figure was dragged from the vehicle and fell to the floor.

Gaijin!

Gaijin!

GAIJIN!

There were no journalists, no policemen, they had melted into the crowd, joined the screaming mob and were thrusting towards the cowering, blood-covered bundle.

Pedestrians, packed tight against him, began to join the chorus from the sidewalk as Jeremy caught sight of the Scotsman's fearful face, caught the doomed man's eye, saw the flicker of recognition before the official managed to cover himself once more against the blows, but the mob was relentless, was beating him, crushing the life from him.

Jeremy tried to move, he began to feel faint, he closed his eyes, and his head began to swim. He could hear the screaming and the cursing, the cars' horns, even the distant sirens once more and they filled his world, rang in his ears, had taken over his being.

The flashing neon lights of the shops and bars burned through his eyelids, forced him to open his eyes, Jeremy was helpless, and he knew it, his body was floating, it was beyond his will. He felt sure that he had left this place, that, when he opened his eyes, he would be elsewhere, but he was not. He was still pinned, helpless by the throng, fighting to draw breath, but he felt a little less afraid and he looked at the Embassy man, tried to lend him strength as a hush descended upon the crowd.

Heads turned.

Jeremy tried to turn, to twist around but then, as the crowd melted away to his right, he felt suddenly alone, vulnerable. He felt a drop of sweat run, cold, down his back and tried to hide himself, to burrow back into the crowd, to become a part of it, but again, as though he were the carrier of a dread disease, people shrank from him, melted away as a man in a white robe swept past.

The figure halted, his back to Jeremy and slowly turned. Eyes cold and hard, it was the man from the bar, the man who had spoken to Jeremy in the street. Jeremy felt no surprise, it seemed somehow right and there was a spark of recognition from the man, almost a smile as he turned away, walked into the road, the crowd parting silently to let him pass.

His world spinning, Jeremy wanted time to pass, but it would not; it was slowing, crawling as if through treacle and he raised his head. The Japanese man was in the road, standing in front of the Embassy car, the bloody Gaijin moving his head feebly from side to side, his body sprawled across the bonnet of the vehicle, arms and legs pinned by the crowd around him.

Jeremy shook his head, could not comprehend what was happening, felt numb, this was unreal. The sound had died away, the crowd was hushed, and he could hear the fabric of the Embassy man's clothing rubbing against the car, his feet scrabbling weakly for a purchase on the metal of the bonnet. Jeremy tried to look away, but he was too slow, he caught the Embassy man's eye, read the confused, fearful message that the man knew he was about to die.

Jeremy struggled to comprehend as the white-clad Japanese man smiled, reached to his waist. His knuckles whitened against the black of a handle and, in one smooth action, he pulled a large sword from its scabbard.

Jeremy could take no more; he began to shut down.

Shock would protect him from the worst of it, spare him from what he was about to see as, without hesitating for a second, his movements fluid, the Japanese man raised the sword above his head, held it for an instant, then brought it slicing down, every ounce of his weight behind it.

Turning his head, shutting his eyes with an effort, Jeremy heard no scream, no metallic clang of blade against bonnet, just an intake of breath from the crowd, a hush and then the bump, bump, bump of something rolling, uneven, across a metal surface followed by sharper crack as, hard and heavy like a coconut, the object fell to the floor.

Nothing and then, Jeremy's eyes still tightly closed, it began again
    Gaijin!
    Gaijin!
    GAIJIN!

GAIJIN!

The hate-filled chant echoed from the buildings, carried easily to the Ginza shops, its art galleries and boutiques, was ignored by their clientele, their stylish liberalism in the eyes of some an unspoken insult to Japan, but Jeremy, his heart pounding hard in his chest, was deaf to all but the rush of his own blood in his ears.

Rooted to the spot, his arteries, his veins must surely burst but Jeremy, his eyes still tightly closed, could not move. He was too tall, stood out, was fatally different. What was left of his life permanently changed, he rounded his shoulders, willed himself into the ground, shrink into himself, into nothing.

Seventeen

The wait had been a little tiresome, but the take-off, when it came, had been uneventful. Now Davie had the ship and Colonel Warner shifted in his seat, stretched his legs, felt the bones in his feet crack, as he pressed down hard on the floor of the cockpit, methodically worked his muscles and headed off the threatening cramp. Unbroken blue before him, he smiled. July 16th. It had been quite something, had changed his life forever!

The Trinity Site, had it really been less than three weeks ago? Warner had been privileged to be there, he knew that. The Brass had broken with protocol, he had got the invitation, had spent two days there, had seen it all.

It had been a beautiful, cloudless, New Mexico day when he had arrived at the McDonald ranch house on the Alamogordo

Bombing and Gunnery Range late in the afternoon of the fourteenth of last month. Little more than an abandoned shack, Warner had nodded and smiled to please his hosts as they had showed it to him, but his mind had already been on other things.

Sure, they had assembled it there in that very building, they had machines, grey boxes, brown boxes, they said that they could still detect traces of the bomb, but when all was said and done, it was just a windblown farmhouse and, to the extent that he had noticed it at all, he had been disappointed.

It had gotten dark quickly in the desert, earlier than he had expected and the day had been over almost before the visit had begun. Still, the morning had promised much, much more and he had found it difficult to sleep.

On the fifteenth he had met Jumbo, and things had become rapidly more interesting. A huge tank, as big as a large railway coach and forged from specially strengthened steel and shaped like a gigantic water bottle, was meant to contain the explosion, to stop the chemicals being spread around the desert, but it had not been used and Warner was grateful for that, had wanted to see what the bomb could really do, was pleased when he had heard that they were going to do it in the open.

It had been another beautiful day, hot and dry.

Again, Warner had spent hours nodding and smiling as various processes had been explained to him. He had understood little of it, but he had been impressed, had been swept up in the achievement of these strange men and it brought it home to him; this was their war now. The Germans were out of it, the Brits had been sidelined, the Russians exhausted, leaving them, the Americans, to run the show. Now, they, and their eggheads, would deal with the Japanese on their own terms. There had been more brass on the site than a fourth of July parade and he had looked around, had begun to concentrate on the people rather than the science and had sensed a growing anticipation laced with fear, the fear that this would not work. Heads would have rolled if the thing had failed but, as it was, the scientists need not have worried; the device had worked to perfection.

As he had been told earlier, it had been assembled on site, at the McDonald ranch house, had been thought too dangerous to transport otherwise, and now Warner had one of his own, was risking the lives of his crew with the Tennessee Flyer's every jolt and turn.

Warner had not seen the Alamogordo bomb in the flesh; none of the visitors had, they had had to rely on photographs showing how it had been hauled to the top of a spindly looking tower where it had sat, godlike, snared by wires and shielded by a purpose built canopy from the blazing sun and, he remembered, he had felt a flash of worry, had shared the scientists' concerns; would it work?

But it had worked!

The following morning, Warner had risen at 2.30am.

There had been a violent thunderstorm overnight and again he had scarcely slept, but everything had gone smoothly, according to plan. The journey to Compania Hill had passed in silence, the bunker itself impressively safe. Warner had noted the thickness of the concrete, his curiosity had driven him on, but the test had been postponed! Warner had been disappointed, simply had to see it for himself, but then it had been back on, delayed only until 5.30am.

They had been nearly twenty miles from Ground Zero. Even after the countdown had started, Warner had still had his doubts and, at twenty miles distant, had worried that there might be nothing to see.

By half past five, Warner had feared that it might be a

dud, had felt a fool, had been about to ask permission to remove his darkened glasses when the bomb had exploded.

Like a gigantic magnesium flare throwing jagged shadows against the walls of the shelter it had hung on the horizon for an age, surely a minute but in reality nearer to two seconds, before it had begun to fade, orange and red.

Still, it had filled the horizon like nothing that he had ever seen before, had changed the colour of the few clouds visible against its brilliance and had competed with the rising sun itself and it had been then that Warner had felt the force, the immense, mind-bending power, the heat against his cheek. Even at that distance it had been like opening an oven door on a cold morning, and he had looked on in amazement, his eyes, protected by his glasses, screwed almost shut against the glare as the shock wave hit the shelter, wore itself out against its concrete walls and he had imagined his aircraft, the Tennessee Flyer, being shaken like a toy by this force about which he knew so little.

He had flinched, had closed his eyes, and could only imagine the forces nearer to the blast. Would they smash his plane? Crush her like an eggshell? Or would he be thrown from his seat to dash out his brains against her side, his belt, digging hard into his thighs and shoulders but unable to restrain him?

Magnificent. The clapping, the cheering in the bunker, Warner had been swept up in the emotion of the moment, had almost cried. It had been all and more than he had ever imagined, had ever hoped for yet how much more powerful, how much more impressive would it be when he saw it for real, when he, Charles Warner, unleashed its ferocious, indiscriminate power upon the crawling masses of the Japanese capital beneath him?

The memories still vivid, Warner checked the clear sky

before him, nodded slowly; he had truly watched history being made. Before him, a massive cloud of dust and debris had been pulled up into the air, piled, layer upon layer, built in seconds into a monstrous column, thousands and thousands of feet high, a living tower of ash that had continued to grow silently, the forces within it defying gravity until it stood, quivering, a cauldron of boiling dust, the outer edges moving no higher, the inside spilling outwards, cascading, peeling downwards like the skin of a banana.

Yet now, Warner was sure, it had not been a banana; it had been more of a mushroom.

****

In the centre of Cambridge, it was lunchtime and the market below Great Saint Mary's church was in full swing. Housewives, swaddled against the easterly wind, were buying fruit and vegetables and office workers and students and other academics were picking over the second-hand books and bric-a-brac. The freshmen, not a month into the University, had begun to find their feet and were sifting through the junk, searching for the used tweed jackets and flannel trousers sported so persuasively by second and third year students and the beggars were out in force.

No one flinched when the fireworks began to crackle from the direction of Queens College and, although the occasional dull boom did turn heads, few people gave it a second thought.

When Major Young, the senior SAS man on site, had received the final order to proceed from his Regiment's Colonel in Chief, Colonel Sir Ian Dunne, he had been relieved. Special Branch had briefed them on the Tangen facility well but maintaining the readiness of his men was both tiring and dangerous. When the Branch had finally handed the situation over, Young had instinctively known what to do.

By the standards of the Regiment, this was a big job.

Ten four-man teams were to take part and, before his orders had come through, the tall officer had paced up and down the large trailer for almost forty minutes. He had known that his men, still checking and re-checking their weapons, were in danger of losing it, had begun to suspect a stand-down when, at last, it had been made clear; the civilian authorities were to cede the situation to the military. Young and his men were to occupy the building as rapidly as possible using whatever force was necessary.

There had been a final briefing, and it had been made clear; this was not a drill. The Brass were worried, weapons of mass destruction had been mentioned, and, at the first sign of armed resistance, all measures were to be taken to prevent the operation of machinery, computers or handheld devices of any sort and Young had understood fully; it was a license to kill.

More than that, it had been an order to kill. Young and his men were to assume that all occupants were potential saboteurs, and that the facility was booby-trapped. Standard operating procedure but, after the first signs of armed resistance, it was unlikely that any prisoners would be taken, it was simply too dangerous.

Alive, even fatally wounded, they could detonate hidden bombs or use concealed weapons of some sort. Once again, in the heat of an engagement, he and his men would be treading a fine line; do their job well and their reward would be to slip back unnoticed into anonymity but do it badly? Then they could be left to twist in the wind, forced to answer to the criminal justice system, the tea and sherry brigade and the full weight of the law would be brought to bear against them. They would be pilloried, blamed for their failure, decried as the unthinking martial arm of an overbearing State.

The risk of compromise had rendered a full reconnaissance of the facility impossible. No covert listening devices had been planted, they had no idea as to where the x-rays were located, nor even their numbers, so Young and his men had had no choice, had fallen back on their training, had hit everything hard and fast and, initially, it had gone well.

Three individuals, challenged in the grounds, had drawn weapons; they had been shot. A police radio, found on one of the bodies had appeared to explain the disappearance of the policeman, meant that entry had to be immediate.

Windows had already been identified on two sides of the building through which an entry could be gained. Pre-prepared shaped charges had been attached to them and they were quickly blown, the glass, window frames and a significant amount of brickwork crumpling and falling inwards as the sound of the explosions echoed around the grounds, followed quickly by the sharper, less significant cracks of the 'flash-bangs', non-fatal concussion grenades, the momentary brilliance of their explosions casting jagged shadows around the darkened, smoke filled rooms.

The building had seemed to shake and, as the last of the debris tumbled from the windows, a dense, steady stream of black smoke began to billow out. Something was burning and Young's men went in. Immediately, the crackle of automatic gunfire broke the silence.

Young looked around him; inside now, something about this was not right. The first rooms had been too easy to clear, a few double taps, one guy screaming and blazing with an automatic, but the inner walls seemed to be hardened; they were facing a building within a building, some sort of core, with no external walls, no obvious entry points.

Young recognized they risked losing momentum.

'No-Legs, where's the plastic?'

'Twelve, maybe ten seconds...'

'Soonest,' said Young, his respirator now on, the equipment made more cumbersome by the thermal imaging gear hanging around his neck, attached but not yet in position. He forced himself to smile, turned to Carter Lockyer. 'Not cricket I'm afraid; just stick close.'

The Major turned away, frowned. He disliked having to carry passengers, but this one, American, an ugly character, a fighter, scrapes all over his face, seemed to know what he was doing, had handled his M16 well. He'd taken out a couple of x-rays, one an easy-conscience kill, the second a classic one-on-one and the American had head-jobbed him in an instant; he knew what he was doing.

Nine seconds.

Young breathed hard as shadows danced on the wall and a short man, a non-standard-issue AK47 strapped across his shoulders, bundled past, his arms laden with ordnance, wires and detonator cords trailing. Major Young said nothing, left him to his work. His men knew their jobs and, as No-Legs slumped by the inside wall of the building, he tore the caps from several aluminium tubes. He wedged two of them deeper into the bundle that he was carrying and, in one long, continuing movement, he placed the ordnance on the floor and rose partially to his feet, scuttled towards the Major and Carter Lockyer.

'Out! Out! OUT!'

Major Young turned, his vision impeded by his respirator, slapped Carter Lockyer on the shoulder, half dragged him from the room which erupted an instant later, seared their heels, dust, furniture and rubble flying out of the door, smashing into the furthermost wall of the room in which Young and the others had scrambled for shelter.

'Don't you guys ever knock?' said Lockyer. He was covered head to foot with a fine dust.

'No need, I think they heard us,' said Young, his ears ringing from the blast. He pulled himself to his feet and clambered over the broken furniture back into the badly damaged room. The reinforced wall against which the explosives had been placed was no longer there but heavy steel bars, bent and twisted by the blast, still blocked their progress.

The concrete wall was reinforced; this was bad. The Major fell to the ground, pulled his radio from his belt as another booming explosion from the opposite side of the building shook the ground. 'Heavy cutting gear needed, rooms three and six.'

'Have that,' said the voice in his respirator.

Flashes, the sound of small arms, and Young rolled to one side as the men behind him clambered for position, began to pour suppressing fire into the gloom and swirling dust of the interior of the building. 'Reinforced inner walls, believe movement in inner building.'

'Have that; wait one.'

Young opened his mouth to aid his hearing above

the sound of his own breathing and the gunfire around him. He could still see movement in the inner building. The radio spluttered: 'Cutting gear thirty seconds, vital neutralize x-rays soonest, repeat neutralize x-rays soonest.'

'Have that!' Young did not hesitate; he knew his men had heard the order. He rose to his feet, pulled his Heckler & Koch MP5 to his shoulder. 'Slot them all.

Have two entry points, mind the copper...'

There was less movement in the dusty interior of the facility now, but soon Young had a shape; it moved, and the Major smoothly lined up his weapon, felt his stomach flutter; the x-ray was wearing a gas mask. Young tracked his mark, squeezed the trigger of the MP5 and the shape jerked backwards. Clear the room, pan to the right, another shape, squeeze, mark down, move on.

From his side, Young could hear the sharp cracks of individual shots, a burst from Lockyer's M16, but still flashes in the dusty interior and incoming. Young squeezed the trigger of the MP5 again; another shape fell, its arm outstretched, and a small object traced a path across the dust, clattered to the floor. 'Grenade!'

Young reacted instinctively, fell to the ground, pulled Lockyer with him as the sharp crack of a grenade rang out.

From his right. 'Gas, gas, gas!'

A plop and a fizz, tear gas going in.

His respirator stifling, fast filling with sweat, Young raised his head as more canisters traced into the inner room, sensed someone behind him. No-Legs. The cutting gear had arrived, the machine sparked into life, chewed at the metal of the bars, but still there was hostile fire and one of the engineers stumbled to the ground, clutched his stomach, protected by his body armour, but still hurt.

Another took his place, and the barrage of automatic fire continued to pour into the interior of the building. The incoming fire was lessening, a bar crashed to the ground; then another and Young grabbed roughly at one of the engineers, pulled him backwards, jumped over him and into the building's interior blinded, despite his mask, by the dust and debris.

'Night-sights!'

'NIGHT-SIGHTS!'

Young pulled the thermal imaging sights around to the front of his mask and his world turned green. The flashes were a risk, but his men knew better than to blind each other. He held his breath, could still see very little, but sensed men following him, muzzle flashes confirming their presence and then the air began to clear.

The second breach was directly opposite, the crouching shapes entering the interior occasionally visible through the swirling gas and dust, white and orange flashes flying before them, years of training in the close quarter combat house in Hereford put to the test and Young was firing his weapon himself.

Now little seemed to be moving and gradually a silence descended on the inner room. The Major could see the warm shapes on the floor, dead x-rays, a much lighter green through his thermal sights, pools of liquid around them, dead he was sure, but no chances could be taken.

The bodies jerked occasionally as bullets went in. Then one moved; it rolled over; it had a gun. Instinctively, Young raised his MP5, but he was too slow, saw the pistol line up on him and he knew it well, would recognize it anywhere, it was a Browning and he knew that he was dead, was more certain of it than anything in his life but then he felt the hand in his back, the shove that saved his life, and the gun flashed. Young felt the bullet tear the air by his face, but did not hear the sound, drowned by Lockyer's M16 as the shape on the floor jerked and died.

Young flushed, turned to Carter Lockyer, nodded, held up his hand.

In the inner room of the facility, the dust continued to swirl, caught by the weak sunlight streaming in from the two gaping breaches in its walls. It glittered yellow and green in the deathly quiet and Young opened his mouth again, held his breath, strained to listen and looked around him. There was no movement. He relaxed fractionally.

He and his men were in a very large, high-ceilinged room, about a hundred feet long, perhaps eighty wide, rows of work-benches, banks of computer equipment and other machinery, much of it now smouldering after the intensity of the assault. The floor was thick with bodies, far more than could be accounted for by the firefight and no wounded. Young glanced at Lockyer.

'Suicide?' Lockyer was speaking for the benefit of those monitoring their conversations outside the building. 'Sixty? Eighty?'

Young nodded. 'Looks like.'

None of the interior of the building looked anything like the plans that the Major had received earlier. Doubtless, the Cambridge City Council had done their best, but the inner room had not been marked at all and there was no upper story as the plans had suggested. The room that he was in was as tall as the building was itself, there was nothing above them, but there could be a lower floor.

Young indicated the ground with his finger and his men began to search amongst the debris for any exit out of the large room, down to a lower level.

'Door!'

Young raised his head sharply, picked out the man pointing to the ground and spoke into his radio. 'We have a door to a lower level.' He crossed to the man, looked at the door, well concealed, flush to the surface; no handle, it appeared to be of solid metal.

'Have that, please wait,' crackled the voice in Young's earpiece; then. 'Secure access immediately. Standing orders remain.'

Young looked around him, he could read his men, knew that they had heard the message; they began to move about their tasks, but he was worried; the whole operation was taking too long.

'No-Legs? NO-LEGS?'

The squat soldier had already left the inner room, he returned seconds later, his arms once again laden with bundles and wires, three of the engineers hard on his heels dragging a pneumatic drill, its extended air hose attached to a compressor outside the building.

Young nodded, looked at his watch. No-Legs and the sappers busied themselves and he reached for his radio again. 'Inner room clear, still no access underground.'

'Understood. Prisoners?'

The deafening hammering of the pneumatic drill filled the room. 'NEGATIVE.'

No-Legs, bouncing and shaking like a toy, refusing to let go, quickly brought the drill under control, battered holes around the trapdoor into which the two engineers squeezed what looked like thick, grey, dough, attached wires and, abruptly, the noise stopped; the squat man dropped the drill, held up his hand, spread his fingers and thumb twice.

Ten seconds.

Young raised his arm, circled his hand. 'Everybody out.'

The squat man already bolted, barrelled from the room, men streamed through the holes into the outer building and Young turned. Slapped the last man hard on the back. 'OUT, OUT!'

Hands reached through the hole, dragged Young through and he crashed to the floor, scrambled to the side and away from the expected line of the explosion as a flash lit up the room around him, a blast filled his ears.

The building shook. Newly settled dust rose from the floor, chunks of plaster crashed from the walls, tiles from the ceiling onto the crouching soldiers.

No-Legs opened his eyes slowly, grinned and blinked back the dust. 'That's the hatch gone, then!'

'Get in there!' shouted Young, rising to his feet. He pushed his way back through into the inner room, slotting a fresh magazine into his HK MP5 as he did so. Walking briskly, dark shapes pushing past him, he pulled out the fifteen shot Sig-Sauer pistol that he preferred for close work to the Browning.

'Who the fuck put that there?' No-Legs was on the floor, he scrambled to his feet, fell again and tore at his trousers, freed his leg from the sheared off metal bar that had caught him, and Young turned away, certain that he was not seriously hurt.

A curtain of dust and smoke, much thicker than before had reduced visibility in the inner room to a couple of feet but the thermal sights lent them much better vision; nothing seemed to be on fire, but Young ducked his head sharply.

An automatic reaction beyond his control, then the 'zip, zip, zeep' of bullets and he ducked again. 'INCOMING!'

The green dust around him flashed as his men opened fire. Something brushed Young's cheek, scorched it, then a second bullet tore through the loose clothing beneath his arm, and he cursed. Still, he could see nothing, then a shadow traced across the cloud of dust, and then another and another as the concussion grenades flew through the air into the gaping hole where the door had been and down into the lower level.

'Grenade!'

'GRENADE!'

The muzzle flashes around him intensified. Young was firing his weapon himself, the hail of bullets viciously whipping up the dust on the floor near the hatch, dissuading attempts to throw back any of the bombs, but still an arm appeared, a dark round object clutched in the hand, and the bullets from a dozen guns tore it to shreds. The object fell back and the floor beneath the soldier's feet lurched violently one, two, three times.

'Gas!'

'Get in there!'

More objects, hissing and fizzing, men following them underground, weapons momentarily silent. Major Young was towards the front, but No-Legs was past him again, below ground now, scuttling forward when he appeared to take a bullet or a splinter in his thigh. He grunted, twisted to his side by the force of the impact and fell heavily against Carter Lockyer.

Young jumped over the prostrate body. He squeezed off a couple of shots from the Sig, put No-Legs out of his mind. The bullets that they were putting down must surely destroy everything before them, but from the flashes elsewhere in the large room, he knew that he and his men were not alone. They began to fan out in the dusty gloom and the firing became more sporadic.

'Clear here, Major!'

'Clear here!'

The dust in the room was beginning to settle but the visibility was still poor, and Major Young felt his stomach begin to knot.

'Clear here!'

'Clear here!'

Young breathed slowly, weighed the situation. 'Benjy, Five Brains, get No-Legs out of here!' Behind him, movement but Young did not turn. 'Mr Lockyer, are you OK?'

'Having a ball, I'm to your left,' said Lockyer. He seemed to lose his balance, tried to move his foot and looked down and Young followed his eyes, the pool of liquid around the American's left foot highlighted bright against a dark floor by his night-sights. The front of the Lockyer's boot had gone, mashed up toes visible through an ooze of blood. The American tried to smile. 'Not a no-shots-fired incident?'

'God forbid,' said Young. He looked away, gestured to someone out of Lockyer's line of sight. 'Get this man out of here.'

Hands grabbed at the wounded American, pulled him rapidly backwards. More hands looped under his thighs, formed a seat, raised the bumping feet from the floor and Lockyer was gone and Young turned back to the interior of the room. It was clear, but he could feel his worry continue to build.

The bunker echoed to the laboured breathing of his men, but that was all. There was no groaning, no tell-tale coughing from a stunned enemy confused in the clouds of teargas and still the single cracks from his men's handguns broke the silence. Maybe it was over?

'Major Young-San?'

The Major started, he spun towards the voice, levelled his MP5 one handed, the Sig now held in his left.

Active ops, shoot first, questions later, but he had no target. Fresh blisters of sweat prickled on his back. 'Make yourself known!'

'Yours is a noble death, Major Young.'

Young fired a four-shot burst from his MP5. He had seen a white clad shape, but nothing fell to the ground. 'Identify yourself!' Young raised his left arm, the Sig still in his hand and circled it in the air, motioned his men back towards the door to the upper floor.

'The disgusting excesses, Major. The bribery, the corruption, filth endemic throughout, they all die,' said the voice, everywhere and nowhere. 'What is a solution for one becomes a solution for all...'

A shape became momentarily distinct, and Young was aware of a smile. White overalls, orange material of some sort at the neck and Young brought down the Sig, shot it, twice in the head, twice in the body, but it was gone, no corpse fell to the ground and his mind began to race. Worry threatened to overwhelm him, but he pushed it from his mind; he could only do what he could do, but something was wrong, very wrong.

'He just disappeared!' said a voice to Young's side, and the Major knew what to do.

'Get out!'

A shimmer of white and the figure was there. 'Goodbye Major.'

'Out, out, OUT!'

The figure was gone; Young turned for the shattered stairs and his world slowed, a blur of green shapes, dust and smoke, but once again, his men were ahead of him, were pouring up into the main fortified inner room, but he knew that it was too late, far too late and, when the explosion came, it was almost a relief, an instant and it was over.

The blast shattered the already weakened building. The walls shuddered; crows rose, complaining into the bitter blue sky as the explosion built, grew with a dreadful intensity, rumbled through the large inner room, the smaller outer rooms and lifted the entire structure into the air.

It appeared to hang, graceful, feet from the ground then reversed the direction of its movement crashed to earth with a tremendous force, began to crumple in on itself before the blast of the shock wave caught the weakened outer walls, smashed them, blasted masonry, furniture and glass in every direction.

Eighty yards from the blast, Carter Lockyer raised his head, watched, unable to move as the debris and rubbish tumbled towards him and then the blast was upon him.

His hair almost torn from his head, he was flying, spinning across the grass, the streetlights and beech trees around him bent, snapping where they would not give and then the blackness. Roof tiles, debris and human remains rained around him for almost a minute and then there was silence.

Eighteen

The Tennessee Flyer cut through the endless blue and Warner thought back to the explosion, tried to imagine its power, but still he found it difficult to comprehend. It had turned the sand to glass, and he smiled, spoke without turning his head. 'We'll finish it, Davie. We'll finish it today!'

The two young pilots had been silent with their thoughts for some minutes, but Warner meant it; this was their war now, new, like nothing ever seen but Campbell did not answer.

The radio crackled. 'Colonel Warner?'

Warner reached forward, flicked on the radio. 'Warner here.'

'Weather report, Colonel. Cloud cover less than two tenths at all alts,' said the male voice. Warner and Campbell exchanged glances. Both men knew what was coming next. 'Advice, bomb primary.'

'Repeat?' said Warner calmly, he looked at Davie Campbell. Both men had heard the report perfectly well.

'Weather over target clear at all altitudes. Advice bomb primary.'

'Message received and understood,' said Warner. He flicked off the radio, turned to Davie Campbell and nodded. Those were their final instructions, they should expect to hear no more. They had received the official order to test the results of the Manhattan Project in the field. Warner spoke into the intercom. 'Johnson, Bonetti? Big Daddy all set?'

'Armed and ready!'

It was Frankie Bonetti's voice and Warner could picture him, toying nervously with his rosary beads. 'Roger that! ETA, eleven minutes. Let's do it!"

Warner looked at the brilliant blue summer sky; it was a beautiful day. He reached over, smiled, patted Davie on the shoulder and settled down for the ride of his life.

****

Jeremy Whittleton was lying on his hotel bed fully clothed. It was almost midnight, and he was sweating, could not control his trembling and he felt sick. His eyes were closed, but he could not banish the images from his mind.

Earlier, the crowd by the Prime Minister's residence had thinned after the killing and Jeremy had not been threatened. Shunned, it was as though nothing had happened and maybe, he had hoped, it had not?

Jeremy had left the scene in a dream. He could have imagined it, a nightmare brought on by lack of sleep, by stress. He had slipped away, headed back into Akasaka, had stood for almost an hour in the first taxi queue that he had found, but there had been no further problems, no whispered 'Gaijin', and, by the time that he climbed into the new Toyota, his world was a different place.

Back in his room in the Hotel Seiyo Ginza, Jeremy wanted to go home, wanted to see Caroline, hold the girls again, but he could not. He knew that he should ring the British Embassy. It had not been a dream, one of their men had died, the card that the man had given him only that afternoon was still in his pocket, but surely the driver had survived, must have reported the murder?

Jeremy screwed his eyes more tightly; he wanted so badly for it to have been a dream, to be his subconscious cruelly torturing him, all a hideous creation of his mind. He had laid on his bed, not switched on the television, had clung to his ignorance like a drowning man, but now, as he opened his eyes, slowly looked down, he shuddered. The flecks of blood on his trousers, his shirt must have been powerfully sprayed, arterial blood pumped by a redundant heart, brown now in the warm room.

This was real.

****

In Downing Street, a grave Prime Minister Donald Berwick put down the telephone. It was 3pm and Colonel Sir Ian Dunne of the SAS had been briefing the Cabinet Room regularly by phone on the storming of the Tangen Facility in Cambridge. Now, Berwick was seated with Julian Ryde, Susan Burnell and Peter Whinney, the Director General of MI5, and his colleagues, were waiting for him to speak.

Berwick looked around the room, his eyes settling on the desk in front of him, on his hands, on his fingernails.

They were clean, but too long. He hadn't had time to cut them, but it would have taken how long, a minute? He raised his eyes, looked at Julian Ryde. 'The facility has been destroyed by an explosion.'

Silence.

'The troops?' said Ryde. 'And the police officers?'

'A single blast, apparently,' said Berwick. 'Not one of ours, but they had begun an evacuation, the wounded had been brought out earlier...'

'Survivors?' The Prime Minister said nothing, and Ryde cringed. 'And what about the site?'

Berwick looked at the telephone. 'The facility's been completely levelled, but there's no sign of a fire. The brigade's foaming down the site, something about a flammable jelly, it looks as though it might have been meant to go up in flames, but it's OK, not enough oxygen under the rubble.

'Forensics want to preserve the site, but there could be more survivors. Jones is trying to keep the Press off the scene.' Berwick paused and turned to the MI5 Director General. 'Peter, get me the President would you please.'

'Good result, Donald?' said President Sutton on the secure line from Washington a few moments later.

'We lost a lot of men,' said Berwick. 'It's too early to be sure, everything will be moved from the site, the examination of the contents has only just begun. Your people will obviously have access to the investigation, if they can physically take part, then so much the better, but we want to keep the material on one, or at most two sites for the sake of security.

'Until we know just what was in there, we don't know whether this is over or not and even then, we won't know if there is a mirror site somewhere else or whether the know-how to build another facility has survived.'

'You sound like a lawyer, Donald,' said President Sutton and Berwick smiled; Sutton was a lawyer himself. 'We've got forensic guys at our airbases less than half an hour from Cambridge, we'd like them to be involved.'

'No problem.'

Sutton paused. 'Nothing's fallen on Tokyo; I guess that's a good sign?'

'That's true,' said Berwick. 'But we think that they knew we were coming. There were signs of a mass suicide. Maybe they simply weren't ready.

'We're transcribing the conversations between the troops via their radios and the early signs are that the officer leading the assault saw the man who detonated the device.'

President Sutton nodded. 'What do the scientists have to say?'

'They don't want to be drawn, but they seem to be disappointed, seem to believe that the facility has been destroyed.'

'They can be as disappointed as they like,' said Sutton. 'Just so long as they're right. So, what now?'

'Let our investigators tell us what was in the building and take it from there,' said Berwick. 'And pray that this was the one and only site.'

'We'll be with you Donald. I'm sorry about your man in Tokyo.'

'You're well informed, George,' said Berwick. 'A nasty incident. We hear that Dr Whittleton's husband was involved again, but she doesn't know, and we'll keep it that way for the moment. I hear you've lost two.'

President Sutton nodded, the line to Washington

died, and Prime Minister Berwick turned to the documents before him; several copies of the transcripts of the conversations between the members of the SAS team that had stormed the Tangen Industries site had arrived. He read them silently then raised his head, looked directly at Julian Ryde.

The Home Secretary had finished reading his own copy, turned down the corners of his mouth. 'The disappearing man?'

Berwick turned to Peter Whinney. 'Peter, I believe that you have a theory?'

'It may have been Dr Yoshi Kasaga,' said Peter Whinney. 'He's a director of Tangen, quite recently on the scene, has been a personal adviser to Benny Natsumo's for a year and a half now. He's some sort of guru.'

'He's been in Britain. How come we're just finding this out?' said Julian Ryde.

'We had no reason to believe Kasaga was in the UK,' said Whinney firmly. 'He's just one of several non-executive directors of a company that we've never considered a problem.'

'OK, Peter,' said Prime Minister Berwick, his tone conciliatory. 'Then could you just tell us why you're looking at him now?'

'We've had intelligence from the Koancho, the Public Security Investigation Agency in Tokyo, in the last hour,' said Whinney. He coughed, glanced at Julian Ryde. 'Hirohata's been leaning on them to share more information with us. Apparently, this man Kasaga's become involved in the overseas operations of Tangen only relatively recently. The Koancho believe that he left Japan six weeks ago, initially visited the US. They put someone on him, followed him to New York, but they lost him, unfortunately. They also lost one of their men, but they now believe that Kasaga may have travelled on from the States to the UK where he...'

The Director General of MI5 stopped in mid-sentence as Prime Minister Berwick answered the ringing telephone on the desk before him. 'Yes, give us a few moments.'

'Ambassador Hirohata?' asked Susan Burnell.

The Prime Minister nodded, frowned and looked back at Burnell. 'Get some rest Susan.'

'Donald, I'm OK.'

'You let me be the judge of that, Susan. We need everyone on peak form, and you'll be fully briefed, I promise. Just get a couple of hours.'

Burnell pursed her lips, nodded. She rose and left the room.

'We think that Kasaga might be the effective force behind Tangen,' said Whinney, returning to the Prime Minister's earlier question. 'The Japanese are saying that, although he was only a non-executive director of the company itself, he was increasingly influential.

'We're examining Brinefleet Security's CCTV footage; we believe that he was there, but there's no news on a body to match his description.'

'Is this man dead or not?' said Ryde. Whinney remained silent and the Home Secretary raised an eyebrow.

There was a knock at the door; Berwick did not authorize entry to the room, but still the DG of MI5 said nothing. He rubbed his upper lip then slowly shook his head. 'We don't know, sir. If he's behind these events, then it's possible that he was, well, moved, may even have moved himself.'

Ryde glanced at the Prime Minister, nodded. 'In which case, he would return to the same spot. Dr Whittleton has always said that the location at which disappeared objects reappeared would be unchanged. Although we could not know when.'

'The hell with that,' said Berwick. He rose from his seat. 'It maybe that we can't influence the timing, but we can seal the site, watch it day and night, forever, if necessary, then we could catch him...'

'We can't watch it forever, Donald...'

'Then brick it up!'

'But the scenes of crimes people, forensics?'

'Let them finish, but make it quick, build the whole site over. Let the man re-materialize, or whatever the hell he does, inside a block of concrete.' The Prime Minister stared hard at the desk before him before continuing. 'In the meantime, make our people aware that he could come back on the same spot, at any moment, that he might even be there now!

'Tell them that any man of oriental appearance in the area is to be apprehended, shot if there's any resistance, he's a danger to thousands of people.'

Ryde nodded. 'The Japanese Government is sending some of their scientists over, we'll keep them away from the site and see to it that everyone there looks distinctive, wears bright clothing of the same colour, purple or orange. That way if Kasaga turns up unannounced, he should at least stand out, draw attention to himself.'

Prime Minister Berwick nodded, and Ryde gestured towards the door with his chin. Peter Whinney rose and left the room, and the Home Secretary turned back to Berwick.

'I'm sorry to say that the body of Constable Marshall

has been found. It appears that he was dead before the building was stormed.'

'So, we were expected?'

Ryde did not reply. He had had more time than Donald Berwick to digest the news, weigh the implications and the Prime Minister's face clouded as he drew his own conclusion, that the site had been stripped. 'There has to be another facility.'

Ryde nodded.

Berwick took a deep breath and pressed the button on his desk. The inner of the double-doors to the private office opened and Ambassador Michio Hirohata was ushered in; he was limping noticeably.

Despite his prosthetic leg, the Ambassador usually walked with the spring of a much younger man, but today he was walking with the aid of a stick and, as he forced a smile, his normally friendly eyes bleary and red, the scar tissue on his face caught the light.

'Good afternoon, Michio,' said the Prime Minister rising to his feet. He shook the Ambassador's hand, the grafted skin cool to the touch. 'Thank you for coming.'

'It's an honour, Prime Minister,' answered Hirohata, his two years as a post-graduate student in Liverpool some twenty-five years earlier immediately noticeable.

'Make it Donald, please,' said Berwick. He liked Hirohata, had considered that the two men were relaxed in each other's company, firmly on first name terms, but it was only to be expected, the Ambassador would revert to formality at times.

'Donald, I'm so sorry,' said Hirohata. He twisted his mouth, tried to smile again, but the grafted skin around his mouth made it difficult, the action seeming to pull his eyes wider apart. 'These Japanese nationals, they are bringing shame on our country.'

'All of that can wait, Michio,' said Berwick, dismissing the Ambassador's apology with a wave of his hand, his eyes not leaving the Japanese man's face. He had always found Hirohata difficult to read, had not known him before the car bomb and the surgery had taken away what little emotion had ever showed itself from his face. The Ambassador gave nothing away, glanced briefly at the floor and Berwick inched forward imperceptibly in his seat. 'What do we know about Yoshi Kasaga?'

'I have spoken to Tokyo several times today,' said the Japanese Ambassador, his speech a little stilted. 'I now have much more information than I did this morning. Kasaga is thirty-nine years old. He has no formal education past sixteen. He...'

'We were told he was a doctor,' interrupted Julian Ryde.

Ambassador Hirohata raised an eyebrow. 'Self-taught,' he said. 'He has a directorate in the history of religion. For a time, he was a Shinto monk, but it didn't work out for him, and he became involved with mainstream politics. His lack of education closed some doors, and he became more extreme, was jailed for the possession of explosives.

'It was thought that he had planned to attack an abortion clinic. He spent eighteen months in jail and, when he was released, he joined the Aum Shinrikyo, the group that attacked the Tokyo subway system in 1995. We believe that he was expelled, his views too extreme but, whatever happened, he left the Aum on bad terms.'

Berwick felt his face begin to flush, fought for control. Had Hirohata misled them? The Ambassador had been active in the suppression of the Aum himself, had infiltrated the organization. Surely he would have known Kasaga. At least known of him.

Berwick watched as the Ambassador raised a hand to the scar tissue on his own face then raised his eyes and looked at Berwick, his fingers edging up towards the deeper, pitted scar by his left eye and he continued. 'Kasaga picked up a serious facial injury and his eyes were damaged. He appears to have borne a grudge and there is some speculation that he was the source of the information that led to the rapid rolling up of the Aum after the Tokyo subway incidents.'

The Ambassador paused, and Donald Berwick resisted the urge to glance at Julian Ryde. When he allowed himself a smile, it was tinged with bitterness. Hirohata had stood before them only hours earlier and said nothing; yet he had acted against the AUM from within, must have known this man. He turned back to his guest. 'Please go on, Michio.'

Hirohata did not avoid eye contact. He cleared his throat and continued. 'Whatever happened, Kasaga may have thought the Aum to be too reactive, that they should have taken their vision to the people, forced it upon them, violently, if necessary, that they should not simply have reacted to perceived threats.

'It would explain why they expelled him and, after the Aum were badly damaged, the next we heard of him was several years later when he reappeared at Tangen.'

Berwick might have imagined it, but there was an unfamiliar edge to Hirohata's voice. The Ambassador could be apologizing, could be acknowledging that he had betrayed a trust, but the Prime Minister still felt that Hirohata knew more than he was prepared to say. He tilted his head and caught Julian Ryde's eye once more.

'How easy is it for a man with a criminal record to simply disappear in Japan?'

'Not easy,' said the Ambassador, unblinking. Berwick allowed the pause to lengthen, and Hirohata continued. 'He, well, he might have enjoyed some protection...'

'Protection?' It was Julian Ryde who had spoken.

'Japan.' Hirohata rolled the word slowly, turned to the Home Secretary and then back to Donald Berwick and, for a moment, the Prime Minister believed that he would not speak again. The Ambassador's eyes clouded. 'Japan is a great nation, be in no doubt that I love my country George, that I would die for it. It has achieved so much yet, yet there is always a risk, a risk that a darker force, an ancient force will prevail, that our people will yield to the demands of the past. We must be forever vigilant against that, George and, for whatever reason, it was decided that Kasaga was not a high priority...'

'For God's sake why not?' said Berwick.

Hirohata did not answer, and the Prime Minister allowed the pause to lengthen. Berwick did not doubt that the Ambassador was an accomplished liar. He must have known Kasaga, at least known of him and yet he had not said a word, had not turned a hair at the mention of the man's name earlier, but now Berwick was sure that he was speaking from the heart, was pained by what had happened. For whatever reason, the Ambassador's successors in the Koancho had allowed Kasaga to remain free.

Hirohata blinked, he said nothing for several seconds, allowed the question to remain hanging in the air and then he lowered his eyes, seemed to pick out a spot on the carpet and stared at it hard, his nostrils flared. He seemed to be personally suffering. When he spoke, his voice was scarcely audible. 'Donald, I do not know...'

'Michio,' said Donald Berwick, his voice, no louder than that of the Ambassador. 'You do know, you must know.'

Hirohata said nothing, did not raise his eyes. He shook his head and, when he spoke, his voice was little more than a whisper. 'Kasaga had a small number of close followers. Culture and heritage were fashionable, tradition was back and there were allegations of mind control and extortion. Many of the cult member's families complained.'

'This is old ground, Michio.'

Hirohata nodded. 'Some escapees were murdered. One of the cult's beliefs was that redemption could be achieved through suffering and a great effort was made to redeem these reluctant members. Parts of them were found all over Tokyo.'

Donald Berwick caught Julian Ryde's eye, unsure where the Ambassador was going. 'Please go on, Michio. You mentioned that he had close allies?'

'That's right,' said Hirohata. He was avoiding the Prime Minister's eye. 'They may have helped him in the past and they may be helping him now. He was aided in his rise within Tangen, was helped to get close to Mr. Natsumo, to the heart of one of Japan's leading technology companies, an overseas advertisement for the country. It is all very unsatisfactory...'

Ambassador Hirohata's voice trailed off and Donald Berwick raised his eyes from the study of his hands. He looked directly at the Ambassador, wanted to believe him, but knew that Hirohata had misled them, could still be lying, but it was obscene, a former terrorist allowed to, even encouraged to, wield the power of one of the world's largest combines, and to what end?

Berwick felt Julian Ryde's eye on him, but did not turn his head. The major and fundamental achievement of the post war era had been the successful integration of Germany and Japan into the family of civilized nations, but was that under threat? And even if it was, what could Kasaga or anybody else realistically hope to gain from an attack on Tokyo? 'What does he want?'

'He does not want money,' said Ambassador Hirohata. 'He does not want anything that you can give him, nor anything that I or the Government of my country can give him, not directly at least. He wants change. I believe that he wants to reunite our people with their past.'

'So the lack of any financial or other demands?' said Ryde breaking the silence, his words calculated. He spread his hands. 'What do we draw from that?'

'I think you know,' said Ambassador Hirohata. He looked from the Prime Minister to Julian Ryde.

'He wants the bomb to explode?' said Ryde. 'Your people against the Americans?'

'More,' said Hirohata. 'Much more. It would reawaken memories long since dead, tear the fabric of our society, threaten our links with the West.'

Duncan Berwick studied his hands. 'This man's a monster, Julian. Concrete the site.'

****

Less than two hours later, leaves eddying in the bitter wind that had picked up from the east, cement trucks tearing up the scorched earth, the devastated Tangen site was alive with activity as the Prime Minister's instructions were carried out.

The site was brightly lit, almost shadowless, but, away from the main bustle of activity, a bundle of white clothing fell, unnoticed, from a man's hand. One of many similarly dressed, he pulled the collar of his bright orange overalls closer to his face, adjusted his industrial goggles, checked that the bulk of his long hair was out of sight, gathered beneath his hard hat. The man had a large purple number thirty-one stitched onto the back of his overalls, an electronic tag secured to his wrist, another to his ankle and, at the edge of the site, from the heights of a hastily erected wooden-tower, several men with powerful binoculars stood observing and recording his movements along with those of his orange-clad colleagues.

Intrigued by the excitement in his supervisor, G. B. Singh's voice, Malcolm Hoover had been called to the Tangen facility just under an hour ago, had been allocated number thirty-one, but had not lived to warm his clothing for his body lay in the woods near his home in Grantchester to the south-west of Cambridge.

The strange overalls with the hideous purple numbering on the back and the electronic tags had arrived by motorcycle courier and Hoover had put them on as he had been instructed to do. An expert in disaster recovery, he had left his house intensely curious as to what had happened, but sure that it must involve a serious, possibly even fatal, accident.

He had been right but, although he was an investigator, a trained observer, he had not seen the car behind him as he walked towards his motorbike, nor had he noticed the three Japanese men leave it when it stopped some little way behind him.

****

His poor sight a burden he must always carry, Yoshi Kasaga surveyed the ruins of the Tangen facility before him. The site was crawling with armed men, men who would kill him, yet he felt supremely confident, knew that he could not be caught, how could he be?

Had he not already avoided the explosion, protected himself from the safety of the future? And now, leaden footed, they would pour their concrete, create their tomb, but he was free, free to visit upon his children that which would cleanse them. In the distance, he could hear a motorcycle. It had been his destiny to survive...

****

From the tower the Special Branch officer with responsibility for numbers thirty-one through thirty-six scratched his head. Kenneth McKenna flipped open the booklet in front of him and scrolled down the list. He read Malcolm Hoover's details, looked at Kasaga. The man he appeared to be the correct height and build, but why was he gazing into space?

Was he a threat? If he was then what was the correct response? Should he shoot him? Could he really pull the trigger? As he weighed these questions, McKenna stooped, picked up the Heckler and Koch MP5 machine gun by his side.

McKenna had never known anything like it. He and his colleagues were to monitor the movements of everyone on site, ensure everyone wore their numbered orange overalls at all times and to detain immediately any men of Oriental appearance without question, shoot them if they resisted, was it a test, some sort of joke?

As the motorcycle approached, number thirty-one turned slowly to the temporary watchtower, raised his head further and took off his industrial goggles. He squinted and McKenna blinked. Time slowed, the Special Branch officer seemed to have left his body, he watched as his own hands began to level his weapon, raise it to his shoulder, but something was not right.

McKenna felt the hair rise on the back of his neck and frowned. The stock of the MP5 pushed into his shoulder, it felt like some sort of electrical discharge, but McKenna had his orders. His left eye was beginning to close but there were men, orange-clad figures to the left and right of his mark, their proximity meaning that he could not just point and press, obliging him to aim his weapon. The Japanese man smiled and McKenna squeezed the trigger.

'Kenny?'

The officer who had been standing by McKenna's side turned around. From the corner of his eye, he had seen McKenna raise his weapon, felt that something was wrong, but then he was gone, must have fallen from the tower.

The officer gripped the handrail, shook it hard and, as Yoshi Kasaga walked calmly towards the approaching motorcycle, he looked over the side. Kenneth McKenna was nowhere to be seen.

****

Caroline Whittleton had heard the SAS's assault on the Tangen Industries facility to the southwest and had been puzzled by the noise of fireworks. After all, it was broad daylight, quite sunny, but she had thought little of it and had been horrified when she had heard of the actual events, the probable loss of life.

Nevertheless, Caroline could not deny the shiver of excitement that she felt at the possibility of examining the equipment that had been retrieved from the Tangen site. She had shared her thoughts with Professor Jobber, the American looking increasingly dishevelled, unshaven, his tie hanging several inches below the collar of his coffee-stained shirt and Caroline looked at him now. He had not uttered a word since speaking at length with Professor Klutz several hours earlier.

'Damned waste!' he said causing Caroline to start. 'Losing the men who built the machines I mean, not the soldiers.' Caroline said nothing and the Professor continued. 'Some of it might have survived, of course, but I guess if they had wanted to destroy it then they would probably have been able to do so, even if they were being attacked by the SOS.'

'SAS,' corrected Caroline. She had not been able to stop herself.

'Whatever!' said Jobber. 'But we might still be able to tell what they were using as an energy source, maybe even get some idea as to how they directed it, how they located their targets.'

Caroline slumped back in her chair. Jobber was a boor, a thoughtless bastard, but his words had served to highlight just how little they knew, and she found it profoundly depressing. She needed some fresh air. She turned her back to the Professor, took off her lab-coat, nodded to one of the now permanently present security men and walked out into the grounds, her hands thrust deep into the pockets of her trousers.

The cold immediately penetrated the thin cotton of Caroline's blouse, but she scarcely felt it. Nor did she register the beauty of the day, the crisp perfection, as she brushed through the gathering leaves, contemplated their progress or lack of it, more like.

Caroline was no fool although they knew so little. How much energy was necessary to transport an object? How was the energy generated, how was it directed and how were the targets located, gathered up? In fact, what did they know? Only that a theoretical link between energy and time existed, yet even that was disputed by some. And sometimes it did seem impossible. How could individuals located in a fluid continuum be brought through time? This was no hoax. Surely no one would go to such lengths, gather a diverse group of individuals, be ruthless enough to kill dozens of people, just to give the impression of time travel?

Everything was too real; the language that the men in Yorkshire had spoken, the way that the Germans in Poland had fought to the last man. No, someone out there really had made the giant leap. They had to hope that they had targeted the right site for destruction; and that it was the only one ...

Caroline had stopped walking, became aware that she was no longer alone and looked up, afraid of what she might see, but it was Malcolm McCurran, some five or six yards to her left and she smiled, reassured. McCurran smiled back, but then he was looking past her and his face clouded. He was about to speak when Caroline heard a woman's voice.

'Caroline?'

'Ignore them, Dr Whittleton,' said McCurran moving towards her. 'We'd best be getting back...'

'Over here, Caroline,' said the woman's voice, more insistent. 'Who was in the ambulance, Caroline?'

They knew her name!

Caroline had been deep in thought, must have strayed towards the wire fence that separated the Science Park from the open countryside beyond, had forgotten about the journalists, but they had seen her. A figure at the front of a substantial crowd was waving at her.

'Over here, Caroline!' The woman put the telephoto lens back to her eye, cupped her free hand to her mouth. 'Just a few words.'

McCurran took Caroline's arm. He was in front of her now, shielding her from the journalists and Caroline caught his eye; he appeared concerned, and she tried to smile, but she could not, he looked worried. He pushed her more forcefully now, bundled her backwards towards the laboratory, until they rounded the corner of one of the storerooms. McCurran smiled as the words of the journalists passed over them.

'Who was in the ambulance, Caroline?'

'Who was hurt, Dr Whittleton?'

'Was he dead?'

'Is she married?'

'Where's Jeremy, Caroline?'

'Was it Jeremy, Caroline?'

'He's in Tokyo, isn't he Caroline?'

'Are you worried about him?'

'Was it one of the girls in the ambulance?'

'What are you working on, Caroline?'

'Where are they, Caroline? Where are your little girls?'

Caroline felt as though she had been struck in the stomach, felt her eyes begin to fill with tears then a hand on her shoulder. A gentle hand, it was guiding her backwards, but she could not move her feet, almost fell and McCurran took a hold of her shoulders, began to speak, but Caroline did not hear his words.

****

In the distance, a motorcycle screamed past, but Caroline did not hear it and she entered the laboratory in a daze, Malcolm McCurran remained outside.

Professor Jobber was whistling tunelessly as Caroline sat down. She moved the mouse on her computer, interrupted the screensaver and peered at the figures, still so incomplete, on the screen. She shook her head and looked up. Jobber caught her eye and nodded towards her computer screen; she had mail.

It was a bitter blow; the underground room at the Tangen site was burning, had been damaged, initially by the explosion, but now there were signs of a fire, the flames fed by an oxygen source, deep within the building. There would be no more survivors, little more evidence but still, they had got something.

The bulk of the material recovered from the site must have been located on the ground floor and was easily identifiable. Large numbers of readily available computer monitors, they would have been fed remotely, presumably from the underground room and that was gone, but Caroline had found one aspect of the investigation intriguing. Some of the objects retrieved had defied identification.

Caroline had not seen them, but forensic examiners had described thin slivers of metallic-type materials and, without prompting, they had speculated that they could be non-terrestrial, space-junk, some man-made but other fragments of meteorites or larger objects that had struck the earth.

Caroline had been reluctant to leap too far but Jobber had immediately pushed for more. Could the objects be from a space-exploration museum? Tangen funded one and Caroline, in common with a majority of fellow scientists, had always said that, in the vastness of space, there could exist unidentified elements, exotic materials, sources of negative energy, dark matter, but now she felt dizzy, as though she had pushed too far, had twisted logic until it no longer had any meaning. She pushed her spectacles up onto her head, her hair holding them in place.

The human cost of the operation had been horrific.

Caroline had had to know, had suspected that they would try to keep the information from her, but they had not for, initially at least, there had been considerable hope as injured men had been pulled from the rubble of the building. Now, however, there were only bodies and soon those too would be lost to the flames. The Press had been prevented from obtaining photographs of devastated site. An attempt to over-fly the site in a helicopter had been thwarted and the Press had had to channel the official data, had reported an industrial accident, resulting in no injuries, but a contamination of the site which was likely to prevent civilian access to the area for some time.

Caroline did not hear Professor Jobber approach her.
'Are you unwell?'

Caroline looked up. Jobber was observing her peculiarly. He put one of the two cups of coffee that he was carrying down on the workbench in front of her.

'There's so much of it that we don't understand.'

'Don't understand yet,' said Jobber. 'Although it's starting to make some sense.'

Caroline raised her head, she hated being obliged to tease information out of people, found it deeply annoying. 'Do go on.'

'Tagnen, whatever it was called, the company, has mining operations in all the right places. Near the earth's fault lines, in Siberia, in South Africa, in New Guinea and it collects space-junk.' Jobber paused but before Caroline could interject, he continued. 'Where would you look for exotic materials?'

Caroline nodded, was too tired to object. 'You think this was the only site?'

'No way of knowing, of course,' said Jobber, taking the change of subject in his stride. 'But I rather doubt it. If Japanese perpetrators and a Japanese target, then why England?'

Jobber paused, but Caroline did not speak, she found talking to Jobber draining. She smiled without conviction. 'Expertise is here?'

'Yes?'

Caroline looked across at the American Professor, the conversation once again broken down. 'Do you think they could succeed in moving an airplane?'

Jobber scratched his head, slid his spectacles back up to the bridge of his nose and pushed a lock of hair behind his ear. 'Certainly, a challenge.' He screwed his face, almost in pain. 'A challenge to move tens of tons of metal moving at several hundred miles an hour. They did the vehicle in Poland I suppose. So, it's likely possible, but not yet. If they could do it, then they would have done it already.'

Caroline nodded. Jobber was right.

****

When Caroline next looked at her watch, it was nearly 10pm and she leaned back in her chair, rotated her head slowly, the small bones in her neck grating, then stood up. She felt dazed, was exhausted and struggled to gather her thoughts. She spoke briefly with Jobber, left the laboratory and, dreamlike, began to walk slowly to the second house in the grounds of the Science Park and it was then that she heard it, movement.

Caroline's stomach tightened into a knot, but she walked on. Could they reach her? Kill her at any time? Take her from her children?

She was past the first house now comically fenced with yellow tape, still some distance from the second and she doubted that her legs would carry her when she looked up saw the Special Branch officer, McCurran, closing on her from behind.

A wave of relief overwhelmed Caroline's feeling of foolishness and she tried to smile, but she could not, was too tired and felt changed, somehow diminished by the experience of the last three days.

The smile slipped from the Special Branch officer's face. 'Give it time.' He nodded towards the first courtesy house. 'It'll fade.'

Caroline's breath billowed white about her head, and she gathered her strength, smiled weakly and walked to the door of the second house. She nodded to the Special Branch detective then turned sharply away as her chin begin to crumple, tears burning her eyes. She sensed the officer take a step towards her, held up her hand

and opened the door. She entered the house and leaned against the door as it closed behind her.

Caroline raised her hand to her head, massaged her temples. Her eyes began to clear, and she breathed out long and full, steadied herself and looked up, a red light blinking by the side of the telephone and she checked the answering machine. There were two messages from the girls saying that they were enjoying themselves, were at the seaside. They did not say where and, whilst relieved, Caroline shuddered; this was really happening, she and her family were at risk.

Yet there was nothing from Jeremy. Caroline took out her mobile; she had not missed any calls, would surely have heard if there had been any problems, but he hadn't rung; couldn't he imagine how worried she must be?

Caroline checked her watch; it would be early morning in Tokyo, she would ring him before she went to bed.

All the lights already on, Caroline walked to the kitchen, felt her skin crawl. The security men would have checked the building, this had to be one of the safest houses in England, but still Caroline did not want to be alone.

Caroline flicked on the kettle and quickly made a cup of tea, her eyes settling on the microwave; she needed to eat. The freezer was packed with single meals. She picked out a vegetable curry, programmed the microwave. She was being protected, being looked after by a team of professionals yet she jumped when the microwave pinged. Her hunger quickly returning, she steadied herself, pulled open a drawer by the sink, took out a fork, peeled back the pierced plastic cover of her meal and turned on the television.

The news was still playing; more dreadful stories from Tokyo filled the screen. An official from the British Embassy had been killed, other foreigners were missing and Caroline resolved once again to ring Jeremy. He owed it to his family to be careful, yet she was worried. It was not unusual for him to fail to ring but, as Caroline looked back at the television, her attention was drawn to the scenes playing on the screen behind the shoulder of the smiling presenter.

The story was no longer about Japan and Caroline turned up the volume. She could not believe what she was hearing, felt suddenly very sick. The plastic container slipped from her fingers and fell, unnoticed, to the floor.

Nineteen

'*Prepare to open the bomb doors. ETA four minutes.*'
Colonel Warner flicked off his radio. He would make history, would kill the Emperor, and he was content. He would turn his divine majesty's world to glass, it was real, and he would do it. The farm boy from Minnesota would kill the Emperor of Japan!

Warner smiled, mirthless, determined and shook his head. Yokohama, Shimbashi, and Ginza. They were secondary targets, they interested him little, he was indifferent to their fate, cared not for the thousands, the hundreds of thousands of ant-like creatures beneath him. The Emperor of Japan was his target, and he would seek him out, kill him.

Warner screwed his eyes slightly and there it was, the enemy coastline visible through the summer haze, beyond *it the smouldering pyre that was Tokyo, the fires from the previous raids for the best part extinguished, but the tons of ashes rising lazily into the otherwise clear blue of the summer sky still visible for many miles and Warner nodded.*

The time to bring the fires back to life was nearly upon them as, thirty-one thousand feet below the labouring aircraft, still some 20 miles distant, the people of Tokyo struggled to make it through another day and the equally desperate but ultimately futile search within the Government for a way to end the war with dignity continued.

His smile broadening, Warner glanced at his watch; it was shortly before noon. He knew little about the pitiful existence of the ordinary people of Tokyo, cared even less but he had few illusions; life would be returning to what passed for normality but the politicians, the very mechanism of evil lay before him and they deserved to die. With them would perish the women queuing for food, the Korean guards, the children playing around their feet, the bloodied and bowed Chinese prisoners of war, but Warner was untroubled. Such was the price that they had chosen to pay.

****

By the fish market on the Sumida-gawa River, a laughing group of children continued with their game. Saburo Matsushima, at twelve, older than his friends by almost a full year, surely old enough to fight, pointed at the three tall gaijin prisoners, men without honour, jabbed at them forcefully with his finger and he felt no fear.

True, a surly Korean guard with a rifle, his bayonet fixed, was standing by the side of the prisoners, but Saburo's lack of concern rose from deep within. He could not, would not, fear these people. His brothers had died fighting for their Emperor, and they had made him proud, strong; he would gladly do the same. He looked slowly from the puffed-up Korean to the foreigners.

The gaijin were Australians he had heard tell, Englishmen in Asia, in Japan's back yard but they would be made to pay. For the moment, they were white filth guarded by yellow filth. They were no threat to him.

Saburo smiled, pitiless, wicked and one of the Australians pulled a face. Saburo thrust out his chin, felt himself begin to flush, bent down and picked up a stone, sharp edged, put there by the Gods to use against these foreign devils.

The pig had fouled him, smeared him with his look. Saburo pulled back his arm, prayed for the strength to redeem his honour when he heard the noise in the sky. He hesitated, tore his eyes away from the hideous red-haired gaijin and looked up, a small group of planes approaching lazily from the southeast.

****

Colonel Charles Bertrand Warner glanced at the fish market then past it, further into the city, the Government districts of Ginza and Kyobashi easily identifiable. In seconds he would be upon them and the politicians in both Tokyo and Washington would not have to worry about the War much longer. Charles Warner would end it for them and his name would live forever...

'What the hell's that?' said Campbell.

Warner's eyes focused immediately. He turned to his co-pilot, followed the pointing finger to the front of the aircraft, the blazing blue sky beyond, but he saw nothing save the blinding blue, the odd splash of very light cloud, mountains in the distance, but then a flash. He frowned. 'It's just the light, Davie. The sun's still low...'

'But it isn't, Charlie. It's lunchtime, it's more than that...'

Campbell raised his hand, shielded his eyes and pointed again and then Warner had it, a light, many lights, illuminating the sky, moving, searching, looking for something, looking for them and then it had found them.

From nowhere, it was all around, everywhere at once and Warner flinched, his mind flying, as the bright, silvery blue fingers filled the cockpit.

The bomb!

He had felt nothing, heard nothing, but the lights were like the Alamogordo, the same colours and intensity. Had the bomb exploded, were they dead? Is this what death felt like? No pain, a simple end to everything? But no, he was aware of Davie by his side then the rush of his own blood in his ears, the tearing, splitting of his very being and the first stab of pain.

****

Caroline did not feel the plastic food container strike her foot, nor the hot Chinese food that burnt her ankle. She was transfixed, staring at the television in disbelief.

The screen flickered momentarily. Caroline feared that it would fade, but it did not, and the camera panned from a large building, past an aircraft, past several airmen hastily erecting a large screen then stopped to frame a grinning woman holding a microphone.

'Flight 19 consisted of five Grumman TBM Avenger aircraft,' said the reporter, her voice now grave. 'It took off from Fort Lauderdale, Florida, at 2pm on 5th December 1945, but contact was lost with the aircraft later that afternoon, the planes swallowed up somewhere in the Bermuda Triangle by forces that have never been explained. Yet here, in Florida, some sixty years after the event, one of the aircraft has finally completed its journey!'

The reporter nodded seriously, and the camera edged above her shoulder, focused on the aircraft hangar, the canvas screen now nearly up and the aircraft hidden from sight. 'No-one from the USAF is prepared to talk,' the reporter said, her voice less strident, more confidential. 'But here we are fortunate to have the Bermuda Triangle expert Professor Gilbert Dyke.'

Caroline had never heard of a Professor Gilbert Dyke, but the director cutting back to the studio, the man's head and shoulders filling the screen, she found herself nodding. He was bald and his glasses were suitable thick. 'Well, Eleanor...'

'Helen!' corrected the reporter sharply. She turned, smiled sweetly at the camera.

'Well Helen,' said the Professor nodding sagely, 'the forces at play here are almost beyond our comprehension....'

The man was right, thought Caroline. She was well ahead of him, but his audience would doubtless assume that he was talking rubbish. She checked her watch, this was one of the last items, one of those slots usually reserved for singing dogs or for the tearful reunion of long lost twins and nobody in his or her right mind would believe the suggestion that a propeller driven General Motors torpedo bomber, a Grumman TBM Avenger from Flight 19 had taken off in December 1945 to land today, at a small airbase near Fort Lauderdale in Florida.

But Dr Caroline Whittleton believed it to be true,

believed it more than anything that she had believed before, knew that the healthy young pilot, likely in his twenties was, in fact, a pensionable eighty years old plus, his aircraft an antique and the implications were only too obvious. She left the remnants of her dinner on the floor, grabbed her coat and rushed back the short distance to the laboratory.

It was past 10.30pm but, as Caroline brushed almost unnoticed into her lab, Professor Jobber and most of the other scientists were still there. They had not watched the television reports, did not know what had happened and Caroline envied them their ignorance.

She cleared her throat, attracted Professor Jobber's attention and was about to speak when the telephone rang. A white-coated figure answered it, screwed his eyes and looked around the room. 'I think she's left...'

'I'm here,' said Caroline, sure that the call was for her.

'It's the Prime Minister's office.'

All eyes on her, Caroline walked from one side of the laboratory to the other and took the telephone from the outstretched hand. She raised it to her ear, nodded several times, replaced it to its cradle and looked at it closely, spoke without raising her head. 'The Prime Minister would like to speak to me and Professor Jobber immediately. He wants to discuss the new news.'

Professor Jobber broke the silence. 'Sure, that would be fun. More quantum physics for eight-year-olds, but what new news?'

Caroline briefly relayed the story of the Grumman Avenger and Professor Jobber steadied himself, sat down heavily in his chair. The TV reporter had wound up her story with some general Bermuda Triangle patter, her grinning and winking at the camera denuding the story of what little credibility it had possessed but still, the implications of what had happened were not lost on Caroline's colleagues.

They had done it.

They had targeted a moving aircraft and there had to be a mirror site, possibly more than one.

'So, this is it?' asked Caroline, breaking the silence that had descended upon the room. It was a rhetorical question, and she chewed her lower lip, an affectation that she had suppressed for nearly twenty years, but did not notice. 'Do they really have the ability to pluck fast moving, large objects from the air and move them through time?'

Caroline looked at Professor Jobber, felt close to him, but he did not reply, did not need to. The authorities had to find the second facility and find it quickly. They would not be rescued by science. The gap was too great, and they needed help. These people had had years, maybe decades, to perfect their theories, had had the first mover advantage throughout.

'Excuse me, Dr Whittleton?' The voice was small, it hardly intruded into Caroline's consciousness, but she looked around, refocused her eyes on the near distance. 'Flight 19 consisted of five aircraft, didn't it?' said the voice. It belonged to Stevie Tanner, a recent addition to Caroline's team. Maybe thirty years old, small, nondescript, he had something of a reputation as an expert on the bizarre. He continued, seemed to grow in confidence. 'Five Grumman TBM Avengers, the same plane that President Bush senior ditched in during the Pacific War and one of the rescue planes was also lost.'

Caroline caught Professor Jobber's eye; he shrugged, and Tanner continued. 'The Avengers took off from Fort

Lauderdale Naval Air Station early in the afternoon of 5th December 1945. They radioed in reports of compass malfunctions and unidentified lights in the sky but were never heard from again.

'One PBM patrol plane also failed to return to base later the same evening although a fireball reported in the vicinity of the search suggested an explosion. They all became part of the Bermuda Triangle myth.'

Caroline shook her head; she was exhausted, could scarcely take it in. Tanner was ahead of her. He continued. 'So where are the other Grummans and the rescue plane? They're not here, not now at least so where are they?

'Could they have been destroyed, expended in practice?

The 1945 fireball suggested an explosion; maybe the technique for capturing moving aircraft still hadn't been perfected when it was taken? They might even have destroyed the Tennessee Flyer when they tried to gather her up.'

Tanner shifted uneasily, he looked exceedingly uncomfortable, and Professor Jobber was staring directly at him. 'It's possible,' said Jobber. The admission appeared to pain him. 'Although the bomb had already been armed. Unless someone in a burning aircraft was able to disarm it, then it should still detonate inside the aircraft when it hits the ground wherever, or whenever, that happens.'

Tanner nodded. 'But the Tennessee Flyer was also much bigger than the Grumman's, wasn't it? Something like ten times the weight, a fully loaded 150,000 pounds against 15,000.'

'If that's true,' said Caroline, 'then there's still hope.'

Her voice lacked conviction and Tanner continued.

'The Avengers were slower as well, easier to pick up; that could help. They had a top speed of about 280 miles per hour against about 360 for the Superfortress although the Tennessee Flyer would have been doing nearer its cruising speed when it disappeared...'

Professor Jobber held up his hand. He had been picking at his teeth, an irritated look on his face for some time. 'Mere detail.' Tanner shrank visibly and Jobber continued. 'What about the last message received from the Tennessee Flyer before she disappeared?'

Tanner said nothing.

'What was it?' asked Caroline.

'They had problems,' said Tanner, his words beginning to trail. 'Mechanical interference, some sort of unidentified lights in the sky.'

****

Prime Minister Donald Berwick replaced the telephone handset and shook his head. 'So, he can do it?'

Julian Ryde smiled, continued to trace the line of his nose with his index finger. 'It all makes perfect sense, Donald. It can't be long.'

Berwick nodded. 'The Americans?'

'Knew before we did,' said Ryde. 'They've spoken to Peter and Robert. The aircraft looks genuine.'

'And Hirohata,' said Berwick. His hand began to shake, he raised it to his face, steadied it, rubbed his chin hard. 'Does he know how close we might be?'

'He's back at the Embassy. Needs a secure site from which to communicate with Tokyo. He's promised to return here as soon as he's able.'

Berwick nodded and looked away. The mention of Hirohata had brought back the hurt of his deception, but he pushed it from his mind, tapped his front teeth with his fingernails. The Ambassador's scarred face had given little away, but Berwick chided himself on his sentimentality, knew that it was a weakness that he could ill afford.

Still, to the best of their knowledge, the ends desired by Michio Hirohata coincided with their own. The Ambassador had devoted his life to the integration of Japan into the West, to cementing its chair in place at the table of civilized nations. He had lost his wife and children in the pursuit of that goal, was surely a true ally.

Trying to shake the doubt from his head, Berwick considered the files before him, but could not focus his attention; what did anyone, even a Prime Minister ever really know for certain?

What could one truly believe?

MI6 had been busy, had gathered what information they could in their world of half-truths, of innuendo, rumour, but the Prime Minister, tired and susceptible as he was, felt inclined to believe them, remembered Michio's eyes. They had been the eyes of a different man, cold, dead, the eyes of a man who had known Kasaga. Though more than ten years the madman's senior, Hirohata had known him well.

The campaign against the AUM had been limited in scale, but nasty. What the authorities had needed to do had been done and Ambassador Hirohata had played a central role. He had infiltrated the organization, the stories were agreed, but some went further, suggested that he had become a trusted cult member, even an enforcer, chilling references made to the future Ambassador's calm acceptance of violence as a necessary tool.

Before the bomb that has almost wiped out his family, Hirohata himself had been attacked, almost killed by his former colleagues, his injuries making him a natural ally of Kasaga, a friend even and the two men had been expelled together, but no hard data had ever been forthcoming to prove a continuing link and Berwick did not want to believe that one existed. Much of the intelligence that came across his desk was little more than gossip, could be chaff, even deliberate disinformation; but he could not ignore it.

Donald Berwick looked at the documents in front of him again then leaned back in his chair, scratched his head and tried to push away the clawing paranoia.

****

It was now 7pm in Washington and, once more seated behind his desk in the Oval Office, President Sutton was drawing the meeting with his senior advisers and Chiefs of Staff to a close. He caught Gerry Buchanan's eye. 'So he can put a B29 over Tokyo?'

'He may already have done it.' President Sutton raised an eyebrow and Buchanan continued. 'The last message from the Tennessee Flyer said that she was caught up in some sort of electrical storm, this may have all already happened.'

The President turned, slowly shook his head. He turned to his Defence Secretary, Dick Turner. 'We can't allow ourselves to don't believe in fate. Is the Thomas Jefferson able to help?'

'She's back in Tokyo Bay,' said Turner; he stood a little taller. The USS Thomas Jefferson was the most recently built of the US Navy's nuclear powered Nimitz Class aircraft carriers. One of the largest warships ever built, weighing in at over 100,000 tons fully laden, home to more than 6,000 personnel. Costing almost $5bn, one of the most expensive single structures on the planet, she could launch one of her 85 aircraft every 20 seconds. She had been exercising with the Japanese Navy and had been less than half a day from Tokyo when she had been ordered back to the Japanese capital.

'How about shooting down a B29?'

'Very, very easy,' said Turner without hesitation.

'In addition to the ground based F16s and the ground-to- air missiles in Tokyo itself there are dozens of naval aircraft, F14 Bobcats, F18 Hornets and more on the Jefferson. The ship's Phalanx machine guns or its sea- to-air missiles should be enough to bring down a relatively slow-moving intruder on their own and it would be quick...'

'Quick enough?'

Turner shrugged, shook his head. 'There's no way we can be sure, George. Maintaining readiness at the missile batteries and radar stations should be relatively simple, they can lock and fire automatically but keeping the aircraft in the right place at the right time would be more difficult, and we don't know whether we could guarantee to damage the bomb sufficiently to prevent it from exploding when it hit the ground.'

Turner paused, looked around the room, met the searching eyes and continued. 'The best way to do that would be to hit the aircraft from the air. Keeping sufficient aircraft above Tokyo is technically possible, of course, but it would be expensive, disruptive to civilian air-traffic, noisy on the ground. Still, it could be explained as a training exercise if...'

'If we knew how long this situation was going to last,' said President Sutton.

'That's right, sir.'

President Sutton pursed his lips. 'How quick is quick?'

'A few seconds, probably,' said Turner. 'A minute at the most. We'll have in place an optimal range of weaponry shortly but ground-based F16s might be the best for the job. They're manoeuvrable, all-weather capable and durable, but they might be simply too fast, could be past the B29 too quickly to use their weapons against her, hence the need for other delivery mechanisms, ground to air and air to air missiles.

'Those on the ground could be programmed to respond automatically but would obviously pose a significant threat to civilian air traffic and a few moments' notice of the B29's approach might be needed. That can't be guaranteed and, even after launch, ground to air missiles would take between 15 and 20 seconds to hit an aircraft at 31,000 feet...'

'That's too long,' said Sutton. He paused, turned to Buchanan. 'Gerry, what do we know about the Tennessee Flyer's disappearance?'

'The records from 1945 don't help us too much,' said the CIA chief after a moment's silence. 'The senior staff from the time are all dead, we only have the written record. There were no tapes kept of the pilot's last conversations and the post war enquiry is full of holes...'

'Explain.'

'The B29 was lost within ninety seconds of its target. With hindsight, the suggestion that the plane had ditched in the sea unrealistic. It would have taken it between sixty seconds in free fall and several minutes in a glide to descend from 31,000 feet to sea or ground level so where was the wreckage? After all, she was headed inland; her problems may have begun over water, but, unless she turned around, she must have gone down over land.'

President Sutton looked at the papers before him and shook his head. Buchanan continued. 'So why didn't the bomb explode when the aircraft hit the ground? It had been primed, made ready. It should have detonated.

'Aside from a fault in the bomb itself, the plane could have been hit by anti-aircraft fire, the bomb smashed, but the testimony of the pilots riding shotgun would've mentioned it in their reports and there would have been traces of uranium around the site...'

'The official report is garbage.' It was President Sutton who had spoken. He raised his eyes from his hands. 'Gerry alluded to it earlier on and we've got to face facts. We were on the point of winning the war and the Russians were in Manchuria so let's be realistic, this report was at the top of nobody's priority list.'

Gerry Buchanan did not reply. The silence built until President Sutton continued. 'So, we have an armed bomb and a dedicated and professional crew ready, willing and able to deliver it. We have little idea as to timing and hitting it, when it arrives, will be a challenge, but we may only succeed in hastening its detonation. What's more, if we're successful, if we destroy the bomb and the aircraft in which it's being carried, then we will still be unable to avoid showering uranium on central Tokyo.'

The President's advisers remained silent, and Sutton rose to his feet, turned, looked out of the window. 'Larry, keep the Brits informed and speak to the Japanese. Sound them out about us keeping several of the Thomas Jefferson's aircraft in the air three or four miles offshore.

Permanently if necessary.'

Edelman turned to delegate the order and caught Linda King's eye. She glared at him, and he turned to Daniel White instead. The special adviser nodded.

'And Daniel,' said President Sutton as White rose to leave the room. 'Make sure that Tokyo is aware of the logistical difficulties we're facing. We can't afford for them to be under any illusions. They might like to consider their options.'

'An evacuation?'

President Sutton's face remained impassive. He nodded. Daniel White left the room, and the President continued. 'We've got to play for time, people. We need to make contact, offer this man anything that he wants. If we find the second facility, we might be able to make some progress, give our advisors something to work on and bring this man to the table, deal with him on a human level.

'Any more on the energy pulse that the Japanese recorded when the Grumman Avenger appeared in Florida?'

'It was traced to Tokyo,' said Edelman. 'The authorities there have cancelled all police leave, have brought in troops. They're putting it down to the need to control the crowds, the financial demonstrators and the Brits have sent over details of the Tangen facility in Cambridge, but it's expected to be of only limited use. Most of the material was badly damaged and they're still not sure what they're looking for.'

'Thanks, Larry,' said Sutton. He turned to Alex Reinhardt. 'Putting the risk to life to one side for the moment, what's the damage assessment, Alex, the financial impact? Do we have estimates, any earthquake projections, floods?'

Alex Reinhardt, the President's bookish, fifty-three-year-old adviser on economic policy, rose slowly to his feet. Brilliant, apolitical, he coughed, smoothed his hair then pulled out a pale blue handkerchief. He studied it carefully, then, unused, returned it to his pocket before he spoke. 'There are disaster projections, sir,' he said, his mid-western accent reassuring. 'I re-read them when Tokyo was first mentioned but they're based on a series of natural catastrophes with a level of damage that wouldn't begin to compare with that that which would be caused by a nuclear weapon.'

The President watched Reinhardt shift from foot to foot, his blue shirt already dark with sweat beneath his jacket. The adviser seemed unwilling to continue, and President Sutton spread his hands. 'Details, Alex?' Reinhardt pursed his lips and continued. 'On the ground, a period of shock, of course, but the financial markets would react almost immediately. The rebuilding cost, the cost of cleaning up Tokyo would have to be priced into the global economy, and it would happen very quickly.

'The Japanese could afford it, but they would have to draw on their savings, empty their piggy bank globally, sell foreign equities and bonds, any liquid assets.

They would likely start the slide themselves, but world stock and bond prices would fall to head them off and international interest rates would rise, as it would be assumed that the Japanese would raise their own rates to attract capital.

'Perceived future demand from Japan would push up prices of raw materials and commodities, oil, aluminium, even foodstuffs and there would be a real risk of inflation. Most of this would happen in the first few minutes after the explosion and a global recession would almost certainly result.'

President Sutton steepled his fingers, looked over them at his economic adviser, Reinhardt once again silent. 'Suggestions?'

'In an open world, there isn't a great deal that we could do in the short term,' said Reinhardt. He pulled out his handkerchief once more and mopped his brow. 'We could suspend trading in Treasury Bonds and the most liquid equities, but overseas markets would retaliate immediately, and it would just force the selling pressure elsewhere, to the US real estate market, for example.' Reinhardt hesitated, tried to smile. 'We just can't close our economy. It failed in the '30's, heaven knows we're much more open now and the Japanese own large chunks of everything in this country, from Hollywood right through to Park Avenue and it would be a global phenomenon. Europe's position would be similar to North America and in the Far East it could be worse...'

President Sutton resisted the desire to wring his hands. 'What if we did close the financial markets?'

Reinhardt paused, weighed his answer. 'It would stem the capital outflow in the short term, but I would suggest that it would equate to financial and political suicide.

'We'd have to re-open Wall Street eventually and there would simply have to be a global transfer of wealth from the rest of the world to Tokyo. It would happen one way or the other and it would destroy confidence in our financial markets if we tried to stop. The Fed Funds rate would be driven higher for decades to compensate for the risk that we might do it again.'

Sutton nodded. 'How would it compare with other disasters, the 1923 Tokyo earthquake, surely the Second

World War was on an altogether larger scale?'

Again, Reinhardt took a few seconds before he answered. 'Yes,' he began, 'you're right, of course. The collateral damage would be much less severe than that during World War Two, but things are different now, shocks are much more quickly transmitted. and, in 1945, the political landscape was very different.

'We had command economies across the world; relatively low levels of international trade and much lower cross- border capital flows and even then, the upheaval was such that the Brits were rationing food into the 1950's and tens of millions of German and Japanese citizens spent their lives rebuilding their countries. In the eastern part of Germany, they still haven't finished.

'Now, the Japanese have been running a trade surplus for decades, saving for a rainy day while the rest of the world, ourselves included, have been spending. A fifty-year rebuild simply won't wash with them and, if this is their rainy day, they might want their money back.'

Tuesday 30, October 1999
Twenty

Gripped by the light, Colonel Warner's movements slowed. He was driving his limbs through water, thicker, more like treacle, a delay between the instructions sent to his hands and their sluggish movement, but for the moment he could think. He turned to Davie Campbell, jagged shadows playing on the younger man's face and extended his arm, flicked on the radio.

'Warner here, trouble with the instruments, over.' The sound of his own disembodied voice reassured him, but he felt himself slipping, the lights blinding, there was no answer, but then the radio buzzed. It crackled, feigned life but still nothing. 'Compasses malfunctioning, lights over the target, over.'

Still the radio did not answer. His head heavier than it had ever been, Warner felt his shoulders begin to sag, struggled to keep his eyes open. 'Davie?' The foreign, alien, word resonated through Warner's body. He felt his stomach churn, heave up within himself but then the pain began to ebb. There was nothing, but the light.

****

It was almost 1am in Cambridge and Caroline Whittleton was staring, unseeing at her computer screen. Her head was throbbing, the worst of the migraine had passed, but the dizziness lingered. She felt sick, blinked hard, tried to focus, looked around the laboratory, but still the thought would not leave her.

He could do it!

He could really do it!

Kasaga had the capability to move aircraft. He had done it once, proved that it was possible, and the mood in the laboratory had darkened. Even Professor Jobber had sensed it, something was very wrong, and he had found the words. 'It was only a matter of time.'

Yes,' said Caroline sharply. 'It means that they're there already, they can do it, size and speed are just refinements.'

'And it makes it more obvious why we haven't been targeted,' said Jobber. Caroline thought that she could detect a note of petulance in his voice, but she said nothing, and Jobber continued. 'It's either because he wants us alive or because we're no threat to him.'

Caroline turned away. She did not want Jobber to see her face, but he was right. Kasaga could have killed any one of them at any time; but he hadn't. Instead, he had watched them, running like rats from a shadow. He must have known about the suicide, must have known that the

Japanese man would warn her yet he had let it happen.

Why? Because Jobber was right, they were destined to fail, and their failure would cost the lives of thousands.

Suddenly tired, Caroline shook her head and looked at her watch; it would be just after 10am in Tokyo and she felt a sudden emptiness, a yawning gap in her life. She needed her family. She would go back to the house, ring Jeremy, force him to come home. She rose to her feet, took off her lab coat and walked to the laboratory door. It was locked, she looked around her and a man, plain clothed, but doubtless a policeman, appeared from nowhere. He produced a key and Caroline walked out into the night.

As she opened the door to the courtesy house, Caroline felt the depression push through her tiredness. Dark, heavy, she tried to fight it off, but she could not. In the house, the television was off, all traces of the Chinese meal gone from the floor, but it barely registered. Caroline felt numb, blanketed by something heavy and clinging, something that blurred her thoughts, slowed her movements and she walked to the sink, filled the kettle. She threw her coat onto an over-stuffed armchairs in the sitting room, sat down and her eyes began to close, but there was something that she had to do. She rose to her feet, struggled to think. She must ring Jeremy.

There were no further messages on the answerphone in the kitchen and Caroline pulled her mobile from her handbag. Jeremy's number rang busy, and she sat down. She had fallen into a fitful sleep when the phone in her hand rang some minutes later.

'Caroline?'

Jeremy's voice sounded strange, distant and Caroline, eyes wide, momentarily unaware of where she was, looked around the unfamiliar kitchen, checked her watch. It was 1.40am. She had been asleep, was still in Cambridge, on the science park and then it flooded back. 'Jeremy, are you all right?'

'Fine,' said Jeremy and Caroline frowned; Jeremy's voice was too casual, perhaps he'd had a heavy night. 'I'm sorry I didn't ring earlier. It's been a bit tough.'

In Cambridge, Caroline wanted more than anything to tell Jeremy to come home. She brushed her hair back from her eyes. 'Yes, maybe you could...'

'Don't say it Caroline,' said Jeremy. 'I can't ask people to stay out here if I won't stay myself.'

'It's only a job, Jeremy, the girls are worried; they miss you. The reports on the television frighten them.'

Jeremy said nothing and Caroline sensed that her moment had passed. 'Most of the people here have got families too,' said Jeremy. He continued, the edge to his voice gone. 'They're here, in Tokyo. I've got to stay, but don't worry, if things get bad, they'll pull us out to Hong Kong or Singapore.'

Jeremy's voice trailed off, but in that moment, Caroline knew that he would not come back. He sounded unsure, worried, but it was his job, and Caroline felt her eyes begin to mist. Words failed her, and she felt frustrated, hated not being able to express her concerns. Should she tell him? It could be a recorded line, but she did not care, the Hell with it; she sniffed back the tears.

'Don't cry, Caroline,' said Jeremy softly. 'It's not that bad, just a few windows broken, nothing too dramatic, honestly. Still, I'm looking forward to getting back; things haven't been easy, we'll get away...'

Caroline said nothing. She wanted to tell Jeremy about the project, about the suicide, tell him that the girls were safe, that they were expecting another baby;

it would only take a moment, but the words would not come. 'Jeremy...'

'I've got to go, darling,' said Jeremy, not unkindly.

Caroline could hear something in his voice; it might have been fear, but she knew that he would never admit it, not even to himself. 'Don't be upset, I'll ring you back this afternoon. I love you; tell the girl's that nothing's worth crying about.'

Yes, it is you fool, thought Caroline, the burr of the deadline echoing in her ear, yes it is.

****

Little more than four hours later, Caroline's worry-creased face looked back at her from the bathroom mirror and she felt weak, somehow unworthy. Unable to picture her husband's face, unable to see him clearly in her mind, Caroline had slept in front of a hissing television, had woken in time to drag herself to bed shortly before her alarm clock had gone off, and she felt dreadful, almost drunk, distinctly hung over.

She closed her eyes, shut out the image in the mirror and felt a familiar wave of nausea wash over her. She couldn't go on, yet she had no choice. Letting the nausea pass, Caroline breathed deep and looked again at the familiar face before her, scanned it for some sign that this was a dream, a harmless fantasy but she knew that it was not. Her husband had been threatened, her family was at risk and things were moving too fast, much too fast and she could not keep up. No one could. She and her colleagues were hurtling, headlong down a slope, blind, lacking comprehension, struggling to stay upright and they knew virtually nothing.

How long was the ride? Was it smooth; without turns; a gentle easing of the gradient towards the end or would the slope end in a cliff, a bottomless precipice, the very ground beneath their feet falling away as they span into the unknown?

Caroline shook the thought from her head, washed quickly, dressed and left the house, the cold clawing at her as she walked the short distance to the laboratory that had so recently been hers alone. She wiped her eyes. The cold had made her weep and she entered the lab. Inside, many of the newcomers, from other Cambridge facilities, from elsewhere in the UK and from the US, were already at their workbenches. Several looked towards her, but Professor Jobber did not.

'Good morning, Professor.'

Jobber grunted. He was tie-less and unshaven, his hair wilder than it had been the previous evening, but he had changed his shirt; the ink stain beneath his breast pocket was of a slightly different shade. Caroline looked at her watch then back at Jobber; it was 7.15am.

'Do you sleep here?'

'I've tried to give that up,' said Jobber. The corners of his mouth turned slightly upwards.

Had it been a joke? Caroline looked at the Professor, but all trace of the smile had gone. He was looking at her again. 'Is there anything the matter, Professor?'

'Not aside from the obvious,' said Jobber. He looked down at the papers in front of him, shuffled them while Caroline slipped off her coat. 'At least I don't think there is. We had another conference at 5am. The politicians...'

'Why didn't you wake me?'

'You didn't miss much, just more ways of saying the same thing, but I did send somebody to the house. They got no answer when they knocked,' said Jobber, almost human in his reaction to Caroline's sharp words. 'Then we rang you. Still no answer and we concluded that you needed the rest. It was your Prime Minister who made the final decision not to wake you.'

'OK,' said Caroline, mollified. 'So, what has happened?'

'The police in Japan are searching all the buildings within a two-square-mile area of downtown Tokyo,' said Jobber. He pushed his spectacles back up to the bridge of his nose. 'They've cross-referenced the pulse when the plane turned up in Florida with known Tangen sites. Nothing's shown up and two square miles is a big area.

'It might take a week to search but I don't think we've got that long. Some SOS soldiers have been sent out overnight although what they can do when they get there I really don't know. In any case, they won't arrive until lunchtime and I...'

Caroline did not have the energy to correct Jobber's reference to the SAS, her mind now wandering, her attention span shortened by her lack of sleep. She sat down, tried to think.

What did they know and how could they use what little information they had? They knew now that Kasaga had operated at least two facilities, one in Cambridge and one in Tokyo and he might be operating more. He must have known that once the authorities knew what they were looking for, a facility would be good to use only once, and the conclusion was depressingly obvious. He was not intending to use the Tokyo site again.

****

In Downing Street, tie-less and badly needing a shave,

Prime Minister Donald Berwick rubbed his eyes hard. It was 8.45am, he had grabbed a little sleep, had insisted that his advisers did likewise yet still he struggled to focus.

The door to the Cabinet Room opened, Julian Ryde and Susan Burnell entered, and Donald Berwick nodded, tried to smile. Both had had some sleep and Berwick noted that Burnell looked much the better for it; he had been right. He indicated the chairs beside him.

'Any news?' said Ryde a little too quickly. Excited, he couldn't hide it.

'They found the facility, but haven't moved in,' said Berwick. 'Nothing that you could have done Julian, I'd have woken you if there was. They thought that it was too easy to find, was right where the data suggested that it should be and they feared a dummy, but it looks genuine. It's in Kanda, in the University district, close to the Tennessee Flyer's target drop...'

'Target the bomb on themselves, go out with a bang, some sort of ritual?'

'That was their first thought.'

'Could they have built a shelter?'

'That was their second.' Berwick smiled, nodded.

Julian was with him, ahead of him even and he turned to Susan Burnell, felt he should expand. 'Suicide's often not the only way out for these people. The Aum, for example, seemed to consider that Armageddon was not for them, they'd been building shelters to protect their own and Tangen is a major civil engineer.

'It's been involved in tunnelling work in Tokyo for decades and the authorities over there are considering whether Kasaga could have constructed sufficient underground protection for his own people. They're coordinating their search in Kanda with recent building work carried out by Tangen as well as with the Tangen sites...'

Blanched almost white, Susan Burnell looked physically sick. 'Can it get any worse?'

'It could be looked on as a recruitment incentive,' said Ryde. 'An offer of protection, it certainly wouldn't do their membership numbers any harm.'

Berwick nodded. 'The Japanese want to attack the facility in Kanda before the American troops arrive...'

'I think they're right,' said Ryde. He smiled grimly; he didn't interrupt the Prime Minister often. 'They've got what details we have about the Cambridge site?'

Berwick nodded again. 'Time is the key but they're worried that Kasaga might press the button as soon as the building is stormed...'

'So, what's the choice?'

'That's just it,' said Berwick. 'I don't think we have one. They can't just take the building out, flatten it completely. They're not sure that he's even there but the people on the ground have been instructed to kill him on sight, to kill anyone who looks like him, anyone who's close to him.

'As regards the Tennessee Flyer, the Thomas Jefferson has instructions to shoot first and ask questions later. The Japanese have given the same instructions to their own people and civilian air traffic has been cleared from the area. There will be a dozen F16s in the air before we hit the building.'

Susan Burnell shook her head, closed her eyes.

'It's a risk Susan,' said Julian Ryde. 'But if this is going to happen, then surely it must be better to do it at a time of our choosing?'

'Then why now?' Susan Burnell looked at her watch. 'It's 9.05am, 6.05pm in Tokyo. It's the rush-hour, half or more of the city's workforce will be out of doors.'

Julian Ryde did not reply. Prime Minister Berwick responded for him. 'To wait three or four hours is too great a risk, Susan. They're going in.'

****

Twenty minutes later, Prime Minister Berwick was alone with Julian Ryde in his private office when the first reports from Tokyo came in. Torn wires, junction boxes, some LCD monitors had pointed to the site having been recently used and, in a lower, basement room, this one stripped of all equipment, there had been bodies, nearly eighty of them, longhaired, but clean-shaven individuals, dressed in simple white silk robes. They appeared to have died by their own hand.

Donald Berwick slowly shook his head, raised his hands to his eyes and rubbed them wearily, his breath hissing out as the red and orange patterns danced before him. 'We need more time.'

'You think we have any?'

Berwick looked up, caught Julian Ryde's eye, but when he spoke, he spoke softly, almost to himself. 'This is a nightmare. Well organized, well financed, a huge, legitimate company, ahead of us technologically, harnessed and used by a madman.'

'We can still stop him, Donald.'

'Let's hope so, Julian,' said the Prime Minister.

'But this is a man who knows what we're going to do even before we know it ourselves.'

'A technicality,' said Ryde. He smiled thinly. 'We've

stopped making records and all's not lost. It's always easier to destroy than to build.'

'So why hasn't he targeted us?' It was a rhetorical question and Berwick continued. 'It suggests that he doesn't care what we do, that he knows he'll achieve what he wants whether or not we try to stop him.' Ryde raised an eyebrow, but Berwick had not finished, looked directly at him. 'Do you think Hirohata knew, might have been expecting something like this?'

Ryde exhaled gently, shook his head. 'Fearing it certainly but expecting it? Possibly, but where does one draw the line between the two?'

The Prime Minister rested his chin on his fingers.

'His surviving children, they're in Tokyo?'

Ryde nodded, began to rise from the table and gasped, flinched visibly. His knees weakened he put his hand to his side and straightened, was quickly back in control.

He glanced apologetically at the Prime Minister.

'Can you continue, Julian?'

Ryde nodded and looked away, didn't speak. He steadied his breathing and turned to face the Prime Minister, tried to smile. 'The pain's usually manageable when I'm on my feet. It just takes a little longer every day...'

With difficulty, Berwick held his friend's eye. He had caught something there that he had thought he would never see. Fear. Julian Ryde was afraid, but for himself or for what he would leave behind?

It was infectious, a threat and Berwick tried to stamp it from his mind. What chance did he have if Julian, his rock, the man on whom he relied upon more than any other, could be afraid? He felt a weight bear down on him, spoke brusquely. 'Keep me informed.'

Ryde nodded. 'The pain's a little more acute, I've been passing a little blood, but I'm OK. The medication helps, but there will come a time when I'll need you to tell me to stand down. They can't, or won't, tell me when, but things could move rather quickly. We're not buying any Christmas cards.'

Berwick nodded, looked away and the Home Secretary continued, his voice barely audible. 'There's always so much to do, Donald. The children both newly married, the first grandchild on the way, it's due in the spring...'

Eyes still averted, Donald Berwick felt a wave of sadness wash over him. He had known Julian for thirty years, was a friend, a true friend, but he would only ever be a gravestone to the child. He looked back and, when he spoke, his voice was level. 'You should be at home, Julian. Spend some time with Jenny.'

'I'd just get under her feet,' said Ryde. He paused then continued. 'I can cope, for the moment at least, but keep an eye on me, don't take any bullshit. I wouldn't want to bugger things up for you.'

'I appreciate that Julian,' said the Prime Minister. He would speak to Jenny, could surely do something, but the telephone rang, and he pressed the answer button, leaned forward again and flicked it onto the speakerphone.

'We've got a call coming in from President Sutton, sir; will you take it?'

'Of course, put him through,' said Berwick. It was a breach of protocol, these calls had to be planned, stage-managed but he had spoken to the US President twice during the night, Gerry Buchanan as well; they had been the source of his information from Japan. The line clicked several times.

'Donald, I think we have a problem.' President

Sutton's voice, digitally dismembered, encoded and reassembled in an instant, echoed around the room. It was not yet dawn in Washington, but George Sutton sounded very much awake. 'More planes have turned up in Florida, the remaining four Grumman Avengers along with the rescue aircraft. Two of the aircrew are dead, the others are sick, but they landed the aircraft, seemed perfectly able to function as pilots; for a time at least.'

'Could he try to bring more aircraft back? How many did you lose over Tokyo during the War?' said Berwick. He looked at Ryde, gestured with his chin towards a second telephone and Ryde picked it up, dialled an internal number and whispered into the handset, patched in Susan Burnell.

President Sutton paused before he answered. He seemed to recognize the implication behind Donald Berwick's question. 'Fifty-seven recorded losses, Donald. Most of them seen to hit the ground, but Gerry's let us into another little secret. Our actual losses were nearly four times that number...'

'So, more could have disappeared?'

No reply from Washington. Julian Ryde broke the silence. 'Why understate your losses? Surely that's inconsistent with what you said regarding the stockpiled bombs?'

'Over to you, Gerry,' said President Sutton, a distinct edge to his voice.

'On the face of it you're right, Mr Ryde,' said the CIA chief, a slight distortion lending an unearthly tone to his voice. 'Partly it was an attempt to protect morale, but the two sets of disinformation were put out at different times. When we understated our losses over Japan we were still fighting in two theatres, and we hadn't perfected the bomb. The Russians, pouring through Eastern Europe, scared us. They could have beaten us to Paris, and we felt that we had to minimise their perception of our losses.

'We knew that they had people in our industrial plants in the States, they knew our production capacity. They also had a pretty good idea of our losses in the west, but they had much less information in the Pacific. So that was the only area in which we could mislead them.

'As we went into '45, particularly after the Battle of the Bulge, morale wasn't a problem and, certainly by July of that year, we knew that the bomb worked, and we'd knocked the Germans out. We'd had a chance to dig in on the Elbe and across the Continent and we knew that, if a confrontation with the Russians couldn't be avoided, then that was the time, before we'd demobilised the bulk of our troops in the west, for it to happen...'

'Thanks Gerry,' said Sutton. 'So, we've to expect more than one plane appearing over Tokyo, Donald?'

'It has to be a possibility,' said Berwick in London leaning forward to speak into the star-shaped telephone on the desk before him. 'Certainly, from Kasaga's point of view, it would improve the Tennessee Flyer's chances of getting through. How many ground-to-air missiles can you get in the air at the same time?'

The line to Washington was quiet; Berwick could hear breathing, a distant conversation. The line was not dead. 'Not enough to be sure,' said Dick Turner, the US Defence Secretary. 'We'll get more there, and we have shoulder-held weapons but they're better at lower altitudes. We'd certainly have trouble getting more than a dozen or so, we'll get the news conveyed to Tokyo.'

'Of course, success could pose a further problem,' said Julian Ryde.

Donald Berwick looked at his Home Secretary. 'Go on Julian.'

'Mr Ryde is right,' said Dick Turner from Washington. 'If we hit several aircraft, then the sky above Tokyo will be full of blazing wreckage; that's obviously a danger, ordnance will spill out, fall to earth, but it would render heat seekers less useful. We can program them to target certain heat signatures, but many of them would hit the burning aircraft time and time again...'

'Could they be brought down by aircraft with visual contact,' said Donald Berwick.

'It's possible,' said Dick Turner, 'but the ordnance could still be live...'

'We'll get more F16's there,' said President Sutton, talking over his Defence Secretary. 'We can call it an exercise or something, but we'll have to keep them in the air.'

The line fell silent. A cough from Washington and Donald Berwick looked at Julian Ryde then sharply back at the speakerphone. 'George, it must be today.'

'Donald?'

'Kasaga must know what conclusion we'd draw when the remains of Flight 19 appeared in Florida. He must know that we'd move more ordnance to Tokyo, don't you see? He had to do it now. Put the Tennessee Flyer and the other aircraft there now, before we have any more time to prepare.'

Silence, then President Sutton spoke. 'You're right, Donald but we only need a few more hours...'

'That's more than a lifetime,' said Julian Ryde, his voice barely audible. 'More than a quarter of a million lifetimes.

****

In Tokyo, a Japanese man of medium height stared without seeing at a large video screen hung on the wall of his simple office. He acknowledged the Westerner's understanding, he understood it, had expected it, and he raised his hand to his face, gently stroked his upper lip, the cruelly broken skin, almost translucent. It reflected the flickering candlelight unnaturally and his dark eyes glittered. On the screen before him, the black and white images of uniformed men moving cautiously through a building, dogs at their feet. 'You have been patient, my children,' said the man softly. He turned, his eyes screwed tightly shut, and nodded. A figure by the wall melted from the room. 'You will lead the way.'

Yoshi Kasaga smiled, slowly opened his eyes. The screen flashed brilliantly, and the picture died.

Twenty-one

Saburo Matsushima shielded his eyes from the glare and puffed out his chest, but he could no longer see it. Two planes were still visible, but he was sure that there had been a third. A filthy Gaijin trick, he was sure then one of the Australians laughed and Saburo span to face him. The man was still pointed at the children, but his smile had frozen on his face. He dropped his hand and Saburo stooped, picked up a broken fence post. He had his honour to protect.

****

Still, light had filled the cockpit of the B29, and Colonel Warner had felt himself melt, slip, slide like the grains of sand in a timer through an infinitely small hole and he could no longer see Davie's face. Now, he tried to think, to make out the familiar shapes around him but he could not.

There was only the light and then, that too, was gone and he was floating, he had no shape, no weight, was at one with the blackness around him and he knew that he was dead, that the bomb had exploded, that every atom in his body had separated, that he had been vaporized in an instant and he had failed, had failed himself, his family and his country.

The young pilot tried to shrug his shoulders, he had done his best, but it was not possible; he had no shoulders to shrug, was a part of the void and could sense nothing. But then he could. He was sliding back towards the light.

****

In Downing Street, the line to Washington was open, but silent when the red light began to flash on the second telephone. Donald Berwick reached across, picked up the receiver. Susan Burnell and Julian Ryde, the Home Secretary in pain, his teeth gritted, his breath hissing between his teeth watched him, tried to lend him strength.

'Yes,' said the Prime Minister, his voice firm. 'Come back to me.'

'Donald?'

'Another pulse,' he said quietly. 'The biggest yet.'

****

Charles Warner closed his mouth, blinked hard and shook his head. A piercing, splitting headache like nothing he had known before, dominated his being, but he could see again, the shapes around him were beginning to come into focus and he could hear it, feel the vibration of the aircraft's powerful engines all around him.

Blood, metallic in his mouth and he looked down; he had hands. Alien, remote, they were resting in his lap and he turned them over, checked his fingers, began to believe that they were really his and his tongue flicked across his dry lips. His vision continued to clear, his chin set hard and, he was sure. He was Colonel Charles Bertrand Warner, the pilot of the Tennessee Flyer.

Davie Campbell, his co-pilot and friend was by his side, and it was flooding back, memories cascading through time. He had a mission and the means with which to do it.

And there was more. Warner felt a relief, an immense wave of relief that he had not failed yet surely something had changed. He looked at Davie Campbell, registered his fear and knew that Davie had felt it too, the lights, the loss of radio contact, the attempt to confuse them, but it had failed; they would do their job and he raised his hands, gripped the controls before him, pushed any redundant thoughts of failure from his mind and allowed the relief once more to wash over him.

Warner took a deep breath, knew that he had to lead. He nodded to Davie, twisted his face into a grotesque smile and leaned forward, slapped the radio hard.

Squinting against the building pain in his head, he strained to listen. It had been dead for what seemed like hours, but now there was something. Music. It was music and he shifted in his seat, a little slow in his movements and tried to gather his thoughts, clear his mind.

The lights had gone. The 'Flyer's instruments were normal, and they had their mission, could still complete it, but it was dark, suddenly very dark, and this was no storm, it was as dark as night. Warner glanced at Davie Campbell, caught the younger man's eye. Davie was frightened, Warner knew it and he had to be strong, not just for himself but for his crew, for his family in the sky.

But what should they have expected? They had been told that the Japanese would throw everything that they had at them, that they might see things that they had never seen before and that they should be prepared. Yet now, their course was correct, their altitude was fine, they were a touch higher, nothing unreasonable, but it was dark and the two B29s that had been flying shotgun had gone. Worse, the radio was still out, but they had their orders, and he would carry them out. They had been cleared to drop.

Warner craned his neck, squinted and smiled. It was still there, the enemy coastline visible as a darker, more solid body against the lighter gloom of the sea and he raised his hand, pointed to the blur of the unfamiliar sodium lights above the gigantic city before them. 'There she is Davie, Tokyo and see the glow? She's still burning!'

Campbell nodded, but Warner's smile had set on his face; By God, Tokyo had changed! It had grown and, his eyes screwed almost shut, he was sure; the city was not burning, it was brightly lit!

Amazing! Ridiculously, fatally foolish but the blacked-out centre, its huge buildings towering into the sky, was surrounded by vast rings of illuminated suburbs and the huge avenues of open ground, the firebreaks which criss-crossed Tokyo, created by tearing down over half a million houses, appeared to be no longer there.

Warner looked across at his co-pilot again and Davie tried to smile but he could not. The younger man leaned forward, nodded towards the radio with his chin, tried to keep his voice steady. 'What do we do Charlie? The radio? What do we do?'

'You know what we do, Davie,' said Warner looking back out of the cockpit as they made to cross the Japanese coastline. His voice firm, authoritative, he felt supremely calm. Whatever the enemy had done, tried to interfere with the Flyer's radio, light up their city to mislead them, mask the avenues of rubble and mud used to counter the firestorm that he would unleash, it had not been enough. He had never felt so sure of anything in his life. 'We've got our orders.

We over-fly the site and make the drop, one kilometre to the east of the Imperial Gardens; simple! ETA ninety seconds.'

'But that's not Tokyo,' said Campbell, the struggle against his wavering voice now lost. He pointed to the port side of the aircraft, a bridge clearly visible. Across it a train was moving rapidly, it's engine clear of smoke and steam. 'Everything's different...'

'It is Tokyo, Davie,' said Warner flatly.

It was where it should be. They had followed the correct course. He had checked it himself. It had to be Tokyo, yet Davie was right; it was different.

A fleck of blood on the corner of his mouth, Warner's jaw set once more, he shook his doubts from his mind. They had their orders, knew what they had to do, what they would do, and he tried not to despise his friend for his weakness. It was natural, understandable; Davie had a right to be concerned. They were about to make history.

'Even the train, Charlie?'

'It's a mock-up,' said Warner. A sharp edge had crept into his voice. 'Dummy bridge, fake locomotive, but what does it matter? It won't be there for long...'

****

Some 31,000 feet below the Tennessee Flyer, some little way to the west, Jeremy Whittleton had never met Sanetoki or Tsukiyama Hirohata. That Ambassador Hirohata's surviving son and daughter, having just spoken to their father, were at that moment sitting, hand in hand in a room in Jeremy's own hotel would have interested him little yet he was being drawn towards them, was to share their fate. He scraped back his office chair and rose to his feet. It was nearly 7pm, he had made some progress, might only have to spend one more day in Tokyo but he was tired, was ready to leave for the evening.

He had spoken to Declan O'Donnell during the afternoon, had agreed to meet him here, at Stretton's offices, and share a cab back to the Hotel Seiyo Ginza for dinner. Denying it, even to himself, he was still shaken, had had a taxi waiting outside for almost half an hour.

The day had started, fresh and bright and Jeremy had forced himself to face his demons, had walked to the office from his hotel that morning alone and had faced the streets again at lunchtime. The windows on the ground floor of Stretton's offices now repaired, things had appeared to be getting back to normal and he had begun to relax but a cab ride up to Ueno at the suggestion of one of the ex-pats had left him strangely uneasy.

The park, beautiful in the spring when the cherry blossom was out, the heavy boughs of some of the older trees supported by wooden beams, had seemed somehow oppressive, dangerous even and the cardboard city of homeless people had been difficult to ignore.

Jeremy had felt the stares of the washed-up, hopeless people, the debris of a successful society and they had been accusing, conveying to him that their plight was his fault, that he was a foreigner, a Gaijin.

Fortunately, he had not left his cab but, back in Stretton's offices after a shortened lunch, Jeremy's day had deteriorated further. The Japanese financial markets had slumped further during the afternoon and there had been more worried talk amongst the ex-pats of a resurgence of attacks on foreigners. A siege mentality had begun to develop, the humour very black and the rumour that Narita International Airport had been closed, later proven to be correct, spread quickly.

Noisy aircraft flying low overhead, military, had added to the feeling of paranoia, the near certainty that a terrorist attack of some sort was imminent and another power cut during the afternoon had effectively shut down the whole office. Jeremy still had no idea how much information had been lost and the day, which had shown such promise, had effectively been over.

Jeremy checked his watch, leaned back in his chair and, an unwelcome flush of guilt preceding the thought, his mind turned to Caroline. He'd promised that he'd ring, he hadn't got around to it and she'd be worried. He reached for the telephone but, as his hand closed on the receiver, it rung. Jeremy jumped, grabbed the handset. It was Declan.

'I'm downstairs, you fit to leave. The cab won't wait forever!'

'Two minutes,' said Jeremy. He checked his mobile, would ring Caroline from the restaurant. He turned off his computer, pulled his jacket from the back of his chair and took the elevator down to reception. Outside, the air fresh but tainted by aviation fuel, somehow charged, expectant, he ignored Declan's scowl and got into the taxi beside him.

****

'You actually saw it?'

Declan's mouth hanging open, Jeremy had just related the events of the previous evening. He had not embellished his report, had tried to sound casual, to keep the worry from his voice but he had failed. 'He was no further from me than you are now, Declan. Some guy in a white robe breezes up and, well, swish...'

Jeremy brought down his hand in a chopping motion and Declan shook his head. 'Jeez!'

The cab pulled away from the kerb but, almost immediately, it slowed to walking pace. The roads increasingly clogged, jets still tearing the sky above them, Jeremy and Declan abandoned it a short block from the Hotel Seiyo Ginza and began to edge their way towards the hotel. All around them office workers and shoppers were struggling to get home, thronging the pavements, pushing their way to the subways and Jeremy took in the scene.

There were more policemen than there had been the previous evening but otherwise the busy street scene appeared thoroughly normal. Aside from the commuters, the bars and restaurants were beginning to fill up and even the shops, although preparing to close, were trading well.

Jeremy's eyes clouded and, the face of the man from the British Embassy in his mind, he shuddered, unconsciously strained his ears, but there was nothing out of the ordinary, the odd raised voice, but no shrieking, no chanting, no wild-eyed mob, everything was normal but then the ground shook.

It was nothing dramatic, like the underground rumble of a subway train, but Jeremy stopped in mid stride. He frowned and then he heard it; the dull crack of what sounded like an explosion ahead of him and he felt his chest compressed by what he imagined to be a pressure wave following the blast.

Echoing around the Nihombashi canyons created by the skyscrapers around them, the sound began to fade, and Jeremy turned to Declan, tried to look casual, to seek the large Australian's assurance that he was not going mad. The puzzled look on Declan's face broadly mirroring his own he shrugged, turned down the corners of his mouth and beat Jeremy to it. 'What the hell was that?'

Jeremy did not answer but around them, commuters were sniffing the air, heads angled upwards. The noise had come from Kanda, but the echoes made it difficult to be sure and soon, though the noise had been of some passing interest, the everyday fight of the day workers to get out of the city was resumed but then Jeremy felt it.

A crackle, static in the air and the lights were gone. The neon signs, the streetlights, the lights in the shops and offices, everything had gone in an instant. It had been light during the last power cut but now it was as black as hell, deathly quiet but then the complaints began as a thousand people began to speak at once.

'Christ, Dec! Tokyo is falling apart!' said Jeremy. He could see Declan, a slightly darker shade against the night sky and he reached out his arm, grabbed a hold of his jacket, but the shadow of the Australian raised its hand, put a finger to its mouth, tapped its ear and Jeremy strained to listen. Nothing and then he thought he had something, could just out another, different, noise distinctly audible above the angry buzz of the crowd around them.

It was overhead, had arrived quite suddenly, it was an aircraft, then several aircraft, not the jets that had been criss-crossing the air above the city for most of the day, but something older, different, somehow less threatening. Jeremy peered into the dark sky, his vision improving, aided by the lack of lighting around him and there they were, dark shapes moving slowly across the lighter clouds in the night sky high above them.

Jeremy looked at the commuters around him. They seemed not to have heard, and most were pushing robotically for the sub-ways, but then others were gazing skyward, hands cupped to their eyes and the tone of the conversations around them seemed to change. Jeremy turned back to Declan, questions crowding his mind and he felt a flutter in his stomach; an unexplained fear but he struggled to control it, to fight it down, but he could not.

Then the first of the commuters near to the Yaesu underground arcade began to point at the sky. Jeremy followed the outstretched arms, it was too hard not too and the angry, complaining tone of the crowd had gone, had been replaced by an excited, infectious whispering that began to bring commuters back up from the surrounding subways, out of the shops and onto the already crowded pavements. Within moments, Jeremy felt the pressure around him beginning to build, memories of the death of the Embassy man flooding back; there was no light, and he was afraid. His rising panic unseen, he struggled to draw breath into his lungs.

Then the streetlights flickered back on.

As he sucked in a lungful of air, the dazzling neon of the shop signs burnt star shapes onto Jeremy's eyes. He looked at Declan, felt his head begin to spin as the oxygen kicked in, felt drunk as a terrific display of fireworks erupted into the sky, rockets shooting from the rooftops around the entire area.

From the Tokyo Stock Exchange, from the roof of the All-Nippon Airways building, from the top of the Bank of Japan, from the Mitsukoshi Department Store and from the unseen US warship in the harbour, rockets tore into the air and Jeremy felt the ground shake beneath his feet.

He could smell the fuel, taste it on his tongue as the massive fireworks snaked higher and higher and then the smaller, somehow more modern aircraft screamed in from the sea.

Jeremy's heart was pounding, and he looked around him.

He was worried, could not explain it but Declan, his mouth hanging wordlessly open then grinning inanely, seemed to be enjoying the spectacle.

A ripple of applause broke out. Still the rockets climbed higher, and the applause grew, drew more wide-eyed commuters up from the steps of the Kyobashi and Takaracho subway stations. Word spread quickly. Many of the government workers packing Kasumigaseki station began to turn, to push their way back up to the surface to join the throng.

Now the pavement was packed. The crush built and Jeremy Whittleton began to sweat. The buildings were emptying and those workers choosing not to stay crowded the streets were pressed against the glass of their building's untested windows as the first brilliant fireballs burst against the sky, grew, attracted more of the rockets until the entire sky seemed to be illuminated by a fantastic cascade of explosions, pockets of brilliance.

Jeremy flinched as the first of the chest shuddering booms from within the fireballs rent the air and more of the powerful fireworks detonated within the original bursts. The spectacle put the very grandest displays that Jeremy had ever seen into the darkest shade and now the smaller aircraft, faster, more modern were weaving in amongst the balls of fire and the sound of more explosions added to the brilliant display.

Declan clapping heartily beside him, his shirt sticking to his back, his face flushed, Jeremy felt a sudden chill, felt the hairs on his arms begin to rise but still he could not explain it. And then he had it; this was too real!

These were real aircraft, this was no display and then Jeremy was sure that he could see it, a sprinkling of dust against the sky as the contents of more than a dozen B29s, ripped apart by the first hail of missiles and including instruments, payloads and lifeless crew, began their fifty-five second fall to earth. Like confetti, the lighter debris fluttered from side to side, but other objects, whistling shrilly but invisible against the night sky, fell faster.

Without conscious thought, Jeremy pulled out his telephone. He had to speak to Caroline, had to be near her. He could hear little above the crowd but needed to hear her voice, at least to know that it was there. He hit the speed-dial for Caroline's mobile, but it was useless, he could hear nothing. Caroline may or may not have answered, but Jeremy could feel her presence, shouted into the telephone, ignored Declan's frown, told Caroline that he loved her, that he would come home. He ended the call and, nine time zones to the west in Cambridge and set to mute, the vibrating telephone stopped its unseen rotation on the laboratory bench.

****

'ETA twenty seconds,' said Davie Campbell turning in his seat. 31,000 feet above the admiring crowd, Colonel Warner had begun to shake, and Campbell frowned. 'Are you OK?'

Warner did not reply. His breathing short, he felt unwell, not normal, numb, almost drunk but still, he would do his duty. He nodded, raised his hand and pointed out of the cockpit window as an object, several objects, moved quickly towards them, picked up speed, streaked across the sky. Too fast, much too fast, they looked like no aircraft that he had ever seen before. 'What the hell?'

Campbell shook his head, said nothing as the first of the rockets, smoke trailing behind it, carved its way towards them, others following and then the sky was full of them and Warner gasped, felt the hairs on his arms rise and a tremendous pain in his chest. Less that a second had passed and Warner looked around him as if in a dream, could not believe his eyes. There were B29s, Superfortresses, everywhere, lumbering ungainly against the smaller aircraft, fifteen, twenty, maybe twenty-five of them, conjured from nowhere.

Then, almost before they had arrived, Warner watched, helpless, as the first of the magnificent aircraft erupted into a ball of flames. He had seen aircraft die before, had seen them plucked from the sky, but this was different, more shocking and then another, and another aircraft was hit, massive, gasoline fuelled explosions filling the air, followed by the secondary, more powerful blasts of the high explosives within the planes' bellies and then he knew for sure.

They were decoys, planes sent to crowd the enemy, to improve the Flyer's chances of getting through, a proper escort, but then the first of the shock waves hit them and the Flyer lurched violently to one side.

Charles Warner smiled as, below him, Tokyo spread for miles in every direction. 'Boney, Johnson? ETA fifteen seconds; acknowledge, please.'

'We hear you.'

It was Frankie Bonetti. Warner could picture him clearly. The New Yorker's rosary to hand, his fingers busy, he would nod to Johnny Johnson, feign a lack of concern and go about his job, but the youngster would be frightened, blind to what was going on in the skies around them, but he trusted in his family, his family in the sky, and Warner could sympathize but, for the moment, he did not care, needed only for the boy to focus on the release lever. It had to be within easy reach; even a dead man must be able to pull it.

A shattering explosion and Warner looked to his left.

Another aircraft had been hit but they were doing the job, drawing the enemy's fire.

Still, Warner cursed. He had been on difficult raids before. Those over Germany in the middle of '44, before the Luftwaffe had been effectively put out of action, had been sticky, but this was much worse, was like nothing that he had ever seen before, the ground to air fire targeting the aircraft around him with a frightening accuracy, the shells and rockets bending and turning as they travelled through the air.

Now B29s were being hit to their right as well, and above and beneath them, shattered planes hit again and again as they spilled their contents into the night, the ordnance, fluttering black against the once more brightly lit city beneath them. The blackout had been short lived, but now aircrew were falling, mute, arms and legs spinning against the sky, bouncing against the fuselage of their aircraft as they fell, gasped their last and still there were no parachutes.

Warner turned his head. He felt sick, dizzy and the pain surged back into his chest, held his lungs in an iron grip, kept the breath from him. Maybe the light that had engulfed them earlier had been a weapon, some sort of poison?

Warner swallowed back the bile, the bitter acid that had risen in his throat and set his mind. He would ignore it, push the pain away and fulfil his mission, but still he was awed.

This was the shit storm to end all shit storms, but he felt detached, invulnerable, somehow safe in the carnage, but then his seat shot from beneath him, his harnessed body pulled downwards with a terrific force an instant later, as another B29 was hit above them, the shock wave almost separating the Flyer's body from her wings. Then a second and a third explosion as the dying aircraft was hit again and again and time slowed to a crawl as a missile, that could not possibly have missed the Tennessee Flyer, slipped past, attracted at the last moment by the heat of the blazing wreckage above them to slam into the burning hulk.

Smoke, flames and debris flew in every direction.

Warner gripped the Flyer's joystick, parts of the dead

B29 from above them spattering and clanking against his plane's fuselage, but she steadied, the engines were OK.

Less than five seconds surely?

She was a tough old bird, but Warner's gunners were exposed. 'Give me your names!' The names came back, curses and jokes, they were all alive and Warner smiled, felt an intense relief. It was his job to keep them that way and nothing else mattered. Except, perhaps, for one thing. 'Three seconds.

'Boney, you ready?'

'Ready!'

Warner jerked his head backwards involuntarily as something flashed past, then a second movement caught his eye, a dot moving towards them, growing rapidly, an aircraft? It took shape quickly, smoke and flame shooting from its wings and the image of the Stars and Stripes flashed through Warner's mind as the plane was gone, the turbulence from the F16's missiles shaking the Flyer before they hammered into a B29 burning a quarter of a mile behind them.

Warner coughed, pulled off his mask, spat out a mess of blood-flecked phlegm and shook his head. 'Jesus!'

Campbell, his eyes wide, gestured at Warner's mask. 'Charlie, you OK.'

Blood bubbling from his nose, Warner replaced his facemask, but started to gag, struggled to compose himself. They couldn't fail, they were too close, had come too far. He had seen the bomb in New Mexico and wanted, needed, the others to see it now. Warner pulled off his mask, held the radio to his mouth. 'Boney, drop it now!'

Deep within the belly of the aircraft, Frankie Bonetti opened his blood-gummed eyes, flinched as a rattle of smaller debris rained against the bulkhead of the aircraft but he knew what to do. His mask back on, he flicked at the vomit on his chest, gritted his teeth and raised his head.

A bead of perspiration traced the line of his cheek where the smooth skin ended and the stubble of his chin began and he looked at the silent, strangely harmless grey metal cylinder before him. His strength fading, he shook his head sharply, crossed himself and pulled himself forward in his seat.

Bonetti's hand was trembling as his knuckles brushed the vulcanised rubber that covered the handle of the release mechanism, and he steadied it against the bulkhead of the plane. He breathed deep, fought against the heaving of his stomach and flicked off the first safety catch. He squeezed, twisted and released the second catch.

'Boney?'

Bonetti pulled the now visible lever down sharply.

'Frankie, what's happening?'

Frankie Bonetti watched, mute, as Big Daddy hung for an instant, then swung slowly downwards from the front, its massive fins ensuring that it fell nose first even during the first few seconds of its flight.

Gracefully, it slipped from sight.

'Bomb's away, Colonel. Two seconds down.'

Colonel Warner felt a massive surge of relief. It was done! They were making history! The science didn't interest him, but he knew what mattered. In fifty-five seconds, five miles beneath the Tennessee Flyer, four or five miles to its rear, a charge of conventional explosives would blast a block of Uranium 235 into a larger block of the same material, causing critical mass and an explosion the like of which few in the world had ever seen.

Warner smiled, wrenched hard on the joystick and pulled the Tennessee Flyer into a steep turn to the northeast, a clockwise turn, away from the bomb, putting it somewhere to their left and behind them and turned to Davie Campbell.

He opened his mouth but said nothing. In the sky to the front of the aircraft, the lights had started again, brilliant white, then violet, then blue.

Seconds later, across the sea of time, shadows danced across the instruments in the cockpit of the Tennessee Flyer. They rose and fell, tore at the feeble bodies of the men and then stopped abruptly. Colonel Warner looked at the controls before him.

The spinning compass settled, once again read northeast and, his mind numb, Warner recognized it to be correct, but there was more, much more. Outside, it was light, and the anti-aircraft fire had stopped as suddenly as it had begun.

Behind the blood-smeared glass of his facemask, Warner's eyes began to dull as the bile rose once more into his throat. He struggled to think. Something was wrong, it was very, very wrong and pulled off his facemask, spat onto the floor of the cockpit and glanced at Davie Campbell, then past him, glazed-eyed, at the remaining aircraft now showering their bombs onto the crippled city below.

The burnt shells of several aircraft were falling to earth, some crumpled, burning rags and others spiralling gracefully, trailing oily smoke-black ribbons behind them, but then Warner had it; the bomb!

Twenty seconds surely?

Nothing could touch Big Daddy now and the first

pinprick circles of dust were rippling on the ground below. The package would be safely delivered, but the buildings were different again. Taller, more of them, they covered a larger area.

Warner scowled, tried to twist his face. Was it the better light?

Another trick?

His stomach beginning to heave, Warner pushed the worry from his mind. He was ill, might be dying and felt a dreadful weight press down on him, cloud his mind, but he knew that he should rejoice. He had brought them through, completed their mission, but he felt cheated, they should be safe, and more than 30,000 feet above the souls gasping for breath in the heat and smoke on the ground below, men, women and children being blasted this way and that before being consumed by the fire storm that would surely develop in their wake, his boys deserved to live.

Thirty seconds?

It could be no less, but Warner's vision was beginning to cloud as the first parachutes flowered against the blue of the horizon.

Poor bastards!

The thought had entered his mind. The falling airmen following the largest bomb ever built to earth would be incinerated in an instant.

Forty seconds?

Red flashes of fire now as the pinpricks on the ground began to merge, but Warner could not breathe. He gagged, sucked in a breath and looked across at Davie Campbell, his co-pilot nervously chewing on the knuckles of his left hand. Warner struggled to raise his hand, tapped his watch. He nodded and looked behind him and to their left, but there was nothing. He tried to speak, but the words would not come, and he coughed again.

The fabric of his body coming apart, the pain beginning to build, Warner knew that he was dying, but he had to see it through, would not, could not, let his crew down. He would scar the sprawling city beneath them and leave his mark.

Fifty seconds?

Campbell, a bubble of bloody mucus inflating and deflating from his nose, raised his hand, pointed at his watch and Warner began to level off, the horizon straightening before them. Perhaps ten B29s, their ordnance gone, wheeling, like the Tennessee Flyer itself, away from the target, filled the sky before them and Warner could see figures in the aircraft closest to his own, faces drawn and grey.

A figure raised its arm, waved, but then it was gone, the pilot and his plane engulfed in flames and Warner flinched. Numb, his senses slipping, he felt the heat of the explosion sear his face through the glass of the cockpit window.

'What the Hell?'

Davie Campbell turned, opened his mouth, but did not speak as the crimson and black flowers erupted violently against the blue of the sky around them. He held out his hand, touched Warner on the shoulder as the Tennessee Flyer was hit, and in an instant, the world in which they lived was torn apart.

For an age, the mass of flame and vaporized fuel flew on lifeless, carried by its momentum like some huge beast struck lifeless in mid-stride until, at last the near perfect ball of fire began to slow and fade. And then there was nothing. Only a thousand nameless parts that began to tumble and spin to earth.

****

On the ground, Jeremy Whittleton closed his gaping mouth, shook his head in disbelief. The planes and rockets had gone. The laser display that had thrilled the crowd had ended as abruptly as it had begun and the applause echoing around the skyscraper canyons was now the only sound that split the night.

The virtual aircraft, clever holograms that the newspapers would describe in detail the following morning, created by thousands of lasers positioned in and around the city centre had disappeared at the same moment as most of the simulated rockets that had been streaking towards them. Perfectly coordinated, it had been a truly awesome spectacle and unaware of his actions, Jeremy found himself grinning, clapping along with the enthusiastic crowd. Gradually, the applause faded as the commuters, in ones and twos and then in greater numbers resumed, just a little less heavy hearted, their difficult journeys home. Some people even smiled on the underground trains as the last few surface-to-air missiles, lacking targets, detonated impotently forty thousand feet above the city.

Remarkably, the falling fragments caused no deaths, but angry letters of complaint would tumble onto the desks of the local newspapers for many weeks. The display had been in bad taste, they would maintain.

The proud and resurgent Japan of today did not need, did not want, to be reminded of its humiliation at the hands of the Americans more than half a century earlier, but the complaints would be ignored, swamped as they were by the deluge of parental requests for a second showing. But it was not to be, not for the moment, at least.

It was unfortunate, the authorities would say. The rehearsal, for such it had been, had revealed serious problems, dangerous, even life-threatening faults in the way that the holograms had been created that would make it impossible to create them again.

Epilogue

It was late November and the few remaining leaves on the large chestnut trees that edged its gravel drive were being sorely tried by the swirling wind as the Prime Minister's bullet proof black Jaguar swept into the grounds of the beautifully landscaped Saint Ignatius Hospice five miles from Stockton-on-Tees. Above the site loomed the flat-topped Cleveland Hills, now carpeted with a blanket of snow, which few of the facility's patients would live to see melt.

George Sutton's predecessor had opened the tastefully converted Georgian building some eight years earlier and it was currently helping nearly two hundred seriously ill patients to come to terms with their own mortality, helping them to move, with what dignity they could muster, from this world to the next and the Prime Minister closed his eyes, tried, without success, to push the thoughts of the last month from his mind.

He owed it to Julian to do so, but he could not, it still filled him with dread. It was impossible, but it had happened; the bombs had disappeared. Neither the Big Daddy nor any of the conventional ordnance that the authorities were sure had been released above Tokyo had hit the ground, but it had happened, was happening still and the scientists maintained, and the threat posed to the city by the first ever nuclear device dropped in anger remained immense.

Every moment in time was equidistant from every other moment, they had said, but some went further; time was layered upon itself, they insisted. Everything that had ever happened and everything that was to happen in the future, was happening now, was ever-present, making the threat to the city permanent, indelible. The bomb was halfway to earth, they said, and Donald Berwick had been in no doubt as to what that would mean; it would hang above the heads of the people of Tokyo for all time, influence their behaviour, change them forever.

Yet in Japan, there had been no panic. The riots had abated, calm had returned to the streets, but foreigners had continued to leave the country. They had no longer felt welcome, they had maintained, and the government of Mr Hiro Tanaka had made no efforts to persuade them otherwise.

Japan's financial markets had fallen further, helped in part by aggressive selling from overseas. The domestic Press had highlighted several unfortunate incidents, attempts by US and European banks to profiteer, to make money from Japan's misfortune and the attitude towards foreigners had hardened further. The Gaijin were fickle, they had no loyalty, no honour, said the newspapers. They were not necessary, were not wanted and there had been calls to liquidate the country's foreign assets.

Frozen gravel crunching beneath its wheels, the Prime Minister's car slowed to a halt. Donald Berwick did not open the door, he knew the routine, could see the two black Range Rovers parked discretely at either end of the spacious car park, several men in dark suits standing by their sides, wires taped to their necks and disappearing beneath their shirts and he heard a faint crackle from the earpiece of the Jaguar's front seat passenger.

The man turned, nodded, and the car's door opened from the outside. A group of men half-circling him immediately, the Prime Minister got out, sniffed at the frosty air, registered the concern on the faces of those around him and smiled as best he could. He waited for the nod then walked to the main entrance of the hospice, opened the door and entered the building. Warm but not stifling, it smelled like what it was. A death factory.

Berwick acknowledged the suited man by the door, again he tried to smile then he turned, noted the arrowed room numbers discretely stencilled onto the wall and walked down a well-lit corridor before halting by a beige painted door. He checked the number, raised his hand, hesitated then knocked twice. He was about to knock again when a smartly dressed woman opened the door.

Jennifer Ryde must be what, fifty-three, fifty-four but she looked younger. Handsome now, rather than beautiful, she had been crying, averted her eyes and Donald Berwick leaned forward, took her arm by the elbow. 'Jenny, I'm most dreadfully sorry.'

'Thank you for coming, Donald.' Jennifer Ryde stepped into the hallway, closed the door softly behind her and put her free hand on the Prime Minister's own. 'He wanted to see you, but he hasn't had a good night, he's very weak.'

Berwick smiled, sensed that there was more. He said nothing and Jennifer Ryde hesitated before she continued. 'The medication's very strong and he, he. Well, I just wouldn't like you to think any less of him.'

Donald Berwick squeezed Jennifer Ryde's arm, kissed her lightly on the cheek. 'That's not possible, Jenny. You know me better than that.'

Jennifer Ryde tried to smile, but her lip began to quiver, and she stood slightly to one side. The Prime Minister squeezed her hand again, then gently let it go and entered the room, left his former Home Secretary's wife standing in the corridor outside.

Berwick had expected worse, the scent of death perhaps, but the room was light and airy, the smell of flowers hanging in the air. He raised his eyes, looked at the bed that dominated the room. 'Julian?'

The crumpled figure that lay before him did not respond and Berwick moved closer. Cadaverous, skeletal, words flooded Donald Berwick's mind, he could not keep them out. Julian Ryde seemed to have shrunk, his body no longer able to fill his skin. 'Julian?'

The figure stirred, opened its eyes, distant, rheumy and yellow and, at first, the Prime Minister thought that there had been some terrible mistake, that he did not know this man. But then the eyes sharpened and Julian Ryde raised his head, tried to speak, but slumped back, wheezed, then raised a hand from the sheets, pointed towards the half-filled jug on the low cabinet by the side of his bed.

Donald Berwick poured a glass of water, held it out, but Ryde did not respond, and the Prime Minister put the glass down. He reached forward, put his hand under Ryde's shoulders, helped him to lean forward in bed, the former Home Secretary's shoulder blade pushing, knife-like, through his pyjamas against the Prime Minister's hand.

Berwick raised the glass, and the shrunken man sipped a little water then eased himself back against his pillow, his eyes, once again, closed

Several seconds passed before he tried to speak again. When he did his voice was dry, hoarse, filled with the dust of ages. 'Good of you to come...'

'I thought I'd look in on you while I was in the constituency.' Berwick's own seat was close by but this had been a special journey. 'How are you feeling?'

Ryde twisted his lips into a smile; grimaced. 'Not good.'

'Is there anything I can do?'

'No. Loose ends practically all tied up,' said Ryde. His eyelids fluttered and he winced. He opened his eyes. They briefly sparkled but faded quickly. 'What about yours?'

'Still loose,' said Berwick. 'Consequences?' The Prime Minister paused for several seconds. Should he lie, deceive a dying man? No, he could not. Julian knew most of it, deserved to know the rest, but still Berwick paused before he spoke, pondered his words carefully.

Over the last few days and weeks, the Government of Prime Minister Tanaka in Tokyo had changed. The rioting on the streets had intensified but had been stamped out in early November and, more worryingly, Japan's approach to its neighbours and the West had begun to change.

But surely that was to be expected, Japan's relationship with the outside world could never be quite the same again. Like that between one spouse and another after a dark secret had been revealed, they would have to live with the change, but Berwick had feared that it was more than that. On the streets, openly nationalist sentiments were beginning widely aired, were becoming acceptable.

Donald Berwick blanked his face, turned to his former Home Secretary. 'Very much as we had thought, Julian. Ambassador Hirohata has been recalled to Tokyo, there's work for him to do there ...'

'I know,' said Ryde weakly. The crow's feet around his eyes built into a smile at the memory. 'Came to see me.'

The Prime Minister inclined his head slightly to one side. He went on. 'The Americans have raised their interest rates again, the markets in Japan steadied, but they're still under tremendous pressure and the Yen is in free fall. We've taken the appropriate action...'

'Sold Yen?' Prime Minister Berwick nodded but Ryde's eyes were closed, he held up his hand. 'He knew you know...'

Berwick nodded again, affirmed Ryde's comment for the benefit of nobody but himself. 'Hirohata?'

Ryde opened his eyes, gathered his strength and nodded. He paused then went on. 'The bomb. It's where they want it...'

'What do you mean?'

The Home Secretary seemed not to have heard the interruption. He continued. 'Hirohata brought me a book,' he said. His voice was fainter still and the Prime Minister leaned forward, struggled to catch his words. 'Japanese mythology, a village, a Camelot built in the shadow of a volcano...'

Ryde paused, but the Prime Minister did not speak, he looked away. Outside, the wind whistled faintly, the thin, leafless branch of a tree scraped against the window and Julian Ryde's eyelids flickered. The former Home Secretary focused his eyes on Berwick, tried to smile. 'Don't you see?'

Ryde's voice was little more than a whisper and Berwick leaned further forward, the faintly sweet smell of medication, the breath of a dying man upon his face and he shivered, felt afraid, afraid for his friend, and for himself. Ryde eyes were closed, his lips began to move, but Berwick struggled to catch his words. 'Their own sword of Damocles, a permanent threat, reminder of mortality, Donald. They became fatalistic, accepted their lot, gave everything, what little they had, for their honour.' Ryde opened his eyes, smiled without humour and, for a moment, the Prime Minister registered the presence of his friend as he had been, as he would like to remember him. 'They were unpleasant, brutal, sadistic even, but they were the best warriors of their time, became an icon for some in Japan in the years after the tale was first told.'

Berwick waited, but Ryde's eyes were closed once more and for a moment he thought that he might have gone but he had not. The former Home Secretary's eyes flickered and he tried to cough but barely moved. The specks of dust caught by the winter sun, low in the sky, were undisturbed by the faint puff of air that escaped from his lungs and, his lips pursed, Donald Berwick put his hand on Julian Ryde's shoulder, fought the urge to recoil from the bones. He shuddered and Ryde's eyes opened fully. They were beginning to fade, and the Prime Minister felt a wash of guilt.

Ryde lips moved and Berwick leaned closer. 'The village was called Kasaga-matsu.'

Donald Berwick felt his cheeks begin to flush. They had been blind, and he shook his head, raised the glass once more to Ryde's grey lips, an obscene slit in the terrible, drained face of a living corpse and he felt alone. Julian would leave him. He felt the tears begin to well in his eyes, tried to push away the selfish thought.

Julian was too brave to die like this, but it was humbling; as it was in birth, so it was in death, so few people, no matter their status, were able to choose the timing or the manner of either, though it was often chosen for them, by parents or strangers; doctors, midwives or friends; and by others, others like Yoshi Kasaga…

'Kasaga was born Yoshifumi Iwamoto,' said Berwick. He looked back at Ryde, held his eye. 'The Embassy told us yesterday. He changed his name to Kasaga eleven years ago.'

Ryde nodded, slipped back and sank into his bedding, swallowed by the loose cloth. 'Find the village and you find the man…'

'You're right, my friend,' said Berwick. He put his hand on Ryde's shoulder again, felt the skin chase and slither from his fingers, but he did not flinch. 'But it's a myth, Julian.'

'Perhaps,' said Ryde, his eyelids beginning to flutter. 'Maybe just never found. After all, the volcano erupted; the fire took them. The earth became liquid beneath their feet, their bodies gone, buried but they lead the way to salvation, the Divine Way. Don't you see? They were pure. It was the threat that kept them pure…'

Also from Hit the North

Always Adam by Mark Brumby

London-based financial journalist Spencer Beck is obsessed with billionaire biotech prodigy, Adam Reid, orphaned in his mid-teens when his parents died in a tragic murder-suicide in New York City. A shadowy informant with MI5 connections promises Beck unfettered access to the mysterious Reid and introduces him to Daniel Flanagan, a retired Big Apple detective who investigated the deaths of Adam's mother and father. Spencer's initial scepticism, fed by the suspicions of the former police officer, turns to excitement when Reid reveals the truth about himself and his altruistic ambitions to protect society from a deadly virus with a powerful vaccine he's developed. But when Beck's entire world starts to implode, he discovers Reid harbours a vendetta that, left unchecked, threatens not only his survival but that of an entire species.

After the Bridge by Andrew J Field

Two suicidal strangers, failing actor Owen and traumatised Ukrainian refugee Becky, postpone death on the Humber bridge to honey-trap married men. They make easy money until they reach Manchester when a corrupt civil servant dies on Becky in a hotel room. Owen steals the dead man's identity to con a small fortune from a brain-damaged hero's trust fund. His impersonation is good, but doesn't fool a cynical cop or the deceased's self-harming granddaughter. As their blackmail scam spirals out of control, Owen and Becky must confront their own personal demons or risk drowning in a sea of corruption and criminality.

All Down the Line by Andrew J Field

Manchester 2017: Cain Bell thinks he has finally found happiness with April Sands, a celebrated chef and the love of his life. But on the night he proposes, April reveals a shocking secret: the man who confessed to killing Cain's daughter in a hit-and-run accident two decades ago was not the real driver. As Cain seeks answers, he discovers April harbours many more dark secrets — one of them ties her to the very tragedy that has haunted him for years. Caught between seeking vengeance and turning the other cheek, Cain must navigate the blurred lines between right and wrong in pursuit of a truth that will either renew or destroy him.

Without Rules by Andrew J Field

China is fighting back against her abusers. She knows she must win, whatever the cost, otherwise she is mincemeat. Sexually abused as a young teen, China fears her young daughter is next the gang's next victim unless she can finally permanently break free from her abusers. But she can only do this if she is more ruthless than her evil amoral abusers. When her initial plan ends up in a bloodbath, she must team up a cold-blooded killer suffering from PTSD and forget all the rules if she and her daughter are to survive the wicked games of evil men.

Visit www.hitthenorth.info